61,065, 61,170

3.5 gal   *¢1,346*

7.8 gal

4.2 gal **Celebrate . . . If You Dare!**

KIM HARRISON

introduces us to a younger Rachel Morgan—an under-graduate witch-in-training—who naively resurrects a spirit and sparks a terrifying showdown with a deadly undead adversary.

Two Ghosts for Sister Rachel

LYNSAY SANDS

serves up a scrumptious stew of Yuletide suspense when, in order to escape from a determined stalker, a beautiful, reluctant shape-shifter must assume different forms.

Run, Run, Rudolph

T Shirts Only *1-800-346-4407*

MARJORIE M. LIU

keeps a petite-but-powerful government agent's hands full when she must join forces with a hunky necromancer to prevent an unholy brotherhood of terrorists and vampires from ringing in the New Year with blood.

Six

VICKI PETTERSSON

brings a former superhero—an elite Zodiac warrior—back to the mortal world for a Thanksgiving reunion with her equally hated and beloved enemy to do battle for the lives of her imperiled children.

The Harvest

W9-BRW-153

By Kim Harrison

FOR A FEW DEMONS MORE • A FISTFUL OF CHARMS
EVERY WHICH WAY BUT DEAD
THE GOOD, THE BAD, AND THE UNDEAD • DEAD
WITCH WALKING
DATES FROM HELL
(*with Lynsay Sands, Kelley Armstrong,*
Lori Handeland)

By Lynsay Sands

BITE ME IF YOU CAN • A BITE TO REMEMBER
A QUICK BITE • DATES FROM HELL

By Marjorie M. Liu

TIGER EYE • SHADOW TOUCH
THE RED HEART OF JADE • DARK DREAMERS
EYE OF HEAVEN • SOUL SONG
A TASTE OF CRIMSON • X-MEN: DARK MIRROR
WILD THING

By Vicki Pettersson

THE TASTE OF NIGHT • THE SCENT OF SHADOWS

KIM HARRISON

LYNSAY SANDS

MARJORIE M. LIU

VICKI PETTERSSON

Holidays Are Hell

HARPER

An Imprint of HarperCollinsPublishers

HARPER

An Imprint of HarperCollins*Publishers*
10 East 53rd Street
New York, New York 10022-5299

"Two Ghosts for Sister Rachel" copyright © 2007 by Kim Harrison
"Run, Run, Ruldolph" copyright © 2007 by Lynsay Sands
"Six" copyright © 2007 by Marjorie M. Liu
"The Harvest" copyright © 2007 by Vicki Pettersson
ISBN: 978-0-06-123909-0
ISBN-10: 0-06-123909-7

First Harper paperback printing: November 2007

HarperCollins® and Harper® are registered trademarks of Harper-Collins Publishers.

Printed in the United States of America

Visit Harper paperbacks on the World Wide Web at
www.harpercollins.com

10 9 8 7 6 5 4 3 2 1

Contents

Two Ghosts for Sister Rachel

Kim Harrison

Chapter 1

I stuck the end of the pencil between my teeth, brushing the eraser specks off the paper as I considered how best to answer the employment application. WHAT SKILLS CAN YOU BRING TO INDERLAND SECURITY THAT ARE CLEARLY UNIQUE TO YOU?

Sparkling wit? I thought, twining my foot around the kitchen chair and feeling stupid. *A smile? The desire to smear the pavement with bad guys?*

Sighing, I tucked my hair behind my ear and slumped into the kitchen chair. My eyes shifted to the clock above the sink as it ticked minutes into hours. I wasn't going to waste my life. Eighteen was too young to be accepted into the I.S. intern program without a parent's signature, but if I put my application in now, it would sit at the top of the stack until I was old enough, according to the guidance counselor. Like the recruiter had said, there was nothing wrong with going into the I.S. right out of college if you knew that's what you wanted to do. The fast track.

The faint sound of the front door opening brought my

heart to my throat. I glanced at the sunset-gloomed window. Jamming the application under the stacked napkins, I shouted, "Hi, Mom! I thought you weren't going to be back until eight!"

Damn it, how was I supposed to finish this thing if she kept coming back?

But my alarm shifted to elation when a high falsetto voice responded, "It's eight in Buenos Aires, dear. Be a dove and find my rubbers for me? It's snowing."

"Robbie?" I stood so fast the chair nearly fell over. Heart pounding, I darted out of the kitchen and into the green hallway. There at the end, in a windbreaker and shaking snow from himself, was my brother Robbie. His narrow height came close to brushing the top of the door, and his shock of red hair caught the glow from the porch light. Slush-wet Dockers showed from under his jeans, totally inappropriate for the weather. On the porch behind him, a cabbie set down two suitcases.

"Hey!" I exclaimed, bringing his head up to show his green eyes glinting mischievously. "You were supposed to be on the vamp flight. Why didn't you call? I would've come to get you."

Robbie shoved a wad of money at the driver. Door still gaping behind him, he opened his arms, and I landed against him, my face hitting his upper chest instead of his middle like it had when we had said goodbye. His arms went around me, and I breathed in the scent of old Brimstone from the dives he worked in. The tears pricked, and I held my breath so I wouldn't cry. It had been over four and a half years. Inconsiderate snot had been at the West Coast all this time, leaving me to cope with Mom. But he'd come home this year for the solstice, and I sniffed back everything and smiled up at him.

"Hey, Firefly," he said, using our dad's pet name for me and grinning as he measured where my hair had grown to.

"You got tall. And wow, hair down to your waist? What are you doing, going for the world's record?"

He looked content and happy, and I dropped back a step, suddenly uncomfortable. "Yeah, well, it's been almost five years," I accused. Behind him, the cab drove away, head-lamps dim from the snow and moving slowly.

Robbie sighed. "Don't start," he begged. "I get enough of that from Mom. You going to let me in?" He glanced behind him at the snow. "It is cold out here."

"Wimp," I said, then grabbed one of the suitcases. "Ever hear about that magical thing called a coat?"

He snorted his opinion, hefting the last of the luggage and following me in. The door shut, and I headed down the sec-ond, longer hallway to his room, eager to get him inside and part of our small family again. "I'm glad you came," I said, feeling my pulse race from the suitcase's weight. I hadn't been in the hospital in years, but fatigue still came fast. "Mom's going to skin you when she gets back."

"Yeah, well I wanted to talk to you alone first."

Flipping the light switch with an elbow, I lugged his suit-case into his old room, relieved I'd vacuumed already. Blow-ing out my exhaustion, I turned with my arms crossed over my chest to hide my heavy breathing. "About what?"

Robbie wasn't listening. He had taken off his jacket to show a sharp-looking pinstripe shirt with a tie. Smiling, he spun in a slow circle. "It looks exactly the same."

I shrugged. "You know Mom."

His eyes landed on mine. "How is she?"

I looked at the floor. "Same. You want some coffee?"

With an easy motion, he swung the suitcase I had dragged in up onto the bed. "Don't tell me you drink coffee."

Half my mouth curved up into a smile. "Sweat of the gods," I quipped, coming close when he unzipped a front pocket and pulled out a clearly expensive bag of coffee. If the bland, environmentally conscious packaging hadn't told me what was in it, the heavenly scent of ground beans would have. "How did you get *that* through customs intact?" I said, and he smiled.

"I checked it."

His arm landed across my shoulders, and together we navigated the narrow hallway to the kitchen. Robbie was eight years older than me, a sullen babysitter who had become an overly protective brother, who had then vanished four-plus years ago when I needed him the most, fleeing the pain of our dad's death. I had hated him for a long time, envious that he could run when I was left to deal with Mom. But then I found out he'd been paying for Mom's psychiatrist. Plus some of my hospital bills. We all helped the way we could. And it wasn't like he could make that kind of money here in Cincinnati.

Robbie slowed as we entered the kitchen, silent as he took in the changes. Gone was the cabinet with its hanging herbs, the rack of dog-eared spell books, the ceramic spoons, and copper spell pots. It looked like a normal kitchen, which was abnormal for Mom.

"When did this happen?" he asked, rocking into motion and heading for the coffeemaker. It looked like a shrine with its creamer, sugar, special spoons, and three varieties of grounds in special little boxes.

I sat at the table and scuffed my feet. *Since Dad died,* I thought, but didn't say it. I didn't need to.

The silence stretched uncomfortably. I'd like to say Robbie looked like my dad, but apart from his height and his spare frame, there wasn't much of Dad about him. The red hair and green eyes we shared came from Mom. The earth magic skill I dabbled in came from Mom, too. Robbie was better at ley line magic. Dad had been topnotch at that, having worked in the Arcane Division of the Inderland Security, the I.S. for short.

Guilt hit me, and I glanced at the application peeking out from under the napkins.

"So," Robbie drawled as he threw out the old grounds and rinsed the carafe. "You want to go to Fountain Square for the solstice? I haven't seen the circle close in years."

I fought to keep the disappointment from my face—he had been trying to get tickets to the Takata concert. Crap. "Sure," I said, smiling. "We'll have to dig up a coat for you, though."

"Maybe you're right," he said as he scooped out four tablespoons, glanced at me and then dumped the last one back in the bag. "You want to go to the concert instead?"

I jerked straight in the chair. "You got them!" I squealed, and he grinned.

"Yup," he said, tapping his chest and reaching into a pocket. But then his long face went worried. I held my breath until he pulled a set of tickets from a back pocket, teasing me.

"Booger," I said, falling back into the chair.

"Brat," he shot back.

But I was in too good a mood to care. God, I was going to be listening to Takata when the seasons shifted. How cool was that? Anticipation made my foot jiggle, and I looked at the phone. I had to call Julie. She would die. She would die right on the spot.

"How did your classes go?" Robbie said suddenly. His back was to me as he got the coffeemaker going, and I flushed. Why was that always the second thing out of their mouth, right after how tall you've gotten? "You graduated, right?" he added, turning.

"Duh." I scuffed my feet and tucked a strand of hair behind my ear. I'd graduated, but admitting I'd flunked every ley line class I had taken wasn't anything I wanted to do.

"Got a job yet?"

My eyes flicked to the application. "I'm working on it." Living at home while going to college hadn't been my idea, but until I could afford rent, I was kind of stuck here, two-year degree or not.

Smiling with an irritating understanding, Robbie slid into the chair across from me, his long legs reaching the other side and his thin hands splayed out. "Where's The Bat? I didn't see it in the drive."

Oh . . . crap. Scrambling up, I headed for the coffeemaker. "Wow, that smells good," I said, fumbling for two mugs. "What is that, espresso?" Like I knew? But I had to say something.

Robbie knew me better than I knew myself, having practically raised me. It had been hard to find a babysitter willing to take care of an infant prone to frequently collapsing and needing shots to get her lungs moving again. I could feel his eyes on me, and I turned, arms over my chest as I leaned back against the counter.

"Rachel . . ." he said, then his face went panicked. "You got your license, didn't you? Oh my God. You wrecked it. You wrecked my car!"

"I didn't wreck it," I said defensively, playing with the tips of my hair. "And it was my car. You gave it to me."

"Was?" he yelped, jerking straight. "Rache, what did you do?"

"I sold it," I admitted, flushing.

"You what!"

"I sold it." Turning my back on him, I carefully pulled the carafe off the hot plate and poured out two cups. Sure, it smelled great, but I bet it tasted as bad as the stuff Mom bought.

"Rachel, it was a classic!"

"Which is why I got enough from it to get my black belt," I said, and he slumped back, exasperated.

"Look," I said, setting a cup beside him and sitting down. "I couldn't drive it, and Mom can't keep a regular job long enough to get a month's worth of pay. It was just taking up room."

"I can't believe you sold my car." He was staring at me,

long face aghast. "For what? To be able to dance like Jackie Chan?"

My lips pressed together. "I was mad at you, okay?" I exclaimed, and his eyes widened. "You walked out of here after Dad's funeral and didn't come back. I was left trying to keep Mom together. And then everyone at school found out and started pushing me around. I like feeling strong, okay? A car I couldn't drive wasn't doing it, but the gym was. I needed the money to get my belt, so I sold it!"

He looked at me, guilt shining in the back of his eyes.

"You, ah, want to see what I can do?" I asked hesitantly.

Robbie's breath came in fast, and he shook himself. "No," he said, gaze on the table. "You did the right thing. I wasn't here to protect you. It was my fault."

"Robbie . . ." I whined. "It's not anybody's fault. I don't want to be protected. I'm a lot stronger now. I can protect myself. Actually . . ." I looked at the application, my fingers cold as I reached for it. I knew he wouldn't approve, but if I could get him on my side, we might be able to convince Mom—and then I wouldn't have to wait. "Actually, I'd like to do more than that."

He said nothing as I pulled the paper out like a guilty secret and shoved it across the table. My knees went weak, and I felt the hints of lightheadedness take over. God, how could I ever hope to be a runner if I didn't have enough nerve to bring it up with my brother?

The sound of the paper rasping on the table as he picked it up seemed loud. The furnace clicked on, and the draft shifted my hair as I watched his gaze travel over the paper. Slowly his expression changed as he realized what it was. His eyes hit mine, and his jaw clenched. "No."

He went to crumple the paper, and I snatched it away. "I'm going to do this."

"The I.S?" Robbie said loudly. "Are you crazy? That's what killed Dad!"

"It is not. I was there. He said so. Where were you?"

Feeling the hit, he shifted to the back of the chair. "That's not fair."

"Neither is telling me I can't do something simply because it scares you," I accused.

His brow furrowed, and I grabbed my cup of coffee, sliding it between us. "Is this why you're so hell bent on those karate classes?" he asked bitterly.

"It's not karate," I said. "And yes, it puts me ahead of everyone else. With my two-year degree, I can be a full runner in four years. Four years, Robbie!"

"I don't believe this." Robbie crossed his arms over his chest. "Mom is actually letting you do this?"

I stayed silent, ticked.

Robbie made a derisive noise from deep in his chest. "She doesn't know," he accused, and I brought my gaze up. My vision was blurring, but by God, I wasn't going to wipe my eyes.

"Rachel," he coaxed, seeing me teetering in frustration. "Did you even read the contract? They have you forever. No way out. You're not even twenty yet, and you're throwing your life away!"

"I am not!" I shouted, my voice trembling. "What else am I good for? I'll never be as good as Mom at earth magic. I've tried flipping burgers and selling shoes, and I hated it. I hate it!" I almost screamed.

Robbie stared, clearly taken aback. "Then I'll help you get a real degree. All you need is the right classes."

My jaw clenched. "I *took* the right classes, and I *have* a real degree," I said, angry. "This is what I want to do."

"Running around in the dark arresting criminals? Rachel, be honest. You will never have the stamina." And then his expression blanked. "You're doing this because of Dad."

"No," I said sullenly, but my eyes had dropped, and it was obvious that was part of it.

Robbie sighed. He leaned to take my hand across the table, and I jerked out of his reach. "Rachel," he said softly. "If Dad was here, he'd tell you the same thing. Don't do it."

"If Dad was here, he'd drive me to the I.S. office himself," I said. "Dad believed in what he did with his life. He didn't let danger stop him; he just prepared for it better."

"Then why did he let himself get killed?" Robbie said, an old pain in his pinched eyes. "He'd tell you to expand on your earth witch degree and find something safe."

"Safe!" I barked, shifting back. *Damn it, now I'd never convince Mom.* I needed her signature on the application, or I'd have to wait until I was nineteen. That meant I'd be twenty-three before I was actually making money at it. I loved my mom, but I had to get out of this house. "If Dad was here, he'd let me," I muttered, sullen.

"You think so?" Robbie shot back.

"I know so."

It was silent apart from my foot tapping the chair leg and the ticking of the clock. I folded up the application and snapped it down between us like an accusation. Reaching for my coffee, I took a swig, trying not to grimace at the taste. I don't care how good it smelled, it tasted awful. I couldn't believe people actually enjoyed drinking this stuff.

Robbie stood, startling me as the chair scraped and bumped over the linoleum. "Where are you going?" I asked. *Not home for five minutes, and we were arguing already.*

"To get something," he said, and walked out. I could hear him talking under his breath, and the harsh sound of a zipper as he opened his suitcase. His bedroom door slammed shut and the familiar stomp of his feet in the hall as he came back was loud.

I knew I was wearing that same unhappy, ugly look he had when he dropped a heavy book on the table in front of me. "Happy solstice," he said, slumping into his chair.

I waited, not knowing what to say. "What is it?"

"A book," he said shortly. "Open it."

I scooted closer and tucked my hair behind an ear. It was as big as a dictionary, but the pages were thick, not thin. The stark brightness told me it was new, but the charms in them . . . I'd never even heard of them.

"That's an eight-hundred-level textbook from the university in Portland," he said, voice harsh. "Now that you have your two-year degree, I wanted to ask if you would come out with me to take classes."

My head came up. He wanted me to go out to the West Coast with him?

"Mom, too," he added, and then his expression shifted to pleading. "Look at those spells, Rachel. Look what you can do if you apply yourself and invest some time. If you go into the I.S., you won't ever be able to do charms like that. Is that what you want?"

Lips parted, I looked at the pages. I was okay with earth magic, but these looked really hard. "Robbie, I—"

My words cut off and I stared at the page. "Oh wow," I breathed, looking at the charm.

"See," Robbie coaxed, his voice eager. "Look at that stuff. It's yours if you want it. All you have to do is work for it."

"No, look!" I said, shoving the book across the table and standing to follow it around. "See? There's a charm to summon the wrongfully dead. I can ask Dad. I can ask Dad what he thinks I should do."

Robbie's mouth dropped open. "Let me see that," he said, bending over the book. "Holy shit," he breathed, long fingers trembling. "You're right." He was wearing a smile when he pulled his gaze from the pages. "Tell you what," he said, leaning back with a look I recognized, the one he used to wear when he was getting me into trouble. "You do this spell to summon Dad, and ask him. If it works, you do what he says."

My pulse quickened. "You said it was an eight-hundred-level spell."

"Yeah? So what?"

I thought for a minute. "And if he says I should join the I.S.?"

"I'll sign the application myself. Mom gave me your guardianship right after Dad died."

I couldn't seem to get enough air. It was a way out. "And if I can't do it? What then?"

"Then you come out to Portland with me and get your master's so you can do every single charm in that book. But you have to do the spell yourself. Front to back. Start to finish."

I took a deep breath and looked at it. At least it wasn't in Latin. How hard could it be?

"Deal," I said, sticking my hand out.

"Deal," he echoed. And we shook on it.

Chapter 2

Squinting, I crouched to put my gaze level with the graduated cylinder, knees aching with a familiar fatigue as I measured out three cc's of white wine. It was this year's pressings, but I didn't think that mattered as long as the grapes had been grown here in Cincinnati, in effect carrying the essence of the land my dad had lived and died on.

My mom's light laughter from the other room pulled my attention away at a critical moment, and the wine sloshed too high. She was cloistered in the living room with Robbie under the impression that I was making a last-minute solstice gift and the kitchen was totally off limits. Which meant I was trying to figure out this crappy spell without Robbie's help. See, this was why I wanted to be a runner. I'd be so damn good, I could afford to buy my spells.

I grimaced as I straightened and looked at the too-full cylinder. Glancing at the hallway, I brought it to my lips and downed a sip. The alcohol burned like my conscience, but when the liquid settled, it was right where it was supposed to be.

Satisfied, I dumped it into Mom's crucible. She had gone over it with a fine-grit sandpaper earlier this afternoon to remove all traces of previous spells, as if dunking it in salt water wasn't enough. She had been thrilled when I asked to use her old equipment, and it had been a trial getting everything I needed amid her overenthusiastic, wanting-to-help interference. Even now, I could hear her excitement for my interest in her area of expertise, her crisp voice louder than usual and with a lilt I hadn't heard in a long time. Though Robbie being home might account for that all on its own.

I leaned over the textbook and read the notes at the bottom of the page. WINE AND HOLY DUST ARE INVARIABLY THE BUILDING BLOCKS OF CHOICE TO GIVE SPIRITS SUBSTANCE. Scratching the bridge of my nose, I glanced at the clock. This was taking forever, but I'd do anything to talk to my dad again, even if the spell only lasted until daybreak.

It was getting close to eleven. Robbie and I would have to leave soon to get a good spot at Fountain Square for the closing of the circle. My mom thought Robbie was taking me to the Takata concert, but we needed a whopping big jolt of energy to supplement the charm's invocation, and though we could find that at the concert, the organization of several hundred witches focused on closing the circle at Fountain Square at midnight would be safer to tap into.

I had really wanted to go to the concert, and sighing for the lost chance, I reached to snip a holly leaf off the centerpiece. It would give the spell a measure of protection. Apparently I was going to open a door, and holly would insure my dad's essence wouldn't track anything bad in on the soles of his feet.

Nervousness made my hands shake. I had to do this right. And I had to do it without Mom knowing. If she saw Dad's ghost, it would tear her up—send her back to the mess she was in almost five years ago. Seeing Dad was going to be hard enough on me. I wasn't even sure by the description of "desired results" how substantial a ghost he'd be. If we both couldn't see him, Robbie would never believe that I'd done it right.

Standing at the table, I used my mom's silver snips to cut the holly leaf into small segments before brushing them into the wine. My fingers were still shaking, but I knew it was nerves; I hadn't done enough to get tired, low fatigue threshold or not. Steadying the crucible with one hand, I started grinding the holly leaves with all my weight behind it. The lemon juice and yew mix I had measured out earlier threatened to spill as I rocked the table, and I moved it to a nearby counter.

Lemon juice was used to help get the spirit's attention and shock it awake. The yew would help me communicate with it. The charm wouldn't work on every ghost—just those unrestful souls. But my dad couldn't be resting comfortably. Not after the way he died.

My focus blurred, and I ground the pestle into the mortar as the heartache resurfaced. I concentrated on Robbie's voice as he talked to my mom about how nice the weather was in Portland, almost unheard over some solstice TV cartoon about Jack Frost. He didn't sound anything like my dad, but it was nice to hear his words balanced against Mom's again.

"How long has Rachel been drinking coffee?" he asked, making my mom laugh.

Two years, I thought, my arm getting tired and my pulse quickening as I worked. *Crap, no wonder my mom quit making her own charms.*

"Since you called to say you were coming," my mom said, unaware it was my drink of choice at school as I struggled to fit in with the older students. "She is trying to be so grown up."

This last was almost sighed, and I frowned.

"I didn't like her in those college classes," she continued, unaware that I could hear her. "I suppose it's my own fault for letting her jump ahead like that. Making her sit at home while she was ill and watch TV all day wasn't going to happen, and if she knew the work, what harm was there in letting her skip a semester here or there?"

Brow furrowed, I puffed a strand of hair out of my face and frowned. I had been in and out of the hospital so often the first four years of public school that I was basically homeschooled. Good idea on paper, but when you come back after being absent for three months and make the mistake of showing how much you know, the playground becomes a torture field.

Robbie made a rude noise. "I think it's good for her."

"Oh, I never said it wasn't," my mom was quick to say. "I didn't like her with all those damned older men is all."

I sighed, used to my mom's mouth. It was worse than mine, which sucked when she caught me swearing.

"Men?" Robbie's voice had a laugh in it. "They're not much older than her. Rachel can take care of herself. She's a good girl. Besides, she's still living at home, right?"

I blew a strand of my hair out of the mix, feeling a tug when one caught under the pestle. My arm was hurting, and I wondered if I could stop yet. The leaves were a gritty green haze at the bottom. The TV went loud when a commercial came on, and I almost missed my mother chiding him. "You think I'd let her live in the dorms? She gets more tired than she lets on. She still isn't altogether well yet. She's just better at hiding it."

My shoulder was aching, but after that, I wasn't going to stop until I was done. I was fine. I was better than fine. Hell, I'd even started jogging, though I threw up the first time I'd run the zoo. All those hills. Everybody throws up the first time.

But there was a reason there were very few pictures of me before my twelfth birthday, and it didn't have anything to do with the lack of film.

Exhaling, I set the pestle down and shook my arm. It hurt all the way up, and deciding the holly was pulped enough, I

stretched for the envelope of roots I'd scraped off my mom's
ivy plant earlier. The tiny little roots had come from the
stems, not from under the ground, and the book said they
acted as a binding agent to pull the lingering essence of a
person together.

My head came up when the TV shut off, but it was only
one of them turning on the stereo. Jingle Bells done jazz.
One of my dad's standbys.

"Look, it's snowing again," Robbie said softly, and I
glanced at the kitchen window, a black square with stark
white flakes showing where the light penetrated. "I miss
that."

"You know there's always a room here for you."

Head bowed over the mortar as I worked, I cringed at the
forlorn sound of her voice. The spell had a pleasant wine-
and-chlorophyll scent, and I tossed my hair out of the way.

"Mom . . ." Robbie coaxed. "You know I can't. Everyone's
on the coast."

"It was just a thought," she said tartly. "Shut up and have
a cookie."

My knees were starting to ache, and knowing if I didn't
sit down they'd give way in about thirty seconds, I sank into
a chair. Ignoring my shaking fingers, I pulled my mom's set
of balances out of a dusty box. I wiped the pans with a soft
rag, then recalibrated it to zero.

The wine mixture needed dust to give the ghost something to build its temporary body around, kind of like a
snow cloud needs dust to make snowflakes. I had to go by
weight since dust was too hard to measure any other way.
Robbie had collected some from under the pews at a church
while out shopping for a coat, so I knew it was fresh and
potent.

My breath made the scales shift, so I held it as I carefully
tapped the envelope. The dust, the wine, and the holly would
give the ghost substance, but it would be the other half with

the lemon juice that would actually summon him. Yew—
which was apparently basic stuff when it came to communing
with the dead, the ivy—to bind it, an identifying agent—
which varied from spell to spell, and of course my blood to
kindle the spell, would combine to draw the spirit in and bind
it to the smoke created when the spell invoked. There wasn't
anything that could make the situation permanent, but it'd last
the night. Lots of time to ask him a question. *Lots of time to
ask him why.*

Guilt and worry made my hand jerk, and I shook too
much dust from the envelope. *Please say I should join the
I.S.,* I thought as I alternately blew on the pile of dust and
held my breath until the scales read what they should.

Moving carefully to prevent a draft, I got the tiny copper
spell pot with the lemon juice and carefully shook the dust
into it. I breathed easier when the gray turned black and
sank.

The box of utensils scraped across the Formica table, and
I dug around until I found a glass stirring rod. It was almost
done, but my pleased smile faltered when Robbie asked,
"Have you given any thought to coming out with me? You
and Rachel both?"

I froze, heart pounding. *What in hell? We had a deal!*

"No," she said, a soft regret in her voice, and I stirred the
dust in with a clockwise motion, paying more attention to the
living room than to what I was doing.

"Dad's been gone a long time," Robbie pleaded. "You
need to start living again."

"Moving to Portland would change nothing." It was quick
and decisive. When she used that tone, there was no reason-
ing with her. "Rachel needs to be here," she added. "This is
her home. This is where her friends are. I'm not going to
uproot her. Not when she's finally starting to feel comfortable with herself."

I made an ugly face and set the stirring rod aside. I didn't have many friends. I'd been too sick to make them when younger. The girls at the community college treated me like a child, and after the guys found out I was jail bait, they left me alone too. Maybe moving wasn't a bad idea. I could tell everyone I was twenty-one. Though with my flat chest, they'd never believe it.

"I can get her into the university," Robbie said, his voice coaxing. I'd heard him wield it before to get both of us out of trouble, and it usually worked. "I've got a great two-room apartment, and once she's a resident, I can pay her tuition. She needs to get into the sun more."

We had a deal, Robbie, I thought, staring at the empty hallway. He was trying to work an end around. It wasn't going to work. I was going to do this spell right, and he was going to sign that paper, and then I was going to join the I.S.

"No," my mom said. "Besides, if Rachel wants to pursue her studies, Cincinnati has an excellent earth magic program." There was a telling hesitation. "But thank you."

"Did she tell you she's taking martial arts?" she said to change the subject, and I smiled at the pride in her voice. The lemon half was done, and I reached for the mortar with the wine and holly mix.

"She got her black belt not long ago," my mom continued as I stood to grind it up a little bit more, puffing over it. "I wanted her to tell you, but—"

"She sold The Bat to pay for it," Robbie finished glumly, and I grinned. "Yeah, she told me. Mom, Rachel doesn't need to know how to fight. She is not strong. She never will be, and letting her go on thinking she can do everything is only setting her up for a fall."

I froze, feeling like I'd been slapped.

"Rachel can do anything," my mom said hotly.

"That's not what I mean, Mom . . ." he pleaded. "I know she can, but why is she so fixated on all these physical activities when she could be the top witch in her field if she simply put the time in? She's good, Mom," he coaxed. "She's in there right now doing a complicated charm, and she's not batting an eye over it. That's raw talent. You can't learn that."

Anger warred with pride at his words on my skill. My mom was silent, and I let my frustration fuel the grinding motions.

"All I'm saying," he continued, "is maybe you could get her to ease up on trying to be super girl, and point out how some guys like smart chicks wearing glasses as much as others like kick-ass ones in boots."

"The reason Rachel works so hard to prove she's not weak is because she is," my mom said, making my stomach hurt all the more. "She sees it as a fault, and I'm not going to tell her to stop striving to overcome it. Challenge is how she defines herself. It was how she survived. Now shut up and eat another damned cookie. We get along just fine here."

My throat was tight, and I let go of the pestle, only now realizing my fingers had cramped up on it. I had worked so hard to get my freaking black belt so the I.S. couldn't wash me out on the physical test. Sure, it had taken me almost twice as long as everyone else, and yeah, I still spent ten minutes at the back of the gym flat on my back recovering after every class, but I did everything everyone else did, and with more power and skill than most.

Wiping an angry tear away, I used the stirring rod to scrape every last bit off the pestle. Damn it. I hated it when Robbie made me cry. He was good at it. 'Course, he was good at making me laugh, too. But my shoulders were aching beyond belief, and a slow lethargy was taking hold of my knees once more. I had to sit down again. Disgusted with myself, I sank into a chair, elbow on the table, my hair making a curtain between me and the rest of the world. I wasn't that much stronger now than when they kicked me out of the Make-A-Wish camp. I was just getting better at feeling it coming on and covering it up. *And I wanted to be a runner?*

Miserable, I held my arm against the ache, both inside and out. But the spell was done apart from the three drops of witch blood, and those wouldn't be added until we were at the square. Mom and Robbie had lowered their voices, the cadence telling me they were arguing. Pulling a second dusty box to me, I rummaged for a stoppered bottle to put the potion in.

The purple one didn't feel right, and I finally settled on the black one with the ground glass stopper. I wiped the dust from it with a dishtowel, and dumped the wine mix in, surprised when I found that the holly and the ivy bits went smoothly without leaving any behind. The lemon half was next, and my fingers were actually on the copper pot before I remembered I hadn't mixed in the identifying agent.

"Stupid witch," I muttered, thinking I must want to go to the West Coast and bang my head against the scholarly walls. The spell wouldn't work without something to identify the spirit you were summoning. It was the only ingredient not named. It was up to the person stirring it to decide. The suggested items were cremation dust, hair . . . hell, even fingernails would do, as gross as that was. I hadn't had the chance this afternoon to get into the attic where Dad's stuff was boxed up, so the only thing I'd been able to find of his was his old pocket watch on my mom's dresser.

I glanced at the archway to the hall and listened to the soft talk between Mom and Robbie. Talking about me, probably, and probably nothing I wanted to hear. Nervous, I slipped the antique silver watch out of my pocket. I looked at the hall again, and wincing, I used my mom's scissors to scrape a bit of grime-coated silver from the back. It left a shiny patch, and I rubbed my finger over it to try to dull the new brightness.

God, she'd kill me if she knew what I was doing. But I really wanted to talk to my dad, even if it was just a jumbled mess of my memories given temporary life.

My mother laughed, and in a sudden rush, I dumped the shavings in. The soft curlings sank to the bottom, where they sat and did nothing. Maybe it was the thought that counted.

I gave the potion another quick stir, tapped the glass rod off, and poured the mess into the glass-stoppered bottle with the wine. It was done.

Excited, I jammed the bottle and a finger stick into my pocket. The book said if I did it right, it would spontaneously boil when I invoked it in the red and gray stone bowl I'd found in the bottom of a box. The spirit would form from the smoke. *This had to work. It had to.*

My stomach quivered as I looked over the electric-lit kitchen. Most of the mess was from me rummaging through mom's boxes of spelling supplies. The dirty mortar, graduated cylinder, plant snips, and bits of discarded plants looked good strewn around—right somehow. This was how the kitchen used to look; my mom stirring spells and dinner on the same stove, having fits when Robbie would pretend to eat out of what was clearly a spell pot. Mom had some great earth magic stuff. It was a shame she didn't use it anymore apart from helping me with my Halloween costume, her tools banished to sit beside Dad's ley line stuff in the attic.

I dunked the few dishes I had used in the small vat of salt water used to purge any remnants of my spell, setting them in the sink to wash later. This had to work. I was not going to the coast. I was going to join the I.S. and get a real job. All I had to do was this one lousy spell. Dad would tell me I could go. I knew it.

Chapter 3

The temporary lights of Fountain Square turned the falling snow a stark, pretty white. I watched it swirl as I sat on the rim of the huge planter and thumped my heels while I waited for Robbie to return with hot chocolate. It was noisy with several thousand people, witches mostly, and a few humans who were good with ley lines or just curious. They spilled into the closed-off streets where vendors sold warmth charms, trinkets, and food. The scent of chili and funnel cakes made my stomach pinch. I didn't like the pressing crowd, but with the fridge-sized rock that the planter sported at my back, I found a measure of calm.

It was only fifteen minutes till midnight, and I was antsy. That was when the lucky seven witches chosen by lot would join hands and close the circle etched out before the fountain. The longer they held it, the more prosperous the following year was forecast to be. My name was in the hat, along with Robbie's, and I didn't know what would happen if one of us was drawn. It would have looked suspicious if we hadn't added our names when we passed through the spell checker to get into the square.

I had known about the spell checker, of course. But I'd never tried to sneak a charm in before and had forgotten about it. Apparently a lot of people tried to take advantage of the organized yet unfocused energy that was generated by having so many witches together. My charm was uninvoked, undetectable unless they searched my pockets. Not like the ley line witch ahead of me who I had watched in horror while security wrestled him to the ground. It was harder to smuggle in all the paraphernalia a ley line spell needed. All I had was a small stoppered bottle and a palm-sized stone with a hollowed-out indentation.

My heels thumped faster, and in a surge of tension, I wedged my legs under me and stood above the crowd. Toes cold despite my boots, I brushed the snow from the ivy that grew in the small space between the rock and the edge of the planter. I searched the crowd for Robbie, my foot tapping to Marilyn Manson's "White Christmas." He had set up on the far stage. The crowd over there was kind of scary.

Fidgeting, my gaze drifted to the only calm spot in the mess: the circle right in front of the fountain. Some guy with CITY EVENT blazoned on his orange vest darted across the cordoned-off area, but most of the security simply stood to form a living barrier. One caught my eye, and I sat back down. You weren't supposed to be on the planters.

"Take a flier?" a man said, his voice dulled from repetition. He was the only person facing away from the circle as he moved through the crowd, and I had prepared my no-thanks speech before he had even gotten close. But then I saw his "Have you seen me?" button and changed my mind. I'd take a stinking flier.

"Thanks," I said, holding out my gloved hand even before he could ask.

"Bless you," he said softly, the snow-damp paper having the weight of cloth as I took it.

He turned away, numb from the desperate reason for his search. "Take a flier?" he said again, moving off with a ponderous pace.

Depressed, I looked at the picture. The missing girl was pretty, her straight hair hanging free past her shoulders. Sarah Martin. Human. Eleven years old. Last seen wearing a pink coat and jeans. Might have a set of white ice skates. Blond hair and blue eyes.

I shoved the flier into a pocket and took a deep breath. Being pretty shouldn't make you a target. If they didn't find her tonight, she probably wouldn't be alive if and when they did. I wasn't the only one using the power of the solstice to work strong magic, and it made me sick.

A familiar figure captured my attention, and I smiled at Robbie in his new long coat. He had a hesitant, stop-and-go motion through the crowd as he tried not to bump anyone with the hot drinks. Besides the new coat, he now sported a thick wool hat, scarf, and a pair of matching mittens that my mom had made for him for the solstice. He was still in his thin shoes, though, and his face was red with cold.

"Thanks," I said when Robbie shuffled to a halt and handed me a paper and wax cup.

"Good *God* it's cold out here," he said, setting his cup beside me on the planter and jamming his mittened hands into his armpits.

I scooted closer to him, jostled by some guy. "You've been gone too long. Wimp."

"Brat."

A man in an orange security vest drifted past, the way opening for him like magic. I busied myself with my drink, not looking at him as the warm milk and chocolate slid down. The bottle of potion felt heavy in my pocket, like a guilty secret. "I forgot tapping into the communal will was illegal," I whispered.

Robbie guffawed, taking the top off his drink and eyeing me with his bird-bright eyes brilliant green in the strong electric lights that made the square bright as noon. "You want to go home?" he taunted. "Come to Portland with me right now? It's freaking warmer."

He was getting me in trouble, but that's what he did. He usually got me out of it, too. Usually. "I want to talk to Dad," I said, wiggling my toes to feel how cold they were.

"All right then." He sipped his drink, turning to shield me from a gust of snow and wind that sent the crowd into loud exclamations. "Are you ready?"

I eyed him in surprise. "I thought we'd find a nearby alley or something."

"The closer, the better. The more energy you can suck in, the longer the magic will last."

There was that, but a noise of disbelief came from me. "You really think no one's going to notice a ghost taking shape?" It suddenly hit me I was stirring a white charm in a banned area to get into the I.S. *This will look really good on my employment essay.*

Robbie gazed over the shorter people to the nearby circle. "I think you'll be all right. He's not going to be that substantial. And that's assuming you do it right," he added, teasing.

"Shut up," I said dryly, and I would've bobbed him but that he was drinking his hot chocolate.

Marilyn Manson finished his . . . really odd version of "Rudolph the Red-Nosed Reindeer" and the people surrounding the stage screamed for more.

"They're drawing names," Robbie said, watching the circle instead of the stage.

Excitement slithered through me, and as the crowd pressed closer, I levered myself back up onto the planter wall. No one would make me leave now for standing on it. Robbie moved so I could steady myself against his shoulder, and from the new vantage point, I watched the last of the names pulled from the informal cardboard box. I held my breath, both wanting to hear my name blared from the loudspeaker and dreading it.

Another man with a city event vest put his head together with an official-looking woman with white earmuffs. The two spoke for a moment, her head bobbing. Then she took the wad of names and strode to the stage where Marilyn was blowing kisses and showing off his legs in black tights. The crowd turned like schooling fish, the noise growing as a path parted for her.

"Can you see?" Robbie asked, and I nodded, bumping my knee against his back.

A wave of expectation grew to make my fingertips tingle. With my back to that huge rock and high above everyone, I had a great view, and I watched the woman stand at the stage and peer up at the band. Someone extended a hand to help her make the jump to the plywood. A laugh rippled out when she made the leap, and the woman was clearly flustered when she tugged her coat straight and turned to face the crowd. Marilyn handed her a mike, giving her a word or two before the straitlaced woman edged to the middle of the stage.

"I'm going to read the names now," she said simply, and the square filled with noise. She glanced shyly behind her to the band when the drummer added to it.

Robbie tugged at my coat and I missed the first name— but it wasn't me. "You should start now," he said as he peered up, his cheeks red and his eyes eager.

Adrenaline spiked through me to pull me straight, and my gloved hand touched the outside of my pocket. "Now?"

"At least set it up while everyone is looking at the stage," he added, and I nodded.

He turned back around and applauded the next person.

Here, on our side of the square, there were already two people standing in the middle of the circle, flushed and excited as they showed their IDs to security. I glanced at the people nearest to me, heart pounding. Actually, Robbie had picked a really good spot. There was a narrow space between that big rock and the edge of the planter. No one else could get too close, and with Robbie in front of me, no one would see what I was doing.

The snow seemed to swirl faster. My breath left me in little white puffs as I dropped the egg-shaped red and white stone to the ground and nudged it into place. The shallow dip in it would hold a potion-sized amount of liquid. It was one of my mom's more expensive—and rare—spelling utensils, and I'd be grounded for a year if she knew I had it.

The last name was read, and the crowd seemed to collectively sigh. Disappointment quickly turned to anticipation again as the last lucky few made their way to the circle to sign their name in the event book and become part of Cincinnati's history. I jumped when the big electric lights shining on the square went out. Expected, but still it got me. The tiny, distant lights from the surrounding buildings seemed to shine down like organized stars.

Tension grew, and while the noise redoubled, I dropped to a crouch before the stone and pulled my gloves off, jamming them into a deep pocket. I had to do this right. Not only so Robbie would get me into the I.S., but I didn't want to go to the West Coast and leave my mom alone. Robbie wouldn't be so mean, would he?

But when he frowned over his shoulder, I didn't know.

My fingers were slow with cold, and in the new darkness, I twisted the ground-glass stopper out, gave the bottle a swirl, then dumped the potion. It silently settled, ripples disappearing markedly fast. I couldn't risk standing up and possibly kicking snow into it, so I could only guess by the amount of noise that the seven lucky people were now in place.

"Hurry up!" Robbie hissed, glancing back at me.

I jammed the empty bottle in a pocket and fumbled for the finger stick. The snap of the plastic breaking to reveal the tiny blade seemed to echo to my bones, though it was unheard over the noise of the crowd.

Then they went silent. The sudden hush brought my heart into my throat. They had started the invocation. I had moments. Nothing more. It was in Latin—a blessing for the following year—and as most of the people bowed their heads, I jabbed my index finger.

My fingers were so cold, it registered as a dull throb. Holding my breath, I massaged it, willing the three drops to hurry. One, two, and then the third fell, staining the wine as it fell through the thinner liquid.

I watched, breathing in the heady scent of redwood now emanating from it. Robbie turned, eyes wide, and I felt my heart jump. I had done it right. It wouldn't smell like that if I hadn't.

"You did it!" he said, and we both gasped when the clear liquid flashed a soft red, my blood jumping through the medium, mixing it all on its own.

Behind us, a collective sound of awe rose, soft and powerful. I glanced up. Past Robbie, a bubble of power swam up from the earth. It was huge by circle standards, the shimmering field of ever-after arching to a close far above the fountain it spread before. In the distance, the faint resonating of Cincinnati's cathedral chimes swelled into existence as the nearby bells began ringing from the magic's vibration, not the bells' clappers.

We were outside the circle. Everyone was. It glittered like an opal; the multiple auras of the seven people gave it shifting bands of blues, greens, and golds. A flash of red and black glittered sporadically, red evidence of human suffering that made us stronger, and black for the bad we knowingly did—the choice we all had. It was breathtaking, and I stared at it, crouched in the snow, surrounded by hundreds, but feeling alone for the wonder I felt. The hair on the back of my neck pricked. I couldn't see the collective power rolling back and forth between the buildings—washing, gaining strength—but I could feel it.

My eyes went to Robbie's. They were huge. He wasn't watching the stone crucible. Mouth working, he pointed a mittened hand behind me.

I jerked from my crouch to a stand and pressed my back to the stone. The liquid in the depression was almost gone, sifting upward in a golden-sheened mist, and I held a hand to my mouth. It was person-shaped. The mist clearly had a man's shape, with wide shoulders and a masculine build. It was hunched in what looked like pain, and I had a panicked thought that maybe I was hurting my dad.

From behind us, a shout exploded from a thousand throats. I gasped, eyes jerking over my brother's head to the crowd. From the far stage, the drummer beat the edge of his set four times to signal the start of the all-night party, and the band ripped into music. People screamed in delight, and I felt dizzy. The sound battered me, and I steadied myself against the stone.

"Blame it all to the devil," a shaky, frightened voice said behind me. "It's Hell. It's Hell before she falls. Holy blame fire!"

I jerked, eyes wide, pressing deeper into the stone behind me. A man was standing between Robbie and me—a small man in the snow, barefoot with curly black hair, a small beard, wide shoulders . . . and absolutely nothing on him. "You're not my dad," I said, feeling my heart beat too fast.

"Well, there's one reason to sing to the angels, then, isn't there?" he said, shivering violently and trying to cover himself. And then a woman screamed.

Chapter 4

"Streaker!" the woman shouted, her arm thick in its parka, pointing.

Heads turned, and I panicked. There were more gasps and a lot of cheers. Robbie jumped onto the planter beside me and shrugged out of his coat.

"My God, Rachel!" he said, the scintillating glow from the set circle illuminating his shock. "It worked!"

The small man was cowering, and he jumped at a distant boom of sound. They were shooting off fireworks at the river, and the crowd responded when a mushroom of gold and red exploded, peeking from around one of the buildings. Fear was thick on him, and he stared at the sparkles, lost and utterly bewildered.

"Here. Put this on," Robbie was saying. He looked funny in just his hat, scarf, and mittens, and the man jumped, startled when Robbie draped his coat over him.

Still silent, the man turned his back on me, tucking his arms into the sleeves and closing the coat with a relieved quickness. Another firework exploded, and he looked up, mouth agape at the green glow reflected off the nearby buildings.

Robbie's expression was tight with worry. "Shit, shit, shit," he muttered, "I never should have done this. Rachel, can't you do a damned spell wrong once in a while?"

My heart dropped to my middle, and I couldn't breathe. Our bet. Damn it. This wasn't Dad. I'd done something wrong. The man hunched before me in bare feet and my brother's new coat wasn't my dad.

"I speculated hell was hot . . ." he said, shivering. "This is c-cold."

"It didn't work," I whispered, and he fixed his vivid blue eyes on me, looking like a startled animal. My breath caught. He was lost and afraid. Another distant boom broke our gaze as he looked to the snowy skies.

From nearby came a shrill, "Him. That's him right over there!"

Spinning, I found the woman who had screamed earlier. Security was with her, and they were both looking this way.

"It's an outrage to all decent folks!" she said loudly in a huff.

My eyes went to my brother's. Crap. Now what?

Robbie jumped off the planter. "We have to go."

The small man was scanning the crowd, a look of wonder replacing his fear. At my feet, Robbie grabbed my mom's stone crucible and jammed it in his pocket. "Sorry everyone!" he said with a forced cheerfulness. "Cousin Bob. What an ass. Did it on a dare. Ha, ha! You won, Bob. Dinner is on me."

I got off the planter, but the man—the ghost, maybe—was staring at the buildings. "This fearsome catastrophe isn't hell," he whispered, and then his attention dropped to me. "You're not a demon."

His accent sounded thick, like an old TV show, and I wondered how long this guy had been dead.

Robbie reached up and grabbed his wrist, pulling. "It's going to be hell if we don't get out of here! Come on!"

The man lurched off the planter. All three of us stumbled on the slick stone, knocking into people wearing heavy winter coats and having red faces. "Sorry!" Robbie exclaimed, all of us in a confused knot as he refused to let go of my wrist.

I squinted as the wind sent a gust of snow at me. "What did I do wrong?" I said, too short to see where we were going. The fireworks were still going off, and people in the square had started singing.

"Me, me, me," Robbie cajoled, shoving the ghost ahead of us. "Why is it always about you, Rachel? Can you move it a little faster? You want to end up at the I.S. waiting for Mom to pick you up?"

For an instant, I froze. *Oh, God. Mom.* She couldn't find out.

"Hurry up! Let's go!" I shouted, pushing on the man's back. He stumbled, and I jerked my hands from him, the sight of his bare feet in the snow a shocking reminder of where he had come from. *Holy crap, what have I done?*

We found the blocked-off street with an abrupt suddenness. The smell of food grew heavy as the crowd thinned. My lungs were hurting, and I yanked on Robbie's sleeve.

His face was tight in bother as he turned to me, but then he nodded and stopped when he saw me gasping. "Are you okay?" he asked, and I bobbed my head, trying to catch my breath.

"I think they quit following," I said, but it was more of a prayer than a true thought.

Next to me, the man bent double. A groan of pain came from him, and I lurched backward when he started in with the dry heaves. The people nearby began drifting away with ugly looks. "Too much partying," someone muttered in disgust.

"Poor uncle Bob," Robbie said loudly, patting his back gingerly, and the man shoved him away, still coughing.

"Don't touch me," he panted, and Robbie retreated to stand beside me where we watched his hunched figure gasp in the falling snow. Behind us, the party continued at the square. Slowly he got control of himself and straightened, carefully arranging his borrowed coat and reaching for a nonexistent hat. His face was almost too young for his short beard. He had no wrinkles but those from stress. Silently he took us in as he struggled to keep his lungs moving, his bright blue eyes going from one of us to the other.

"Robbie, we have to get out of here," I whispered, tugging on his sleeve. He looked frozen in his thin shirt with only his mittens, hat, and scarf between him and the snow.

Robbie got in front of me to block the man's intent gaze. "I'm really sorry. We didn't mean to . . . do whatever we did." He glanced at the square, arms wrapped around himself and shivering. "This wasn't supposed to happen. You'll go back when the sun comes up."

Still the man said nothing, and I looked at his bare feet.

Over the noise came an aggressive, "Hey! You!"

My breath hissed in. Robbie turned to look, and even the man seemed alarmed.

"We need a cab," my brother said, grabbing my arm and pushing the man forward.

I twisted out of his grip and headed the other way. "We won't get a cab five blocks from here. We need a bus." Robbie stared blankly at me, and I yelled in exasperation, "The main depot is just over there! They can't close it off. Come on!"

"Stop!" a man's voice shouted, and we bolted. Well, Robbie and I bolted. The guy between us was kind of shoved along.

We dodged around the people with little kids already leaving, headed for the bus stop. It took up an entire block length, buses leaving from downtown for all corners of Cincy and the Hollows across the river. No one seemed to notice the small man's feet were bare or that Robbie was drastically underdressed. Song and laughter were rampant.

"There," Robbie panted, pointing to a bus just leaving for Norwood.

"Wait! Wait for us!" I yelled, waving, and the driver stopped.

The door opened and we piled in, my boots slipping on the slick rubber. Robbie had shoved the man up the stairs ahead of me, falling back when the driver had a hissy about the fare. I stood a step down and fumed while Robbie fished around in his wallet. Finally he was out of my way, and I ran my bus pass through the machine.

"Hey," the driver said, nodding to the back of the otherwise empty bus. "If he blows chunks, I'm fining you. I got your bus pass number, missy. Don't think I won't."

My heart seemed to lodge in my throat. Robbie and I both turned. The man was sitting alone beside a center pole, clutching it with both hands as the bus jerked into motion. His bare feet looked odd against the dirty, slush-coated rubber, and his knees were spread wide for balance to show his bare calves.

"Uh," Robbie said, making motions for me to move back. "He's okay."

"He'd better be," the driver grumbled, watching us in the big mirror.

Every block put us farther from the square, closer to home. "Please," I said, trying not to look desperate. "We're just trying to help him get home. It's the solstice."

The driver's hard expression softened. He took one hand off the wheel to rummage out of sight beside him. With a soft plastic rustle, he handed me a shopping bag. "Here," he said. "If he throws up, have him do it in there."

My breath slipped from me in relief. "Thank you."

Shoving the bag into a pocket, I exchanged a worried look with Robbie. Together we turned to the back of the bus. Pace slow, we cautiously approached the man as the city lights grew dim and the bus lights more obvious. Thankfully we were the only people on it, probably due to our destination being what was traditionally a human neighborhood, and they left the streets to us Inderlanders on the solstice.

The man's eyes darted between us as Robbie and I sat down facing him. I licked my lips and scooted closer to my brother. He was cold, shivering, but I didn't think he was going to ask for his coat back. "Robbie, I'm scared," I whispered, and the small man blinked.

Robbie took his mittens off and gripped my hand. "It's okay." His inhale was slow, and then louder, he said, "Excuse me, sir?"

The man held up a hand as if asking for a moment. "My apologies," he said breathily. "What year might this be?"

My brother glanced at me, and I blurted, "It's nineteen ninety-nine. It's the solstice."

The man's vivid blue eyes darted to the buildings, now more of a skyline since we weren't right among them anymore. He had beautiful, beautiful blue eyes, and long lashes I would have given a bra size for. If I had any to spare, that is.

"This is Cincinnati?" he said softly, gaze darting from one building to the next.

"Yes," I said, then jerked my hand out of Robbie's when he gave me a squeeze to be quiet. "What?" I hissed at him. "You think I should lie? He just wants to know where he is."

The man coughed, cutting my brother's anger short. "I expect I'm most sorry," he said, taking one hand off the pole. "I've no need for breathing but to speak, and to make a body accept that is a powerful trial."

Surprised, I simply waited while he took a slow, controlled breath.

"I'm Pierce," he said, his accent shifting to a more formal sound. "I have no doubt that you're not my final verdict, but are in truth . . ." He glanced at the driver. Lips hardly moving, he mouthed, "You're a practitioner of the arts. A master witch, sir."

The man wasn't breathing. I was watching him closely, and the man wasn't breathing. "Robbie," I said urgently, tugging on his arm. "He's dead. He's a ghost."

My brother made a nervous guffaw, crossing his legs to help keep his body heat with him. We were right over the heater, but it was still cold. "That's what you were trying to do, wasn't it, Firefly?" he said.

"Yes, but he's so real!" I said, hushed. "I didn't expect anything but a whisper or a feeling. Not a naked man in the snow. And certainly not him!"

Pierce flushed. His eyes met mine, and I bit back my next words, stunned by the depth of his bewilderment. The bus shifted forward as the driver braked to pick someone up, and he almost fell out of his seat, grabbing the pole with white hands to save himself.

"You drew me from purgatory," he said, confusion pouring from him even as he warily watched the people file on and find their seats. His face went panicked, and then he swallowed, forcing his emotions down. "I suspected I was going to hell. I suspected my penance for my failure was concluded, and I was going to hell. I'll allow it looks like hell at first observance, though not broken and lacking a smell of burnt amber." He looked out the window. "No horses," he said softly, then his eyebrows rose inquiringly. "And you bricked over the canal, nasty swill hole it was. Are the engines powered then by steam?"

Beside me, Robbie grinned. "He sure uses a lot of words to say anything."

"Shut up," I muttered. I thought he was elegant.

"This isn't hell," Pierce said, and, as if exhausted, he dropped his head to show me the top of his loose black curls. His relief made my stomach clench and burn.

I looked away, uncomfortable. Thoughts of my deal with Robbie came back. I didn't know if he would think this was a success or not. I did bring a ghost back, but it wasn't Dad.

And without Dad saying yes to the I.S., Robbie would probably take it as a no. Worried, I looked up at Robbie and said, "I did the spell right."

My brother shifted, as if preparing for an argument. My eyebrows pulled together, and I glared at him. "I don't care if it summoned the wrong ghost, I did the freaking spell right!"

Pierce looked positively terrified as he alternated his attention between us and the new people calmly getting on and finding their seats. I was guessing it wasn't the volume of my voice, but what I was saying. Being a witch in public was a big no-no that could get you killed before nineteen sixty-six, and he had clearly died before then.

Robbie frowned in annoyance. "The deal was you'd summon Dad," he said, and I gritted my teeth.

"The deal was I would do the spell right, and if I didn't, I would come out to Portland with you. Well, look," I said, pointing. "There's a ghost. You just try to tell me he isn't there."

"All right, all right," Robbie said, slouching. "You stirred the spell properly, but we still don't know what Dad would want, so I'm not going to sign that paper."

"You son of a—"

"Rachel!" he said, interrupting me. "Don't you get it? This is why I want you to come out with me and finish your schooling." He gestured at Pierce as if he was a thing, not a person. "You did an eight-hundred-level summoning spell without batting an eye. You could be anything you want. Why are you going to waste yourself in the I.S.?"

"The I.S. isn't a waste," I said, while Pierce shifted uncomfortably. "Are you saying Dad's life was a waste, you dumb pile of crap?"

Pierce stared at me, and I flushed. Robbie's face was severe, and he looked straight ahead, ticked. The bus was moving again, and I sat in a sullen silence. I knew I was heaping more abuse on Robbie than he deserved. But I had wanted to talk to my dad, and now that chance was gone. I should've known I wouldn't be able to do it right. And as much as I hated myself for it, the tears started to well.

Pierce cleared his throat. Embarrassed, I wiped my eyes and sniffed.

"You were attempting to summon your father," he said softly, making nervous glances at the people whispering over Pierce's bare feet and Robbie's lack of a coat. "On the solstice. And it was I whom your magic touched?"

I nodded fast, struggling to keep from bawling my fool head off. I missed him. I had really thought I could do it.

"I apologize," Pierce said so sincerely that I looked up. "You might should celebrate, mistress witch. You stirred the spell proper, or I expect I'd not be here. That I appeared in his stead means he has gone to his reward and is at peace."

Selfishly, I'd been wishing that Dad had missed me so much that he would have lingered, and I sniffed again, staring at the blur of holiday lights passing. I was a bad daughter.

"Please don't weep," he said, and I started when he leaned forward and took my hand. "You're so wan, it's most enough to break my heart, mistress witch."

"I only wanted to see him," I said, pitching my voice low so it wouldn't break.

Pierce's hands were cold. There was no warmth to him. But his fingers held mine firmly, their roughness stark next to my unworked, skinny hands. I felt a small lift through me, as if I was tapping a line, and my eyes rose to his.

"Why . . ." he said, his vivid eyes fixed on mine. "You're a grown woman. But so small."

My tears quit from surprise. "I'm eighteen," I said, affronted, then pulled my hand away. "How long have you been dead?"

"Eighteen," he murmured. I felt a growing sense of unease as the small man leaned back, glancing at Robbie with what looked like embarrassment.

"My apologies," he said formally. "I meant no disrespect to your intended."

"Intended!" Robbie barked, and I made a rude sound, sliding down from my brother. The people who had just gotten on looked up, surprised. "She's not my girlfriend. She's my sister." Then Robbie's expression shifted. "Stay away from my sister."

I felt the beginnings of a smile come over my face. Honestly, Pierce was a ghost and too old for me even if he was alive. At least twenty-four, I'd guess from the look at him. All of him.

I flushed as I recalled his short stature, firmly muscled and lean, like a small horse used to hard labor. Glancing up, I was embarrassed to see Pierce as red as I felt, carefully holding his coat closed.

"If the year is nineteen ninety-nine, I've made a die of it for nearly a hundred and forty-seven years," he said to the floor.

Poor man, I thought in pity. Everyone he knew was probably gone or so old they wouldn't remember him. "How did you die?" I asked, curious.

Pierce's gaze met mine, and I shivered at the intensity. "I'm a witch, as much as you," he whispered, though Robbie and I had been shouting about spells for the last five minutes. But before the Turn, being labeled a witch could get you killed.

"You were caught?" I said, scooting to the edge of the bus seat as we swung onto a slick, steep road, captivated by his air of secrecy. "Before the Turn? What did they do to you?"

Pierce tilted his head to give himself a dangerous air. "A murder most powerful. I'd have no mind to tell you if you're of a frail constitution, but I was bricked into the ground while breath still moved in my lungs. Buried alive with an angelic guard ready to smite me down should I dare to emerge."

"You were murdered!" I said, feeling a quiver of fear.

Robbie chuckled, and I thwacked his knee. "Shut up," I said, then winced at Pierce's aghast look. If he'd been dead for a hundred and forty years, I'd probably just cursed like a sailor.

"Sorry," I said, then braced myself when the bus swayed to a stop. More people filed on, the last being an angry, unhappy woman with more of those fliers. She talked to the bus driver for a moment, and he grumbled something before waving her on and letting the air out of the brakes. Leaning back, he shut his eyes as the woman taped a laminated flier to the floor in the aisle, and two more to the ceiling.

"Take a flier," she demanded as she worked her way to the back of the bus. "Sarah's been missing for two days. She's a sweet little girl. Have you seen her?"

Only on every TV station, I thought as I shook my head and accepted the purple paper. I glanced down as she handed one to Robbie and Pierce. The picture was different from the last one. The glow of birthday candles was in the foreground and a pile of presents in the back, blurry and out of focus. Sarah was smiling, full of life, and the thought of her alone, lost in the snow, was only slightly more tolerable than the thought of what someone sick enough to steal her might be using her for.

I couldn't look anymore. The woman had gotten off through the back door to hit the next bus, and I jammed the flier in my pocket with the first one as the bus lurched into traffic.

"I know who has her," Pierce said, his hushed, excited voice pulling my attention to him. The lights of oncoming traffic shone on him, lighting his fervent, kind of scary expression.

"Driver!" he shouted, standing, and I pressed into the seat, alarmed. "Stop the carriage!"

Everyone looked at us, most of them laughing. "Sit down!" Robbie gave him a gentle shove, and Pierce fell back, coat flying open for a second. "You're going to get us kicked off."

"I know where she's been taken!" he exclaimed, and I glanced at the passengers, worried. The driver, though, already thought he was drunk, and everyone else was snickering about the peep show.

"Lower your voice," Robbie said, shifting to sit beside him. "People will think you're crazy."

Pierce visibly caught his next words and closed his coat tighter. "He has her," he said, shaking the paper at Robbie. "The man, that . . . beast that murdered me to death. The very creature I was charged to bring to midnight justice. He's taken another."

I could tell my eyes were round, but Robbie wasn't impressed. "It's been almost two hundred years."

"Which means little to the blood-lusting, foul spawn from hell," Pierce said, and my breath caught. Vampire. He was talking about a vampire. A dead one. Crap, if a vampire had her, then she was really in trouble.

"You were trying to tag a vampire?" I said, awed. "You must be good!" Even the I.S. didn't send witches after vampires.

Pierce's expression blanked and he looked away. "Not good enough, I allow. I was there on my own hook with the belief that pride and moral outrage would sustain me. The spawn has an unholy mind for young girls, which I expect he satisfied without reprisal for decades until he abducted a girl of high standing and her parents engaged my . . . midnight services."

Robbie scoffed, but I stared. Figuring out what Pierce was saying was fascinating.

Seeing Robbie's disinterest, Pierce focused on me. "This child," he said, looking at the paper, "is the image of his preferred prey. I confronted him with his culpability, but he is as clever as a Philadelphian lawyer, and to pile on the agony, he informed the constables of my liability and claimed knowledge of the signs."

Pierce's eyes dropped, and I felt a twinge of fear for the history I'd missed by a mere generation. Liability was a mixed-company term for witch—when being one could get you killed. I suspected spawn was pre-Turn for vampire. Midnight services was probably code for detective or possibly an early Inderlander cop. Philadelphian lawyer was self-explanatory.

"Truly I was a witch," he said softly, "and I could say no different. The girl he murdered directly to protect his name. That it was so fast was a grace, her fair white body found in solstice snow and wept over. She could no more speak to save me than a stick. That I showed signs of liability about my person and belongs made my words of no account. They rowed me up Salt River all night for their enjoyment until being buried alive in blasphemed ground was a blessing. This," he said, shaking the paper, "is the same black spawn. He has taken another child, and if I don't stop him, he will foul her soul by sunrise. To stand idle would be an outrage against all nature."

I stared at him, impressed. "Wow."

Robbie crossed his arms over his chest. "Kind of poetic, isn't he?"

Pierce frowned, looking at Robbie with a dark expression.

"I think he's telling the truth," I said, trying to help, but the small man looked even more affronted.

"What would I gain from a falsehood?" he said. "This is the same sweet innocence looking at me from my memory. That damned spawn survived where I didn't, but being dead myself, mayhap I can serve justice now. I expect I have only to sunup. The charm will be spent by then, and I'll return to purgatory. If I can save her, perhaps I can save my soul."

He stopped, blinking in sudden consternation at his own words, and Robbie muttered something I didn't catch.

"I need to study on it," Pierce said softly as he looked out the windows at the tall buildings. "Spawn are reluctant to shift their strongholds. I've a mind that he is yet at his same diggings. A true fortress, apart in the surrounding hills, alone and secluded."

Apart in the hills, alone and secluded was probably now high in property taxes and crowded, right in the middle of a subdivision. "I have a map at home," I said.

Pierce smiled, his entire face lighting up as he held onto the pole. The gleam in his eyes had become one of anticipation, and I found myself wanting to help him until the ends of the earth if I could see his thanks reflected in them again. No one had ever needed my help before.

Ever.

"Whoa, wait up," Robbie said, turning to face both of us. "If you know this vampire and think you know where he is, fine. But we should go to the I.S. and let them take care of it."

I took a fast breath, excited. "Yes! The I.S.!"

Pierce's enthusiasm faltered. "The I.S.?"

Robbie looked out the window, probably trying to place where we were. "Inderland Security," he said, pulling the cord to get the driver to stop. "They police the Inderlanders, not humans. Witches, Weres, vampires, and whatever." His look slid to me and became somewhat wry. "My sister wants to work for them when she grows up."

I flushed, embarrassed, but if I couldn't admit it to a ghost, maybe I shouldn't even try.

Pierce's free hand scratched at his beard in what I hoped was simply a reflexive action. "That was what my midnight profession was," he said, "but it wasn't called such. The I.S."

The bus swayed and squeaked to a stop. Pierce didn't move, holding tight to the pole as Robbie and I stood before the bus had halted. I waited for Pierce, letting him walk between Robbie and me as we got off.

The cold hit me anew, and I squinted into the snowy night

as the bus left. "You want to wait for a bus going back into town?" I said, and Robbie shook his head, already on his cell phone.

"I'm calling a cab," he said, looking frozen clear through.

"Good idea," I said, cold despite my coat, mittens, and fuzzy hat.

"We need to go to the mall," Robbie said, "and I don't want to waste a lot of time."

"The mall?" I blurted as we dropped back deeper into the Plexiglas shelter. "What for?" Then I winced. "You need a new coat."

Phone to his ear and his face red from cold, Robbie nodded. "That, and it's going to be hard enough getting the I.S. to believe we're not nuts coming in with a naked man in a coat."

Pierce looked mystified. "The mall?"

I nodded, wondering if he'd let me pick out his clothes. "The mall."

Chapter 5

Bored, I sat in the comfy brown fabric chair beside Pierce and shifted my knee back and forth. The mall had been a success, but Robbie had pushed us from store to store inexcusably fast, getting us in and out and to the I.S. in about two hours. Pierce was now respectably dressed in jeans and a dark green shirt that looked great against his dark hair and blue eyes. He still had on Robbie's coat, and I swear, he had almost cried when he was able to shift up a half size of boot with the ease of simply pulling another pair off the rack.

But for the last hour, we had been sitting on the third-floor reception area doing nothing. Well, Pierce and I were doing nothing. Robbie, at least, was being taken seriously. I could see him down the open walkway at a desk with a tired-looking officer. As I watched, Robbie took off his new, expensive leather jacket and draped it over his lap in a show of irritation.

Pierce hadn't said much at the mall, spending a good five minutes trying to locate the source of the mood music until he got brave enough to ask. I made sure we passed an electric outlet on the way to get him some underwear. The food court had amazed him more than the electric lights, though he wouldn't try the blue slurry I begged off Robbie. The kiddy rides made him smile, then he stared in astonishment when I told him it wasn't magic but the same thing that made the lights work. That was nothing compared to when he saw a saleslady in a short skirt. Becoming beet red, he turned and walked out, his head tilted conspiratorially to Robbie's for a quiet, hushed conversation. All I caught was a muttered, "bare limbs?" but Robbie made sure we went past Valeria's Crypt so he could see the same thing in lace. Men.

Pierce's silence deepened after finding an entire building devoted to Inderland law enforcement, but even I was impressed with the I.S. tower. The entryway was a fabulous three floors high, looking more like the lobby of a five-star hotel than a cop shop. Pierce and I had a great view of the lower floors from where we sat. It was obvious that the designers had used the techniques of cathedral builders to impart awe and a feeling of insignificant smallness.

Low lights on the first floor created dark shadows that set off the occasional burst of light. Acoustically, the space was a sinkhole, making what would be a loud chatter into a soft murmur. The air carried the faint scent of vampire, and I wrinkled my nose wondering if that was what was bothering Pierce, or if it was that we were three stories up.

A minor disturbance pulled our attention to the street-level entrance as two people, witches, I guess, brought in a third. The man was still fighting them, his arms securely behind his back and fastened with a zip-strip of charmed silver. It looked barbaric, but bringing in a violent ley line witch was impossible unless they were properly restrained. Sure, there were ways to prevent magic from being invoked in a building, but then half the officers would be helpless, too.

Pierce watched until the witch was shoved into an elevator, then he turned to me. His expressive eyes were pinched when he asked, "How long have humans known about us, and how did we survive giving them the knowledge?"

I bobbed my head, remembering Pierce's shock when two witches started flirting in the mall, throwing minor spells at each other. "We've been out of the closet for about forty years."

His lips parted. "Out of the closet . . ."

A grin came over my face. "Sorry. We came clean . . . uh . . . we told them we existed after a virus hiding in tomatoes—a sort of a plague—started killing humans. It dropped their numbers by about a quarter. They were going to find out about us anyway because we weren't dying."

Pierce watched my moving foot and smiled with half his face. "I've always been of the mind that tomatoes were the fruit of the devil," he said. Then he brought his gaze to mine and gestured to take in the entire building. "This happened in four decades?"

I shrugged, twisting my boot toe into the tight-looped carpet. "I didn't say it was easy."

Crossing his knees, he rubbed his beard as if noticing not many men had them. Though very quiet since our shopping trip, he had clearly been taking everything in, processing it. Even his words, few as they had been, were starting to sound . . . less odd.

"Your brother," he said, gesturing at him with his chin, "said you want to devote your life to this?"

I smiled somewhat sheepishly. "The I.S. Yes." A sudden worry pulled my brows together. "Why? You think I shouldn't?"

"No," he rushed. "A daughter's wish to follow in her parent's occupation is proper."

Startled he knew my dad had worked for the I.S., I caught my breath until I remembered our conversation in the bus. "Oh. You heard that."

He ducked his head. "Yes, mistress witch. And who am I to tell you the profession of protecting the helpless is too dangerous? I live for it."

I felt a quiver of connection, that he might really understand. Pierce, though, gave me a wry look. "Lived for it," he amended sourly.

Used to arguing about my chosen profession, I lifted my chin. "I'm stronger every year," I said as if he had protested. "I mean, markedly stronger."

"You suffered an illness?" Pierce asked, seemingly genuinely concerned.

I nodded, and then feeling some honesty was due, added, "I still am sick, sort of. But I'm doing much better. Everyone says so. I have more stamina all the time. I attend classes to keep from slipping back, and I haven't been in the hospital for about four years. I should have died, so I really don't have any cause to complain, but I want to do this, damn it. They can't keep me out because of my health. I got a black belt and everything."

I stopped, realizing not only was I babbling to the first understanding person I'd found, but I was swearing, too. "Sorry," I said, twisting my foot again. "That's probably gutter talk for you."

Pierce made a soft sound, neither accusing nor affirming. He was looking at my middle in a soft puzzlement. "You're passionate," he finally said, and I smiled in relief. I knew he would be gone by sunrise, but I didn't want to alienate him. I liked him, even if he was a ghost. *Oh God, I was* not *crushing on him.*

"I'm in the medical books, you know," I said, trying to get his mind off my bad mouth. "The only survivor of Rosewood syndrome."

He started, turning from where he had been watching Robbie argue with his interviewer. "You . . . Rosewood? You survived? I lost two sisters and a brother to that, passed before they were three months. Are you sure that's what ailed you?"

I smiled because there was no pain in him. The hurt, apparently, was old. "That's what it was. Is. Modern medicine I suppose, or all the herbal remedies they gave me at that Make-A-Wish camp for dying kids. I was there for three years until they kicked me out when I quit dying so fast."

The wonder was stark in his gaze as he settled back as if not believing it. "You're a wonder, mistress witch."

I scoffed and ran my fingernails to bump over the chair's fabric. "I'm not really a witch yet. I haven't gotten my license. You can call me Rachel."

Pierce's subtle fidgeting ceased and I looked up to find him staring. In sudden understanding, I warmed. Crap, giving him my first name might be extremely intimate. He certainly didn't seem to know how to react.

Embarrassed, I focused on Robbie. "I, uh, am sorry for bringing you from your rest," I said. "I was trying to call my dad. See, I had this bet with Robbie. I said Dad, my father, would want me to put my application in to the I.S., and Robbie said if he were still alive, he'd want me to get a higher degree in my earth witch studies. So Robbie challenged me to call him and ask. If I could do it, I promised I'd do what Dad said; if not, I'd go with Robbie and go to school for four more years. I didn't figure on him being at peace. I suppose I should be glad," I said, feeling guilty. "But I really wanted to talk to him."

"Miss Rachel," Pierce said, and my head came up when he took my hand. "Don't weep for your father. I expect he's at rest, watching you and wishing you happiness."

"You don't know that," I said contrarily, pulling away. "You're stuck in purgatory."

But instead of taking that as a brush-off, he nodded as if he liked it.

"You do know the intent behind your brother's challenge

was to prove to you how skilled you are at earth magic, so you will follow that path?"

My mouth dropped open and I looked at Robbie. "The dirtbag," I whispered. "Well, I'm not doing it," I said while Pierce puzzled over the modern phrase. "We don't know if my dad would have approved or not, so the deal is off. I'm not going to Portland. I'm going to stay here with my mother and become the best damned runner since my dad."

Crap, I'm swearing again, I thought, then gave Pierce an apologetic smile. "What do you think I should do?"

The small man leaned forward, startling me with his intensity. "I believe," he said, inches away, "that if you don't follow your passions, you die slowly."

He was holding my hand again. A slow quiver built in me, and I pulled my hand away before I shivered outright. The office chatter seemed to grow loud, and Pierce resettled himself.

"My apologies," he said, clearly not sorry at all. "I've overstepped my boundaries."

Yeah, like I don't want you to? "It's okay," I said, boldly meeting his gaze. "I've held hands with guys before." *And kissed them. I wonder what it's like to kiss a ghost?* God, he had a beard. It would probably be all prickly and nasty. But maybe it was soft?

Yanking my thoughts back where they belonged, I looked down the open walkway to Robbie. He was clearly upset as he talked to the man, his arms moving in sharp angry motions. "I wonder what they're saying," I murmured.

Pierce still had that devilish look, but I liked it.

"Let me see if I can commune with the ever-after," he said. "I've a mind to speak a charm to hear them, though it's wicked to do so." But almost immediately his enthusiasm faltered. "I can't find a line," he said, touching his beard as if nervous. "Being a spectre, one might think it would be easier, not forbidden."

Well, nuts to that. I want to know what Robbie is saying. In a spontaneous motion, I grabbed Pierce's wrist. My focus blurred as I searched for the nearest ley line, finding the university's glowing in my thoughts: a dusky red ribbon of power all witches could tap into regardless of where their talents lay.

Reaching out a thought, I connected to it. Warmth spilled into me in a slow trickle, running to my chi and making my skin tingle. Forcing my vision to focus, I looked at Pierce. My pleased smile faded. Crap, I'd done it again. The small man was staring at me as if I had just taken off all my clothes and was dancing naked on the desks.

"So you can do the spell . . ." I said in a small voice, and took a breath as if only now remembering how to breathe. "Didn't you share lines in your time?"

"Not often," he said, setting a hand atop mine so I wouldn't let go. "But I'm not there anymore. Thank you. Let me . . . do the spell."

He steadied himself, and while I felt like a whore on the corner, he flicked a nervous gaze at me with his beautiful, deep blue eyes. "Well?" I prompted.

"I'm not of a mind to hurt you," he admitted.

"Then don't pull so much," I said, glancing at Robbie. *God, did he think I was a child?*

"Um, yes," he stammered, and I shifted my shoulders when I felt a soft draw through me.

"You're fine," I encouraged, and he pulled more until my hair was floating from static. Intrigued, I watched Pierce close his eyes as if trying to remember something. His lips moved and I heard the faintest hint of Latin, dark and alien sounding. His free hand sketched a quick figure, and then my ears popped.

"A moment," he said, his hand atop mine tightening to keep me from breaking the link.

My gaze shot to Robbie. "Oh, wow," I breathed as his voice came clear, as if I was listening to a phone.

"Wow. Yes," Pierce repeated, smiling from behind his beard, and we turned to listen.

"But I know he took her," Robbie said forcefully, his lips moving in time with the spoken words. "Can't you just get a car out there or something?"

The I.S. officer he was with had his back to us, but I could see he was typing. "Mr. Morgan. I assure you we're giving the matter our full attention."

"Are you?" my brother said. "She'll be dead by sunup if you don't do something. He's done this before. He just made the mistake of taking someone who would be noticed this time."

The man in his wrinkled suit clicked a window on his computer closed. One hand on the mouse, he gave my brother a long look. "And you know this how?"

Robbie said nothing, and I looked at the entryway floor when the vampire turned to see Pierce and me.

"Mr. Morgan," the man said, his voice thick with dismissal. "I've taken twelve statements like yours over the past three hours. We're working on them in turn, but you can understand we can't devote all our manpower to one missing child who is angry she isn't getting what she wants for Christmas and has run away to her daddy."

"I'm not a crank," Robbie said tightly. "My father used to work in the Arcane Division, and I know real from fake. This isn't a joke."

I breathed easier when the vampire focused on my brother again. "Monty Morgan?" he said, and I nodded even as Robbie did.

Pierce's grip on my hand twitched when the vampire stood. The ghost's expression of concern surprised me.

"Wait here," the officer said. "I'll be right back."

Pleased, I smiled at Pierce. "See?" I said, feeling like we were getting somewhere.

But Pierce's brow was creased in a deep worry. "Spawn,"

he muttered, and while I held his one hand, he made a small gesture with the other. I stifled a jump when the energy he was pulling off the line through me shifted. His lips pressed tight, he pointed to the I.S. officer, now bending to speak to another, clearly higher-up, officer.

"Sir, do you have a minute?" Robbie's interviewer said, his voice clear.

I couldn't see the new man's face, but his tone was bothered as he brought his attention up from his paperwork and said, "What?"

"It's the missing girl," the first officer said, fingers moving nervously behind his back.

I caught a glimpse of the supervisor's face when he turned to Robbie. It was smooth and nice looking despite his expression of annoyance. Young. "So?" he said.

Shifting his feet, the older man bent closer. "He knows things not released to the press."

The vampire went back to his paperwork, the pencil skating across the form too fast for a human. "So?" he said again.

"So he's one of Morgan's kids."

I felt a stir of satisfaction when the officer set his pencil down. "Who?"

"The witch in Arcane," Robbie's interviewer prompted. "Died about four years ago?"

But my pride shifted to a stark fear when the vampire looked at Robbie, his pupils swelling to black. Crap, I could see it from here. He was vamping out. But why?

"Morgan's boy?" he murmured, interested, and my pulse quickened. Something was wrong. I could almost taste it. "I thought he was out of state."

Pierce let go of my wrist and I jumped when the connection between us broke. My chi was suddenly overfull, and I forced most of the energy back into the ley line. I didn't let go of the line completely, ready for anything.

"I expect we should leave," the small man said, eyes darting over the three floors to linger on the building's main entrance.

I rubbed my wrist to get rid of the remaining tingles. "What's wrong?"

Pierce eased to the front of the chair and held his coat closed. "It's been my experience that instinct, not what you've been taught, is the clearest indicator of direction. They have a mind that your brother is involved with the girl's abduction and is finding reason to beg clemency by cooperating. We need to pull foot."

"Wait up," I said when he rose and drew me to a stand. "What about Robbie?"

As if having heard me, my brother met my gaze. His face was ashen. Behind him, the two vampires were headed his way. Clearly frightened, he mouthed, "Go!"

"Your brother won't come to any hurt," Pierce said, and I fell into motion when he gripped my elbow and started us toward the wide stairway. "They will give him Jesse until sure of his innocence, but by that time, the sun will be risen. Blame it all, I should have been of a state to fix his flint myself."

I had no idea what he was saying, but Pierce had us on the steps before the first shout. My head whipped around, and I stumbled. Two brutish men were heading our way, and with a little gasp, I pushed Pierce down faster. A chime rang through the air, and my skin prickled. "Lock down!" someone shouted.

"Damnation," Pierce swore, but our feet were still moving, and we had passed the second floor without trouble. My pulse was too fast, and my lungs hurt, but I wouldn't slow down. We wouldn't be caught because of me. Apart from the two guys following us and the uniformed woman standing in front of the doors with her arms crossed over her chest, everyone seemed content to watch. Actually, they were moving back, making room. *Swell.*

"Mistress witch," Pierce said, his tone terse as we neared the ground floor, my steps barely keeping up with his. "I'd respectfully ask that I might commune a line through you." He glanced at me, shocking me again with how blue his eyes were. "To help make our escape. If there were another way, I would use it."

I slid my hand into his, gripping it firmly. "Pull on a line." He shot a bewildered look at me and I shouted, "Commune with the ever-after!"

My breath hissed in as he did, and I squeezed his hand to tell him it was okay. Power burned like ice as we found the first floor, and I felt my tongue tingle. Pierce gathered himself, and with a shout, a head-sized sphere of ever-after enveloped his free hand.

That came through me, I thought in wonder, even as we continued to head for the doors.

Pierce threw the ball. The witch waiting for us yelped and dove for the floor. Green power edged in red and black hit the glass doors, spreading out like slime. A boom shook the air and almost sent me falling. Glass pushed outward in a silent cascade.

"Are you well, Miss Rachel?" Pierce said earnestly when my ears recovered.

I looked up as he steadied me with his grip tight on my elbow. For an instant we stood, focused on each other, linked by way of the line and our need to escape. My inner ear pulsed from the blast. Behind me, shouts started to make sense. Past the shattered doors came the sound of traffic and the crisp cold of a winter night. The witch on the floor looked up from around her fallen hair, shocked. "Wow," I said, and Pierce's concern eased.

Satisfied I had my balance, he let go of my elbow but kept our fingers entwined. "Allow me, mistress witch," he said gallantly, escorting me through the broken glass.

"Hey! Stop!" someone called. My pulse raced, and knowing

my mom was going to "give me Jesse" when she found out, I
nevertheless stepped elegantly over the jagged remnants of the
door and onto the salted sidewalk.

"A moment," Pierce said, turning, and I felt another strong
pull through me when he ran two fingers across both the lin-
tel and threshold of the wide doors and a green sheet of
ever-after swam up from the frozen slush sidewalk to seal
everyone inside. "Now we may depart," he said exuberantly,
the light shining out from the I.S. offices showing his good
mood. "Perhaps a carriage is in order," he said, whistling as
if he had grown up in Cincy, but he had watched Robbie do
the same thing. "I fear we should make an unpleasant haste.
The ward won't last long. And we must stay holding hands
until then."

I grinned. When he was excited, he didn't stop to think
what he was saying and was charmingly elegant. "Maybe we
should walk a few blocks so they don't know what cab we
take?" I suggested. "Otherwise they'll just radio ahead."

Pierce's brow creased, and he waved away the cab that had
pulled up. "Like the music from the boxes?" he said, and I
nodded. It was close enough.

"Then we walk," he said. With a last wave to the angry
I.S. officers behind the green-tinted sheet of ever-after, he
tightened his grip on my fingers, and we strode down the
sidewalk.

My pulse was fast and I felt breathless. I'd never done
anything like this before, and I felt alive. For the first time
in my freaking life, I felt alive—the adrenaline making me
light and airy and my steps long and sure. The snow drifted
down peacefully, and I wished that I could do this forever—
walk with a man's hand in mine, happy and pleasantly warm
with this alive feeling running through me. He wasn't much
taller than me, and our steps were closely matched.

I glanced behind us at the retreating I.S. building, then
shyly at Pierce, but his attention was on the buildings and

storefront displays. I eyed the colored lights and the happy people walking in the snow with last-minute solstice and Christmas shoppers finding a final, perfect gift.

"No beggars," he whispered.

"Well, a few," I said, abruptly seeing the street in an entirely different way. "But they're probably at the square, partying."

Pierce pulled our joined fingers up, mine almost blue from the cold. "I can't keep communing with—ah, pulling a line through you," he said softly. "I'm not one born in the woods to be afraid of an owl, yet to save that child with only my fists I expect is a fool's errand. Do you know . . ." He hesitated, attention flicking from a truck slushing past and back to me. "Do you know a witchy woman or man I might procure ley line charms from?"

"Oh!" I said brightly, determined to keep up with him though my chest was starting to hurt. Of course he'd need something, seeing as he couldn't tap a line himself. "The university's bookstore has an entire floor of ley line stuff. I'm sure they'll have something."

"Magic studies? In the university?" he asked, and I nodded, my free arm swinging. But a frown creased his brow, and leaning to me, he whispered, "I would prefer a smaller shop if you know of it. I don't have even a stick to barter with or a . . . card of credit," he added hesitantly, as if knowing he hadn't gotten the words in the right order.

My eyes widened. "I don't have much money either. Cab fare, is all."

Pierce took a deep breath and exhaled. "No matter. I will suitably impress upon the proprietor my desperate need." His chin rose and a defiant gleam entered his eyes as we continued forward. "I will beg. If they are honorable, they will help."

Beg, eh? I thought, fully believing he would get down on his knees before the night manager at the university bookstore, who would promptly throw him out, not pleased to be working on the solstice. "I've a better idea," I said, praying my mom would go for it. My dad's stuff was in the attic. I knew my mom wouldn't be happy, but the worst thing she could do was say no. Edging us to the curb, I searched for a cab. "I'll take you home," I said, leaning into the street in the universal language of cabbies. "You can look over my dad's old ley line stuff. He worked for the I.S. He probably has something."

Pierce drew me back from the curb, and I blinked at him, surprised. His expression was pinched as he stood in the puddle of streetlight and falling snow, elegant in his long coat and shiny new boots. "Miss Rachel, no. I'm not of a mind to endanger you anymore. I'll escort you home, then go alone to the university. If there are learned men there, they will assist me."

I winced, imagining all Pierce would find right now would be half-drunk students and solstice parties. "Good God, Pierce," I said, when a passing cab saw us standing there and did a U-bangy. "I'm the one that got you involved. Lighten up."

"But—" he said, and I twined my fingers more surely into his as the cab pulled up.

"I'm involved. You're not getting rid of me, so get used to it."

Pierce's grip tightened on mine, and then he relaxed. "Thank you," he said, and in those two words, I saw how lost he was. He had until sunrise to save both the girl and his soul, and I was the only one who could get him through this nightmare that I lived in.

Chapter 6

The cabbie drove away from my house slowly, the sound of his car muffled from the piled snow. In the Hollows there would be bonfire parties and neighborhood howls, but here, on my street, it was quiet. Pierce's steps were almost silent next to mine as we left prints on the walk to the porch. It had stopped snowing, and I looked up at the red-bottomed clouds through the cold, black branches of the maple tree I had planted for my dad upon his death. My throat closed and I touched the tree in passing. I was glad he was at rest, but it would have been nice to have had him back again as solid as Pierce was—even if just for the night.

Pierce hung back as I went up the three cement steps and twisted the knob to no avail. "My mom must be out," I said, swinging my bag around to look for my keys. The porch light was on, and her prints showed where she had gone to the garage and not come back. Maybe some last-minute shopping? Maybe down to the I.S. tower to pick up Robbie? I had a bad feeling it was the latter.

"This is a very beautiful house," Pierce said, facing the

neighborhood and the bright lights and snowmen keeping guard.

"Thanks," I said as I dug in my jeans pocket for my house key. "Most witches live in the Hollows across the river in Kentucky, but my mom wanted to live here." Finding my keys, I looked up to see a faint bewilderment in his gaze. "Both she and my dad were in high school during the Turn, and I think she likes passively making trouble when she can get away with it—like living in a predominantly human neighborhood."

"As is the mother, so the daughter?" he said dryly.

My key was warm, and I slipped it into the lock. "If you like."

Only now did Pierce come up the steps, giving the street a last look before he did.

"Mom?" I called when I opened the door, but I knew from the dull glow of light in the hall coming from the kitchen that the house was empty. Glancing at Pierce on the threshold, I smiled. "Come on in."

Pierce looked at the gray slush on his boots. "I'm not of a mind to soil your rugs."

"So stomp your feet," I said, taking his arm and pulling him in. "Shut the door before you let all the heat out."

The shadow of the closing door prompted me to flick on the hallway light, and Pierce squinted at it. I hated the green color my mom had painted the hallway and living room. Pictures covered the passage to the kitchen: pictures of me and Robbie, slices of our lives.

I glanced back at Pierce, who was still staring at the light but clearly making an effort to not say anything. I hid a smile and wondered how much longer his efforts to not look impressed would win out over his curiosity.

"You have so many rugs," he finally said, following suit as I stomped my feet.

"Thanks," I said, and I shuffled out of my coat.

His eyes finally hit the walls, and he reached out. "And photographs. In color."

"You've seen pictures?" I asked, surprised, and he nodded.

"I've had my picture taken," he said proudly, then reached out. "This is you? It's beautiful," he said in awe. "The expression the artist captured is breathtaking. None of God's landscapes has ever looked so beautiful."

I gazed at the picture he was touching in reverence and then away with mixed feelings. It was a close-up of my face among the fall leaves, my eyes as green and vivid as all creation, my hair bringing out all the shades of autumn clustered about. I had just come back from a stint at the hospital and you could see that I was ill by my pale complexion and thin face. But my smile made it truly beautiful, my smile I had given to my dad as the shutter snapped, thanking him for the joy we had found in the simple pleasure of the day.

"My dad took it," I said, looking away. "Come in the kitchen," I said, wiping my eye when I noticed it was damp. *I was supposed to die before him, not the other way around.*

"I don't know how long my mom will be out," I said loudly, hearing his steps behind mine. "But if we can get what we need and leave, it will be all the better. Forgiveness being easier to get than permission . . ."

Pierce entered slowly, hesitating by the laminated table and taking in the ticking clock, the cold stove, and the double-pan sink as I dropped my coat and bag onto my chair. "You and your mother are alone?" he asked.

Surprised at the amount of wonder in his voice, I hesitated. "Yes. Robbie is visiting from the West Coast, but he goes back next week."

His deep blue eyes came back from the ceiling. "California?"

"Oregon."

Pierce looked again at the cold stove, undoubtedly guessing its use from the pot of solstice cranberry tea on it, now scrummed over and cold. "Your mother should be commended for raising you alone."

If he only knew how often it was the other way around. "She should, shouldn't she," I said, going to the coffeemaker and peeking into the filter to find unused grounds. "You want some coffee?"

Taking off his coat, Pierce draped it carefully over a chair. He checked his nonexistent tie, then moved his arms experimentally as if taking in how warm it was. "I'm of a mind, yes, but does our limited time allow for it?"

I flipped a switch and the coffeemaker started. I kind of liked his extra words. It made him sound classy. "Yup. You want to help me with the attic?"

Without waiting for an answer, I went down the other hallway to the rest of the house, Pierce right behind me. "That's the bathroom there," I said as we passed it. "My room is at the end of the hallway, and my mom's is across from it. Robbie has the front room, though it's more of a storage room, now."

"And the servants are in the attic?" he asked as I halted under the pull-down stairs.

"Servants?" I asked, gaping at him. "We don't have any servants."

Pierce looked as surprised as I felt. "But the rugs, the photos, the warmth of your home and its furnishings . . ."

His words trailed off as his hands spread wide in question, and I flushed when I got it. "Pierce," I said, embarrassed. "I'm totally middle class. The closest I've ever come to having a servant is winning a bet and having Robbie clean my room for a month."

The man's jaw dropped. "This is middle class?"

I nodded, stretching up for the pull cord and putting my

weight on it. "Most of the city is." The trapdoor barely moved, and my arms gave out. It snapped shut with a bang, and I dropped back down on my heels, disgusted.

Pierce smoothly took the cord and stepped under the door. He wasn't much taller, but he had more muscle. "I can do it," I said, but my arms were trembling, and I backed up while he swung the ladder down like it was nothing. But then again, it was.

Pierce looked up into the inky blackness spilling cool air down onto us, jumping when I flicked on the light.

"Sorry," I said, taking advantage of his surprise by pushing past him and up onto the ladder. "I'll be right back," I said, enjoying the cooler air up here smelling of wood and dusty boxes. The shush of a passing car from outside sounded odd and close. Arms wrapped around me, I looked over the past boxed up and piled haphazardly about, like memories in a person's brain. It was only a matter of knowing where a thought was and dusting it off.

My eyes lit upon the stack of carefully labeled tomato boxes that had my stuffed animals. A faint smile came over my face, and I stepped over the Halloween decorations to touch a dusty lid. I must have had about two hundred of them, all collected during my stints in and out of the hospital. I had counted them my friends, many taking on the names and personalities of my real friends who never made it out of the hospital that one last time. I knew my mom wanted them gone, but I couldn't throw them away, and as soon as I got my own place, I'd take them with me.

I lifted the first one and set it aside to find the box hiding under them. It was my dad's, tucked away lest my mom throw it out in a fit of melancholy. Some of his best stuff. I dug my fingernails into the little flaps to get a grip, grunting when it proved heavier than I thought. *God, what had I put in here, anyway?*

"Allow me," came Pierce's voice from my elbow, and I spun.

"Holy crap!" I exclaimed, then covered my mouth, feeling myself go red. "I'm sorry. I didn't know you were up here."

Pierce's shock at my language melted into almost laughter. "My apologies," he said, and I shifted to let him to lift the box with enviable ease. "I like attics. They're as peaceful as God's church. Alone and apart, but a body can hear everything. The past stacked up like forgotten memories, but with a small effort, brought down and enjoyed again."

I listened to the cold night and smiled. "I know exactly what you mean."

Watching my footing, I followed him to the stairway. He took the box from me and gestured that I should go before him, and, flattered at the chivalry, I did. My shoulders eased as the warmth of the house slipped over me, and I stood aside when Pierce lightly descended. He handed me the box to fold the ladder back up, but he hesitated at the bare bulb, still glowing in the attic. Without glancing at me for permission, he carefully pushed the light switch down.

Of course the light went out. A delighted smile came over him, and much to his credit, he didn't play with the switch but shoved the collapsible ladder closed and back into the ceiling. I watched his eyes travel over the lines of it as he did, as if memorizing how it worked.

"Thank you," I said as I went before him, back into the kitchen with the box.

The coffeemaker was gurgling its last, and Pierce looked at it, undoubtedly figuring out what it was from the rich scent that had filled the kitchen. "If that doesn't cap the climax," he said, almost missing the table as he took the box from me and set it down. "It made itself."

"I'll get you some," I said as I hustled to the cupboard. It smelled great as I poured out two cups and I handed him one, our fingers touching. He smiled, and something tight-

ened in my chest. *God, I am not falling for him. He's dead.*
But he did have a nice, mischievous smile.

"I hope I'm not making a mistake drinking this," he said.
"How real am I?"

I shrugged, and he took a sip, eyeing me over the rim to
make my breath catch. God, he had beautiful eyes.

His eyebrows shot up, and jerking, he started to violently
cough.

"Oh, golly," I said, remembering not to swear as I took
the cup from him before it could spill. "I'm sorry. You can't
drink, huh?"

"Strong," he gasped, his blue eyes vivid as they watered.
"Really strong."

I set his cup down and took a sip of mine. My mouth tried
to pucker up, and I forced myself to swallow. Crap, my mom
had filled the filter, and the coffee was strong enough to kill
a cat. "Don't drink that," I said, taking his cup and mine to
the sink. "It's terrible."

"No, it's fine."

I froze as he caught my hand. I turned, feeling his light but
certain grip. A slow quiver rose through me, and I stifled it
before it could show as a tremor. I was suddenly very aware
that we were here alone. Anything could happen—and as
the moment hung, his silence and almost-words ready to be
whispered that he was having thoughts, too—I nearly wished
it would. He was different. Strong but unsure. Capable but
lost. He knew I had been ill, and he didn't baby me. I liked
him. A lot, maybe. And he needed my help. No one had *ever*
needed my help before. No one. Especially someone as capable and strong as him.

"It's undrinkable," I said when I found my voice, and he
took his cup from me.

"If you made it, it's divine," he said, smiling like the devil
himself, and I felt my heart thump even as I knew he was
bullshitting me.

His fingers left mine, and my presence of mind returned. I wasn't a fainting debutante to fall for a line like that, but still, to have a man drink nasty coffee to impress me was way flattering. My eyebrows rose, and I wondered how far he would go. I had half a thought to let him drink the nasty stuff.

"Why thank you, Pierce," I said, smiling. "You are a true gentleman."

I turned to open the box, looking over my shoulder in time to see him staring into his mug with a melancholy sigh. Ten to one he was going to spill it, but there was an entire pot to refill his cup with.

The dust made my nose tickle as I unfolded the flaps. A slow smile spread over me as I looked at the stash and saw my dad everywhere. He'd made many of his own ley line charms for work, and being home sick most of the time, some of my earliest memories were of him and me at the table while the sun set and he prepped for a night on the street apprehending bad guys. I had my crayons, he had his chalk, and while I colored pixies and fairies, he'd sketch pentagrams, spill wax in ley line figures, and burn all sorts of concoctions to make Mom wave her hands and complain about the smell, secretly proud of him.

Smiling distantly, I ran a hand over my hair, remembering how it would snarl up from the forces that leaked from his magic as he explained a bit of lore while he worked, his eyes bright and eager for me to understand.

The soft scrape of Pierce setting his cup down by the box jerked me from my memories, and my focus sharpened. "Is there anything here you can use?" I asked, pushing it closer to him as we stood over it. "I'm more of an earth witch. Or I will be, when I get my license."

"Miss Rachel," he said lightly, his attention on the box's contents as his calloused fingers poked around, "only a witch of some repute can summon those at unrest, and only those of unsurpassed skill I expect can furnish them a body." A faint smile crossed his eyes. "Even one as transient as this one."

Embarrassed, I shrugged one shoulder. "It wasn't all me. Most of the energy came from the collective emotions of everyone at the square."

"And whose idea was it to work the charm at the square?" he said, taking out a handful of metallic disks and pins and discarding them into an untidy pile.

I thought back. It had been mine to go to the concert and use the emotion to help strengthen the curse, but Robbie's to use the square's instead. "Robbie's, I guess."

Pierce held a charm up to the light. "Ah," he said in satisfaction. "This I can use."

I looked at the thick silver washer with its pin running through it. Apart from a few ley line inscriptions lightly etched on it, the charm looked like the ones he'd set aside. "What is it?"

The man's smile grew positively devilish. "This likely bit of magic is a noisy lock picker," he said, then set it beside his cup of coffee.

"Noisy?"

Pierce was again rummaging. "It makes an almighty force to jolt the door from its hinges," he said lightly.

"Oh." I peered into the box with more interest and held the flaps out of his way. It was like looking into a box of chocolates, not knowing which ones were good until you took a bite.

A pleased sound escaped Pierce, and he held up another charm, his fingertip running over the symbols etched into it. "This one senses powerful magic. Perhaps it's still working?"

His gaze on the charm, he pulled the pin. The empty interior of the washer-like charm started to glow a harsh red.

Pierce seemed surprised, then he laughed. "Land sakes, I'm a fool. You hold it," he said, handing it over.

I took it, bemused when Pierce backed up, nearly into the hall.

A faint cramping seemed to make my palm twitch, and the harsh red faded to a rosy pink. I glanced at the box of ley line stuff, and Pierce shook his head, coming back and taking it from me. Again it glowed brilliantly.

"It's functioning perfectly," he said, and the spell went dark when he put the pin back in place. "I've no mind to guess how effective it will be if it's glowing like that from me," and he set it gently on the table.

My lips parted, and I looked at him, and then the charms on the table. "You're triggering it? I thought it was the spells."

Pierce laughed, but it was nice. "I'm a spectre, walking the earth with a body that is a faint step from being real. I expect that qualifies as strong magic."

Flustered, I shrugged, and he put his attention back in the box.

"This one is for calling familiars," he said, dropping it onto the table with the discards. "This one for avoiding people who are searching for you. Oh, this is odd," he said, holding one up. "A charm to give a body a hunched back? That has to be a misspelling."

I took it from him, making sure our fingers touched. Yeah, he was dead, but I wasn't. "No, it's right," I said. "It's from a costume. My dad used to dress up on Halloween."

"Halloween?" Pierce asked, and I nodded, lost in a memory.

"For trick-or-treat. I'd be the mad scientist, and he'd be my assistant. We would go up and down the halls of the hospital . . ." My emotions gave a heavy-hearted lurch, and I swallowed down a lump. "We'd hit the nurse's desk in the children's ward, and then the old people's rooms."

I didn't want to talk about it, and my fingers set it down, sliding away with a slow sadness. It seemed Pierce understood, since he was silent for a moment, then said, "You look the picture of health, Miss Rachel. A fair, spirited, young woman."

Grimacing, I picked up the charm and dropped it back into the box. "Yeah, well, try telling my brother that."

Again he was silent, and I wondered what his nineteenth-century morals were making of me and my stubborn determination. He said I was spirited, but I didn't think that was necessarily a good thing back then.

"This is one I'd like to take if I might," Pierce said as he held up a rather large, palm-sized metallic amulet. "It detects people within a small space."

"Cool," I said, taking it from him and pulling the pin. "Does it work?"

Again, that cramping set my hand to feeling tingly and odd. The entire middle of the amulet went opaque, two dots showing in the middle. Us, apparently. "Still works," I said, replacing the pin and handing it to him. "You may as well have it. I've got no use for it."

"Thank you," he said, dropping it into his pocket with the noisy lock picker. "And this one? It also creates a distraction."

I grinned. "Another boom spell?"

"Boom?" he said, then nodded, getting it. "Yes, a boom spell. They are powerful effective. I have the understanding to set one unaided, but I need to commune with the ever-after to do it. This one will suffice."

I had a feeling that most of the spells he was putting in his pocket were ones he knew how to do unaided. I mean, he'd blown the doors in the I.S. tower, and then set a ward over them. I hadn't minded his using me to draw off the line. Which made the next step of wanting to go with him easy. I mean, I could really help him, not just this tour-guide stuff.

"Pierce," I said, fingering the charm to make a hunch-back.

The man's attention was in the box, but he seemed to know where my thoughts lay as his next words were, "There is no need for you to accompany me, Miss Rachel. It has nothing to do with your health, and everything to do with me resolving this on my own." He pulled out a charm. "This is a likely one, as well."

Momentarily distracted, I leaned until our shoulders touched. "What is it?"

Pierce slid down a few inches to put space between us. "It allows a body to listen upon a conversation in a room set apart."

My eyebrows rose. "So that's how they always knew what I was up to."

He laughed, the masculine rolling sound seeming to soak into the corners of the kitchen like water into the dry sand bed of a stream. The house had been so empty of it, and hearing it again was painful as our lack was laid bare.

"Your father was a rascal," Pierce said, not aware I had been struck to the core and was trying to blink back the un-expected tears.

"You say that like it's a bad thing," I quipped. *Why is this hitting me so hard?* I thought, blaming it upon my recent hope to talk to him again.

"Oh look," I said, my hand diving in to pull out a familiar spell. "What's this doing in here? This is my mom's."

Pierce took it from me, our fingers touching a shade too long, but his eyes never flicked to me. "It's a ley line charm to set a circle, but unlike the ungodly rare earth magic equiva-lent, you need to connect to a line to use it."

"My mother is terrible at ley line magic," I said conver-sationally as Pierce collected all the discards and dumped them in, my mom's included. "My dad used to make all her circles for her. She used to set this when she still made his earth magic charms for him."

I saw him stiffen when I reached back in the box, took out my mom's amulet, and placed it around my neck. "I can tap a line. It will work for me."

"No," he said, facing me. "You aren't coming. I've forbidden it."

My breath came out in a scoff. "You forbid it?" I said, tilting my head up. "Look, Pierce," I said, hand going to my hip. "You can't forbid me anything. I do what I want."

"I have forbidden you from accompanying me," he said as if that settled it. "I'm thankful for what you have done, and that you're letting me borrow your father's spells shows how gracious and honorable your spirit is. Now prove it and stay home as you should."

"You little chauvinistic pig!" I exclaimed, feeling my pulse race and my knees start to go weak. Trying to hide it, I crossed my arms over my chest and leaned against the counter. "I can help you, and you know it. Just how are you going to get there, Mr. Man From The Past? Walk it? In the snow? It's got to be at least fifteen miles."

Pierce didn't seem to be fazed by my temper, which ticked me off all the more. He calmly shrugged into his long coat and folded the box closed. "May I still take these?" he asked, eyebrows high.

"I said you could," I snapped. "And I'm coming too."

"Thank you," he said, dropping the last into a pocket. "I will try my best to return your father's belongs to you, but it's unlikely."

He turned to go, me tight behind him. "You can't just walk out of here," I said, my legs shaking from fatigue. Damn it, I hated being like this. "You don't know where you're going."

"I know where he was before. It's unlikely he's moved."

We were in the hall, and I nearly ran into Pierce when he

stopped short at the door, eyeing the handle. "You're going to walk?" I said in disbelief.

He opened the door and took a deep breath of dry, chill air. "I've a mind to, yes."

The cold hit me, and I held my crossed arms close now for warmth. "The world is different, Pierce. We're out, and it's harder to find just one of us now."

That seemed to give him pause. "I will find him," he said, and he stepped out onto the snowy stoop. "I have to. My soul and the girl's both depend upon it."

"You won't find them before the sun comes up," I called after him. *God, what is it with men and their pride?*

"Then I expect I should run."

Then I expect I should run, I mocked in my thoughts, then came out on the stoop. "Pierce," I said, and he turned. There was a whisper of hidden heat in his eyes, shocking the words right out of my head. I blinked at him, stunned that it was there and directed at me. He wasn't amused at my temper. He wasn't bothered by it. He respected it, even as he told me no.

"Thank you, Miss Rachel," he said, and I stumbled back, my eyes darting from his for an instant when my heel hit the frame of the open door. "I can't endanger you any further."

He leaned in, and I froze. My heart pounded. I found my hands against his chest, but I didn't push him away.

"You are fiery and bold," he whispered in my ear, and I shivered. "Like a fey filly who knows her own thoughts and won't be broke but by her will. I don't have a mind to be delicate about it. If I did, I would court you long and lovingly, living for the hour when I would earn your trust and your attentions. I have but this night, so my words must be bold at the risk of offending you and being handed the mitten."

"You didn't," I said, not knowing what my gloves had to

do with it. Tension had me stiff, but inside I was a quivering mix of anticipation. "I'd give anything if you'd kiss me," I said. "I mean," I said when he tilted his head to look at me, his eyes wide in shock, "I've kissed guys before. It's like a handshake these days," I lied, just wanting to know what his lips on mine would feel like. "Almost required if you're leaving."

He hesitated, and my shoulders slumped when his fingers began slipping away.

"Ah, the devil take it," he said suddenly, then rocked back. Before I knew what he was doing, he curved an arm around my back, setting his free hand against the doorframe by my head. He leaned in, and as I took a startled breath, his lips found mine.

A small noise escaped me, and my eyes flew wide. I stood there on my porch in the cold and electric light, and let him kiss me, too shocked to do anything else. His lips were cool, but they warmed against me, and his beard was soft. His hand at my back kept me to him, protective and aggressive all at the same time. It sent a tingling jolt to dive to my middle, settling low and insistent.

"Pierce!" I mumbled, nearly driven to distraction by the sudden passion, but when he threatened to pull away, I wrapped my arms hesitantly about his waist. Hell, I had been kissed before, but they were bad kissers, all groping hands and sloppy tongues. This was . . . exquisite, and it plucked a chord in me that had never been touched.

He felt it when my desire rebounded into him, and with a soft sound that held both his want and restraint, he pulled away. Our lips parted, and I stared at him, shaken to my core. Damn, he was a good kisser.

"You are a most remarkable woman," he said. "I thank you humbly for the chance you have gifted me to redeem my sins."

Redeem sins. Yeah.

I stood there like an idiot as he took the stairs with a purposeful gait until he reached the shoveled walk. Unhesitating, he turned to the left and picked up the pace to run.

Damn . . .

I swallowed, trying to shake it off. Arms going around myself, I glanced up and down the quiet, snow-hushed street to see if anyone was watching. No one was, but I imagined Pierce had looked before he pinned me to the door like that . . . and kissed me senseless.

"Damn," I whispered, then took a deep breath to feel the cold slip in to replace the warmth. He certainly knew what he was doing. Not only had he gotten me to stay, but I wasn't angry with him at all. Must be a charm.

Charm. Yeah, he was charming all right. *Like that changed anything?*

Pulse fast, I went inside. I flicked off the coffeemaker, and then seeing the dusty box sitting there like a red flag waving in the breeze, I scribbled a quick note for my mom, telling her Robbie was at the I.S. and that I had fled with someone I had met at the square who knew who had taken Sarah. I had the car and was going to help him. I'd be back about sunrise.

I looked at it, then added, LOVE YOU—RACHEL.

I shivered as I stuffed an arm into a coat sleeve. I was going to help a ghost rescue a missing child from a vampire. God! A dead vamp, probably.

"This is what you want to do for a living," I muttered as I snatched up a set of keys, my fingers trembling. "If you can't do it now, you may as well go to the coast with your brother."

No way. I felt alive, my heart pounding, and my emotions high. It was a great sensation, and it stayed with me all the way out to the garage. A spring in my step, I yanked the garage door up and into the ceiling with a satisfying quickness. I usually had to have my mom do it.

As I strode to the driver's side, my fingers traced the smooth lines of the beat-up Volkswagen bug I had bought with what had been left over from selling The Bat. It ran most of the time. I got in, feeling how stiff the vinyl seats were from the cold. The temperature had been dropping steadily now that the snow had stopped, and I was freezing.

"Please start . . ." I begged, then patted the steering wheel when it sputtered to life. "Tell me I can't come?" I whispered, turning to look behind me as I backed out with a tinny putt-putt of a sound. Okay, I didn't have a real license yet, but who was going to give me a ticket on the solstice? Scrooge?

Still riding the high, I putted down the street, lights on and scanning the sidewalk. I found him two blocks down. He was still running, but he was in the street now, probably after finding too many of our neighbors hadn't shoveled their walks. I rolled my window down and pulled up alongside of him. He glanced at me, then stopped with a look of ambivalence.

I grinned. "Sorry for ruining your farewell speech. I really liked it. You want a ride?"

"You can drive," he said, his eyes tracing the car's odd shape.

"Of course I can." It was cold, and I flicked the heat on. The almost-warm air shifted my hair, and I saw him look at the drifting strands, making me wonder what it would feel like if he ran his fingers through it.

He stood in the freezing night, not a puff of breath showing as he stood to look charming in his indecision. "It's powerfully difficult to run and not try to breathe at the same time," he finally said. "Do you know the streets to the east hills?"

I nodded, and my grin grew that much wider. His head down dejectedly, he came around the front, the lights flashing bright as they hit him. I stifled my smile when he fumbled for the latch, finally figuring it out and getting in. He settled himself as I accelerated slowly.

"You will stay in the carriage when we get there," he grumbled, stomping the snow from his boots, and I just smirked.

Yeah. Right.

Chapter 7

Faint on the cold air was the singing of Christmas carolers, obvious now that I'd turned the car off. My car door thumped shut, the sound muffed from the mounds of snow the plows had thrown up, and I breathed slowly, pulling the crisp night deep into me. Above, the stars looked especially sharp from the dry air. It had gotten cold, ice-cracking cold. The faint breeze seemed to go right through my coat. It was about four in the morning. Only Inderlanders and crazy humans were up this time of night, which was fine by me.

Pierce's door shut a moment behind mine, and I smiled at him over the car. He didn't smile back, his brow furrowed in an expression of coming nastiness. While he paced around to my side, I leaned against the cold metal and gazed at the house we had parked across from.

We were way up in the hills in the better part of town where the well-to-do had lived ever since inclined-plane railways had made it easy to make it up the steep slopes. The house in question was older than that, making it remote and lonely in Pierce's time. It was a monster of a structure, clearly added to and rebuilt along with the times, with multiple stories, turrets, and a wraparound porch of smooth river rocks: old money, big trees, and a fantastic view of Cincinnati. Bright Christmas decorations were everywhere, flashing in an eerie silent display.

The sound of Pierce's shoes crunching on the frozen slush jolted me into motion, and I pushed off the car and headed to the wide porch.

"I would request you retire into the carriage and wait," he said from beside me.

I kept my eyes forward as we crossed the street. "It's called a car, and you can request all you want, but it's not going to happen."

We reached the shoveled sidewalk and Pierce grabbed my wrist. I jerked to a stop, startled at the strength he was using.

"Forgive me, Miss Rachel," he said, lips pressed thin and tight. "You're full of grit, but I simply will not be able to live with myself if harm comes to you because of me."

My own anger stirred. "Then it's a good thing you're not alive, huh?"

Shaking his head, he started to tug me back to the car. "I'm sorry for using my advantage to force you. Truly I am."

Here comes the him-hoisting-me-over-his-shoulder bit, with me kicking and screaming as he locks me in my own car? Not going to happen. "Let go," I threatened as he pulled me a step. "I mean it, Pierce. Let go, or you're going to be in a world of hurt." But he didn't.

Glad now I didn't have on mittens, I yanked him to a stop, spun my wrist with a loop-de-loop motion into a modified acrobat twin-hold on his palm, stepped under his arm, and flipped him into a snowbank.

He hit it with a puff of snow, staring up at me in surprise. "Land sakes, how did you do that?" he stammered, eyes wide in the low street light.

I stood over him with my hands on my hips, utterly satisfied. "Try to lock me in the car again, and I'll show you."

Pierce started to get up, and I reached to help him. Making a grunt, he accepted, rising to brush the snow from his long coat with sharp, bothered motions.

"I'm going in there," I said, nodding at the house.

"Miss Rachel," he started, and I took a step forward, getting into his face.

"This is what I want to do with my life," I said. "I have a circle amulet. I'm not helpless. And you can't stop me."

Shifting on his feet, he started to look annoyed. "Rachel, I'm schooled for this."

"And you still ended up dead," I shot back.

"That's my very argument. A body can see it's too dangerous." I made a face, and he took both my hands in his, adding sincerely, "I know you're of a mind to help. You're a brave, courageous woman, but you mustn't kick. This vampire is several hundred years dead, and you are eighteen. Consider it logically."

I rather liked his fingers in mine, but I pulled away, not wanting him to make me into putty. Again. "Logically?" I said, starting to get cold. "Yes, let's look at this logically. Training or not, you don't have anything but a few trinkets to help you if you can't tap a line. You don't have a chance to rescue that girl without me, and you know it."

He hesitated, and I surged ahead at the worried slant to his eyes. "Tell me you don't need me," I said, pointing. "That being able to tap a line isn't going to make the difference between saving her or not. Tell me that."

Pierce's gaze went to our feet, then rose. "I can't," he said firmly.

"Then I'm coming with you."

Again I started for the door. Pierce walked a step behind, slow and ponderous. "Now I have to watch for you, too," I heard him mutter, but I didn't care. I was going.

I slowed to slip my hand into his. He started, and I tapped a line. Energy flowed coolly into me to make my hair start to float around the edges of my hat, and I gave his fingers a squeeze. "It's going to be all right," I said firmly, and I shivered when he pulled a thin trace of power into himself.

We were almost up to the wide porch with its stylized Christmas tree when I realized his intent was to storm the front. "Uh, shouldn't we go in the back door or something?" I asked, and he smiled.

"You've listened to too many adventure tales. They never expect the front door."

"Still," I said as he knocked briskly.

"The front door," he said, glancing askance at me and tugging his coat straight. "They undoubtedly have made note of our presence, and it looks foolish to be caught skulking behind the trash bins."

I jumped at the rattle of the doorknob. A surge of adrenaline, and my pulse quickened. I stood wide-eyed beside Pierce as the door opened to show Sarah, standing alone and beautiful in an elegant dress of old lace. Her face was pale, but her look of fear set one of my worries to rest. She hadn't been bitten and bound yet.

Pierce saw her, and he smiled. "And sometimes, it's that easy."

Sarah's mouth opened. "It's a trap!" she shrilled, still standing there. "Help me!"

With a thump, my heart tripped into overdrive. I stumbled back when two men in black came from around the doorframe. One yanked Sarah inside. The other reached past the threshold, and before I could find the breath to scream, jerked us over the threshold.

Now I shrieked, finding myself skating across the hardwood floor to slide into the wall in a crumpled heap.

A loud "Ow!" pulled my head up, and I found Pierce askew on the stairway leading to the upper floors. I got to my feet, tense and hunched. Sarah was gone, but I could hear her crying. Her sobs grew fainter, but never disappeared. A door slammed.

Pierce rose and tossed his black hair out of his eyes. His lips were pressed together, and he seemed mad at himself more than anything else. The remaining man, a vampire by the glint of fang and telltale grace, was fronting him. I stumbled to stand against the wall, and he focused on me.

"Don't touch me," I said, feeling a faint pull from his charisma and a lot of fear.

Pierce touched his lip, surprise widening his eyes when his hand came away red with blood. "Inform your master I wish to parlay," he said, his words almost laughably formal. "We have a small gentleman-matter standing between us."

"Where's the girl?" I blurted, thinking I could hear her under my feet somewhere.

The vampire between us and the door smiled, chilling me. "I'd be more worried about your own neck, little witch," he said to me, but looking at Pierce, clearly the greater threat.

"Christopher!" Pierce shouted, and I felt a wash of dizziness. "Come out of your hole, you disgusting spawn. We have a matter of early interment to discuss!"

The vampire moved. I pressed against the wall as he took a too-fast step to Pierce and smacked him.

"Pierce!" I shouted as the small man fell backwards into the stairs again. "Leave him alone!" I shouted at the vampire.

Standing at the foot of the stairs, the vampire smiled. "Do you have a mommy, little girl? Will she cry for you?"

Fear slid down my spine, pushing out the fatigue and the dizziness. I stood, alive for what seemed like the first time. Too bad it was about to end. Right when it was getting good.

"Pay me mind, not her," said Pierce, picking himself up again.

The vampire took one step to me, and Pierce pulled a

charm from his pocket. I had an instant to prepare, and then he pulled the pin.

The front hallway shook in a *boom* of sound. I cowered as the chandelier swayed, and the windows in the door blew out. Falling into a ball, I crouched in the corner where the wall met the stairway, feeling my ears throb.

Someone touched my shoulder. Panic gave me strength. Wide-eyed, I turned to strike, stopping at the soft pull of ley line running through me.

Pierce.

Exhaling in a wash of relief, I found him close and worried. He crouched beside me and fingered another amulet. "Grit your teeth, and close your eyes," he said. "Forgive me if it's too much."

I nodded. Hunching down, I tried to become one with the floor. My breath caught as a silver-lined ribbon of ever-after iced through me to leave the taste of tinfoil in my veins. The soft presence of Pierce's body covered mine, sheltering me.

A second boom of sound pulsed over us, and in a visible cloud, the scent of dust and broken wood rose. Coughing, I looked up as Pierce slipped his hand in mind and helped me stand. The vampire was out cold against the wall beside the door. But even more startling was the four-foot-wide hole in the floor between us.

Pierce peered into my eyes, striking me silent with how concerned he was. "Are you well? Did I hurt you?"

I shook my head. "There's a hole in the floor."

Pierce pulled me to it. "I'll catch you."

I held my breath as he nonchalantly stepped off the edge of the floor and dropped from sight. From across the room came a soft groan, and the vampire moved.

Pulse hammering, I sat on the floor and dangled my feet. "Here I come!" I warned him, then dropped.

I stifled a shriek, but it came out as a yelp when he caught me and we fell in a tangle of arms and legs. We were in a lower living room with soft carpet and lighting, and expensive paintings on the walls. An entertainment center stood in one corner. There were two doors, one beside us, the other across the room.

"You're heavier than you look," Pierce puffed, and I scrambled off of him.

"Yeah, well, you're a lousy catch." I glanced up at the hole in the floor, then back to the TVs. There were a couple of them, and my lips parted when I recognized a black and white shot of my little car looking funny out there against the expensive estates. Closer to the house was the imprint in the drift where Pierce hit. It made me glad we'd come in the front.

A frightened whimper caught my attention. Together Pierce and I looked to a far corner dusky with a soft light. My hope withered to nothing as I saw Sarah in the grip of a small man dressed in casual sophistication. His silk-clad arm was wrapped around her, covering her mouth. Tears marked her face, and she was terrified.

"Gordian Pierce," the vampire said in a soft, almost feminine voice. "You should have stayed dead."

I pressed back into Pierce, then realizing it made me look afraid, I rocked forward. I was still holding his hand. I was telling myself it was so he could do his magic, but the real reason was I was as scared as Sarah.

"You haven't changed," Pierce said, a new accent coloring his words. "Still the same Nancy boy forcing your putrid self on little girls, I see."

Sarah made a heartbreaking sound, and the vampire, Christopher, I guess, stiffened. His knuckles went white where he pressed his hand over her mouth. "I saw you in the ground," he said bitterly. "You shouldn't be here."

Pierce's hand clenched on mine in a bitter anger. "Your first mistake was putting me in blasphemed ground," he said shortly. "It left me in a mind to return. Eliminating your filth of existence is worth postponing heaven for."

Christopher's chin rose, and a snarl curved his lips up. I knew he was several hundred years old, but he looked thirty. Witch magic at its finest.

"Good," he said, shoving the girl to a nearby couch, where she collapsed to sob. "I'll enjoy hearing your screams again between the beautiful thumps of dirt hitting your casket."

I felt a chill, imagining it. Pierce's hand on mine went damp with sweat. Mine probably.

"You foul bastard," Pierce said, his voice shaking. "I will not leave without the girl."

Intuition and the shifting of light pulled my attention to the hole in the ceiling. "Look out!" I cried, pulling Pierce and myself back when the two vampires from the front door dropped down. Pierce's free hand started making gestures behind his back, and my pulse raced to make me light-headed. Smiling like death, they started to advance.

"No!" their master shouted, and they hesitated. "Let them stand." He flicked his eyes to the one who had carried Sarah down here earlier. "You, man the outside grounds," he said, then turned a disparaging look at the other. "You mind the stairs. From outside. I don't want to be disturbed."

He turned to Pierce and me, and I thought I heard the small man beside me mutter a curse. "I enjoy trespassers," the vampire said. "The law is going to see you dead again, Pierce. All you have brought to me is more terror to lap up. What a timely gift. Thank you."

He nodded curtly at the two vampires, and they slipped away, one through the door and stair behind us, the other jumping straight up through the hole in the floor. Sarah was still crying, and the twin clicks of two doors shutting were ominous. Great. I think it was about to get ugly.

"Believe me," Pierce whispered, his hand giving mine a quick squeeze.

I flicked a look at him, then back to the vampire. "What?"

Pierce angled to get in front of me. "He's going to kill me, but I'm already dead. Trust me. As soon as he thinks I'm dead, I'll move against him. Get the girl out. Please."

I didn't want to leave him here. I wouldn't! "Pierce . . ."

But his fingers slipped from mine.

A jolt of line energy burst in me as I took the entire line myself. Pierce had been siphoning off of me, and I hadn't even known it. Stumbling back, I barely saw Pierce jump away from me, shouting curses at the vampire.

Lips curled to show his teeth, Christopher went to meet him.

"Pierce, no!" I shouted from where I had fallen to one knee, transfixed when they met. The man didn't have a chance. My heart pounded in fear as they grappled, the vampire finding his neck and sinking his teeth.

Pierce's groan struck through me, and I almost panicked. "This can't be happening," I whispered. "This can't be happening!"

I jumped when the girl darted across the room, a white shadow fleeing. She clutched at me, her tear-streaked face pleading up at me. "Get me out," she whispered, as if afraid he would hear. "Please, get me out!"

I looked at Pierce, slack in the vampire's grip. The animal hung over him, sickening me.

"Help me!" she sobbed, trying to drag me to the door, but I knew what was behind it.

Jaw clenched, I pried her grip off my arm and shoved her behind me. "Give me a minute," I muttered. My heart was pounding too fast, and my knees were going weak. Striding to the nearest wall, I lugged a picture from it, staggering at its unexpected weight.

"Get off him!" I shouted, dropping it on the vampire.

Glass cracked and it slid off his back. Snarling, the vampire let Pierce fall, turning with a look on his face to send a ribbon of fear-laced adrenaline through me. Slowly I backed up. Maybe I should've taken my chances with the vampire behind door number one.

His mouth red with Pierce's blood, the vampire started for me, hunched and looking as if he was in pain. "Stupid, foolish witch," he said, wiping his mouth and then licking the blood from his hand. "Your species will thank me for taking you out before you can breed. The too smart and the too stupid are all culled first. I don't know which one you are."

"Stay back," I said, hand raised as I almost tripped on the rug.

From behind me the girl gasped. My gaze darted to Pierce as he moved. Hope surged, and sensing it, the vampire turned around.

"How many times do I have to kill you?" he snarled when Pierce pulled himself upright, and with a dark grimace, tugged his coat straight. His neck was clean. Not a mark on it.

I didn't understand. I had seen blood. But had it been real? He was a freaking ghost!

"Once was enough, and I expect it will be your undoing, God willing," the man said raggedly, and my breath came in with a hiss when a ball of green ever-after swirled into existence between his two hands. He flung it at the vampire. The vampire lunged sideways, and the green, red, and black mass smacked into the wall, harmless.

My short-lived hope vanished, and I looked at Pierce across the living room. I knew it had been everything he had stored in his chi. He had gambled everything on that one throw. There was nothing left. He was helpless unless he could reach me and refill his chi. And there was a vampire between us.

Christopher seemed to know it, and he started to laugh. "I may not be able to kill a ghost," he said in perverted glee. "But I can still tear your fucking head off."

I backed to the door with the girl. Nothing left. Pierce had nothing left but those stupid ley line charms of my dad. I felt my expression go slack in thought. The ley line charms . . .

My hand went up to grip the charm around my neck. It would make a circle only I could break. Sarah and I would be safe, but Pierce . . .

Pierce saw my hand, trembling as it gripped the spell. "Use it, Rachel," he said, falling into a crouch. "Invoke the amulet!"

I tried to swallow, failing. I pulled the charm from around my neck, the chain catching my hair and tugging free. The vampire lunged to catch Pierce. He cried out in pain.

"Hey, prissy face!" I shouted, voice trembling. "You're a pathetic excuse of a bat, you know that? Can't get your fangs wet without a glass of milk? Come and get me. He doesn't have any blood in him."

The vampire turned and hissed, and my stomach did a flip-flop. *Shit.*

"Rachel, no!" Pierce cried, but the vampire tossed him into a wall like a rude book. I winced when he hit and slid down to stare at me in fear.

"Trust me," I mouthed, and he scrambled up. But he was too far away, and he knew it.

Pulse hammering, I fell into a crouch and beckoned the vampire to me. "You're nothing but a sorry-assed, hide-in-the-ground child molester," I taunted, and the vampire went almost choleric.

"I'm going to kill you slow," he said, advancing slowly.

"Great," I said, estimating the distance between us. "But first, catch this!"

His hands flew up as I pulled the pin and threw the amulet. It thumped into the vampire's grip, and he sneered at me. I smiled back, and as smooth and pure as water, a wash of gold-tinted ever-after flowed up and around him, trapping him.

"No!" the vampire screamed, throwing the amulet, but it was too late. My eyes widened and I fell back in shocked awe as the vampire seemed to devolve into a raving lunatic, hammering at the barrier between us, almost spitting in frustration. Howling like a mad thing, he threw himself against it, over and over. And it held.

Shaking, I leaned against the back of a couch. "Stupid ass," I muttered.

"Miss Rachel!" Pierce cried out, and I blinked when he grabbed me, spinning me to face him. His hands heavy on my shoulders, he looked me up and down, his blue eyes searching me. "Are you well?"

I blinked again at him. The adrenaline was wearing off, and I was feeling woozy. "Sure. Yes. I think so."

The girl screamed, and a vampire dropped into the room through the hole in the ceiling. From behind the other door, the thumping of feet said the other was coming, too, drawn by Christopher's furious shouts.

Pierce took me in a brief, surprising hug. "You're grit, Rachel. Pure grit," he said, rocking me back. "But you should have used it to save yourself and the girl. All they have to do is throw you into the bubble, and it will fall."

"Nonsense," I said, hearing my words slur. "Just pull some more power from me and blast them back to hell."

His eyes widened, and he held me upright as the door behind us opened to show the second vampire. The girl was at our feet, sobbing. I might have joined her, but I had a feeling I was going to pass out soon, anyway. Damn it, I hated this. I was just kidding myself that I could do this for a living.

I pushed from Pierce, unsteady as I put my hands on my hips and looked from one vampire to the other. I felt like I was drunk. Faint through the broken ceiling came the wail of sirens. "You all better go," I said boldly, sounding like John Wayne to my ears. "Or my friend here will blast you all to hell. He can do it. Can't you?"

But Pierce was watching the monitors with the strength of hope in his grip as he held me upright. I wavered as the two vampires exchanged a knowing look. The master vampire trapped in the circle hesitated in his tantrum, going white-faced when his two servants gave him a short, nervous bow.

"Don't leave me!" the master vampire shouted, hammering on the invisible barrier. "I will hunt you down and take your last blood, then kill you again!"

I smirked, muscles going slack. Pierce caught me with a little grunt. On the monitor were several I.S. cruisers, a news van, and, Lord help me, my mother in her Buick. Robbie got out first, having to be restrained from storming the house on his own. "That's the I.S.," I said, my words running into each other in a soft, slow drawl. "I left my mother a note. She's probably got half the force behind her." Blinking, I struggled to focus on the two vampires. "Don't mess with my mom. She'll kick your . . . ass."

The two vampires looked at each other, and as their master howled, they levered themselves back out through the ceiling. There was a faint thump of feet overhead—and they were gone.

"I think I'm going to pass out," I said, breathless, and Pierce eased me to the carpet. My head lolled, and the edges of my sight grayed. "I'm sorry," I started to babble, feeling light and airy. "I shouldn't have come down here. I'm no good at this."

"You are exceptional at this." Pierce held my hand and fanned me with a magazine. "But please, Miss Rachel, don't pass out. Stay with me. At least a little longer. If you succumb, your circle might fall."

"That's not good," I mumbled, struggling to keep my eyes open, but damn it, I had overtaxed my body and it was shutting down. When the adrenaline had flowed, it had been fantastic. I had been alive and strong. I felt normal. Now all that was left was the ash of a spent fire. And it was starting to rain.

"Rachel?"

It was close, and I pulled my eyes open to find Pierce had cradled my head in his lap. "Okay," I breathed. "Are you okay?"

"Yes," he said, and I smiled, snuggling in so I could hear his heartbeat. Maybe it was mine. "Stay with me," he said. "Just a few minutes more. They're almost here."

Distantly I heard the sound of thumping feet overhead and loud voices. The heater clicked on, and the warm breeze made my hair tickle my face. Pierce brushed it off me, and I opened my eyes, smiling up at him blissfully.

"Holy shit!" a deep voice said. "There's a hole in the floor."

The girl revealed us with a little sob. Standing under the hole she peered up, screaming, "Get me out of here! Someone get me out of here!"

"My God, it's the girl!" another man said. "Damn, he was telling the truth."

"Just a little longer, Miss Rachel," Pierce whispered, and I closed my eyes again. But an icing of fear slid through me, almost waking me up when my mom's voice cut through the babble, high-pitched and determined.

"Of course Robbie was telling the truth. You smart-assed agents think you're so clever your crap doesn't stink, but you couldn't spell your way out of a paper bag."

"That's my mom," I whispered, and Pierce's grip on me tightened.

"Rachel?" she called, her voice getting louder, then, "Get your sorry ass out of my way. Rachel! Are you down there? My God, she circled a vampire. Look what my daughter did! She got him. She got him for you, you lazy bastards. Ignore my kids when they come to you, huh? I bet the news crew would like that. You either drop the charges on my kids, or I'm going out there and give them what they want."

I smiled, but I couldn't open my eyes. "Hi, Mom," I whispered, my breath slipping past my lips. And then to Pierce, I added, "Don't mind my mother. She's a little nuts."

He chuckled, raising my head and rocking me. "I expect a body would have to be to raise you properly."

I wanted to laugh, but I couldn't, so I just smiled. There was the brush of wind against me as people moved about us. Someone had finally gotten Sarah out of here, and the sound of two-way radios and excited chatter had replaced her blubbering. "I'm sorry," I said, feeling like I'd failed them. "Someone needs to circle him. I'm passing out."

"Rest," Pierce whispered. "They have him. Let your circle down, Miss Rachel. I've got you."

I could hear a faint call for an ambulance and oxygen, and I had a fading thought that I was going to spend the last half of my solstice in the hospital, but we had done it.

And with that, I let go of the line and let oblivion take me, satisfied to the depths of my soul.

Chapter 8

They say when you're ten, you think your parents know everything. At sixteen, you're convinced they know nothing at all. By thirty, if you haven't figured out they really did know what they were doing, then you're still sixteen. After watching my mom work the I.S. like a fish on a line, I was suitably impressed that she knew everything in the freaking world.

Smiling, I tugged the wool blanket tighter around me and scooted my folding chair closer to the small fire Robbie had started in the backyard. My mom was beside me, pointedly between my brother and me as we toasted marshmallows and waited for sunrise. I hadn't been outside very long, and my breath steamed in the steadily brightening day. It was a few hours past my normal bedtime, but that's not why my arms shook and my breath was slow. Damn, I was tired.

I'd fully expected to wake up in the hospital or ambulance, and was surprised when I had come to in the back of my mom's car, still at the crime site. Wrapped in an I.S. blanket, I had stumbled out looking for Pierce to find myself in a media circus. Robbie and I had stood in the shadows and watched in awe as my mother worked a system I hadn't even known existed. Through her deadly serious threats disguised as scatterbrained fussing, she not only managed to get the charges against me for willful destruction of private property dropped, but got them to agree that I didn't have anything to do with their doors being blown out, much less fleeing their custody with an unknown person. The I.S. personnel were more than happy to give my mom whatever she wanted if she would keep her voice down, seeing as three news crews were within shouting distance.

Apparently the vampire I'd helped bring in had a history of such kidnappings, but because of his clout, he'd been getting away with it for years. I hated to go along with the shush work, but I didn't want a record, either. So as long as my mother, Robbie, myself, and the girl kept quiet—her parents being placated with enough money to put Sarah through the university and therapy of her choice—the vampire would be charged with kidnapping, not the stiffer crime of underage enticement.

It didn't bother me as much as I'd thought it would. He was still going to jail, and if vampire justice was like any other kind, he'd probably wake up one night with a wooden spoon jammed through his heart. Vampires didn't like pedophiles any more than the next guy.

So Robbie's and my trip to the I.S. had been dulled to an anonymous tip, making the I.S. out to be the heroes. Whatever. Along with the notoriety went any charges they might file against me. Mom had grounded me, though. God, I was nearly nineteen and grounded. What was up with that?

Of Pierce, there had been no sign. No one remembered seeing him apart from my mom.

A sigh shifted my shoulders, coming out as a thin mist catching the pink light of the nearing sunrise.

"Rachel," my mom said, reaching to tug the blanket closed

around my neck, "that's the third sigh in as many minutes. I'm sure he will be back."

I grimaced that she knew where my thoughts were, then searched the sky and the strips of clouds throwing back the sun in bands of pink. I'd known he'd be gone by sunrise, but I wished I'd had the chance to say goodbye. "No," I said, bobbing my marshmallow in and out of the flame. "He won't. But that's okay."

My mom gave me a sideways hug. "He looked like he really cared. Who was he?" she asked, and a hint of alarm slipped through me. "I didn't want to ask in front of the I.S. because he rushed off as if he didn't want to be noticed." She huffed, taking my stick with the now-burning marshmallow. "I don't blame him," she muttered as she blew the little fire out. "They would have probably tried to pin the entire kidnapping on him. I don't like vampires. Always shoving their nastiness under a rug or onto someone else's plate."

Fingers gingerly taking the burnt marshmallow off, she smiled, her eyes brilliant in the clear light. In witch years, she wasn't that much older than me, always dressing down to make herself match the other moms in the neighborhood. But the morning light always showed how young she really was.

"So was he someone from school?" she prodded, a small smile dying to come out.

I gestured for her to eat the sticky black mass if she wanted it, and while she was occupied, I glanced nervously at Robbie. He was ignoring me. "Just a guy I met at the square," I offered.

My mother huffed again. "And that's another thing, missy," she said, but it was Robbie who got the thwack of the back of her hand on his shoulder. "You said you were going to the concert."

Robbie shot me a black look. "Aw, Mom, I had to scalp the tickets to get your solstice gift."

It was a lie, but she accepted it, making happy-mom sounds and giving him a marshmallowy kiss on his cheek.

"That's where we met Pierce," I said to give some truth to the story. "If we hadn't helped him, no one would."

"You did the right thing," my mom said firmly. "If I toast you a marshmallow, will you eat it, honey?"

I shook my head, wondering if she knew exactly *how* we had made his acquaintance. Probably, seeing as by the time I got into the kitchen, all evidence of my spelling had been boxed up and was back in the attic.

Robbie took the stick and put a new marshmallow over the fire. He liked them so light brown it was almost not worth doing. "So, I imagine your little adventure has cured you of wanting to go into the I.S.?" he asked, and my head jerked up.

Shocked he would bring it up in front of Mom, I stared at him from across her suddenly still figure. "No."

Silent, my mom eased back into her chair and out of the way of the coming argument.

"Look at you," my brother said after a cautious glance at our mom. "You passed out. You can't do it."

"That's enough, Robbie," Mom said, and I flicked my gaze at her, surprised at her support. But Robbie turned in his seat to face her. "Mom, we have to look at it logically. She can't do it, and you letting her believe she can only makes it worse."

I stared at him, feeling like I'd been kicked. Seeing me floundering, Robbie shifted awkwardly. "Rachel is a damn fine witch," he said, suddenly nervous. "She stirred a level eight hundred earth magic arcane spell. Mom, do you know how hard those are? I couldn't do it! If she goes into the I.S., it's going to be a waste. Besides, they won't take her if she passes out at the end of a run."

It had been an arcane spell? He hadn't told me that. Surprise kept my mouth shut, but it was that damned fatigue that kept me in my seat and not pummeling him into the snow. He'd told her. He never said he wouldn't, but it was an unwritten rule, and he had just broken it.

"You put a level eight hundred arcane spell in front of her?" my mom said crisply, and I paled, remembering her equipment used without her knowledge.

Robbie looked away, and I was glad I wasn't under her angry expression. "I can get her into a great school," he said to the ground. "The I.S. won't accept her, and to keep encouraging her is cruel."

Cruel? I thought, tears starting to blur my vision. Cruel is throwing my hopes in the dirt. Cruel is giving me a challenge, and when I meet it, telling me I lose because I fell down after it was done.

But he was right. It did matter that I had fainted. Worse yet, the I.S. knew it. They would never let me pass the physical now. I was weak and frail. A weak prissy face.

I sniffed loudly, and my mom glanced at me before turning back to my brother. "Robbie, can I have a word with you?"

"Mom—"

"Now." Her tone was sharp, brooking no complaint. "Get in the house."

"Yes, ma'am." Pissed, he stood, dropped his marshmallow and stick into the fire, and stomped inside. I jumped when the screen door slammed.

Sighing heavily, my mom took the stick out of the fire and rose. I didn't look at her when she handed the marshmallow to me. It was all out now, and I couldn't even pretend I had the ability to do what I wanted, do what made my blood pound and made me feel alive.

"I'll be right back," she said, giving my shoulder a squeeze. "I was saving these for the sunrise, but I want you to open them now—before the day begins."

Her thin but strong hands drew from her coat pocket a card and small present, which she set into my lap.

"Happy solstice, sweetheart," she said, and a single tear slipped down my cheek as she followed Robbie into the house. I wiped the cold trail away, heartbroken. It just wasn't fair. I had done it. I had summoned a ghost, though not Dad. I had helped save that little girl's life. So why was mine in the crapper?

Setting Robbie's marshmallow to burn, I took off my mittens and ran a cold finger under the seal of the card. Eyes welling, I opened it up to find my I.S. application, signed by my mother. Blinking furiously, I shoved it back in the envelope. I had permission, but it didn't mean anything anymore.

"And what are you?" I said to the box miserably. "A set of cuffs I'll never get to use?" It was about the right size.

I stared at the brightening pink clouds and held my breath. Exhaling, the fog from my lungs seemed to mirror my mood, foggy and dismal. Setting the envelope aside, I opened the box. The tears got worse when I saw what was in it. Cradled in the black tissue paper was Dad's watch.

Miserable, I glanced back at the silent house. She knew what spell I had done. She knew everything; otherwise why give me the watch?

Missing him all the more, I clenched Dad's watch in my hand and stared at the fire, almost rocking in heartache. Maybe things would have been different if he had shown up. I was glad he was at peace and the spell wouldn't work on him, but damn it, my chest seemed to have a gaping hole in it now.

A warm sensation slipped through me, and startled, I sniffed back my tears and sent my eyes to follow a small noise to the side yard. A pair of hands was gripping the top of the wooden fence, and as I wiped my face, a small man in a long coat vaulted over it. Pierce.

"Oh, hi," I said, wiping my face in the hopes he couldn't tell I'd been crying. "I thought you were gone." I dried my hand on my blanket and folded my hands in my lap, hiding my dad's watch and my misery all at the same time.

Pierce looked at the house as he approached, boots leaving masculine prints in the snow. "After seeing your mother at that spawn's house, I had a mind to heed the better part of valor."

A faint smile brought my lips curving upward despite myself. "She scares you?"

"Like a snake to a horse," he said, shuddering dramatically.

He glanced at the house again and sat down in Robbie's spot. I said nothing, noting the distance.

"I couldn't find your home," he said, watching the fire, not me. "The drivers of the public carriages . . . ah . . . buses, won't be moved by pity, and it took me a space to figure the Yellow Book."

I sniffed, feeling better with him beside me. "Yellow Pages."

Nodding, he looked at the still-burning wad of Robbie's marshmallow. "Yes, Yellow Pages. A man of color took pity on me and drove me to your neighborhood."

I turned to him, aghast, but then remembered he was over a hundred years dead. "It's polite to call them black now. Or African-American," I corrected, and he nodded.

"They are all free men?"

"There was a big fight about it," I said, and he nodded, eyes pinched in deep thought.

I didn't know what to say, and finally Pierce turned to me. "Why are you so melancholy, Miss Rachel? We did it. My soul is avenged and the girl is safe. I'm sure that when the sun rises, I will go to my reward." A nervous look settled in the back of his eyes. "Be it good or bad," he added.

"It will be good," I said hurriedly, my hands gripping the watch as if I could squeeze some happiness out of it. "I'm thrilled for you, and I know you will land on the good side of things. Promise."

"You don't look thrilled," he muttered, and I scraped up a smile.

"I am. Really I am," I said. "It's just that—It's just that I tried to be who I wanted to be, and I—" My throat closed, as if by admitting it aloud, there was no way it could happen. "I can't do it," I whispered. Fighting the tears, I watched the fire, forcing my breathing to stay even and slow.

"Yes, you can . . ." Pierce protested, and I shook my head to make my hair fly around.

"No, I can't. I passed out. If you hadn't been there, I would have passed out, and he would have gotten away, and it would have been all for nothing."

"Oh, Rachel . . ." Pierce slid to my mother's chair. His arms went around me and he gave me a sideways hug. Giving up my pretense, I turned into him to make it a real hug, burying my face in his coat. I took a shaky breath, smelling the scent of coal dust and shoe polish. He had a real smell, but then, I'd heard most ghosts did.

"It's not bravery you lack," he said, his words shifting the hair on the top of my head. "That's the most important part. The rest is incidental. Real strength is knowing you can live with your failure. That sometimes you can't get there in time and that your lack might mean someone dies. It was cleverness that captured the vampire, not brute strength. Besides, the strength will come."

It sounded so easy. I wanted to believe him. I wanted to believe him so bad, it made my chest hurt. "Will it?" I said as I pulled back to see his own eyes damp with tears. "I used to think so, but I'm so damned weak. Look at me," I said derisively. "Wrapped up like a baby, my knees going shaky when I get up to turn the TV channel. I'm stupid to think the I.S. would want me. I should give it up and go out to Portland to be an earth witch, set up a spell shop and . . ." My eyes started to well again. *Damn it!* "And sell charms to warlocks," I finished, kicking a snow clod into the fire.

Pierce shook his head. "That's the most dang fool idea I've heard since having ears to hear with again, and I expect I've seen and heard a few fool things since you woke me up. If I might could talk to the dead, I'd ask your father, and I know what he would say."

His language was slipping again; he must be upset. I looked up from where my kicked snow had melted, dampening out the fire to show a patch of wood. "You can't know that," I said sullenly. "You've never even met him."

Still he smiled, his blue eyes catching the brightening light. "I don't need to. I expect a man who raised a young lady with such fire in her would have only one answer. Do what your heart tells you."

A frown pressed my lips together. "I'm too weak," I said, as if that was all there was to it. "Nothing is going to change. Nothing."

I didn't want to talk about it anymore. My hands were cold, and I dropped the watch in my lap to put my mittens back on.

"Hey!" Pierce said, seeing it. "That's mine!"

My mouth dropped open, but in a moment, I looked at him in understanding. "No wonder the charm didn't work. It's your watch?" I hesitated. "Before it was my dad's? Maybe I can try again," I said. But he was shaking his head, clearly wanting to touch it.

"No," he said. "You're his daughter, and your blood that kindled the charm is a closer bond than a bit of metal and fancy. If he had been in a position to come, he would have." An eager light was in his eyes, and, licking his lips, he asked, "May I?"

Silently I handed it over.

Pierce's smile was so beautiful that it almost hurt to see it. "It's mine," he said, then quickly amended. "Pardon me. I meant that it once had been. I expect it was sold to pay for the stone they used to keep me from rising up to avenge my wrongful death. See here?" he said, pointing out a dent. "I did this falling into a post to avoid a nasty-tempered nag of a horse."

I leaned to look, finding a small comfort in his history.

"I wonder if my sweetheart's silhouette is still in it," he said, turning it over. My eyebrows rose when he wedged a ragged fingernail into a tiny crack and whispered a word of Latin. The back hinged open, and a folded paper fluttered to the ground.

"That's not it," he said with a sigh, and I picked it up, handing it to him.

"What is it?" I asked, and he shrugged, handing me my dad's watch to unfold the off-white scrap of paper. But then my heart seemed to stop when the scent of my dad's pipe lifted through my memory, rising from the paper itself.

Pierce didn't see my expression, and he squinted at the words. "My little Firefly," he said, and tears sprang into my eyes as I realized who had written them. "I write this on the evening of our day in the leaves as you sleep. You're still a child, but today, I saw the woman-to-be in you—" Pierce's words cut off, and he brought his gaze to my swimming eyes. "This is for you," he said, extending it. His expression looked tragic as he shared my heartache.

"Read it to me," I said, catching a sob. "Please."

Pierce shifted awkwardly, then began again. "Today I saw the woman-to-be in you, and you are beautiful. My heart breaks that circumstance will probably keep me from seeing you reach your full strength, but I'm proud of your courage, and I stand in awe at the heights you will achieve when your strength builds to match your spirit."

I held my breath to keep from crying, but my head started to hurt and a hot tear slipped down.

"Don't be afraid to trust your abilities," he said, voice softening. "You're stronger than you think. Never forget how to live life fully and with courage, and never forget that I love you." Pierce drew the paper from his nose and set it in my lap. "It's signed 'Dad'."

I sniffed, smiling up at Pierce as I wiped my eyes. "Thank you."

"Little Firefly?" he questioned, trying to distract me from my heartache.

"It was the hair, I think," I said, bringing the paper to my nose and breathing deeply the faded scent of pipe smoke. "Thank you, Pierce," I said, giving his hand a soft squeeze. "I never would have found his note if it hadn't been for you."

The young man smiled, running a hand over my hair to push it out of my eyes. "It isn't anything I did a'purpose."

Maybe, I mused, smiling brokenly at him, the spell to bring my dad into existence had worked after all—the only way it could, his love bending the rules of nature and magic to bring me a message from beyond his grave. My dad was proud of me. *He was proud of me and knew I could be strong.* That was all I had ever wanted, and I took a gulp of air.

I was going to start crying again, and, searching for a distraction, I turned to find my mom's gift. "My mom signed my application," I said, fumbling with the envelope beside me with a sudden resolve. "I'm going to do it. Pierce. My dad said to trust in my abilities, and I'm going to do it. I'm going to join the I.S."

But when I turned back to him with my signed application, he was gone.

My breath caught. Wide-eyed, I looked to the east to see the first flash of red-gold through the black branches. From across the city came the tolling of bells, celebrating the new day. The sun was up. He was gone.

"Pierce?" I said softly as the paper in my grip slowly drooped. Not believing it, I stared at where he had been. His footprints were still there, and I could still smell coal dust and shoe polish, but I was alone.

A gust of wind blew on the fire, and a wave of heat shifted

my hair from my eyes. It was warm against me, comforting, like the touch of a hand against my cheek in farewell. He was gone, just like that.

I looked at my dad's watch and held it tight. I was going to get better. My stamina was going to improve. My mom believed in me. My dad did, too. Fingers shaking, I folded up the paper and snapped the watch shut around it, holding it tight until the metal warmed.

Taking a deep breath, I sent my gaze deep into the purity of the morning sky. The solstice was over, but everything else? Everything else was just beginning.

Born and raised in Tornado Alley, *New York Times* bestselling author **KIM HARRISON** now resides in more sultry climates. She rolls a very good game of dice, hangs out with a guy in leather, and is hard at work on the next novel of the Hollows.

For more information, go to *www.kimharrison.net*.

Run, Run, Rudolph

Lynsay Sands

Chapter 1

"Beth?" Jill peered down the stairs that disappeared into darkness and frowned. She'd looked everywhere in the house for her errant niece before noticing the cracked-open door to the basement. Now she stood on the landing, biting her lip as she looked into the black pit and wondered if her niece could possibly be down there.

Her brother, Kyle, had obviously forgotten to lock the door. That was unusual. With all the experimental equipment—including the molecular destabilizer—he housed in the basement, he was fanatical about locking it. However, it wasn't locked now.

Surely a toddler wouldn't go down into the dark on her own, though?

A faint rustle from the stillness below answered the question. Beth was definitely down there. And shouldn't be. She could get hurt.

Flipping on the light, Jill started down, calling, "Beth? Honey? You aren't supposed to be down here. Come to Aunt Jill. Your breakfast is ready."

Pausing on the bottom step, Jill waited for some sound to give away the girl's location, but there was nothing. Her gaze slid around the room, skating over gleaming metal surfaces and glass-fronted cupboards containing all sorts of scientific-type paraphernalia. She'd never been down here before, but it looked just like she'd imagined, like every lab she'd ever seen when she visited her brother at work.

A faint scraping sound drew her gaze to the far corner of the room and Jill peered toward the large glass chamber that took up the end of the basement. It held the molecular desta-bilizer Kyle had spent so much of the last five years rebuild-ing . . . And the door into the small glass room was open.

Alarm rising in her, Jill hurried toward the open door. "Beth? Enough. You aren't supposed to be down here. Your mommy and daddy will be mad," she said firmly. When she reached the door without receiving an answer, she added pleadingly, "Come out, honey. Your breakfast is ready."

The only answer was another rustle, this time from be-hind the machine. Breathing out a sigh, Jill approached the front of the destabilizer. It was huge, stretching from one wall to the other. There was no room to slip between the machine and the wall to peer behind it. That left crawling under the table set up below the telescope-like apparatus that the beam shot from. At least Jill thought it probably came from there. She was no scientist, but didn't see any-where else it could come from.

She eyed the crawl space under the table, unhappy at the prospect of crawling under it but seeing no alternative. She had to get Beth back upstairs.

Cursing Kyle for carelessly leaving the door unlocked, Jill started to climb under the table, pausing when she bumped it and it shifted slightly. Noting it was on wheels and could move in and out, she straightened and wheeled the table out of the way to make more room, then crawled into the space to peer behind the machine.

"Beth," she said with relief. The child was sitting in the narrow space between the machine and the back wall. Spying Jill, she giggled and clapped her hands with glee. It was a grand game to the tot.

Jill was less entertained. She was very aware that she was now kneeling directly under the destabilizer beam, exactly where Beth's mother, Claire, had been when a crazy coworker, determined to try the molecular destabilizer on humans, had zapped her. Claire had survived the exposure to the destabilizer, as had Kyle when he'd run into the beam to pull her out, but now the two of them were different. They could both shift their shapes, taking on the facial features and body shape of others. A cool trick to be sure, and one Jill had first thought she might like herself, but that was before she'd heard Kyle's fears. The destabilizer had done what it was meant to, made their molecules unstable and changeable, but they weren't sure how unstable and feared the possibility of the cells collapsing, leaving them to die in a puddle of human slime, or worse yet, not die, but be alive and aware as a puddle of human slime. That possibility was enough to kill any desire to be zapped.

That thought in mind, Jill started to lift her head to glance nervously toward the beam, but instead cried out as pain shot through her skull and everything went black.

Jill moaned and slowly opened her eyes. At first she didn't know where she was. She stared at the dim bulb overhead, then blinked and lowered her gaze as she felt a soft patting on her cheek.

"Beth," she whispered. The child was seated on the floor beside her, patting her cheek, a worried look on her little face.

Jill offered her a reassuring smile and then sat up, her gaze sliding around the glass chamber as she tried to sort out what had happened. She recalled coming down in search of Beth, crawling under the machine, and then lifting her head and *bang*, unbearable pain had hit her. Obviously she'd slammed her head into the telescope thing and knocked herself out. Brilliant. She always had been the clumsy one in the family.

When Beth made a gurgle of sound, Jill got carefully to her feet. Much to her relief, while she felt a little weak, she didn't appear to be suffering any other side effects from the encounter.

Letting her breath out slowly, she glanced down to her niece, then carefully bent and picked her up. The action made her woozy, and she stood still for a moment, hugging the child close until her head cleared again. Once she felt steadier Jill started across the basement to the stairs. She had just put her foot on the first step when she heard a car engine and the crunch of tires on gravel.

Pausing, she glanced toward the nearest window at the top of the basement wall just in time to see the bottom of a blue car moving past.

Kyle and Claire were home . . . And she had a few choice words for her brother about leaving the basement unlocked. Scowling, Jill carried Beth upstairs and into the dining room. She set the child in her high chair and was spooning cereal into her mouth by the time the front door opened and Claire's laughter drifted up the hall.

"I love you too," Claire was chuckling. "And that's why we aren't getting a motorcycle."

"Ah, honey. Think how cool it would be to ride down the highway on the back of a hog, the wind in your hair and—"

"And my maternity top flying over my head," Claire interrupted dryly.

Jill smiled at the mental picture. Claire was more than seven months pregnant with their second child, very close to giving birth and showing it. Jill had been a little surprised that they were continuing to have the "date" nights that gave her the opportunity to babysit her niece, but it seemed the pregnancy wasn't cooling their ardor.

"Your coat would hold your maternity top down, and—Oh, hey Jill," Kyle interrupted himself as the couple reached the dining room door.

"Still trying to talk her into getting a motorcycle?" Jill asked with amusement. Her brother had been trying to talk Claire into getting one when they left for their "date" the night before.

"'Try' being the key word," Claire said, laughing as she entered the room and picked up her daughter. Lifting the child high in the air, she blew a raspberry on her cheek and cuddled her close. "Hello, beautiful. Were you a good girl for your aunt Jill?"

"She was a very good girl," Jill assured her, and then turned a scowl on her brother as she added, "Unlike her father, who left the door to the basement unlocked so that nosy little miss could crawl down there."

"What?" Kyle's eyes widened in shock as Claire turned an alarmed glance his way. "I locked it. I always lock it."

"Well, apparently last night you forgot," Jill assured him. "I put Beth in front of the television this morning while I got her cereal and when I came back she was gone. The door to the basement was open and she'd managed to get down there." Jill frowned even as she said the words and then added, "I don't know how she got down there on her own. Those stairs are pretty steep for a two-year-old. But I found her down behind the molecular destabilizer."

There was a moment of silence as all three of them peered at Beth and then Claire turned a concerned gaze his way and Kyle sighed.

"I was sure I locked it," he said apologetically, then added, "But we can't take a chance. I'll go to the hardware store and get one of those locks that lock automatically when a door closes. I'll do it right after I bring our bags in."

Claire smiled and reached out to squeeze his hand, then withdrew it quickly to grab for her daughter as Beth suddenly leaned toward the bowl of cereal on the table and made disgruntled sounds.

"She's hungry. Let me finish feeding her," Jill suggested.

"I'll do it," Claire said, setting the child back in her high chair. "I know you want to get to the shop for that parade this morning."

"Oh!" Jill's eyes widened with alarm and she shot to her feet. She'd forgotten all about the Christmas parade this morning. It was starting on the street where she had her store and she, along with many of the other storeowners, was expected to help with it.

"It's after ten o'clock and you said you had to be there by eleven," Claire reminded her, then gave a laugh and added, "I can't believe you forgot. You were so excited that Mr. Handsome Shoes was playing Santa."

"Mr. Handsome Shoes?" Kyle asked with bewilderment.

"He's the guy who opened a shoe store next door to Jill's clothing store six months ago," Claire explained. "He's apparently very good looking. All the women in town are gaga over him, but he's only showing interest in your sister."

"Are you two dating?" Kyle asked with a frown. "Why haven't you mentioned him before? Is there something wrong with the guy?"

"We aren't dating," Jill said quickly and then scowled at him as she added, "And there is nothing wrong with Nick."

Claire smiled faintly and said, "They aren't dating officially, but they *do* have lunch together every day *and* have exchanged store keys in case there are problems."

"A shoe store owner, huh?" Kyle asked slowly, and then added, "And you've exchanged keys but only eaten lunch together every day? For six months?" He arched an eyebrow, then pursed his lips and said, "He's got to be gay."

"Kyle!" Claire cried with dismay, but Jill just scowled at

her brother and hurried out of the room, heading for the spare room to collect her things. Nick, or Mr. Handome Shoes, as Claire called him, couldn't be gay. She just wouldn't believe it. She was already half in love with the man.

Jill frowned. She was sure she'd know if he was, but while Nick was always charming and interesting and seemed to enjoy being with her, he'd never taken that step to move the relationship from friendship to actual dating.

Maybe he *was* gay. Her shoulders slumped at the possibility. Wouldn't it be just her luck to fall for a guy who couldn't possibly have any interest in her as anything more than a friend? She didn't have a great track record with men lately.

Sighing unhappily, she snatched up her purse and overnight bag and headed out of the room. If he were gay, then today was going to be a total bust. The only reason she'd agreed to play Mrs. Claus to his Santa in the Christmas parade was to spend more time with the man in the hope that he would finally move the relationship to the next level. It had been Bev's idea. Bev owned and operated a hair salon farther up the street. She was also the friend she tended to moan to the most about Nick. Bev seemed to think Nick was just shy.

In charge of the parade preparations, it was Bev who had suggested that seeing each other away from their stores and actually playing Mrs. Claus to his Santa might be just the push Nick needed to get him over his shyness and make him ask her out.

Ever hopeful, Jill had decided to give it a go. And it seemed to be working. He hadn't yet asked her out, but— where on the lunches they were prim and proper, sharing their thoughts, but careful not to invade each other's space— at the meetings for the parade, they'd been much more relaxed, both of them laughing and joking as they worked at the preparations.

There had also been a good deal of "accidental" touching

going on, hands meeting as they each grabbed for the same item, bodies brushing as they passed. And last night as they'd worked on the preparations, they'd been left alone in Bev's kitchen for several minutes and Jill was positive Nick'd been about to kiss her before Jay, one of the elves, had entered, interrupting them.

Jill had been disappointed at the interruption, and was hoping today he'd actually finish what he'd nearly started, claim the kiss and ask her out. It was their last chance before the parade was over and they went back to their rushed lunches in the middle of busy workdays.

Sending up a quick prayer that Nick asked her out today, Jill started downstairs, pressing close to the wall as Kyle started up with suitcases in hand.

"Have fun with Mr. Gay Shoes," he teased as she rushed past.

Jill stuck out her tongue and kept going, pausing only long enough at the dining room door to wish Claire a good day before rushing out of the house, her knapsack over one shoulder and purse over the other.

Jill had parked on the street when she'd arrived the night before to prevent blocking in Claire and Kyle's car when they went to leave or being blocked in by it when they returned. Unfortunately, the closest empty parking spot she'd found had been halfway up the street. Now she hurried up the sidewalk, her thoughts already on the day ahead and Nick.

Distracted as she was, Jill was nearly at her car before she noticed the man leaning against the front grill of her little Toyota. Pausing abruptly, she watched with a frown as the man straightened to face her. He was tall, dark-haired, not bad looking, but there was something about his mouth and eyes that made him look hard and cold. She was instantly wary.

"Can I help you?" she asked, her hand tightening on her bags. The only thing she could think was that it was his house she'd parked in front of and he didn't care for her parking there. "Is it about my parking here?"

"Parking here?" he echoed with bewilderment, then seemed to understand. Flashing a smile that didn't reach his eyes, he said, "Oh, of course, you don't know who I am. I'm John Heathcliffe. I used to work with your brother."

Jill stiffened, the hair on the back of her neck suddenly standing on end as she recognized the name of the crazy co-worker who had zapped Claire with the destabilizer.

"You've heard of me," he said with apparent pleasure.

"What do you want?" she asked, her gaze slipping back the way she'd come.

"You didn't think I'd zap you with the destabilizer and then just leave you alone?" he said with amusement.

Jill jerked her head back around.

"Zap me with the destabilizer?" she echoed blankly, wondering what on earth he was talking about. He shouldn't even know about the destabilizer. No one knew Kyle had rebuilt it in his home. As for zapping her with it, the only encounter she'd had with it was banging her head as she . . .

Jill frowned as she suddenly recalled the flash of light that had accompanied the pain before she'd blacked out.

"You zapped me?" she asked in a choked voice.

John nodded with a wicked grin that quickly turned bitter. "Did Kyle really think I'd let him just take the machine away from me? I worked on the original prototype as long as he did. It's as much mine as his," he proclaimed, taking a step toward her. "Dr. Cohen may have believed that nonsense about it not working and allowed him to talk him into shutting down the experiment, but I can't believe Kyle really thought I was stupid enough to swallow it."

"You zapped me with the destabilizer?" Jill repeated faintly.

John nodded again, appearing amused by her stunned state, and then announced, "Once the project was shut down I started to watch Kyle. I saw the materials he brought into the house and realized he was rebuilding it. Some nights I even watched through one of the basement windows as he worked." He smiled with disdain. "Kyle really should have covered the windows. It was rather silly of him not to. I suppose he thought it was private enough with the high fence around the property, but anyone could climb the fence and look in . . . like I did."

Jill remained silent, her mind still reeling under the possibility that she'd been hit by the shape-shifter beam. She found herself suddenly doing a silent self-assessment, checking to see if she felt different. She didn't. She'd felt a little weak directly after waking up in the basement, but— Her thoughts stopped dead as she realized she'd woken up in the middle of the basement floor, nowhere near the destabilizer.

"You pulled me out from under the machine?" she asked uncertainly.

John nodded. "Once I'd estimated you'd been exposed long enough, I turned it off. You collapsed like a limp noodle." He shrugged. "I had to be sure I hadn't given you too much and accidentally killed you, but I couldn't take your pulse all crumpled under the machine as you were."

Jill stared at him with disbelief. He was standing there admitting that he hadn't been at all sure the beam wouldn't have killed her and he'd gone ahead and zapped her anyway. Why would he do such a thing?

"Now," John continued. "If you'll just come with me, we'll go to my house and I can start running tests on you."

"Tests?" she asked with surprise.

"Yes. Why else do you think I zapped you? You're going to be my guinea pig."

"Are you nuts?" Jill cried, tugging her arm free of the hard hold he suddenly had on her wrist. "Stay away from me or I'll tell my brother."

Okay, as threats went it was pretty lame, Jill thought as soon as the words left her mouth, but let it go and merely pushed past him to get to the driver's door of her car. Before she could get it unlocked, he was there, grabbing her by the arm again.

"I said you're coming with me!" he snarled, trying to pull her away.

Jill didn't think, she just reacted. Allowing her self-defense classes to kick in, she struck backward sharply with her elbow, driving it into his stomach. She then turned and drove her knee sharply into his groin. John collapsed on the street, groaning in agony, one hand clutching his stomach, the other cupping his groin.

Leaving him rolling around on the pavement, Jill unlocked the driver's door, threw her bags in, and leapt inside. She hit the button to lock the doors the moment the door closed, and then struggled briefly with her keys. Her hands were shaking and by the time she managed to turn on the engine, John was crawling to his feet beside the car.

"Hey!" He lunged for the driver's door even as she shifted into drive and hit the gas. He thumped furiously against the side window as she tore away up the street.

Eyes shifting between the street and the rearview mirror, Jill reached for her purse. She opened it one-handed, felt around until she found her phone and glanced in the rearview mirror as she pulled it out, only to curse again as she spotted a black van rushing up the street behind her. She *knew* it was John.

Mouth tightening, Jill pushed her foot down harder on the gas and raised the phone in front of her eyes. She needed to call Kyle. She didn't know what else to do. Jill was afraid to call the police and bring them into the matter. She didn't know how much damage the man could do to Kyle if he blabbed about the machine in his basement. She should have just pulled into Kyle and Claire's driveway and made a run for the house. Unfortunately, the car had been pointing in the opposite direction. Also, unfortunately, she wouldn't be calling her brother for advice. She'd forgotten to recharge her phone again. The battery was dead.

Cursing, Jill tossed it aside and glanced in the rearview again. The van was gaining on her. She needed to lose the crazy idiot and either drive back to Claire and Kyle's, or find a phone. Calling seemed her safest bet. Jill didn't really want to lead trouble back to Claire and Kyle's door. She didn't know just how crazy John Heathcliffe was or what he'd do.

Where to call from was the problem. Jill suspected her house would be high on John Heathcliffe's list of places to look. Even if he didn't already know where she lived, all he had to do was look in a phone book to find her address.

He might overlook her shop though, she thought. In fact, he might not even know about it. He'd said he'd been watching her brother's house, not that he'd been following her around. Her store might be a safe place to go to call Kyle.

Mouth thinning with determination, Jill tightened her hold on the steering wheel and increased her speed. She then suddenly spun the wheel, taking a sharp and abrupt right that almost saw her car on two wheels. Managing to maintain control, she shot up the street, watching the rearview mirror as much as the road ahead.

"Yes," she breathed with relief when she saw the van shoot past the end of the street, wheels squealing as he tried to bring the vehicle to a halt to follow her. Jill was already turning left down another street by the time he managed to bring his car around.

Jill lost sight of him as soon as she turned the corner and her attention was again divided between the rearview mirror and the road ahead, grateful it wasn't a busy area. The last thing she needed was to hit someone in her efforts to escape her pursuer.

When there was still no sign of the van behind her before she turned up the next street, Jill felt her shoulders relax the smallest bit. But she continued to drive a little faster than she should and continued to take turns right and left and right again to be sure she'd lost the man before heading for her store.

Due to the parade, the streets around her store were all blocked off. The closest Jill could park was in the lot at the end of the road from where the parade was to launch. It was blocked to the public today, open only for parade participants to park. There were several tents set up at one end for everyone to don costumes and do their makeup.

Jill bit her lip as she gazed over the floats and costumed people milling about as she parked her car. If she hurried to the store, called Kyle, and then changed into her costume, there was really no reason she couldn't come back and be a part of the parade as planned. Surely Kyle could handle John, she reasoned. It wasn't like there was anything she could do. Besides, she'd committed herself to the parade and had her costume in her knapsack. She could hardly just leave them without a Mrs. Claus. But she had to make that call first, Jill decided as she got out of the car.

Slipping past the tents without running across anyone she knew, Jill hurried up the street to her store. She unlocked the door, slid inside and headed straight for the phone.

A curse slipped from her lips when her call was answered by the answering machine. She listened to her brother's recorded voice, frowning as she tried to sort out where Kyle and Claire could be. Kyle had mentioned going to the hardware store, but surely Claire was still there feeding Beth?

Her gaze slid to the clock on the wall and she frowned as she realized that while the store was only fifteen minutes from Claire and Kyle's house, she'd wasted almost half an hour making sure she'd lost her pursuer. Claire could very well have finished feeding Beth and headed out for some last-minute Christmas shopping.

"Kyle," Jill said when the beep finally sounded. "I need to talk to you. I—" She paused to worry her lip as she realized he wouldn't be able to reach her. Her cell phone was dead and she'd be on a parade float, nowhere near a phone for the next hour or so. Letting her breath out on a sigh, she said, "I'll try calling again later. But it's important."

Unsatisfied with the message, Jill hung up and turned to peer out the front window of the store, stilling when she spotted John Heathcliffe crossing the street headed straight for the front door of her shop.

Cursing, she whirled away from the counter and hurried out the back door, then started up the alley behind the shops, her mind racing. It seemed John hadn't just been watching the house. He must have followed her around and learned where she worked when he'd decided he needed a guinea pig.

"Jill? What on earth are you doing here? I was just heading to my store to try to call you. You aren't even dressed yet."

"Oh, Bev." Jill swallowed guiltily as the woman hurried up the alley to her. "I—"

"You can explain while you dress," Bev interrupted firmly, catching her arm and steering her toward the back door of her salon.

"You don't understand," Jill murmured, glancing nervously up and down the alley, sure John was going to pop up at any moment. "I can't be in the parade."

"The hell you can't!" Bev snapped. Getting the door unlocked, she dragged her inside the dark shop. "Do you know what I went through to make sure you would be Mrs. Claus? Every unattached female shop owner on this street wanted to play the part to get their hands on Nick."

"Yes, but—"

"No buts," she said firmly, flipping on the light and pushing her toward the ladies' room. "Get in there and change."

"But—" Jill's protest died on a sigh as she found herself pushed into the bathroom and the door pulled closed behind her.

"Dress," Bev repeated firmly through the door. "The parade starts in five minutes and you *will* be in it." Without waiting for further protest, she added, "I have to go back and chase a couple other people down. When you're ready, leave through the back door and just pull it closed. It locks automatically."

When Jill didn't respond right away, Bev added grimly, "Don't let me down, Jill. I went to great lengths to see you in this role and I'll never forgive you if you leave me without a Mrs. Claus."

"All right," she said wearily and heard the soft thud of the shop door closing.

Biting her lip, Jill opened the door and peered out. She couldn't be in the parade. The Mrs. Claus costume was a sedate little red dress with faux fur trim, a cute little Santa hat, and red shoes. Unfortunately, there was no mask and she'd be easily recognizable to John should he see her going past on the parade float. That was the last thing she needed. She didn't think he'd drag her off in front of everyone, but he was crazy. Who knew?

But she couldn't let Bev down either. And she really didn't want to miss out on this opportunity to spend time with Nick either.

Cursing under her breath, Jill paced to the front of the salon, her gaze moving up the street to her own store. There was no sign of John, but—Jill stiffened as she realized she wasn't at all sure she'd locked the front door of the store when she'd entered. John could be in there right now searching for her.

Oh, she couldn't do this. And she couldn't not do it. She needed to hide until she could get a hold of Kyle, but where?

Her gaze landed on one of the magazines in the waiting area of the hair salon. Two dozen of them littered the coffee table. Most of them were hair books, but the rest were all celebrity and women's magazines that customers could peruse while awaiting their turn in the chair. The one that caught her attention was a Christmas issue of a fashion magazine. It featured a very sexy brunette Mrs. Claus in a short formfitting red velvet number with white fur trim.

Jill stared at the picture, recalling the day Claire had been zapped by the destabilizer beam and changed into several images from a magazine. If she could do that too . . . well, the best place to hide was often in plain sight, wasn't it?

Grinning, she picked up the magazine and hurried back to the bathroom. Closing the door, she concentrated on the woman on the cover. Claire had told her that she'd simply focused on the image and wished she'd looked like the picture and her body had changed. Jill now tried to do the same thing.

She stared hard, thinking she wanted to look like it, *needed* to look like it, *had* to look like it. But nothing seemed to happen. She didn't feel any sudden tingle or anything. Tossing the magazine aside with frustration, she sagged back against the wall and glared at herself in the mirror, freezing when she found a stranger glaring back.

"But I didn't feel a thing," she murmured, raising a hand and touching her face, eyes widening with disbelief as the brunette mirrored her actions.

It really was her. She'd shifted. She was the magazine Mrs. Claus. Well, mostly. The fur trim was sticking out from under the collar of her t-shirt. She stared at herself for a moment and then began to laugh even as she began to rip off her clothes. As had happened with Claire, her body had taken on not just the other woman's features, but the shape and color of her clothes as well. Her own clothes looked bulky on top.

Removing the last bit of clothing, Jill paused and stared at her new self. She was a brunette with a slim figure that made her smile. But the smile faded to a frown as she realized the costume was clingy and far too sexy for a parade meant for families and children. Concentrating on the hem, she tried to think it a little longer, relief coursing through her when it suddenly lengthened, dropping from mid-thigh to knee length.

It was still rather formfitting, but would have to do, Jill decided. She had to get moving and now it was safe to. Even if he did see her on the float, John Heathcliffe would never recognize her, she thought with satisfaction.

Jill hurried from the bathroom and out of the shop, pulling the door closed as ordered. She paused long enough to be sure it had locked as Bev had said it would, and then hurried up the alley to the parking lot at the end of the street.

There were people everywhere in the parking lot: elves, human reindeer, toy soldiers, snowmen, and people in band uniforms. The elves were made up of a combination of children and little people. Jill was reminded of the presence of several of the dwarves in the parade when someone goosed her and she whirled to find herself staring down at a grinning little man in an elf costume. Only the cigar hanging from his lips ruined the image of one of Santa's elves.

"Jay," she said on an exasperated sigh.

Whatever indecent proposal he'd been about to offer died on his lips and his eyes widened briefly, but then he grinned and said, "I see my reputation precedes me. Who are you, cutie? And why are you dressed up like Mrs. Claus? That's Jill's gig."

Jill blinked in surprise. She'd quite forgotten that she didn't look like herself at the moment until the man had spoken up. Now she forced a smile and said, "Jill was called away. A family emergency. I'm standing in for her."

"Hmmm." Jay didn't look impressed. "Nick isn't going to like that."

"He won't?" she asked faintly.

"Nah. He's sweet on our Jill. Everyone knows that . . . except maybe Jill herself," he added wryly, then tilted his head and asked, "So what's your name, cutie?"

"Name?" she echoed blankly, her thoughts on his claim that Nick was sweet on her.

Jay laughed. "Yeah, you know, what most people call you."

Jill flushed. It hadn't occurred to her that she'd need a name. Her gaze swept around the parade grounds as she searched her mind for a name to offer him. Her eyes landed on one of the painted carolers on the side of the third float. The singer held a sheet of music titled "The First Noel." Relaxing, Jill offered a smile. "Noelle."

"Noelle, huh?" Jay reached up, taking her hand to lead her toward the nearer of the tents set up in the parking lot. "Well, come on, Noelle. Let's go introduce you to Nick and give him the bad news that Jill backed out on him. He won't be a happy guy."

Chapter 2

"Yo!" Jay called out as he led Jill into the tent. "Nick, I found your Mrs. Claus, though not the one you were looking for."

It was late enough that mostly everyone had changed and vacated the tent. There were only a couple of people still inside; one of them was Nick already dressed as Santa and pacing, a worried expression on his face. The worry dropped away to be replaced with a warm smile at Jay's announcement, but that died away to confusion as his gaze landed on Jill.

"Who are you? Where's Jill?"

"Jill had a family emergency," Jay answered for her. "Noelle here is standing in."

"Oh," Nick said and then asked with concern, "A family emergency? But Jill's all right, isn't she?"

Jill hesitated. In truth she wasn't all right at all. She'd been zapped by a madman and turned into a shape-shifter that the madman was now hunting, intending to cage up and perform horrible experiments on. There was nothing all right about her at the moment. She couldn't tell Nick that though, so she forced a smile and nodded. "She's fine."

"Good," Nick said with a sigh and then glanced to the tent flap as Bev sailed in.

"Okay, everything's ready to go. We just need you two on the float." Bev's expression was pinched and anxious as she entered, but became completely alarmed when her gaze landed on Jill. "Who are you?"

"This is Noelle, Bev," Nick answered for her. "Jill had an emergency and asked Noelle to take her place."

Bev scowled. "See if I do that girl another favor. After all the trouble I went to—" Pausing, she peered over Noelle with pursed lips. "Well, that costume won't do. This is a family parade. There are kids out there."

Jill glanced at herself. The costume was more suitable for a bachelor party, she supposed.

"You'll have to wear this." Bev moved in front of her to do up the clasp of the red cape she'd just placed on her shoulders.

Jill ran a hand down the cape's white fur trim and frowned. "Isn't this Santa's?"

"We have both a heavy one and a lighter one so that we're covered whether it's cold or warmer. Its cold today, so old Saint Nick here is wearing the heavier one. You'll have to make do with the lighter one." Finished with the clasp, Bev stepped back to peer at her critically. She didn't look pleased, but said, "It'll have to do. But you're going to be cold in that costume. Jill should have given you the one we made. I swear she's going to hear about this." Whirling to the tent flap, she snapped, "Come on, you two. The parade is already five minutes late in starting."

Jill breathed out a little sigh and silently cursed John Heathcliffe as Nick led her out of the tent.

The parking lot was still full of people rushing about, but now they were all headed in the same direction, toward the row of floats parked at the edge of the lot. Jill and Nick joined the herd, making their way to the middle float that held the small wooden building with the sign "Santa's Workshop" on it. It was a shed really, but quite charming with all its decorations and left plenty of room for the big black bag with gift-wrapped boxes falling out, the fake reindeer standing around and Santa's chair. There were already several people on the float, not one of them taller than four feet. Santa's elves.

"Up we go," Nick urged as they approached the steps that had been wheeled up to the side of the float.

Murmuring a thank you, Jill scampered up the stairs, her gaze slipping nervously around the parking lot as she went, eyes searching for John. While he shouldn't be able to recognize her as she was, she couldn't help fearing that he would.

"This way, cutie," Jay said cheerfully, leading her toward Santa's chair. "You and Nick stand here and smile and wave."

"Thanks, Jay," Jill murmured, following him.

"No problem." He grinned widely and then wiggled his eyebrows and said, "So, if you aren't doing anything later, maybe we could get together and I can show you why us elves are so popular with the ladies."

"Scram, Jay," Nick said firmly, joining them at the chair.

"Ah, come on, Nick. Don't be such a spoil sport," the elf complained. "Why should you get all the babes? Anyway, I thought you were interested in Jill. Don't take it out on me because she stiffed you today and didn't show."

Jill glanced sharply at Nick, her heart leaping with hope when she saw the blush on his face. It seemed he *was* interested in her . . . but then why hadn't he done anything about it?

"Ignore him," Nick suggested. "He's a rude little bugger, but has a good heart for the most part."

"So you aren't interested in Jill?" she asked, unable to help herself.

Nick was silent long enough she didn't think he'd respond, but then he muttered, "Like I said, just ignore him."

She was frowning over that when he said, "I don't know how much Jill explained to you, but the deal is there are boxes of candy canes and treats in the shed. There are two trays. One out here," he gestured to the large tray overflowing with candy canes and toys on the small table beside the throne, then waved to the "workshop." "And one inside that the elves are supposed to use to keep the tray loaded. We throw them to the crowd."

Jill nodded.

"There's also a gas heater in the shed to warm up by if you get too cold, but try to stay on deck as much as possible. The kids want to see Mr. and Mrs. Claus. Okay?"

His glance at her costume suggested he suspected she'd spend more time in the shed than out of it. Feeling self-conscious and stupid, Jill tugged the cape tighter around her, more to hide than because she felt cold.

The truth was Jill wasn't feeling as cold as she knew she should. It was almost at freezing temperature and she should have been shivering in the chill air, but wasn't. Claire and Kyle hadn't seemed to suffer from the heat or cold like other people since being zapped though, so she supposed it had something to do with that.

A shout from the end of the parking lot drew her attention. Bev was at the head of the first float in the parade, waving her arms and gesturing.

"We're about to start," Nick said. "You might want to hang onto this to keep from losing your footing when the float starts moving. You'll get used to the motion quickly, but the first movement might startle you."

Jill moved to his side and took hold of the back of the chair, knowing he was right. Her gaze slid over the float as they waited to move forward, noting that everyone was now on board. There were six elves on their float. Three were children of store owners who'd volunteered to be elves, and the other three were adults, Jay and two of his friends, both little people like himself.

The float started forward, sending everyone swaying where they stood. Once in motion, however, Jill quickly adjusted and was able to stand unaided.

"Okay?" Nick asked as she released the chair back she'd been clinging to.

Jill nodded and offered a smile. "Fine."

"Good." He scooped out a handful of candy canes and whatnot from the tray and passed them to her. "Just smile, wave, and toss treats to the kids."

They worked in silence at first, smiling and waving and throwing candy, but Jill found herself repeatedly glancing toward Nick. This wasn't how she'd expected the day to go. Every time they were together they tended to chat up a storm. She'd rather expected this day to go the same, the two of them laughing and chatting and sharing secret smiles as they tossed the candy and waved, but she wasn't Jill today, she was Noelle, and Nick didn't seem interested in talking to her.

Jill supposed she should be glad. After all, she'd taken on the appearance of a model most men would be drooling over, yet Nick hardly seemed to notice she was there.

They were perhaps halfway through the parade when Jill began trying to strike up a conversation with Nick. She pointed out a child on the side with reindeer horns on and a glowing red nose, but while Nick smiled faintly, it didn't lead to anything. She tried again several times, but the man just wasn't receptive. He was polite enough, but cool in his responses until Jill finally just gave up the flirty attempts and decided to try the direct approach.

"Would you like to go out for dinner after the parade?" she asked suddenly, and was amazed at herself for having the courage to do so. It seemed being someone else gave her courage she'd never had as herself. Jill had never been the sort to ask men out, she always waited for the man to ask . . . which was perhaps why she never ended up dating anyone she was really interested in. Now she waited for Nick's answer, wondering why she'd even asked. She didn't want to date him as stick-thin model Noelle. She didn't even want him to like stick-thin model Noelle. She wanted him to like her, Jill, as herself.

"Look, you seem like a nice woman, Noelle," Nick said gently. "But Jay was right, I *am* interested in Jill."

She sucked in a breath. He'd just said the one thing guaranteed to make her the happiest girl in the parade, maybe even the town. Here he stood, rejecting a woman with the face and body of an international magazine model for little old Jill. She could have kissed him.

Her glee lasted for a very brief moment and then it was pushed out of her brain by questions. If he was interested in her why hadn't he asked her out? Was he just using that as an excuse for him to let Noelle down easy? And if he wasn't interested in Noelle, or Jill, at least not interested enough to ask her out, maybe . . . God! Kyle couldn't be right. Nick wasn't gay, was he?

"What?"

Jill blinked her thoughts away to see that Nick had stopped throwing candy to stare at her. He was frowning under his fake beard as he took in the expressions her thoughts were scribbling across her face and obviously wanted to know what was behind them, she realized. Jill hesitated, but then blurted, "If you're so interested in Jill, why haven't you asked her out?"

She saw his mouth tighten between the white mustache and beard and was sure he was going to tell her to mind her own business, so she quickly blurted, "We're friends . . . and I've been worried about her. You seem to be stringing her along, eating lunches with her, showing interest but not too much interest, never asking her out . . ." Jill watched the play of expressions on his face, then impulsively added, "Her brother thinks you're gay."

"Gay?" Nick's eyes widened in alarm.

"Yes. He thinks that's why you haven't asked Jill out," she murmured quietly, and then added, "If you are you should just tell her so. She'd still be friends with you, but you shouldn't string her along like this."

Nick was frowning now and looking a bit put out. Jill waited, wondering if he'd tell her to go to hell, or actually respond at all, but then he heaved out an exasperated sigh and said, "I'm not gay."

She felt every muscle in her body relax at this news. Jill had told herself she didn't believe he was, but the possibility had bothered her ever since Kyle had brought it up. His answer eliminated the problem, however. Now she just had to find out why—if he was interested in her—he hadn't asked her out. The easiest way was to ask, so she did. "Then why haven't you asked her out?"

Nick pursed his lips and then said, "Because I haven't been free to do so."

Jill blinked at this simple explanation. Not free? Like how? God! He wasn't married, was he? Oh dear God, if she'd gone and fallen for a married guy—

"I was in the middle of a divorce when I opened the store next to Jill's. I've been waiting for the divorce to go through before asking her out. Besides, I didn't want a rebound relationship. The first year after separating from my wife, I dated around a lot, but then I realized I was picking women who were all just like my ex-wife. I decided it would be best to take a year off from dating, give myself that time to deal with all the issues from my marriage, decide what I really wanted in a partner and then consider dating again. The next time I marry I want it to really be 'until death do us part.' "

"I suppose there were lots of women you were interested in during that time," she murmured.

"Yes," he admitted. "There are a lot of attractive women in the world."

"Yes," she agreed with a frown.

"But none of them were as interesting to me as Jill is."

She stiffened, her ears suddenly pricking.

Nick grimaced and shook his head before continuing. "I was halfway through that promised year when I opened the shop here and met Jill. Suddenly, keeping to that year was hard. I actually *like* Jill. It isn't just sexual interest with her. She's normal and sane and funny and smart and sexy . . . everything I've ever wanted in a woman."

Jill sucked in a breath at this news, her heart suddenly bursting with hope.

"Actually, I think this year business turned out to be a good thing for us," he said quietly. "It forced me to be a friend to her first and through that I've found we get along great. We work well together as a team. We like many of the same things . . ." He shrugged. "I didn't even know that much about my wife when I married her. And while I was sure two years ago that I would never marry again, I think I'd be willing to risk it with Jill . . . if she was interested."

"Oh, I'm sure she'd be interested," Jill assured him with a grin. She felt like her heart was bursting. He liked her! And he thought she was funny, smart, and sexy.

"I guess we'll see when I ask her out."

"When will that be?" Jill asked with excitement. "I mean, when is the year up?"

"Both the year and the divorce were final yesterday. I signed the final decree last night," Nick admitted and then gave a dry laugh. "And actually, I had it all planned to ask her out today."

Jill had to grab onto Santa's chair to keep from jumping up and down with glee and squealing.

Nick continued. "I was going to invite her to my sister's Christmas party after the parade. That way there'd be no nervous, first-date jitters, just a relaxed invitation to join me at my sister's. I even invited the others in the parade along too so she wouldn't feel pressured."

"Oh," Jill breathed, thinking he was the most thoughtful man in the world. If he'd asked her out on an actual date the first time, she would have been over the moon, until the first-date jitters set in. Then she would have spent whatever time there was between his asking and the actual date fretting over what to wear, what to say, desperate to have everything perfect.

God, what a clever man he was. His way was so much more relaxed. If he invited her with a bunch of people, she would have been relaxed thinking it was just a group thing and—

Damn! Jill's happiness turned to dismay as she realized that John and his craziness had completely screwed up everything. There wouldn't be any relaxed first date because she wasn't here. Her first date, and probably, finally their first kiss too. Jill had been fantasizing about that first kiss for so long, she doubted the real thing could live up to it. She would have liked to find out though. Dammit! Why had John chosen today of all days to act like a crazy prick and zap her? If not for him she'd be herself up here and she so wanted to be herself right then.

"Say, why is that guy coming out of Jill's store?"

Jill let go of her thoughts and glanced around with confusion. Nick was peering to the left of the float and she followed his gaze, noting that they'd reached their street of stores. The parade was almost over. At the end of this road, they would pull into the parking lot and disband. Her gaze slid along the storefronts until she found her own and she stiffened as she spotted the man now turning away from the door of her store. John Heathcliffe. His gaze slid over the people on the street and then across the floats passing by until it landed on her, where it froze, eyes widening with incredulous recognition.

No, he couldn't recognize her, Jill thought with dismay. She didn't look anything like herself.

"He seems to know you. Who—" Nick's words died as he turned curiously toward her and suddenly froze. "Jesus," he breathed, his wide eyes eating her alive. "Jill? Where did you come from?"

"What?" She peered at him with confusion and then realized he'd called her Jill. Glancing down, she jerked the cape closed with a squeak of alarm as she saw that she'd changed back to herself and now stood on the float with nothing but the cape covering her. She was herself and *naked*. How? She wondered frantically and then realized that she'd been standing there wishing she was herself. Her body had obviously listened.

And, of course, John *had* recognized her. That thought forced any concern for her nudity from her mind and she jerked her eyes back to the bane of her existence. Jill wasn't at all surprised to see that John Heathcliffe was now pushing his way through the crowds, fighting to get to the float.

"Jill? What's going on? Where did Noelle go?" Nick was obviously struggling with confusion, but she didn't have the time to explain.

"I have to go," she muttered, and tried to turn away, but he caught her arm.

"Wait a minute," he said. "How—?"

"I can't explain right now, Nick. Please let me go, he's coming. He'll get me," she cried, panic choking her throat as she saw John break out of the crowd and stumble onto the street next to the float behind their own. As slow as the parade was moving, it wouldn't take him long to reach their float and be on her.

"But the parade," Nick said.

"It's done, we're nearing the end of the street now," she pointed out, tugging at her arm. "Please."

Nick glanced around and saw that they were indeed nearing the parking lot where they would disband. They had two more stores to pass. Frowning, he glanced back to her frantic face, then toward John, who was now running behind the float, reaching for the edge to boost himself up.

Mouth tightening, Nick began to urge her toward the front of the float. "Okay, let's go."

"What?" Jill glanced at him with surprise as he hurried her to the opposite end of the float from where John was trying to board. "You're coming with me?"

"Like you said, the parade is over," he pointed out with a shrug. "And I don't know what's going on . . . but I want to."

"Oh," Jill breathed unhappily, not at all sure she could explain everything to the man. She'd have to explain about her brother and his wife, and the molecular destabilizer and that wasn't her secret to share. Besides, she wasn't sure she wanted to. He said he liked her because she was normal and sane, and she had been until that morning. Now she was anything but normal. Once he found that out, would Nick lose interest in her?

"Hey! What do you think you're doing, buddy?!"

Jill glanced back over her shoulder at that shout from Jay to see him and the other two adult elves converging on the spot where John now hung off the float. His upper body was on it and he was struggling to pull his legs onboard, a struggle made more difficult as the three little men began kicking and hitting him while the children playing elves pelted him with candy canes from a safe distance.

"Jump."

Jill jerked her gaze back around just as Nick leapt from the float, pulling her with him. Biting back the scream that leapt up her throat, Jill concentrated on trying to land on her feet, but she was off balance and landed wrong. Her ankle twisted out from under her and she fell.

"Are you all right?" Nick asked with concern, kneeling at her side.

Jill nodded, then glanced down and blushed self-consciously as Nick suddenly tugged her cape down to cover her upper thighs.

"You really have to explain this to me," he muttered, lifting her to her feet.

Jill didn't comment, concentrating on holding the edges of the cape together as he set her upright.

"Come on." Nick tugged her quickly through the crowd. It took her a minute to realize he was leading her back to his store, then they were there and he was retrieving keys from his pocket and unlocking the door.

Jill shifted from foot to foot and glanced anxiously back toward the float, cursing when she saw that John was now standing on it surrounded by angry elves. He was ignoring them, however, his attention fixed on her.

"Inside." Nick caught her arm and tugged her inside the dark shop.

"He saw us," Jill said anxiously, moving to peer out the window toward the float as Nick locked the door again.

"I know. He's probably headed here then," Nick said grimly and caught her arm to urge her away from the window. "We won't have much time."

"Time for what?" Jill asked with despair. It seemed to her they didn't have any time at all. She should be headed out the back door that very minute and without Nick. He wasn't the one John wanted and should be safe so long as she wasn't with him.

"I'm calling the police."

Startled out of her thoughts, Jill glanced around wildly and realized that Nick had drawn her to the store's back

room and released her to move around the desk and pick up
his phone. Lunging forward, she pressed down on the phone
receiver, hanging up on him even as he started to punch in
the number.

"What are you doing?" he asked with surprise.

"No police," she said, her voice panicky.

"Don't be ridiculous, Jill." He pushed her hand out of the
way. "This guy is obviously bothering you or something.
The police—" His words died and he lifted a disbelieving
expression to her as she suddenly ripped the cord out of the
phone.

"I'm sorry," she said at once. "But I can't let you call the
police. I can't explain, but this doesn't affect just me, but my
family." She glanced down at the cord still in her hand and
dropped it with a sigh. "I'll replace that, I promise."

"Where are you going?" Nick hurried around the desk
after her when she opened the door between the back room
and the shop.

"I'm going to wait until he's looking in the front door and
then slip out the back door. He'll leave you alone then and
come after me. You'll be safe."

"Are you crazy?" Nick pulled her away from the door and
into the middle of the back room, real anger on his face now.
"You must be if you think I'm going to let you draw him off
so I'm safe while you try to handle this on your own."

"He doesn't want you," Jill pointed out on a sigh. "This
is—"

They both fell silent and turned to glance to the front
of the store as they heard someone try the door. As they
watched, John released the knob and used his hands to frame
his face against the window, trying to see inside.

"He can't see us," Nick murmured. "It's dark back here."

Jill bit her lip, watching John with the same fascination
she'd watched a snake about to strike. She then became
aware that Nick had moved away from her.

"What are you doing?" she asked in a whisper as he moved back to the door between the front and back of the shop, then her attention shifted back to the front door as John began to tug at it again as if he could force it open by sheer will. Nick paused too, she noted, but her attention was on watching John try to open the door. Then the scientist suddenly stopped and moved away on the sidewalk, trying to look nonchalant. They understood why when a police officer appeared in front of the store and approached him.

Jill supposed the officer had spotted him working at the door and briefly hoped that he'd arrest him or something, which would leave her and Nick safe and free, but the officer merely spoke to him for several minutes, then turned and continued along the sidewalk. Jill supposed there wasn't really anything he could arrest him for. Trying a door wasn't an offense.

"The cop must be keeping an eye on him," Nick murmured when several moments passed after the policeman moved out of sight, and John didn't return to his efforts with the door. He was merely leaning against the telephone pole out front, his gaze fixed on Nick's storefront. "It looks like he's decided to wait out front for us to try to leave."

"Until he remembers there are back entrances and tries that," Jill said unhappily.

"You're right," Nick muttered and suddenly pushed the door between the back of the store and the front closed. "We'd better be quick."

Hurrying to her side, he caught her arm and urged her toward the back door. "We'll slip out through the alley and—" He paused and turned to frown when Jill didn't budge, but held her ground. "We have to move quickly, Jill."

"Not like this. Santa and Mrs. Claus are too conspicuous. He'd spot us a block away like this," she pointed out.

Nick peered from her red cape to the padded Santa costume he wore and sighed. "You're right."

Jill was about to point out, as patiently and gently as she could, that it was safer for her to go alone, when he suddenly brightened, "I keep a change of clothes here in case of spills or such. They're in my office. You can wear those."

"What about you?" she asked with a frown.

"Unlike you, I have jeans and a t-shirt on under here," he said dryly. "I'll just strip off the costume and beard."

"Oh." She was silent for a minute, then nodded. "Yes. Go find the clothes."

The moment he disappeared into his office, Jill headed for the back door. Despite what she'd said, she had every intention of slipping away. She'd be doing them both a favor. The man had said one of the things he liked about her was that she was normal and sane. If that was so, he'd hardly be interested in her once he knew the truth of what she'd become. There was nothing normal or sane about being a shape-shifter.

No, it was better this way, she decided unhappily. She'd get out of his life before she forced him to break her heart by rejecting her.

Jill's hand was on the door knob to the back door when she spotted the calendar on the wall next to it. Pausing, she stared. It was open to December and showed a couple walking down the city street in warm winter gear. Jill glanced from the picture down to herself and back. She'd be less noticeable in the calendar woman's face and outfit than as herself. And as much as she wanted to spare herself the humiliation of explaining everything to Nick—if she even could—she didn't wish to do so at the expense of getting caught and caged up for the rest of her life by a madman.

Shifting to look like the calendar girl seemed her safest route, and it would only take seconds, Jill assured herself. She'd be changed and gone before Nick got back.

Decision made, she released the door knob and concentrated on the picture, imagining herself looking like that woman. Wanting it. Needing it.

"Jesus."

Jill blinked and glanced toward the door to Nick's office, a small gasp slipping from her lips as she spotted him standing frozen in the doorway. He was beardless and in only his street clothes, the clothes he'd sought for her a bundle clutched to his chest, but it was the shock on his face that concerned her.

She glanced down at herself, not surprised to see that she had changed successfully to the calendar girl. Her only wonder was whether he'd been there long enough to see her change or if his shock was at finding a stranger in the room.

"Jill?" he said with disbelief. "How did you do that?"

Well, that answered her question she supposed, her shoulders sagging. He'd seen her change. Now he knew how unnormal and unsane she was.

It was all so unfair, she thought miserably. Up until this morning her life and everything about her had been boringly sane and normal . . . well, except for her brother and Claire and Beth. Now, because of one idiot mad scientist, everything was topsy turvy and any hope of romance with the one guy she'd really liked in a long time was screwed.

"You changed from yourself to this in like a heartbeat." Nick tossed the clothes he'd collected onto the nearest box and began to walk around her, surveying her from every angle. "The only thing that didn't change is the cape."

Reminded of the cape and knowing she couldn't wear it out of the store for fear of tipping off John to who she was, Jill slid it off and draped it over the clothes on the box.

"Noelle was wearing that cape," he said suddenly.

Jill stiffened and watched unhappily as he put things together in his head.

"Then you were wearing it," he went on slowly. "Then you turned into someone else wearing the cape."

Jill let her breath out on a resigned sigh. She'd always known he was intelligent. It was one of the things she'd liked best about him. She shouldn't be surprised he'd put things together so quickly.

"You're like a . . . What do they call them? Shape-shifter?"

Despite watching him figure it out right in front of her, she still felt a bit shocked when he said the words. She supposed she'd imagined that he'd need her to give him the explanation for what exactly she was now capable of doing.

"Don't look so surprised. I watched *Star Trek* growing up," he murmured, continuing to examine her, then added, "I didn't think shape-shifters were real though."

"Neither did I," Jill muttered under her breath. She really hadn't thought such things were possible, not even when Kyle had explained their work to her. She hadn't believed right up until Claire had got zapped and turned into Brad Cruise.

"Does it hurt? To change like that?"

"No," she said warily.

He didn't look like he believed her, but merely asked, "Can you do it again?"

When her expression became surprised, he said apologetically, "I know it's rude to ask. At least, I think it is, but even though I saw it once, it's hard to believe . . ."

Jill felt her tension return when he suddenly went silent, a frown claiming his mouth. She had a feeling he'd just thought of something, and it was obviously something that didn't please him. She realized why when he said, "I told you— When you were Noelle, I told you—"

"I'm sorry," Jill said at once. "I mean, I'm not sorry you told me. I'm glad you like me. I like you too, but I'm sorry I let you tell me . . ." She paused and sighed, then finished unhappily, "Of course, now that you know this you might not be interested anymore and I'll understand if that's so, but—"

A noise from the front of the store made her pause. They both peered to the closed door between the two sections of the store, then Nick hurried to it, cracked it open, and peered out. Jill was just moving to join him by the door when he closed it again and turned to hurry back to her.

"The cop must be gone. That guy who's following you is trying to pick the lock. We have to go." Nick grabbed her hand as he moved past, drawing her to the back door. Jill allowed him to drag her out of the store, but reached up to grab a long winter coat off the rack by the door as she went. She wasn't cold and appeared to be wearing winter gear, but Nick wasn't. He was now wearing only jeans and a t-shirt. He'd need the coat.

She waited patiently as he locked the door, then handed him the coat and said, "I have to get to my brother."

"Why is this guy after you?" Nick asked as he shrugged into the long coat. "Is it because of what you can do? Does he know you're a shape-shifter?"

"Oh, he knows all right. He's who turned me into one," she said dryly, turning to lead the way up the alley only to find her hand caught as he whirled her back around.

Nick's expression was shocked. "What?"

Jill was silent for a moment, arguing within herself as to whether she should explain everything or not. This wasn't just her secret. Her brother, his wife, who happened to be Jill's best friend, as well their daughter, would be affected by this.

On the other hand, Nick was risking himself to help her, and the cat was already out of the bag, so to speak. It only seemed fair to explain. But they had to keep moving. If John got the door unlocked and got inside the store, it wouldn't take him long to realize that they'd slipped out the back and then he'd be out here after them.

Taking Nick's hand, Jill turned and started up the alley. She paused only long enough to send out a silent apology to her brother, then quickly explained about her brother and Claire's courtship, the experiment they'd been working on and then everything that had happened that morning.

"So your brother and his wife were among the scientists

working on a molecular destabilizer, this John creep zapped her, your brother got zapped pulling her out of the beam, and they both suddenly found themselves able to shift shape?"

Jill nodded.

"I get why they told their boss, this Dr. Cohen, that the machine didn't work and convinced him to break it down. It's obviously dangerous . . . But then why on earth would he rebuild it in his own basement?" he asked with disbelief.

"Kyle and Claire are worried their cells might now be unstable or there might be other problems they can't foresee. Kyle wanted to test the effects on animals with faster metabolisms. They have no idea what pitfalls or problems could be in store for them or Beth and he wanted to find out and hopefully find ways to avoid them," she explained.

"But then why did he bother to convince the company he worked for that the original didn't work? He wasted years rebuilding this new one. Wouldn't it have been faster to just admit that he and his wife had been zapped and were changed?" he reasoned. "He would have been able to experiment right away."

Jill frowned. "He didn't realize it would take so long to rebuild it, and he thought it was too dangerous to let them keep working on the original. He was afraid of what they'd do with such technology. He also feared once they realized he and Claire had been zapped, the two of them might end up the lab animals, being experimented on."

Nick nodded in understanding, and then said, "That John fellow probably took your niece downstairs and placed her behind the machine to get you under the beam."

Jill glanced at him with a start as they paused at the mouth of the alley. "I hadn't thought of that. Do you really think so?"

Nick shrugged. "He tricked your sister-in-law under the beam. And he admitted to you that he wanted to zap you to have someone to experiment on. It probably isn't just a happy coincidence that you ended up knocked out under the beam."

Jill supposed it *was* too much of a "happy coincidence." John probably *had* taken Beth downstairs and used the child to get her under the beam.

"You're right. We can't go to the police," Nick said suddenly, drawing her gaze again. He was looking grim and determined. "We can't risk revealing all this to the authorities and having you and your family locked up in cages to be experimented on. We'll have to deal with this ourselves."

"I need to talk to Kyle," Jill said quietly. "I tried to call him earlier, but there was no answer at the house. He and Claire must have taken Beth and gone to get new locks for the basement door or something. I need to talk to him to figure out what to do."

"Yes, we can—" Nick's hand suddenly tightened on hers. Startled, Jill glanced up to see him looking past her. They were standing at the mouth of the alley and a glance over her shoulder made her suck in a sharp breath as she spotted John weaving his way through the crowd toward them.

Chapter 3

"He must not have been able to pick the front lock," Jill said with alarm.

"More likely the cop scared him off again, so he's coming around to try the back," Nick said dryly.

"We have to hide," Jill said anxiously, catching his hand and trying to pull him away, but he stayed still.

"We don't have to hide. You already *are* hiding," he pointed out, his gaze moving over her face with fascination.

Jill frowned at his expression. She liked this man and didn't want him to see her as some weird creature, but it seemed that's what she now was. Pushing the concern aside for the moment, she said, "Nick, we have to hide. He's been watching Kyle and I think me too. He may have seen me with you. He might know who you are and then know I'm me despite . . ." She gestured vaguely to the form she'd taken.

Nick scowled at this possibility, but then suddenly smiled.

"What?" she asked with bewilderment, her gaze shifting nervously between his expression and the approaching John. Fortunately, he'd been slowed by a group of teenagers goofing around and taking up most of the sidewalk. He was still two buildings away, trying to weave his way around the kids.

"They say the best place to hide is in plain sight."

Nick's words brought her head back around and she opened her mouth to ask what he was thinking, only to gasp in surprise when his lips descended on hers. Jill stood still in his arms for a moment, and then clutched at his upper arms as he suddenly backed her up against the brick wall of the building behind them. She felt the hard, textured brick press into her back and was reminded that while she might appear dressed in winter gear, it was all just her. It was her skin pressing into the cool brick.

Jill shuddered as his hands slid around her waist to her back before dropping down to cup her bottom. Gasping, she rose up on tiptoe as he cupped her there and drew her tight against his body under the coat. His jeans brushed erotically against the naked flesh of her legs and hips and the cotton of his shirt rubbed softly across her breasts, making her nipples tingle. Moaning under the erotic assault, she clutched at his shirt front as his tongue urged her lips apart and slid between them.

Shivering as desire rippled through her, Jill slid her arms around his waist under the coat. Then she let her own hands drop down to his bottom and urged him harder against her, unable to stop her hips from undulating against him.

Nick groaned and ground harder still, then slid one leg between both of hers, forcing a gasp from her lips as his cloth-covered thigh rubbed against her.

"Get a room."

The muttered comment was John Heathcliffe's as he passed them to enter the alley. Jill recognized his voice and instinctively started to pull away from Nick. Seeming to realize that she was about to end their kiss and unintentionally reveal his face, Nick rubbed his thigh against her more firmly, then slid one hand to her breast and squeezed gently to recapture her attention. It worked. His touch drove all thought of others from her head and drew a moan from her throat as she arched into both caresses.

Nick smelled and tasted so good and he felt wonderful, his body taunting hers from beneath his clothes. Jill forgot where they were and that they were hiding from anyone and wished they were both naked without barriers between them. She'd waited so long for this kiss . . . And she'd been wrong, her fantasies hadn't been better. No fantasy could live up to this molten heat and passion. The man was on fire, burning her up with his kisses and caresses. It made her wish they were alone somewhere, that she was herself and they were both naked without his clothes between them.

"Mommy, why is that lady naked?"

"Never mind, Virginia. Don't look. Come on."

Jill heard the exchange, but it didn't really register until an excited stir erupted around them and Nick suddenly stiffened and drew away to peer down with shock.

Dread suddenly a stone in the pit of her stomach, Jill tore her gaze from his to glance down at herself. Much to her horror, she'd somehow shifted back to herself and now stood there on the street, naked for all to see. And they were all seeing. Several people were now yelling, others laughing, and still others just gawking at her.

Nick's mind was acting more quickly than hers. Jill didn't notice his releasing her and shrugging out of his coat. She was still staring stupidly down at herself when he suddenly forced her arms into the coat, and drew it closed around her. In the next moment they were weaving their way through and around groups and couples, then Nick suddenly tugged on her hand and they headed down a side street.

"Where are we going?" Jill gasped, struggling to keep her feet.

"The parking lot. My car's there," he said.

Jill glanced anxiously behind them. At first she thought

they'd given John the slip by veering down this road, but then she heard an alarmed cry and saw a lady stumble into the street and her gaze narrowed on where the woman had come from. Sure enough, John's head popped briefly into view.

"He's still behind us," she told Nick, wondering why she wasn't out of breath. Jill wasn't the most athletic person. Her life revolved around her shop for the most part and she spent a lot of hours there, leaving very little time for other things, including exercise, yet this race wasn't leaving her breathless as she knew it probably should.

Another cry drew her gaze over her shoulder and alarm raced through her as she realized John was gaining on them. The problem was that Nick was trying to avoid people, weaving through the crowds to avoid jostling anyone. John, on the other hand, was charging through the crowd like a football player, sending people stumbling and sprawling in his wake. He'd soon catch them at this rate.

"He's gaining on us," she gasped to Nick and he suddenly veered to the left, dragging her through the door of a store.

"Can I help you?" a clerk asked as they charged past.

"Just looking," Nick called out before dragging Jill behind a rack of sunglasses. He stopped so abruptly then, Jill nearly knocked them both over, slamming into him.

"Do you see him?" she asked as Nick stuck his head around the rack and peered toward the front of the store. "Did we lose him?"

"I'm not sure, he— There he is," he interrupted himself and eased back a bit to make himself less conspicuous as he watched the front window of the store.

"What's he doing?" Jill asked anxiously.

"He's stopped on the sidewalk out front," Nick said, a frown tightening his lips as he watched. "He's looking around the street."

"He must realize we ducked into a store," Jill said with a sigh.

"Yes, but he doesn't know which one."

Jill shifted and drew his coat closer around her as they waited to see what John would do. Oddly enough, she felt more naked now with Nick's coat on than she had when she'd actually been naked but looked dressed. She thought that was strange.

"Is there something I can help you find?"

Jill glanced around sharply. A sales clerk had approached, eyeing them as if they might be shoplifters. Not surprising, she supposed; they were acting oddly after all.

"I— We were just—Umm." Her gaze slid to Nick for help. She was at a complete loss as to what to say to explain their behavior.

"We're just looking," Nick assured her and dragged Jill to the next row to get them away from the woman. Jill immediately picked up one of the boxes on the end display to "look," silently praying the woman would go away. She was so busy trying to look interested in what she held, it took a moment for her to realize it was a box of condoms. Ribbed for her pleasure.

Flushing, she set the box back and asked, "What's he doing now?"

"He's still in front of the store," Nick said on a sigh. "It doesn't look like he's going to move until he figures out where we've gone."

Jill glanced nervously toward the store clerk and noted that the woman was staring narrowly at her naked legs and feet. The phrase *No shirt, no shoes, no service* immediately ran through her head and she felt panic begin to claim her. She was positive the woman was going to throw them out at any moment.

"We can't stay here," she hissed to Nick. "The store clerk is already suspicious. It's just a matter of time before she throws us out."

Nick glanced toward the woman, then picked up a box of

condoms and turned it over as if reading instructions. He then leaned out to glance to the front of the store. His unhappy expression told her John was still there. "We can't leave until he leaves."

"And we can't stay," Jill said firmly, glancing at the clerk out of the corner of her eye. She was sure the woman was just working up the nerve to handle them.

"We have to separate," she decided.

"What?" Nick peered at her with alarm. "But—"

"He knows I'm with you now. It doesn't matter what form I take, he'll follow you if there's anyone with you. We need to let him see us and then separate. He isn't interested in you. He'll follow me."

"But—"

"Once I'm away from you I can change form and give him the slip," she pointed out urgently.

Expression grim, Nick gave a reluctant nod. "How?"

Jill leaned past him to see that John stood on the sidewalk at the opposite end from the entrance. She pictured the storefronts on this street in her mind and then turned to ask the store clerk, "There's a bookstore next door, isn't there?"

The clerk seemed startled by the question, but nodded.

"It's on this side of the store?" She gestured to the right of them.

The clerk nodded again.

"Thank you." Jill turned to Nick. "We'll go out, pause long enough for him to see us, then I'll duck into the bookstore next door while you take off up the street. He'll follow me, I'm sure. I'll slip into an aisle and quick change to give him the slip."

Nick nodded slowly. "I'll head to the parking lot. My vehicle's a big red SUV. Meet me there after you give him the slip."

Jill smiled. Rather than be relieved to be free of her, he was arranging to meet up with her again. She wanted to grab him and plant a big kiss on his lips. Unfortunately, they didn't have time. "I'll head for the parking lot as soon as I can."

"How will I know it's you?" Nick asked with a frown.

Jill grinned and simply said, "I'll tell you."

"Right." He glanced to the front of the store before turning back to ask, "Ready?"

Jill took a deep breath and then nodded. "As ready as I'll ever be."

"Okay." Squeezing her hand, he drew her back the way they'd come, using the aisles to hide them until they'd reached the door. John was still there but his attention was turned in the other direction as they slipped out of the store. Rather than head off right away, Nick urged her toward the door to the bookstore. They'd nearly reached it when John turned and glanced in their direction.

There was one moment when all three of them froze, then Nick took off running. Jill immediately rushed into the bookstore. A glance back as the bell above the door jangled showed John hurrying after her, leaving Nick to escape as she'd expected.

Heart pounding, Jill rushed up the first aisle, then took a sharp left and headed for the back of the store, glancing up each aisle she passed. Jill didn't see John, but she saw a lot of other people. There seemed to be someone in every aisle she passed, which made those aisles useless to her. She could hardly shift in front of witnesses.

Jill was starting to panic when she reached the last aisle and—much to her relief—found it unoccupied. Her relief was short-lived. She hurried up the aisle, wildly scanning the books on display in search of a picture of a person she could turn into. It only took a second for her to realize she would have no luck here. The aisle was filled with Christmas items: cards, calendars, and children's books all featuring elves, doves, Santa, Rudolph . . . Almost every last one was drawn or a cartoon image that was useless to her. At least she didn't think she could turn into a three-dimensional, life-sized cartoon image. And even if she could, John would know at once it was her.

There were only two images that were of actual living creatures. One was a set of cards with a cute little puppy on it. While Jill knew she could probably take on the shape, she somehow didn't think she'd be able to shrink in size to be the creature. Besides, it was cute and cuddly and pretty much defenseless against someone like John.

Her gaze slid to the second image and she stared at the card featuring a real reindeer wearing a glowing red Rudolph nose. Despite the pressure of the moment, Jill couldn't help but wonder how on earth the photographer had gotten the reindeer to stand still long enough to put the nose on, let alone wear it long enough for pictures to be taken.

"Watch it, mister," the woman's voice made her glance anxiously up the aisle. She had no doubt the woman was speaking to John. He was probably barreling up the store's center aisle like a bull as he'd done on the street, pushing people out of the way as he went. And he wasn't far away. He'd be here any moment.

Panic a high-pitched whistle shrieking in her head, Jill turned in a circle. What to do? What to do? John would be here any moment and she was trapped. What to do?

Her gaze slid desperately back to the image of the reindeer. He'd know it was her, of course. He'd hardly imagine a reindeer got loose from the parade and wandered in to pick out Christmas cards. On the other hand, she'd have a lovely pair of antlers to hold him off with, which was more than she had at the moment.

Could she?

"Hey!"

Jill winced and glanced around again. That shout had been much closer than the last. Frighteningly close. Turning determinedly back to the cards, Jill stared at the image of the red-nosed reindeer and closed her eyes. In that moment, she really wanted to be the reindeer. It was big, would be fast, and had large antlers to hold John off.

A gasp brought her eyes open and she peered to the end of the aisle where John stood, a stunned look on his face. The red bulb glowing at the end of her now very elongated nose was her first clue that the shift had worked. Glancing down, she found herself staring at two hoofs sticking out of Nick's coat sleeves.

"Well, you clever little minx," John breathed suddenly. "I never would have imagined you could do this."

He was moving toward her, easing his way as if she was a vicious animal . . . which she supposed she could be now. By rolling her eyes upward, Jill could just see the tips of the long, pointy antlers now crowning her head. They looked deadly and she briefly fantasized about charging at the man and goring him as payback for all the trouble he'd caused her . . . but it just wasn't something she could bring herself to do when she had other options. And she did. Taking advantage of one of those options now, Jill turned to hurry up the aisle away from him. Unfortunately, her brain was trying to run like a human with two legs and she was now on all fours. The new body shape was odd and awkward and left her floundering clumsily for the first few steps. The coat didn't help matters much either; her clumsy hooves kept catching on it as she tried to move.

A sudden jerk on the back of the coat told her John had grabbed it. Fortunately, in all their rushing about, Jill hadn't had time to do it up. Now she struggled to free herself, her feet—hooves—coming free and allowing the long coat to slide off her back.

"Get back here!" John yelled, but she was away.

Reaching the end of the aisle, Jill turned sharply to the right, intending to head for the front of the store, but she hadn't taken her new body into account. Her front hooves turned abruptly on command but her back legs were slower to react and slid out from under her so that her hind end slid along the floor to the side. Jill cursed under her breath as she saw John rushing up the aisle toward her. He'd be on her in a minute. Forcing herself to concentrate on her new body's movement, she managed to regain her feet and immediately charged for the front of the store.

Jill didn't consider the problem the door could be until she was nearly to it. She was just starting to realize that she wouldn't be able to work the door knob when the bells jangled as it was pushed inward by someone entering. It was an older woman who was smiling on first pushing the door open, but who blanched in horror and threw herself to the side, slamming the door against the wall and pinning it there with her body when she saw what appeared to be a huge reindeer charging toward her.

Jill put on a burst of speed and exploded out onto the sidewalk.

Screams and shouts erupted around her and Jill soon rued that she'd changed at all. The antlers were deadly and she wasn't used to them; she could hurt someone very badly if she weren't careful. Fortunately, she wasn't the only one to realize the peril her new shape could cause and everyone was scrambling to get out of her way. Turning in the direction of the parking lot, she broke into a run as the bells on the door behind her chimed. She didn't have to glance around to know it must be John.

"Jill! Get back here!" he roared and she grimaced at the fury in his voice. Did he really expect she'd just docilely allow him to lock her away for his experiments? The man was mad, she thought as he called her name again. "Jill!"

"That's Rudolph!" a child's voice corrected him scornfully, then added, "Run, run, Rudolph! The bad man's coming."

Jill was already running, but put on a burst of speed at the cry. The more accustomed she became to this new shape, the more swiftly she was able to move and everyone was very accommodating in making way for her. They were spreading before her and then closing quickly behind her to stare after her with amazement, which had the added benefit of slowing John down. She quickly left him behind.

Unfortunately, all this attention had its disadvantages and when she heard someone shouting out to call the police or animal control, she knew she had to get herself somewhere out of sight and change again quickly. The problem would be what to change into. If she changed back to herself, she'd be left naked and that was hardly helpful.

A rush of relief ran through her as she broke out of the last of the crowds and found herself on the edge of the parking lot. It was full of people milling about still in their costumes. The parade was over and its members were now laughing and chatting in groups with the relief and excitement that follows a successful venture. Fortunately, they were mostly congregated around the tents and no one seemed to notice her appearance at the edge of the lot.

"Don't let it get away."

"Does anyone have a rope? We can lasso it and hold it until the police get here."

Jill glanced around at that comment, startled to see that some of the people from the crowds had decided to give chase. She should have realized that would be the case, that some civic-minded men would decide to catch the wild reindeer running loose in the streets before it harmed someone, but the possibility hadn't occurred to her.

Cursing, she turned sharply and charged for the end of the parking lot where the parade members had parked. When they reached the cars, she began to weave through them, aware that the men had begun to spread out, trying to surround her.

Pausing between two vans, Jill tried to decide which way to go, but glanced to the side when a muffled bark caught her ear. She blinked in surprise as she found herself face-to-face with a beautiful husky. The dog had climbed right up onto a box on the seat of the van he was in. He stood framed in the window, peering at her with what seemed more to be curiosity than anything else.

"Do you see it?"

Jill glanced behind her, but while the voice sounded close, there was no one there.

"I think it went around that van," someone answered as Jill turned back to peer at the dog again. Knowing she didn't have much time, she concentrated on the animal, wanting desperately to look like it. No one would bother her as a husky. They'd hardly notice her with their attention on finding the reindeer.

"Hey, boy." A hand landed on her rump, rubbing there and bringing her eyes open as two men moved up on either side of her between the vans.

"The reindeer couldn't have come this way, the dog would have stopped it," the second man said as the first man ran his hands over the white fur now cresting Jill's body. She'd shifted successfully and was now a husky.

"Yeah. He must be back further," the first man agreed, straightening and turning back the way they'd come. "Let's backtrack."

Jill released a breath as the two men disappeared around the van, as relieved that the one man wasn't touching her anymore as she was that they'd been fooled by her shape-shifting. The fellow may have thought it was a dog's furry back he'd been running his hand over, but it had felt to Jill like his hand was coursing over her naked skin.

A scratching sound drew her attention back up to the van window and she smiled at the husky as he rubbed his paws over the glass of the window as if to say she should let him out to play with her.

Another time, she thought and hurried toward the opposite end of the parked vehicles, searching for the red SUV where Nick was supposed to be waiting for her. She was relieved when she spotted it and even more so when she saw that Nick was there waiting for her as promised. Some of that relief faded, however, when she saw that he wasn't alone. Bev was there, and judging by her stance and the high angry pitch to her voice, she was in the midst of giving him hell for something.

"I'm sorry, Bev," Nick said apologetically as Jill reached the back end of the SUV. "But it was an emergency and we were on the last leg of the parade. There were only a couple of stores left to pass before the parking lot when we had to leave."

"That's another thing," Bev said. "First Jill's here, then she has to go and that Noelle woman took her place, then suddenly Jill was there on the float, and someone said she was stark naked under the red cape. What the heck is going on?"

"I can't really explain just now, Bev. I wish I could, but . . ." Nick let the word trail away as he glanced worriedly across the parking lot, obviously searching for her, or anyone rushing his way, Jill supposed, since he had no idea what she was going to look like. His action and her own thoughts reminded her that while she may have escaped the concerned citizens hunting the runaway Rudolph, John was probably heading their way and might know it was her when he saw her with Nick.

"Hey, Bev! Where do you want us to put the costumes?"

Bev turned toward the elf who had come around the SUV. "I'll finish with you later," she said over her shoulder to Nick as she started away. "And when you see Jill, you tell her I have a few choice words for her too."

Jill waited until the pair was gone, then hurried to Nick's side, leaning against his leg to get his attention.

"Oh, hello, fellow," he murmured, bending to give her a pat. "I don't suppose you've seen a beautiful redhead that may or may not be herself, have you?"

Jill smiled at the words "beautiful redhead," and then said, "It's me."

She frowned as her words came out very badly slurred. Her jaws were now long and narrow and her tongue felt huge and unwieldly. She supposed she was lucky to be able to speak at all. Dogs didn't.

"Jill?" Nick asked with amazement and knelt to catch her jaw in his hand. He looked her over with disbelief. "How? . . . Why? . . ."

"It's a long story," she said, trying very hard to speak clearly. "We have to get out of here. John—" She paused as Nick suddenly straightened and peered over the roof of the SUV. The curse that slipped from his lips told her all she needed to know. John had caught up.

Chapter 4

"Come on." Nick moved to the driver's door, opened it, and waved her in. Jill immediately bounded into the vehicle, scampering over the driver's seat to the passenger side, where she peered anxiously out the window. She wasn't made any less anxious to see that John Heathcliffe was no more than twenty feet away and moving fast.

She glanced back to Nick as he settled in the driver's seat and slammed his door closed, watched him start the engine, then turned back to the window again. John was running now and had cut the distance in half.

"Are the doors locked?" she asked nervously.

A click sounded as he shifted into gear and the doors automatically locked, then the SUV jerked forward. Jill scrabbled to keep her balance on the passenger seat as Nick accelerated, watching anxiously as John burst forward, shouting as he slammed his fists into the side of the vehicle. It was all he managed, though, before they were tearing out of the parking lot, leaving him behind.

"Do up your seat belt," Nick ordered as he steered them up the road.

Jill turned to him with disbelief to see his gaze shooting between the road ahead and the rearview mirror, which showed the parking lot behind them.

"How exactly do you suggest I do that?" she asked dryly.

Nick glanced at her and frowned. "Can't you change back to yourself?"

"Certainly. If you'd like to drive through town with a naked woman in the front seat."

The smile that slowly curved his lips suggested it wasn't something he'd mind. Sighing, Jill dropped to her haunches on the passenger seat and raised one paw to the door to help balance herself.

Nick was silent for a moment, but now that they were safely away from John, his gaze was moving between the road and where she sat.

Moving uncomfortably under his inspection, she peered into the side mirror on her side of the vehicle, noting that the road behind them was empty. John wasn't following. Yet.

"I don't see him," she murmured.

"No." Nick glanced in the rearview mirror again. "Hopefully by the time he gets his own vehicle and tries to give chase, we'll be far enough away he can't find us."

Jill kept her gaze fixed on the side mirror until they turned a corner without seeing John's black van appear. She relaxed a little bit then and tried to think what she should do now. After a moment's thought, she glanced to Nick. "I need to call my brother."

"Of course. My cell phone is in the glove compartment."

When Jill peered at the glove compartment, but made no move to try to open it, Nick gave a short laugh.

"Sorry, I wasn't thinking. I'll get it for you," he murmured. Pulling to a stop at a red light, he leaned sideways, reaching past her to open the glove compartment and retrieve the phone in question. He started to hand it to her, then paused and shook his head. "I guess I'd better dial for you."

Jill smiled faintly, but forced herself to stop when she realized her tongue hung out of her mouth when she did. Probably not the image she wanted to convey.

"What's his number?" Nick asked as the light turned green.

Jill rattled off the number and watched as he eased the car forward through the light, his concentration split between the phone and the road ahead. Once finished, he didn't hand the phone to her, but placed it to his own ear and listened to it ring.

"The answering machine has picked up," he said after a moment, a frown curving his lips. "What do I say?"

Jill heaved a sigh. "Just hang up. They must still be out."

Nick flipped the phone closed and set it on the seat beside her. Jill stared at the phone with frustration for a moment and then said, "They probably won't be out much longer. If you dropped me off there I could wait for him to get back and—"

"No way," Nick said firmly. "Your brother's house is probably the first place this John guy will look."

Jill grimaced but didn't argue. Now that he'd said it, she realized it was true and she'd rather avoid running into John Heathcliffe again.

"And your place would probably be his next stop," Nick added before she could suggest it as an alternative.

Jill frowned and peered out the window, startled when she saw the husky's face reflected. Turning away from the image, she said, "Well, I have to wait somewhere. You can't just drive me around until my brother and his wife return home. If Claire and Beth have gone too, they could be doing last-minute Christmas shopping. They could stop for lunch or even a matinee movie and be gone for hours."

"Then we'll have to wait hours," he said firmly. "I'm not leaving you alone to be caught by that John guy."

"But you're supposed to be meeting the rest of the parade crew at your sister's place," she reminded him.

"Yes," he said and smiled suddenly. "So that's where we'll go. We'll go to my sister's party. You can keep calling from there."

"I'm not exactly dressed for a party," Jill pointed out dryly.

Nick glanced at her, his smile deepening before he said conversationally, "You know, I would have killed to have a talking dog as a kid."

Jill grunted, not amused.

"Although I probably would have picked a terrier. I always liked terriers best."

"Terriers are small," she pointed out.

When he glanced at her with confusion, she pointed out, "I can shift my shape, but I don't think I can shrink it down to the size of a terrier."

"Oh." He peered at her curiously, and then said, "So I suppose shifting into a mouse so I can slip you into my pocket to enter my sister's house is out, huh?"

"Ha ha," she said dryly and then heaved a sigh and slumped on the passenger seat, resting her head on her front paws with dejection. "I guess I'll have to go as a dog."

It wasn't how she'd imagined a first meeting with his family would be.

Nick glanced at her dejected state and frowned before turning his attention back to the road. When he turned right several moments later, and the SUV bounced slightly as it went over the lip of a driveway, Jill sat up and peered around curiously, expecting to see that they'd arrived at his sister's house. Instead, she found herself staring out at the large parking lot of a mall.

"What are we doing here?" she asked with bewilderment as he steered the car down the ramp into underground parking.

"There's something I need to pick up before we go to my sister's," Nick answered as he pulled into an empty parking spot in the back corner of the complex. Turning off the engine, he glanced at her with concern. "Will you be all right here by yourself for a few minutes?"

"Yes, of course," she murmured, her gaze sliding over the other cars. It was winter and cold out, but there weren't many people around either coming or going from vehicles. Jill supposed when it got cold or inclement, workers of the shops in the mall who started first thing in the morning took up the majority of spaces in the underground parking. Nick had probably been lucky to find an open spot.

"I'll be as quick as I can," he assured her and then slipped out of the truck.

Jill watched him walk across the parking lot to the elevators that would carry him up into the mall itself, then relaxed back on the seat, a little sigh slipping out. Her mind was filled with thoughts. Worrying mostly, about where John was. Was he back at her store, searching it? Checking her house to see if she'd gone there? Or he might be headed to Kyle's house expecting her to head there for help.

That last thought made her sit up anxiously. She wished she'd been able to reach her brother. Something bumped against her paw as she shifted and she found herself peering down at the cell phone Nick had left on the seat with her and stilled. She should try the house again. If John were headed that way, who knew what he'd do to her brother and his family. Jill pawed at the phone and even managed to flip it open using her paws and nose, but punching in the numbers was impossible. The keypads were just too tiny.

Growling in frustration, she peered around the parking garage again, but now that she worried that John was heading to Kyle and Claire's, she was overwhelmed with the desperate need to call there. She peered around the SUV's interior, searching for a pencil or something she could hold in her mouth and use to punch in the numbers, but there didn't appear to be anything like that.

Her gaze slid to the elevator in time to see the doors open as it disgorged a couple of people. Neither of them were Nick. Jill's gaze slid back to the phone. She had to call her brother. If she changed back to herself, she could. She'd also be naked.

Jill shifted on her paws, trying to decide what to do. She couldn't show up at Nick's sister's house naked . . . She needed to warn her brother . . .

Naked. Brother. The two words began to alternate in her mind.

Growling with frustration, she turned on the seat and peered into the back of the SUV, hoping to find something to help her out of this situation. She sighed with relief on spotting the red plaid throw folded neatly on the back seat.

Perfect! she thought happily. She could change back into herself, wrap herself in the blanket and call her brother. Then she could wear the blanket to Kyle's sister's, where he could slip in and maybe borrow something for her to wear. That way she could try calling Kyle right away and hopefully warn him before John got there.

The plan had its flaws, but it was better than nothing, she told herself. Besides, she simply couldn't sit there doing nothing while her family might be in danger.

Mind made up, Jill leapt between the two front seats into the back, dropped onto the floor in front of the seat, and closed her eyes. Just wanting to be herself had been enough to cause the shift while she'd been on the float and on the street, so that's what Jill concentrated on. She wanted to be herself. She repeated that refrain in her mind several times, then cautiously opened her eyes and peered down, relieved when instead of black fur, she found herself staring at her own pale flesh.

"Yes," she breathed and snatched up the folded blanket,

only to freeze as it dropped open and she saw that it wasn't a blanket at all, but a plaid scarf. A large scarf to be sure, measuring perhaps five feet long and a foot wide, but still just a scarf. Jill closed her eyes briefly and groaned.

She should have examined it before carrying out the change. She should have . . .

Really, it was too late for should haves, Jill told herself firmly and forced herself to examine the scarf. It wasn't a blanket, but it was large for a scarf and would just have to do. She shifted the material around in her hands, considering the best way to cover the most she could with the scrap of cloth. Finally, she wrapped it around the back of her neck, brought both sides down over her breasts, and then tucked the ends of the material between her legs. This covered all the vital spots, but just barely. Unfortunately, it was the best she could do and it was too late to change her mind; she didn't have a picture of the dog or anything else to change back into now.

Grimacing, Jill leaned around the back of the front seat and tried to snatch up the phone, but it was farther away than she'd thought and all she managed to do was brush it with her fingertips and send it slipping off the seat onto the floor in front.

"Perfect," she muttered to herself and rose up enough to peer around the parking garage. Fortunately, there didn't appear to be anyone around to witness it, so, muttering under her breath, Jill quickly climbed between the front seats into the front of the vehicle, then dropped onto the floor there to keep out of sight as she searched around for the phone. It took her a moment to realize she'd sat herself on it, but then she found it, flipped it open, and punched in her brother's number.

As had happened every time before this, the phone rang several times before being picked up by the answering machine. Jill hung up as soon as she heard her brother's recorded message and then stared at the phone unhappily, wishing she'd bothered to memorize his cell phone number. Unfortunately, with it programmed into her cell phone, she'd never taken the trouble to memorize it. Why bother when all she had to do was hit contacts, find her brother's name, and hit dial?

Now she peered absently around what she could see of the car interior from her position, running numbers through her mind trying to recall it by memory. She was sure it ended with 1432 . . . or maybe 1342 . . . 1234?

Growling with frustration, Jill lowered her head, then jerked it back up in surprise when the driver's door suddenly opened. Nick peered in, frowning when he didn't see her on the passenger's seat, then froze when he spotted her on the floor.

"You changed back," he said with surprise.

"I'm really worried that John might go to Kyle's. I wanted to try calling him again," Jill explained apologetically, drawing her knees closer to her body to help cover up her near nudity.

"Oh." Nick hesitated, glanced around the garage behind him, then stepped up into the vehicle, dragging a large shopping bag with him as he settled in the driver's seat and pulled the door closed. He then glanced at her again, only to pause and blink. "Is that my scarf you're wearing?"

"Oh." Jill glanced down at herself self-consciously and drew her knees even closer still to her chest. "It was the only thing I could find in here."

He bit his lip, she suspected to keep from grinning, and then said, "Well, I guess it's a good thing I picked this up then."

Jill's eyebrows rose as he now offered her the bag he'd brought with him.

"What is it?" she asked rather than take the bag.

"A dress," he answered quietly. "I thought maybe you'd prefer not being a dog the first time you met my family . . . or

borrowing clothes. I thought you might rather change back
into yourself and wear this to my sister's house."

"Oh," Jill breathed and then lifted shining eyes to his. He
was such a thoughtful man, so smart and clever and caring.
God, she could love this man. Maybe already did. She'd
known him for six months. This certainly wasn't the first
time he'd shown this considerate, caring side. He'd shown
her that and much more since moving into the store next
door. He'd proven himself funny, and smart and insightful
and sweet . . . Yes, she might very well love the man. And
he apparently liked her back. He'd admitted to her when she
was Noelle that he was more interested in her than in any
other woman since leaving his wife. Maybe . . .

"If you keep looking at me like that . . ."

Jill let her thoughts die and blinked at Nick. His expression had gone serious, his eyes hot and intense. It reminded
her of those few passionate moments at the end of the alley,
of his arms around her, his mouth on hers, his hands sliding
over her body . . . and she wanted to experience all that
again, this time as herself, in her own body, not a body borrowed from a calendar.

"If I keep looking at you like that . . . what?" she asked
softly.

Nick was silent, his gaze slipping down over her, taking
in the bit of cloth she'd tried to place so strategically and the
expanse of flesh it didn't cover. Jill felt his gaze like a caress.
Goose bumps began popping up on her skin and she shivered where she sat, her eyelids growing heavy and her mouth
parting on a little sigh.

Suddenly he was leaning forward, seemingly unable to
stop himself from pressing his lips to her invitingly open
mouth.

Jill breathed out a little sigh as his mouth covered hers
and she began to struggle to get her arms free of the cramped
space she'd put herself in so that she could touch him. She

wanted to wrap her arms around his neck and press her body to his as she had at the mouth of the alley, but was trapped by her position. Briefly. Then Nick suddenly caught her by the arms and lifted her up onto the seat.

Jill murmured her relief and gratitude into his mouth as she slid her arms around his shoulders, uncaring that the movement had dislodged the scarf, revealing anything he wished to see. Nick cared though. Breaking the kiss, he pulled back slightly and peered down over her, and she followed his glance, noting that her nipples were already hard and erect, eager for his touch.

As if unable to stop himself, Nick reached out and ran one finger lightly over the exposed tip, then bent his head to cover it with his lips. Jill cried out and arched on the seat, her hand drifting into his hair and holding on as he suckled, but it was too much too quick and she found herself tugging at his hair, urging him back up to kiss her.

Nick gave in to the demand and covered her mouth with his, quickly deepening the kiss with a thrust of his tongue. His hand replaced his mouth at her breast, caressing and teasing the hard peak and making her writhe and moan beneath him.

That seemed to cut loose the last of his restraint, because Nick groaned deep in his throat and propelled himself forward, pushing himself out of his seat and forcing her back against her own as he came over her. She felt the leather against her back, then the seat suddenly collapsed beneath her and she found herself flat on her back with Nick on top, his hands roaming her body as his mouth pillaged hers.

Jill gasped and arched as his hands closed on her skin, each claiming a breast, and this time didn't protest when Nick broke their kiss again and moved his mouth away to begin a trail down her neck.

"I've wanted to do this for so long," he breathed against

her throat as he moved lower. "You don't know how hard it's been not to kiss or touch you all this time."

Jill's answer was to arch and whimper with need as his lips trailed over her collarbone and began to crest the curve of her breast.

"How many times I've sat eating my lunch, thinking how beautiful you are, how much I wanted to touch you and taste you and . . ." His words died as he reached her breast once more and covered her nipple, sucking it into his warm, wet mouth so that his tongue could swirl around it.

Jill's entire body seemed to tighten up in reaction this time, one hand clawing at his shoulder, the other tugging viciously at his hair, trying to make him kiss her again.

Nick ignored the silent demand this time and simply suckled harder as one hand moved to cover her other breast and tease the nipple there.

Jill opened her mouth to beg him to stop it and kiss her again, then nearly bit off her tongue when she felt his other hand begin sliding up her thigh.

A little alarmed at how out of control she felt and at how quickly this was all going, Jill caught his shoulder and tugged hard, relieved when this time he gave in to her and slid up her body to kiss her.

Jill kissed him back passionately, but wanted more. She wanted him kissing her, suckling at her breast, and she wanted to have him inside her. She wanted it all.

Frustrated by the clothing separating them, Jill began to tug at his shirt, dragging it out of his jeans with more desperation than finesse. The moment it was loose, she slid her hands under the material and hungrily ran them over his bare flesh, but it wasn't enough. She'd wanted him for so long—forever it seemed now—and need was exploding inside her, making her demanding as her hands slid down to his jeans and began to tug insistently. When the jeans didn't slide down his body, she changed tactics and managed to squirm her hand into the waistband and find him with her fingers.

Nick groaned into her mouth, his hips instinctively thrusting into the caress as she touched him.

"God," he gasped and pressed his mouth to her neck now, one hand sliding down along her hip as he ground against her.

Jill pressed a kiss to his forehead and ran her fingers over him again. In the next moment, Nick had shifted them both to their sides facing each other. He then used one hand to catch her by the back of the neck and pull her face forward for a masterful kiss as his other hand went searching. As his tongue thrust into her, his fingers found the hot wet core of her and began to explore.

Jill cried out into his mouth and bucked against his seeking hand, her own fingers squeezing hard around him. She thought she'd explode any minute, was almost desperate to do so, then laughter hit her ear and startled her back to awareness of where they were.

It had the same effect on Nick and he suddenly stilled too. They pulled slightly apart and stared at each other briefly, then Nick raised his head and peered out the window. When he didn't say anything, she rose up to peer out as well, and bit her lip as she saw a pair of young men coming from the direction of the elevator and starting along the row of cars toward them.

It was enough to have Jill and Nick scrambling. He shifted back into the driver's seat, and picked up the bag to drag out the dress he'd purchased as Jill slid back to the floor, and out of view of the windows. She began to don it without even really looking at it, managing to tug it on and down over her hips in record time.

"Here." Nick leaned down toward her and Jill stilled, unsure what he was doing until he straightened away with the price tag in hand.

Jill's gaze flickered over the tag and she smiled with gratitude, then pushed herself up out of the small floor space and onto the seat, tugging the dress down over her hips and upper legs as she went.

A glance out the window showed the two young men just passing by the SUV, not seeming to even notice them inside. She watched them walk to a car several down from their own, then let a little sigh slip from her lips. Part of her resented the interruption of what she and Nick had been doing, but another part was confused. She'd liked the man for ages and wondered why he'd never made a move, but now things seemed to be moving in high gear. It was a bit overwhelming.

"Are you all right?" Nick brushed his hand lightly over her cheek, his expression concerned when she turned to peer at him.

Forcing a smile, she nodded. "I—Yes. It's all just a little . . ."

"Intense," he suggested quietly when her voice faltered.

Jill nodded solemnly. Intense was a good word for it. Another word was overwhelming.

Nick leaned forward and kissed the tip of her nose, then hugged her comfortingly.

"It will be all right," he murmured by her ear. "It's just that we've been seeing each other for six months and all these feelings have built up and . . ." He paused to clear his throat, then said, "I'm sorry if I was rushing you."

Jill's breath came out on a soft laugh. "You aren't rushing me. I mean, it's all rather overwhelming, but you didn't do anything I didn't want and . . ." Frowning, she took a breath and admitted, "I want you. I really do. I'm hard pressed not to ask you to make love to me right here and now, but there's so much going on, so much to worry about. I'm worried about what John Heathcliffe is doing right now, about whether Kyle and Claire are safe and—"

"Shh, I know." Nick hugged her a little tighter and rubbed her back soothingly. "I know. It's all happening at the same time. I think that's one of Murphy's laws or something. But we can handle all this together. We'll go to my sister's where you'll be safe in a crowd of people. You can keep calling your brother and his wife until you get through to them and we'll take care of this Heathcliffe character. Then we'll deal with the *us* part of the equation. Okay?"

Jill smiled into his shoulder and nodded. They'd handle it together and then deal with the *us* part of the equation. It had a nice ring to it.

"Okay," she whispered into his shoulder and he pulled back slightly to peer at her.

"We are going to deal with the us part though, Jill," he reassured her solemnly as if she might think he was just putting her off. "We have something special here and my year is up. My divorce is final and I'm now free to pursue you like I want to."

Jill smiled at his expression, and then whispered, "It's about time. Pursue away."

Nick grinned and then kissed her again before saying, "We should get moving."

"Yes," Jill whispered, settling back in her seat and doing up her seat belt.

Nick started the engine and then pulled out of the parking spot, but Jill wasn't paying attention. Her gaze had dropped to the dress she wore and she was examining it with surprise. It was a simple black cocktail dress. Simple, classic, stylish, and tasteful.

"This is nice," she said with surprise.

Nick grinned. "Don't sound so surprised. I happen to have good taste."

"Sorry," Jill laughed, then added uncertainly, "but isn't it a bit dressy for a casual afternoon party?"

Nick shook his head. "The first part of the party is casual, but then most people will leave and at about eight p.m. my sister is having a dinner party."

"Oh." Jill managed a smile. "Then it's perfect. You have good taste."

His eyes caught on her lips briefly, and then he cleared his throat and turned his attention back to the front as they pulled out of the parking garage.

Jill found her eyes slipping over his mouth and hands, re-calling their moments of passion and decided to distract herself. She said, "It was nice of your sister to hold a party for the parade people."

"There was nothing nice about it," he said with a wry smile. "Sue started out having the party for the people she and her husband work with at the psychiatric hospital. But when she found out about you, she told me to invite you along. I pointed out that it might be uncomfortable for you to have our first date be a party with my family, so she opened it up to everyone in the parade too." He shook his head, then went on, "The afternoon is an open party with drinks and snacks for employees of the hospital and parade members, and then at eight it's a proper sit-down dinner with her, her husband, my brother and his wife, and us." He cast her an apologetic glance. "Sorry about that."

Jill merely shrugged. She already knew from their talks that his sister and her husband were both psychiatrists and that his brother was a policeman with a baker for a wife. In fact, she knew a good deal about his whole family and even many of his friends. They'd talked a great deal these last six months. The sister arranging things to meet her didn't sur-prise her so much as the fact that the woman knew about her. Nick had been talking about her to his family.

"What did you say that made her want to meet me?" she asked curiously.

Nick was silent so long she didn't think he would answer, but then he admitted, "That I was pretty sure you were the one."

Jill blinked. "The one?" she echoed faintly.

Nick didn't respond until they reached the first set of lights. Braking then, he met her glance and said quietly, "We've been friends for six months, Jill. I know everything about you. The only thing I didn't know was whether we'd be sexually compatible . . ." He glanced to the light and back, and then added, "Of course, it's pretty obvious now that won't be an issue."

Jill flushed, but merely smiled and reached over to squeeze his leg. This day was turning out to be more than she'd ever expected. All she'd hoped for was being asked out on a date and possibly a first kiss. She was getting much more than that. It was as if the last six months of their lunches and platonic friendship had been dating without it actually being called that, and without kissing or anything else. Now they were moving ahead at an amazing rate. From friends, to almost lovers and being "the one."

She shook her head with amazement. If it weren't for John Heathcliffe's antics this would be the most perfect day she could imagine.

"Here we are," Nick announced and then blew out a whistle. "It looks like we're the last to arrive. We'll be lucky to find parking anywhere nearby."

Jill didn't comment, but was just recalling that she was barefoot when Nick said, "By the way, there are shoes in the bag too."

She glanced at him with surprise and then caught up the bag from where it lay discarded on the floor and retrieved a pair of dressy black shoes. Her eyes widened with surprise as she noted the size.

Nick grinned. "I own a shoe store, love. I can guess a shoe size at a glance and am usually right."

She smiled at the claim and slid on the shoes as he parked, then leaned over and kissed him on the cheek.

"Thank you," she whispered and meant it. He was very thoughtful. Others might not have thought of stopping to get her clothes, let alone shoes. But he had. His consideration was one of the things she liked about him, but there was so much more too.

Nick smiled and reached out to squeeze her hand affectionately, then opened his car door. "Let's go. Time to face the lions."

Chapter 5

"Good Lord! The two of you must be freezing! Come
in!"

Jill smiled at Nick's sister as she opened the door to them,
but then her eyes ran curiously over the large entry, taking
in the gleaming hardwood floors and cream walls. The room
was beautiful and made more so by the tasteful Christmas
decorations.

"Where are your coats?" Maggie asked as she closed the
door behind them.

"We lost them at the parade," Nick murmured.

"Oh. People nowadays," Maggie tutted with a scowl. "You
can't leave anything alone for a minute anymore." She shook
her head. "Well, never mind. I'll loan you both coats before
you go."

"Thanks, Mags," Nick said, giving her a hug. "You're a
sweetie."

"Yes, I am, and don't you forget it," Maggie said laugh-
ingly as he released her. She then turned to beam at Jill.
"Hi, I'm Maggie, Nick's sister, and you must be Jill, the

smart, funny, lovely lady who owns the clothing store next door to Nick."

Jill flushed with embarrassment, her lips tipping wryly as she said, "I take it Nick has mentioned me then?"

"Mentioned you?" Maggie laughed. "It's been Jill this and Jill that for six months. I was beginning to think the divorce would never be over so we could meet you."

"You know," Nick said, scowling at his sister. "If I hadn't already told Jill what I thought of her, I'd be really embarrassed right now."

"I knew you'd tell her before you got here. You've been chomping at the bit for the last couple months. I'm surprised you managed to wait until the divorce was signed," Maggie said with an unrepentant grin and then added, "I plan to help the two of you along by telling Jill all sorts of things today."

Nick rolled his eyes, apparently not surprised at the threat. "Oh, well, if you're just going to embarrass me, I think I'll go find Jill and me a drink. Will you be all right for a minute?" he asked, running a hand down her arm.

She nodded and he pressed a kiss to her cheek, whispering, "She means well."

Jill smiled at the claim as he turned away.

"Don't hurry back," Maggie called after him and then turned to Jill with a wide smile. "Nicky's told me so much about you, I feel I know you already. Of course, that's how I knew he was serious about you."

"It is?" Jill asked, eyes wide. Nick had said as much earlier, but it was still startling to hear it from his sister. As Jay had said, it seemed everyone had known he liked her . . . except for her.

Maggie considered her expression solemnly, then murmured, "It must have driven you wild these last six months, eating lunch together every day, his seeming to like you but never making a move." She grimaced. "I know it would have driven me mad."

When Jill merely smiled crookedly, Maggie said, "I'm afraid he had to. If Michelle—his ex-wife—had caught wind that he was seriously interested in someone, she'd have dragged her feet on the divorce to get more money just to make him miserable."

"Ah." Jill felt her shoulders relax. While she'd believed what Nick had said, she'd wondered why, once he'd decided she was the one, he'd still held to his determination not to reveal his feelings until the year was up. Now she understood.

"She is a horrible woman, grasping, greedy, and spiteful." She shuddered and added, "Nicky would never tell you that, but I'm not as nice. She was horrid."

"She must have had *some* redeeming features," Jill murmured, though she was actually pleased to hear this poor opinion of the first wife. "Nick doesn't seem the sort to marry someone like that."

"He was younger and she was a model, always flying off to some shoot or other." She grimaced. "With her around so little, we were all fooled. Once they were married, though, she dropped out of modeling, was around, and couldn't uphold the image of the sweetheart for long."

"Still out here?" Nick asked as he approached up the hall. Pausing at Jill's side, he handed her a glass of eggnog and then glanced from one to the other. "So, has my sister scared you off yet?"

Jill smiled faintly and shook her head. "Afraid not. I guess you're stuck with me."

"Lucky me," he murmured, slipping an arm around her as he sipped his own drink.

"You make such a cute couple," Maggie commented with a pleased little sigh.

"Maggie, love?"

All three of them glanced up the hall as a man poked his head around the door, a small frown on his face.

"Do we have any more club soda? I can't—"

"I'll find it," Maggie called out, interrupting him and then said, "Lou, this is Nick's friend, Jill. Jill, my husband Lou."

"Hello," Jill greeted him with a smile.

"Hi, Jill," Lou grinned, then gave Nick a thumbs-up. "Nice one."

Maggie shook her head as he disappeared back into the room, then smiled at Nick and Jill. "You two should join the party. I'll catch up with you later."

"Thanks for the warning," Nick teased.

"Ha ha," Maggie muttered as she walked away and then paused and turned back to say, "Oh, I almost forgot, some of the parade people beat you here. Most are in the back room, though there was one fellow hanging out in the front room watching for you."

Nick frowned at this news. "Watching for me?"

"No. It was Jill he asked about."

Jill was aware of Nick stiffening next to her even as ice slid down her back.

"What did he look like?" Nick asked, dread in his voice.

"About your height and build, dark hair. Intense eyes and a bit cold," Maggie answered, frowning now as well. "He followed a group of parade people in. I thought he was with them, but they're all hanging around together and he's sticking to himself . . . Is there a problem?"

Nick's gaze locked with Jill's but he shook his head. "No, I'm sure it's fine."

"Maggie? Lou sent me to ask if you have any ginger ale."

All three of them glanced up the hall to see another male peering around the door frame. He looked like an older version of Nick and Jill knew at once that this must be his brother, Mac, the police officer. The way his gaze was moving over her rather than focusing on Maggie made her suspect Lou had mentioned her presence and he'd come for a look-see at "Nick's friend."

"Mac, Jill. Jill, our brother Mac," Maggie announced, telling her she'd been right. She then continued up the hall saying, "I'll find the ginger ale and club soda." At the door she paused and glanced back to add, "I'll catch up to you two later."

Jill waited until the pair was out of sight before turning anxiously to Nick. "You don't think the guest waiting for me is John Heathcliffe, do you?"

"I don't know," Nick said with a frown. "I suppose he could have overheard the others talking about the party while he was in the parking lot, and then followed a group of them here and entered on their heels."

Jill bit her lip at the prospect. She'd just begun to feel safe again.

"Look," Nick said suddenly. "I think you should wait in the library while I walk through the house and check out the guests. If he's here, we'll leave before he knows you've arrived. If not, we can relax and enjoy the party. Okay?"

When Jill nodded, he urged her to a pair of double doors and ushered her inside.

"You can use the phone to try to call your brother while I'm gone. I'll be quick," he assured her as he pulled the door closed.

Turning away, Jill moved to the telephone on the desk and quickly punched in her brother's number. She wasn't surprised when the answering machine picked up again, and almost hung up, but then changed her mind and said, "Kyle, where are you? I need to talk to you. It's really important. I'll call again."

She hung up, shoulders sagging and head dropping unhappily to her chest. This was the best and worst day of her life. As much good was happening as bad, but all together it was exhausting and beginning to wear on her.

The sound of the door opening made her straighten abruptly. Jill didn't want Nick seeing her looking as defeated as she felt. Taking a breath, she forced a smile and turned, only to freeze when she saw John Heathcliffe moving quickly toward her.

Eyes widening, Jill swiftly shifted around the desk, placing it between them. "Leave me alone. I'm not going with you."

"Of course you are." John started around the desk toward her.

"No, she's not," Nick countered from the doorway. His mouth tightened at John's surprised expression and he said, "I saw you slipping in here. What happened? You saw us arrive and what? . . . Hid in the coat closet to wait until Jill was on her own?"

Ignoring the question, John continued around the desk. "Don't interfere. I'm taking her with me."

"The hell you are!" Nick rushed forward, catching John's wrist before he could touch Jill. He then swung at him with his other hand balled into a fist, but the scientist grabbed his wrist before he could land the blow and the two men began to struggle. They were about the same size, and apparently equal in strength because at first they simply crashed first one way, then the other, neither of them able to pull free or land a blow, but then John suddenly released the hold he had on Nick's wrist and reached into his pocket.

All the breath seemed to leave Jill's lungs when she saw the gun he pulled out. The paperweight she'd picked up from the desk a second before suddenly seemed as effective as a toy and Jill glanced around wildly for something else . . . anything else. Even as she peered around, though, she was wishing she was still the reindeer. She'd gore the man but good were she still the reindeer with those long, deadly antlers.

In the next moment she was. Jill hadn't closed her eyes, and hadn't spent several moments concentrating as she'd thought she had to, she'd just wanted it and suddenly the paperweight was slipping from her mutating fingers and she was dropping to the floor as her body shifted to reindeer form. The sound of tearing cloth accompanied it and Jill grimaced, knowing her lovely dress was being ruined by the new shape. Unable to do anything about that, she glanced to the two men again, relieved to see that rather than shoot Nick, John was swinging the gun at his head. She immediately launched herself forward, a frustrated growl slipping from her lips as Nick fell under the blow before she reached his attacker.

John cried out in surprise when she rammed her antlers into his backside. He crashed to the floor, the gun slipping from his hands and skittering across the hardwood to come to rest under the desk. He didn't go after it, but instead scrabbled across the hardwood himself, trying to get away from Jill and her antlers.

Jill let him go and peered at Nick, relieved when he stirred and moaned. John could have killed him with that blow. That thought brought her anger roaring back and she lifted her head to glower at John. Despite the fact that she was Rudolph in a torn dress, John whimpered and pulled himself into a ball. Before she could go after him the door to the library crashed open and instinct made her drop to her belly on the floor to hide behind the couch.

"Who the hell are you?" Lou's voice was sharp and demanding.

"Where are Jill and Nick?" Mac added, the question assuring Jill that neither she nor Nick were visible from the door. They would be, though, if the men moved farther into the room, she realized and closed her eyes, concentrating on being herself.

Nick's hand on her arm drew her eyes open a moment later to see that he was awake and she was herself once more. Smiling at him worriedly, she helped him to his feet, then grimaced when she glanced down to see the state of her dress. This shape-shifting was obviously going to be hell on her wardrobe.

"What on earth is going on here?" Maggie pushed her way through the crowd that had gathered in the door and hurried around the couch to join them, her worried eyes sliding from Nick to Jill and back as if unsure who was in the worse state. "Nick, you're bleeding, and Jill . . ." Her voice trailed off helplessly as she took in her torn dress. "Are you all right?"

When Jill nodded, Maggie turned her attention back to Nick to fuss over his head wound. Nick suffered it until Mac shifted impatiently by the door and demanded, "What the hell is going on, Nick? How did you get hurt? And why is Jill all beat up? And who the hell is this guy?" he added, gesturing to where John was just getting back to his feet.

Jill lifted her head slightly. She wasn't really beat up. Her dress was a mess and her hair was probably a bit tangled, but other than that she was fine.

Nick slipped an arm around her waist, drawing her to his side as he said, "This guy is John Heathcliffe. He attacked Jill and was trying to force her to go with him. He hit me over the head with his gun when I tried to stop him."

The word "gun" was like an alarm bell. Mac stiffened, his eyes narrowing on John, no doubt searching for the weapon in question.

"He dropped the gun. I think it slid under the desk," Jill said helpfully.

"Take a look and see if it's there, Lou, but don't touch it if it is," Mac said, positioning himself in front of the door in case John had any hopes of leaving that way.

Lou moved to the desk and dropped to one knee to peer under it. He straightened a moment later and nodded solemnly, indicating there was indeed a gun there.

"The man's a nut," Nick said at once. "He thinks Jill is a witch or something."

When Jill glanced at him with confusion, Nick squeezed her hand reassuringly.

"Not a witch, a shape-shifter, you fool," John snapped.

"Right, whatever," Nick said with a meaningful look at his brother-in-law. "And he wants to kidnap her, take her back to his home and torture the evil out of her. He probably has a cage and everything."

"The cage is just to keep her from escaping," John said quickly. "And I wouldn't torture her, just study her. I'm a scientist and we need to experiment on her, do empirical studies to see how her cells respond to various stimuli like cold, heat, or being cut off."

"Cut off!" Jill squeaked with horror.

John nodded. "Yes, painful but necessary. I'll have to cut parts off and see if they change on their own or die and see if the appendage will grow back or your cells simply displace to replace it."

"Well, I've heard enough," Mac said dryly.

"Hmmm," Lou murmured. The psychiatrist came to his wife's side and whispered something that made her nod and move silently out of the room. The moment she was gone, Lou offered John a smile. "These sound like fascinating experiments, John. Science has always fascinated me. Would you tell me more?"

He moved carefully forward as he spoke, his movements slow and cautious, his expression nonthreatening.

John frowned, looking uncertain, but it seemed keeping this all to himself for so long had been terribly difficult. He was eager to tell someone.

"I have a whole list of experiments I wish to try," he blurted, excitement edging into his expression. "I need to test her in cold temperatures and hot to see if it affects her ability to change, and see if she can now withstand freezing temperatures better than normal people. I had a huge walk-in freezer installed for that one," he admitted proudly.

Jill shuddered at the thought. Cutting parts off, freezing her . . . None of it sounded appetizing. She was doubly glad she'd escaped him that morning.

"And then there's fire. We have to see if her cells can now withstand flames."

"Jesus."

Nick's soft horrified whisper drew her gaze to see that he'd gone pale. It seemed he was equally distressed at the "tests" she'd barely escaped.

"Yes, of course," Lou was saying solemnly, his gaze moving to the door as Maggie slid back into the room. She nodded at her husband and his gaze then slid meaningfully to Mac before he put a hand on John's shoulder to turn him away. Walking him toward the windows, he said, "I can see how these would all be necessary. Tell me more."

Jill watched as Maggie and Mac started to move silently forward. It wasn't until they moved past her and Nick that she spotted the syringe the woman held in the hand that had been behind her back since entering. Eyes widening as understanding sank in, she glanced back to John as the man continued his explanations.

"Well," he was saying, "I'll have to see how chemicals affect her now too: poisons, radiation, etc. We have to know just how her cellular basis has been altered and—Hey!" John tried to whirl around but Lou and Mac both grabbed him and held him in place as Maggie pushed down the plunger on the needle she'd just jabbed into his arm.

"What are you doing? Stop that!" John tried to struggle free, but it was too late, Maggie had finished administering the shot and now backed away, leaving the two men to hold the struggling scientist.

"It's all right, John," Lou was saying soothingly. "This is just something to help you relax."

"I don't need to relax. What did you give me?" he asked, his eyes widening with horror as his words began to slur.

"As I said, it's just something to help you relax."

"But you said you understood. You wanted to hear about—" He gasped as his legs suddenly gave out. If not for

Mac and Lou holding him, he would have fallen, she was sure, but the men were holding him and shifted their holds to catch him under the arms and half drag, half carry him to the couch.

"I am most interested in hearing what you have to say, John," Lou assured him. "And we'll have plenty of time for you to tell me all your plans and tests at the hospital when you wake up."

"Wake up? Hospital?" John's voice was soft and confused, then his eyes blinked closed and he appeared to go to sleep.

"Well," Mac said, straightening slowly away from the now unconscious man. "It's handy your being the head of a psychiatric hospital, Lou. I can't think of a better candidate for the place."

"Hmm." Lou nodded solemnly. "The man is obviously delusional. Has he always been?"

Jill's eyes widened as the two men turned in her direction in question. She quickly shook her head and said, "I don't know. I don't know him. I've heard of him, but never met him before today."

"How did you hear of him?" Mac asked with a frown.

Jill glanced nervously at Nick. When he nodded encouragingly and squeezed her hand, she said carefully, "He worked with my brother several years ago on some experiment, but it didn't work and they closed down the lab."

"Hmm." Lou turned back to the man. "Well, his attacking you, plus what he said here is enough to lock him up for seventy-two hours observation. I suspect what he says once he wakes up will be enough to keep him locked up for a while, at least until we can find a drug treatment plan that will stabilize him and rid him of the delusion that you're a witch or shape-shifter or whatever it is."

"But why you?" Mac asked quietly.

Jill glanced sharply at the officer and swallowed thickly.

The man was looking suspicious and she suddenly felt terribly guilty, though she had nothing to feel guilty for.

"If he's never met you before, why did his delusion fixate on you?" Mac asked.

Squeezing her hand again, Nick jumped in to say, "Jill didn't know him, but he told her that he'd been watching her brother Kyle for a while and her as well, didn't he Jill?" he prompted.

"Yes." She nodded quickly. "This morning, when he first tried to kidnap me. He said he'd been watching my brother Kyle and his family since the project ended all those years ago and started following me after he saw me leaving and . . . er . . . finally decided that I was the one he should turn into a shape-shifter and experiment on."

"He tried to kidnap you this morning?" Mac asked with surprise. "Did you make a report?"

"I—No, I—I tried to call my brother right afterward to tell him, but there was no answer and I had promised to be in the parade . . ." She let her words fade to silence, knowing how lame they sounded.

"She thought it was a joke," Nick said, helping her out, then gave a laugh and a shrug. "What else was she supposed to think? She recognized his name from when he worked with her brother, but he was claiming she was some 'creature' and he was going to lock her up and experiment on her." He shrugged. "She thought it was a joke. It was only when he tried to get on our float at the end and then started chasing us around that either of us took it all seriously."

"Ah." Lou nodded as if that all made perfect sense. Even Mac relaxed a bit, though he wasn't looking wholly satisfied.

"The ambulance is here," Jay announced from the doorway and Jill shifted uncomfortably as she was reminded of the presence of all the partygoers. None of them were looking at her with anything but sympathy, however.

"Right," Lou said, drawing her attention back to the two men by the couch. "Let's get this fellow on his way to being settled in the hospital then, shall we."

Nick drew Jill back out of the way as the ambulance attendants entered with a gurney. They lifted John's unconscious form onto the wheeled bed, strapped him down and then took him out with Lou, Mac, and Maggie following.

Jill felt her shoulders sag as the room immediately began to clear.

Nick drew her against his chest. "How are you holding up? Shall we leave and go someplace and relax?"

Jill nodded with relief. "My place. I'd like to bathe and change."

Nick smiled wryly as he took in the ruined dress she wore. "It didn't last long, but it did look good on you while it lasted."

Jill smiled faintly and leaned her head into his chest for a hug, murmuring, "I suspect it may be a good thing that I own a clothing store."

"And I a shoe store," he agreed with a grin and she glanced down to see that she'd lost her shoes once more.

Wrinkling her nose, she peered around the room and then slipped from under his arm to move around the couch. A relieved sigh slid from her lips when she spotted the shoes he'd bought her.

"Here they are," she announced, bending to pick them up and slip them on.

"So it's only your clothes, my coat, and this dress that were lost or ruined in today's excitement," Nick commented. "Not bad all things considered."

"Yes, I could be locked in a cage right now being burnt or frozen," she said with disgust and shook her head at the madness, not to mention cruelty, of John's Heathcliffe's plans for her.

"Not so long as I live and breathe," Nick assured her quietly and slid his arm around her again the moment she straightened.

Jill didn't know if it was because he was finally free to do so, or simply a reaction to the fact that he'd nearly lost her to John Heathcliffe and his madness, but Nick seemed to need to keep her close now, and was always touching her. He had his arm around her as he made their excuses to his sister and promised they'd come back in the next day or so for a meal, then held her hand in the SUV all the way to her place.

Once they'd reached her home the touching took on a different tone. Nick started out just trying to be caring by running her bath while she collected a robe and towel, but then his efforts to help her get the ruined dress off saw them lip-locked. This time there were no sudden bursts of laughter or talking to force them apart and they ended up making love right there on the bath mat. A memorable first time to be sure.

A memorable second time followed when he joined her in the bath.

They were out and drying off when the phone rang. Pulling on her robe, Jill left the towel for Nick and rushed out to the end of the hall to answer the phone.

"Jill? Are you all right? I got your message when we got back. It was followed by a bunch of hang-ups I worried might be you."

"Yes, the hang-ups were me too," Jill admitted with a little sigh, glancing over her shoulder to see Nick walking up the hall to join her with only the towel wrapped around his waist. She smiled softly and relaxed back against his chest as he stepped up to wrap his arms around her from behind.

"What's happened?" Kyle asked worriedly. "You sounded pretty upset in the message."

Jill opened her mouth to speak and then closed it again as all she had to tell him rolled through her mind. This was going to be a long conversation and Jill simply wasn't up to that right now. All she wanted was to collapse into bed and sleep in Nick's arms . . . and . . . she decided she could. John Heathcliffe was safely locked up for at least seventy-two hours. Tomorrow morning she would get up bright and early and go over to her brother's house and tell him everything. For now it would wait.

"Jill?" Kyle asked. "What's happened? What were you calling to tell me?"

She opened her mouth, but again paused, this time because Nick had started to nibble at her neck even as his hands slid around to tug her robe open so his hands could run freely over her body.

"I called to tell you . . ." Jill paused on a soft gasp as Nick's hands closed over her breasts, then finished breathily, "Mr. Handsome Shoes isn't gay."

"Mr. Handsome Shoes?" Nick asked with amusement, pinching her nipples lightly for punishment.

"You were calling to tell me Mr. Handsome Shoes isn't gay?" Kyle asked with disbelief and Jill heard Claire squeal in the background and then cry, "He finally asked her out, didn't he?"

Rather than answer either question, Jill laughed and pushed Nick's hands away, saying, "I'm coming by tomorrow for breakfast."

"Nice of you to invite yourself," Kyle said dryly.

"Trust me, you owe me," Jill responded just as dryly, fending off Nick's roaming hands as she added, "I might be bringing Nick if he wants to come, and believe me, you owe him too. We have quite a bit to tell you."

"I heard that," Claire cried, obviously having picked up another phone in the house. "You can't say something like that and then just leave us in suspense. What do you have to tell us?"

"Tomorrow," Jill said firmly and hung up.

"Hmm . . . Mr. Handsome Shoes," Nick murmured as she

turned in his arms and slid her own around his neck. "No wonder your brother thought I was gay if you've been calling me that."

"I didn't," she assured him, pressing her body close to his. "Claire did."

He grinned. "You talked about me to Claire, did you?"

"And you talked about me to your family," she pointed out, reaching down to undo the towel around his waist.

"Yes. Maybe we should have done a little more talking with each other."

Jill laughed at the claim and began to press kisses to his chest. "Talking is all we did, buddy. It's the other things we should have done more of."

"Oh? Such as?" he teased.

Smiling, Jill pulled away and caught his hand as she began to back her way down the hall. "Come with me and I'll show you."

Smiling, Nick allowed her to lead him into the bedroom, murmuring, "Somehow, I think this is going to be the best Christmas ever."

六
Six

Marjorie M. Liu

To my parents,
with love

Chapter 1

It was an accident that the Foreign Minister's wife was found—her body had been hidden quite carefully, in several different locations—but the fortuitous combination of the harsh Beijing winter and several hungry dogs made her discovery quite immediate, without time for decay, and once the forensic team had finished analyzing the woman's remains it was only a matter of time before the military became involved.

Which explained how, on the eve of Spring Festival, with the thunder of fireworks shaking the streets, Six found herself in a murky massage parlor in the heart of Shanghai, her hands covered in oil as she pounded the brown filthy feet of a man in a wrinkled black suit.

The air reeked. Cigarette smoke, cheap cologne, a multitude of unwashed bodies that had circulated through the room for hours upon hours, for days on end. The scents made Six's nose run, her eyes itch, and though she had held her job for only 360 minutes—by her watch, anyway, which was atomic in nature and government issued—her brief tenure here was more than enough. As far as she was concerned, the other girls who worked in this place—legitimately, without pretense—deserved medals.

Not that Six had met any of them. As per the agreement with the massage parlor's owner—who, according to his file, had long ago given up his Chinese name for the ridiculous foreign moniker of "Lucky John"—Six had remained virtually locked inside this small room, forced to massage the feet and bodies of one man after another. If any of those paying guests asked for a different girl, Lucky John was to insist all the others were busy. And if he did not do exactly that—or if any one of the men discovered Six's true identity—the repercussions had been made quite clear.

Police clear. Prison clear. End of life clear.

Six rolled her shoulders, glancing at the man reclining in front of her on the wide red chair. His eyes were closed, his breathing deep and even. Not asleep, but certainly relaxed. His face was broad and flat; a large mole, replete with long black hair, made a target of his chin. A toothpick jutted from between his lips.

Six slid her thumbs along the arch of his foot, pushing between his toes. She pinched hard on the bone. He jerked, grunting, and she applied more pressure. The man opened his eyes and kicked at her. Six allowed his big toe to connect with her chin, though she angled her head just enough to make it a glancing blow.

"Bitch," he growled, slapping the padded arm of his chair with one hard palm. "Careful."

As Six was supposed to be deaf—like all the other girls of Lucky John's massage parlor—she did not respond. Merely ducked her head, allowing her straight black hair to fall loose past her face, hiding the grim flat smile that passed fleetingly across her mouth.

Just outside the room's painted bamboo door, Six heard

footsteps. Quick, then slow, accompanied by Lucky John's shrill voice. The man beneath her hands tensed. So did Six.

The door opened. Six glimpsed Lucky John's distraught expression, his eyes large and focused entirely on her—stupid of him, a sure giveaway if these men were in any way observant and paranoid—but her view of the old pimp's quick retreat was obscured by a broad chest and skinny tie, and then there was another man in the room and the door closed with a quiet click.

Six glanced up and met a flat gaze, cold as the thick black ice covering the old concrete of her first training installation, a gymnasium near the People's Hall in Beijing, where she had studied alongside the country's Olympic hopefuls before being culled young, no older than five. She still remembered. She remembered training on that ice, out in the blast of arctic wind. Toughening herself. Knowing she had to be stronger than the others, and for a different reason entirely.

The newcomer stared at her. Six dropped her gaze, but not before observing other oddities, such as the man's utter foreignness, a purely physical difference that nonetheless revealed some kind of Asian ancestor through nothing more than the turn of his dark eyes and the prominence of his cheekbones. There was a hint of red in his hair; white man enough, running through his veins. Six could still feel him watching her when he shifted slightly, turned to the man reclining on the chair, and said, "I told you not to call me, Chenglei."

His Mandarin was spoken perfectly, without accent. Smooth tones, full of the North and its soft curves; an elegant voice. More cultured than criminal, certainly educated.

Six continued massaging the foot in her hands. It jerked once, then stilled. "But you came."

"I came because you're trouble," said the foreigner. "I came because I keep my eyes on trouble."

"Trouble." Chenglei's foot twitched again. "Look to yourself, then. Look, and regret."

"I have no regrets."

"All you had to do—"

"I told you no."

"You did," Chenglei said. "But we found *another*. And he did not say no."

The menace in those words was unmistakable, though Six did not understand their meaning. Nor did she need to. She was not an interpreter. Just muscle, a soldier, though at the moment even that did not give her pride. Too much distraction. She could feel the listening wire taped between her breasts. It had been warm, part of her, but now the thin casing was cold—*she* was cold—the whole room like ice, all the heat sucked away in one breathtaking punch that made her shudder with more than a chill.

Six could see her breath. Her breath, clear and white as a ghost puffing from her mouth inside a room where the thermostat was set for sweat.

Her hands stilled around Chenglei's foot. She stood up. Neither man looked at her. She backed away, just enough, and took a slow, deep breath so cold her throat hurt.

The newcomer's gaze flicked in her direction, then settled again on the old man. "There are no others."

Chenglei's smile was strained. He resembled a fat slab of pork, sprawled on his reclining chair. Six watched his hands, his white knuckles, his fingers twitching toward his sides. She recalled his file, old surveillance videos. She knew the signs.

Six moved fast. She grabbed Chenglei's creeping hand and yanked him off his chair, using his momentum to slam two fingers into his throat. He started choking. Spit flecked her cheek. She wiped it away, reached beneath his suit jacket, and removed one gun, silencer already screwed on. Very illegal. Life imprisonment, just on that alone. But for everything else in his file, she could shoot him now and no one would complain.

The room was still cold. Six quickly checked Chenglei for more weapons, then dumped the wheezing man back on his chair. She looked over her shoulder, and met a dark hard gaze. Blown cover, but better than shots fired. Chenglei had been intending to kill this man. And she needed answers.

"Do not try to run," she said quietly.

"I don't run," said the man.

"Over there." Six pointed. "On your knees, hands above your head, palms and forehead flat against the wall."

"No," he said, gaze flicking to Chenglei, whose gasps were quieting. "This isn't over."

"I am with Squad Twelve," Six said in a hard voice. "It could be over with a bullet, if you do not obey me."

"No," he said again, but this time she knew he was not talking to her. She stepped sideways, cautious, and turned to look at Chenglei.

His skin was blue. Cold blue, corpse blue, the flesh around his mouth cracking and flaking. His eyes were wide open, unblinking, and his chest was very still. Not breathing. Six stared. She had not hit him hard enough for that. She had not done anything to cause the rapid physical reaction she was witnessing, which suddenly reminded her of forensics class, time spent in the military's morgue, learning how to understand death, to create death, on an endless supply of corpses. Cold air, cold bodies. Decaying on a schedule. Only Chenglei's schedule appeared to be accelerating in a most unfortunate manner. His eyes were caving into his skull. As was his mouth, lips shrinking inward, shriveling.

"You need to leave," said the man. "Right now. Run."

"I do not run," growled Six, echoing his words. "What is this? A disease of some kind?" SARS had created enough difficulties; it still did, despite government attempts to suppress the disease and keep it out of the media. But that was nothing more than some advanced flu—easy to comprehend. What she was seeing now was something else entirely.

Biological weapons, she thought. *That is what this is all about.*

The wire taped to her chest transmitted a live feed. Just one word, and this place would be overrun by military. Her team was in place. Ready. Quarantine was not an option they had discussed, but it would be just as easily delivered: brutal, swift, the cleanup efficient. No questions asked.

Six opened her mouth to give the order. The man held up his hand—as if he knew what she was about to do—and though she did not trust him, there was something in the urgency of that movement that made her hesitate. That, and the look in his eyes. He stared at her as though he could see right into her heart, and as such, could speak to her heart, and what she heard in his eyes was *Wait, please, wait.*

So she did, feeling a momentary hush that fled with the cold. The air warmed, a flush of heat that curled over her skin and made her nose run. She ignored it. Stared at the man. Tried to watch Chenglei at the same time, which was why she saw his body twitch. Just once. In a manner as subtle as flexing three muscles: in his eyelid, his finger, his naked toe.

"He's alive," Six whispered, horrified. From man to cadaver to a ghost in a shell: she tried to imagine a similar fate, and it terrified her. "He's sick. Poisoned."

"Wrong," said the man, and it occurred to Six that he should really be facedown on the ground, unconscious and drooling. One tap against his head would do it. She had strong bones, good technique.

Except she could not move against him. Choice, instinct: She wanted him able to talk. She needed information. Right now. More than she wanted to be safe. More than she wanted to prevent any attempt to escape.

No chance to ask questions, though. Chenglei moved again. This time, fast. So fast that it was not until much later that Six found herself able to recall any details of what happened—not the flash of his teeth, not the darkness of that shriveled mouth—because in that heartbeat when Chenglei moved, all Six had was training, instinct, and it saved her life.

She ducked. Pivoted low on her right foot, spinning, then launched herself sideways so hard she was able to kick off the wall into the air. Gymnastics, martial arts, a body hardened by years of repetition and exercise; no expense had been spared to turn her into something that could move fast, with accuracy. She saw a blur pass close, gray as dirty ice, and found her feet again, ready to fight.

She did not have to. Chenglei was in the corner, backed against the wall. The young man stood in front of him, hands outstretched, lips moving in a low rumbling chant that made the hairs rise on the back of Six's neck—as did the sight of Chenglei. Only minutes before he had reminded her of a greased wrinkled pig—but the fat was gone, sucked dry, clothes hanging from his frame like rags tied to a line, flapping, flapping, stiff and cold. All bone now, sinew, less even—only a hint of his eyes remained, only a taste of a mouth, only a grinning skull, hissing like the sizzling lines of fireworks burning so effortlessly on the street.

Six forced herself to step close. The young man did not stop chanting. She glanced at him, wary, and had to bite down hard on her tongue. Despite the warming air of the room, his breath still puffed white. Six stared. She did not rub her eyes. She did not call herself crazy. She knew her mind, her training. Her lack of imagination.

The young man looked at her, and though his chanting did not falter, she heard his voice inside her head, clear and strong.

Go, he said. *Please.*

She almost did. Instinct, primal. But she stayed still, swallowing hard, and touched her blouse to feel the wire running beneath. One connection. Lifeline. She wondered how much the others had heard, what they made of it. She wondered why she did not call them in.

She looked again at the man beside her. She could see his eyes past the white cloud of his breath. Black eyes, with a hint of red, like his hair, standing stark and hot. An intense gaze, rocking down to her heart.

Too much. Six turned her focus on Chenglei. Looked hard, deep, and found nothing human. Nothing comparable, not even to an animal. There was too much hunger in that face. Too much violence.

"Tell me," she whispered to the man at her side. He ignored her, still chanting. She touched his arm. Flinched as her fingers burned with electric shock. Little lightning—in her head, as well. She saw a memory. Not her own. A pit of bones and flesh.

The man's voice faltered. Chenglei lunged. Six knocked the young man out of the way and took the blow, dropping and rolling backward, kicking up. She caught Chenglei in the chest, but not before his head snapped close, his gaping, cracking mouth sucking the air around her face. Terror cut, as did disgust; she felt a tug inside her mind, a violent yank like her soul had strings, and then Chenglei was kicked off, slammed into the wall. Not before his hands flung out, though. His nails were long. They scraped her cheek. Six snarled and rolled on her stomach, grabbing the gun she had taken from him. She fired.

It was a good shot. She caught him in the forehead. He went down. But only on one knee. Six fired again. Struck what was left of his right eye. The bullet passed through his head into the wall. She heard screaming outside the room; apparently, she was not the only girl in the massage parlor who still had her hearing.

Chenglei hissed. She glimpsed a tongue inside his mouth. A hand touched her shoulders and she rolled again, bringing up the gun. It was the other man, eyes dark, face white.

He crouched over her. One hand was outstretched against Chenglei. The other hovered above her face. She saw writing on his palm, a circle.

"Back away," Six rasped.

"No," he murmured. "It's too late for that."

He touched her. She tried to shoot him in the shoulder but her finger refused to pull the trigger, and she could not kick him off before his hand grazed her hand. The effect of his touch was immediate, terrifying. Her body stopped working. As did her voice. Muscles locked, trapped. Buried alive in her own body. All she could do was stare into the man's eyes, fighting with all her heart, all her mind.

You are dead, she told herself. *Everything, for nothing.*

"Not yet," whispered the man, leaning close enough to kiss. And then he did kiss her, softly, on the lips.

His mouth was unfamiliar, but hot, like raw ginger. Six found she could close her eyes. She did not want to, but she could not keep them open. She could not see at all. She could not hear.

And when, some time later, her body was lifted and carried by two strong arms, all she could do was wait, and imagine, and plan.

You are dead, she told herself again. *But until then, fight.* Fight to kill. Fight to win.

Chapter 2

Joseph Besud was a quiet man of middling youth—barely out of his twenties, hardly worth being called thirty—and while he had been educated in some of the finest schools in Europe and America, the most enlightening aspects of his life had come from moments such as the one, quite literally, at hand. There was nothing, after all, like carrying the dead weight of an elite counter-terrorist officer to make one appreciate the finer things in life. Like having a car.

He was rather less appreciative of the vampires hunting him, but he knew better than to complain about those parts of his life that could not be changed. And really, given that it was the holidays, he thought he could muster a little good cheer. He was still alive, after all. Whether he lasted long enough to make it home to his family's Spring Festival dinner was another matter entirely.

The woman was small, but heavy. All muscle. Joseph could still taste her lips. Kissing her had been unnecessary, but no one had to know that but him. Frankly, given that she was probably going to attempt murder or arrest after he released her, it was best that he take his chance while he still could. She was cute and tough. He liked that.

The wire taped between her breasts was no longer functional. It had been like that from the moment he stepped into the room. One look into her eyes and he had known what she was, why she was there. It complicated matters, though if Chenglei and his cronies had found someone else to do their dirty work—someone like him—then his life had surged beyond complicated into pure, unadulterated chaos.

No one paid Joseph or the woman in his arms any attention. He made sure of it. A simple mind trick, easy to accomplish given the festivities. No one wanted to pay attention to anything but themselves—or the small bombs in their hands. Firecrackers were technically illegal inside Shanghai, but as with most of China's regulations, the laws were merely guidelines unless someone said otherwise. And given the deafening blasts rocking the streets and sidewalks, no one was saying a word. Not one that could be heard, anyway.

He made it to the car—a tiny red Mini Cooper—beeped it open, and tucked the woman inside the passenger seat. Again, he tried to search her mind to find a name, but all he came up with was a number. Six. Nothing else. No memories of early childhood, unless images of some cold concrete dorm counted. To Joseph, they did not. He wanted warmth, love, some sign of normalcy. Anything to humanize this woman. All he found was solitude, duty, and an unbending sense of honor. Which meant one thing only.

She was going to be very difficult to deal with.

He got in the car, started the engine, and pulled out of the alley beside Lucky John's massage parlor. Inside his head he sensed the edge of an inquisition: Six's team, growing restless with her silence. It was a sign of their faith in her that they had waited so long to check on her status. He could feel it. The men trusted her. Had learned to trust all the women in her unit.

Squad Twelve. China's first all-female counter-terrorist team. Twelve women, hand-picked, trained by the very best. Little had been spoken of them in the media, which made sense, but there was enough government pride in their formation that some publicity had been generated. Enough to instill fear. The women were dangerous. They meant business. Good to know he was skilled enough to take one of them down, though he suspected her distraction was the cause of that. A distraction that concerned him, in more ways than one. He was not comforted that a vampire had almost managed to get the best of Six. Not at all.

Not when the creatures were working with terrorists now.

Joseph drove fast, but traffic was terrible. Too much activity in the streets. The world was red—red lanterns, red lights, red banners etched in gold. New Year's Eve, the edge of Spring Festival. Time for a new start, time to chase the monsters back with sound and fury. Fireworks, making violence and beauty.

Joseph glanced at Six. Her face was more delicate than her body. High cheeks, large eyes, shining hair. A scratch on her cheek. Broken skin. Which was, to use the American colloquial, a real bummer.

He opened himself for a moment, checking the surrounding area for anyone following them, and when he found nothing, snapped his fingers. Six's eyes flew open. Her mouth moved. She could not turn her head, but her gaze flicked sideways to his face, and stayed there.

"Stop the car," she said hoarsely.

"Sorry," Joseph said. "It's not safe."

He felt her consider an impressive list of threats. "Where is Chenglei?"

"Dead. Really dead." Joseph gripped the wheel a bit harder. "I finished killing him."

"Alive would have been better." Six licked cracked lips.

"He is a terrorist. He could have answered questions. I suppose you will have to do."

"I'm no terrorist."

"You were meeting one."

"That's not the same thing. I refused to work for them. You might have noticed that part, if you were listening to our conversation."

"I was." Her eyes narrowed. Joseph tried not to be intimidated. "What did he want with you? Bombs? Plans? Biological weapons?"

Joseph bit back a bitter laugh. "No, though I suppose that last one comes closest."

"Indeed," Six said, with such menace Joseph thought briefly of paralyzing her vocal cords again. "And what I saw . . . what Chenglei became . . . Is that a new weapon? Something that will be used on the Chinese people?"

Joseph said nothing. He was talking too much. Dumping her on some sidewalk suddenly seemed like a good idea. Followed by running like hell. Mongolia was always a good place to hide. As was Russia.

On the other hand, he was in deep now. Deeper than before. So was Six. Even if she did not realize it yet.

"Everyone is in danger," Joseph finally said. "Not just the Chinese."

"The Chinese are all I care about," she said flatly.

He shrugged. "Fine, then. The Chinese are in danger. Happy? Beijing and Shanghai go boom."

Six stared at him. She was very good at it. "You think this is funny?"

"Of course not," he snapped, wondering how one look could make him feel like an asshole.

Six pressed her lips into a hard line. "Who are you?"

"Joseph." He reached over and shook her limp hand. "And you?"

"I do not answer the questions of criminals."

He raised his eyebrows. "Compliment me again. I love it."

Six growled. Joseph bit back a smile. He had never heard a woman growl. Not really. It was kind of sexy, even if it was an indication of how much she wanted to rip out his throat.

A car cut in front of him. Joseph slammed on the brakes and horn. A boom rattled the car; he heard screams of laughter somewhere near, and glimpsed sparks rising into the sky. He opened his mind again, searching for threats. Felt a tickle. Something inhuman, on the move.

"You're in danger," he told Six.

"Really," she said dryly. "What a remarkable surprise."

"Not from me," Joseph replied gruffly. "From men and women like Chenglei. His associates."

He noted a subtle shift in her eyes. Interest. "I am always in danger from such individuals. There is no difference now."

"You're wrong." Joseph reached out, and very gently touched the scratch on her cheek. "You've been poisoned. That makes all the difference in the world."

Her eyelid twitched. "Explain."

Joseph had to look away. Her reaction did not surprise him, not entirely, though its effect was powerful. Tough woman. Real tough. He hoped it would be enough.

The tickle in his brain intensified. Incoming. Close and fast. Not something he was used to, but this whole situation was out of hand. Unexpected rivals were terrible for carrying out long, uneventful lives. Joseph bit the inside of his cheek and glanced at Six. She still watched him, her expression inscrutable.

"I'm not your enemy," he said.

"Your word is not enough," she replied.

"My word and my actions? It'll have to be enough." Joseph held her gaze for one brief moment. "We are going to help each other, Six. You and me."

"You know my name."

"Not your real name," Joseph said quietly. "But then, I'm not even sure *you* know that."

Again, her eyelid twitched. "Where are you taking me?"

"Someplace safe."

"No such thing exists," Six told him. "No place, ever."

She was right, of course. Joseph sighed. "Pessimist?"

"Realist."

"Trust me," he said. "Or don't. But listen. That's all I ask."

"You are not saying anything I want to hear."

Story of my life, he thought, and pulled off the main road, away from the glitter and digital advertisements of several large shopping complexes. He smelled grease, exhaust; his stomach rumbled. They were near the French District; the street rolled into a tree-lined avenue where the architecture was full of quiet clean lines. There were some bars, all lit up, but the fireworks remained, howling and crackling with each ignition. A ball of fire shot into the sky, exploding too low. Sparks rained down the crowd of men and women huddled just outside an iron gate. Joseph saw bottles of liquor. He heard screams. The sensation of being hunted overwhelmed.

"I may have to free you," Joseph said. "Are you going to hurt me if I do?"

"Yes," Six said.

He blew out his breath. "Any way I can convince you not to?"

"No," Six said. "Absolutely, no."

He was close to home. No parking, though. Joseph had to settle for a spot some distance away. Not terribly ideal. He got out, walked to the passenger side, and opened the door. Six could not turn her head to look at him. Not for lack of trying, though. He could feel the force of her will pushing and pushing against the compulsion. If he let her sit long enough, it was possible she might be able to break it. Joseph had never met anyone quite so strong. Or stubborn.

"If you scream," he told the back of her head, "you know I can make you stop."

"And if I simply talk?"

"Talking is good." Joseph unbuckled Six's seat belt and hefted her up into his arms. His back hurt. He needed to lift weights. "Ask me anything you want."

"How long have you been a terrorist?"

Joseph stopped and gave her a look. Six sighed. "Fine, so you are not a terrorist. Perhaps I can believe that. I am not convinced anyone else will, though."

"No one else is going to get close enough to need convincing." Joseph walked fast. His apartment building was a block away. "Besides, I'm going to help you catch the people you're looking for. Once I do that, you'll hopefully be so distracted—and appreciative—you won't *ever* think of hunting down poor me."

"Unlikely." Six narrowed her eyes. "And how will you help? If you know something—anything—it merely substantiates your guilt."

Joseph ignored her. The tickling in his brain was worse. He turned, searching. This was a residential neighborhood, not close to any major shopping center, though the tourist trap of Xin Tian Di was certainly within walking distance. Still, there were quite a few people on the street. Young women, mostly, dressed in skinny jeans and narrow jackets, tall boots stacked with sharp heels. Bodies backlit by bursts of sparks, firecrackers spitting and hissing into the road, dancing beneath the tires of cars, bicycles, scooters dripping exhaust—

"What is wrong?" Six asked.

"Quiet," he murmured, listening hard. He hugged Six close, not even thinking of it until the scent of her hair drifted into his nose. He became aware of roses, warmth. It disconcerted him for a moment, distracted his mind, which suddenly wanted more of Six, less of everything else.

Bad timing. He felt the rush before he saw it and ducked low, dropping Six on the ground, releasing the compulsion that bound her. He expected her to be ready and she was, rolling the moment her muscles were free, and she got on her feet so fast he almost got knocked out before he could explain. No need, though. A black Audi screeched to a full stop on the road beside them. Doors slammed open. Vampires emerged.

There were three of the creatures, making the air cold as ice around their bodies. No way to know for certain how they looked when fully human, but like Chenglei, the flesh had sucked away until all that remained were skeletons racked by skin, hissing as though a great black wind lived inside their mouths. Ugly bastards.

Unfortunately, they also had guns. Guns pointed directly at him.

Joseph never saw Six move. One moment she stood beside him—and in the next she vaulted off the hood of a car, managing a one-two blow with nothing but her feet—practically walking on heads—catching the last creature in the face with her fists as she came down, whirling through the air like a dancer. She was beautiful, a blur, almost as fast as the vampires themselves—and Joseph wondered if it was just their surprise that was letting her go so far, or if she was truly that good.

He flung out his hands and a low rumble rose from his throat, splitting tones like the deep hum of a long mountain horn. The vampires went still. Six grabbed their guns and backed away. She did something with her hands; two of the guns fell into sundry parts, the third she tucked into the back of her pants alongside Chenglei's weapon. Six glanced at him, a question in her eyes, her breath puffing white in the cold air.

Joseph did not answer. Not with his voice, not with his mind. He edged forward, staring at the vampires, matching gazes as his voice coiled hard around them, channeling his will. The vampires were empty on the inside, but with enough spark left that it was hard to bind three at a time. So hard, Joseph did not notice the tickle at the back of his skull until it was almost too late.

Six saved him. He felt her move against his back, heard flesh smack, something crack—a hiss—and then she danced into sight with another vampire hopping and lunging, skin white as ice, hollow and brazen. Joseph's voice remained strong, but it was an effort—nor did he try to extend his control to the fourth vampire. He did not dare. He reached over his shoulder, beneath the neck of his shirt. Touched steel. Listened to the hiss of a sharp edge as he pulled the long dagger free. He felt like his heart was going to fly out of his chest. He had never been attacked like this. No one in his family had, not for years.

Joseph cut off heads, chanting as he killed. The vampires could not fight him, but he felt no remorse. Cold blood, in this case, made no difference. Not when he knew the alternative. Their flesh was brittle, crumbling into clumps of thick ash. No bulky evidence. The remaining sparks of their souls fled.

Six still fought. She did not shoot the guns in her possession; she merely used her fists and feet, never staying in one place long enough to be touched. But her opponent was a vampire—fast—and she was only human. Joseph saw her make a mistake—one pause, a second too long—and he changed the chant, trying to save her life.

Too late. The vampire grabbed her. But Joseph felt no pull, no internal strike to Six's life. Instead, the creature stared at the scratch on her cheek, and touched it with its tongue, delicate, savoring the taste. She struggled, face twisted with disgust.

Joseph pressed harder with his words and the vampire holding her finally froze. Six wriggled free, slamming her fist so hard into the creature's chest, its sternum snapped. The vampire, paralyzed, could not even flinch.

Six backed off. Joseph did not try to touch her. He glanced up and down the street. There were people on the sidewalk, staring. Cars had stopped in the road. Beyond them all, a rain of sparks and fire flooded the night, a series of hard bangs rocking the air. Joseph could feel the explosions in his chest. The sensation felt right at home with his pounding heart.

Joseph did his best. He altered the chant once again, isolating everyone he could see, turning his will on them, spreading a compulsion to leave, forget, to remember only as a dream. He glanced at Six and found her watching him, then the people, who obeyed without question, turning and walking away. Cars started moving again.

He still held the long dagger in his hand. Six glanced from it to the vampire, frowning. She touched her cheek. Her eyelid twitched.

"I need answers," she said, and Joseph sensed she was not entirely speaking of her old investigation.

We both need answers, he told her silently, and Six gave him such a sharp look he wondered if she heard his mental voice. He had wondered earlier, too, at the massage parlor. He had never been able to speak inside another person's mind—not outside the family, at any rate. It required a strong connection.

But even if he did agree with Six, this was not the place to ask questions. Nor did he have the skill to force the vampire back into its human body. That could only be done by choice.

Joseph cut off its head. Six was not fast enough to stop him, though he cheated just a little by slowing her down. He thought she might have tackled him, otherwise. Instead, Six watched that wiry body collapse on itself and blow away in the wind. The ashes mixed with street trash. She turned on him, furious. "Why did you do that? I told you I needed answers. I could have questioned it."

Joseph kicked at the clothes left behind on the sidewalk. "Too much time involved. We need to leave. This place is too exposed."

"Not your decision. I am calling in my team." Six reached for the wire beneath her shirt, then hesitated, looking at him. "You disabled it, didn't you? There was also a tracking device. They would have already been here by now if it was working."

Joseph shrugged, sheathed the dagger, and walked to the abandoned car, which was blocking traffic and generating some very loud honks. Joseph wondered how much the drivers had seen, if any of them had taken pictures with mobile phones. Not that it mattered. Cameras never did well with him.

The car doors were still open. He hesitated, thinking about his apartment with its nice safety features—like walls and doors—and then strode around the sleek hood and slid into the driver's seat. Six leaned into the passenger side and gestured.

"Get out," she ordered. "You are ruining evidence."

"Just a little," he admitted. The keys were still in the ignition. Joseph started the car.

Six stared. "What are you doing?"

"Parking this thing. If I leave it here, the police will come."

"In case you have forgotten," she said coldly, "I *am* the police. In fact, I have far more *authority* than the police, *and* I am better trained."

"So arrest me," Joseph said. "Take me in. Try to explain everything you've seen. Accuse me of terrible crimes. That won't help you catch your terrorists." Nor would it save her life. He stared at the scratch on her cheek. The skin was flushed, slightly swollen.

Six slid into the car. She sat for a moment, staring at him, dark eyes sharp. "You just killed people."

"I suppose," Joseph said warily, recalling the feel of steel cutting through flesh, the crackle of papery skin. "It's complicated, though. I'd hoped you would know that by now."

Six's jaw tightened. No other warning. She grabbed his throat before he could blink, and squeezed so hard he choked. He grappled with her hands, but her fingers were like iron. He struck at her face; she grabbed his wrist and pinched. Fire ran up his arm; he would have cried out if he had a voice.

Her expression never changed. "You need your vocal cords to control me. I could just rip them out. With my fingers. I could do some other things to your body. Nothing pleasant."

Joseph had no doubt of that. Six was stronger than he had imagined.

I understand, he said, using his mind to speak to her. He was not entirely certain the message would go through—he still thought those earlier moments might be flukes—but a furrow formed between Six's eyes and she licked her lips. Joseph remembered kissing her. Felt like a lifetime past. He wondered if he would ever get another chance.

"I heard you," she said softly. "How?"

It's a skill like any other, he told her, feeling inside his chest an unfamiliar sense of panic and warmth. *You know how to do things I don't. I know how to do things you don't.*

Six leaned back. She did not let go of his throat, though her fingers loosened just a fraction, making it easier for him to breathe. "And those . . . things? What Chenglei became?"

The Jiangshi. Hopping ghosts. Vampires.

"No such thing," she said immediately. "Tales of old stupid men who do not know better."

Then call them a virus, if that makes you happy. Think of them as your biological weapon. Your terrorists. Either way, you know they're dangerous. You can't ignore that.

Six's jaw tightened. Joseph did not look away. He studied her eyes as closely as she studied his, and felt her thoughts press against his mind. He tried not to listen. He did not want to. Still, he knew a moment before she acted that her fingers were going to loosen once again, and he fought the urge to rub his throat as her hand slid down to press hard against his chest.

"Drive," she said. "If you try to paralyze me, I will rip out your throat."

"What about destroying evidence?"

"The car is still evidence."

"I'm not turning myself in," he said, keeping his hands in his lap.

Six narrowed her eyes. "All I want are answers. You will drive. I will talk. You will speak only when spoken to."

"Yes, ma'am," he muttered, and put the car in gear. He tapped the accelerator and drove down the street. He took a right at the first intersection, weaving around pedestrians and motorcycles and other cars running the red light. Paper lanterns had been strung across the road; he saw, in front of the shops, men and women sweeping furiously with their brooms. Cleaning out the bad luck, making way for good. He wished it were that easy.

Six said, "What are you? How do you control people?"

"I use my mind," he said.

"Who taught you? Were you part of a government program?"

Joseph almost laughed. "My family taught me."

"So what you do is . . . genetic."

"Somewhat."

Six remained silent. The surrounding buildings became larger, newer, opulent in their modernity, glittering shopping centers and sidewalks crammed with young people. Shanghai—the largest mall in the world, a city devoted to business and commercialism. Shallow, but pretty. Joseph had a weakness for bright lights, especially now, when most of them were red for the New Year holiday. There were fireworks here, too, set off by kids, laughing and screaming in front of monstrous hanging billboards decorated with foreign celebrities hawking watches and designers.

Six's fingers tapped her thigh. "You called them *Jiangshi*. Hopping ghosts. Like in the stories."

"Not quite like the stories," Joseph replied. "Those creatures are *not* lost souls. You can't stop them with a block of six-inch wood at the threshold of a home—they are not scared of sunlight—and you can't hide from them by holding your breath. *That* is fantasy."

"All of it is fantasy," she muttered. "But if I were to pretend it is not, then what of the rest?"

"That they're dangerous? That they kill by stealing a person's life essence?" Joseph gritted this teeth. "That, unfortunately, would be true. It's why I call them vampires."

"Western folklore. Vampires steal blood."

"World folklore," Joseph corrected her. "And blood is the same as life, no different from energy."

Six studied him. Her hand was still on his chest. Her palm felt warm. "How do you know all this? Did your family teach you?"

Joseph glanced at her. "Yes."

"And these . . . creatures? What do they want with you? And what do they have to do with the terrorists? Chenglei—"

"Was unexpected," he interrupted. "That man was not always a vampire. In fact, the last time I saw him, he was very human. He worked in conjunction with a terrorist organization run by members fresh out of Central Asia, Indonesia, and Xin Jiang. Business matters. A money man. No ethical qualms, either. Chenglei himself was not a native Chinese. He was born in Jakarta. His uncle could be considered one of the most radical clerics in Southeast Asia."

"I know most of this," Six said. "We had Chenglei under surveillance for quite some time. We wanted his contacts."

"You didn't get them, I assume."

"Some. Not enough. Tonight, after seeing who he was meeting with, I planned on bringing him in. Permanently."

"Ah," Joseph said. "Too late now. Not that you need to worry. I suspect everyone you're looking for will be easy enough to find."

"And why is that?"

Joseph sighed. "Because the man the vampires recruited wants me dead. And you're becoming one of them."

Chapter 3

When Six was only five years old, she remembered quite clearly being led into a small office that was extraordinary in its luxury. Two wooden chairs with patched cushions on the seats; a dark wide desk covered in pens and paper, one lamp; a small ink painting of a tea pot; and best of anything, a window with a view beyond the gray concrete walls of the gymnasium training center. She remembered caring more about that view than the people she had been brought to see.

There were three adults in the office. Two men. One woman. All wearing dark pants and dark jackets, buttoned just so with their short collars straight and pressed flat against their throats. The men wore caps. The woman had black hair shot with silver, cut to her chin. Six had never seen any of them before.

"That's the one," said the woman. "Her family?"

"None."

"Her name?"

"None. Our recruiter found her in Shandong Province a year ago. The village was feeding her. She wandered there from the hills. They called her Six, because that was the date they found her."

"Skills?"

"Some. No artistry. But she's fast."

The woman knelt in front of Six. She poked the girl's forehead with one hard finger. It hurt. She began to do it again. Six knocked her hand away. The woman tried one more time, faster. Six stepped out of reach, her hand raised again. The woman smiled.

"Good," she said. "We'll take her."

Six remembered the woman. She remembered that the woman never had a name. She was simply *Aunt*. The Aunt who ran a small school for girls, where, in addition to being taught reading, math, and science, they were also educated in a variety of physical activities, many of which involved hurting people. Or at least, people wrapped in layers of protective padding. The real fighting came later. When she was thirteen.

But what struck Six, as she sat in the passenger seat of a strange car, beside a strange man with her hand pressed against a strange chest, was that for the first time in twenty years, she remembered what it felt like to be *herself* again. The self she had been as a child, hungering for more, knowing her place and dissatisfied with it, looking and looking for that high view of something beyond her life.

She had lost that. She had forgotten that. But now she remembered, and it was the only reason she did not subdue the man at her side. It would have been easy, despite his skills. She had a sense of him now. Somewhat ruthless, but not hard. Not toward her.

But she wanted more. More than answers. What she had stumbled upon was a mystery beyond that which she had set out to solve, and the outcome mattered. She had a chance to see over the wall. She had a view. But the view now was not enough.

Six studied the man. His face was full of planes and angles, shadows dancing over his skin as the lights of the shopping district flickered, burned. His expression was mildly stressed, his mouth set in a hard line. Six remembered the taste of his lips.

"You said earlier that I had been poisoned." Six touched her cheek. It hurt. The skin felt hot. She recalled the wet tip of a tongue, and suppressed a shudder. "Poisoned by a scratch?"

"That's all it takes," Joseph said.

"So you believe I will become . . . like them?" Six could not say the word. Not *Jiangshi*, not *vampire*.

Joseph looked at her. It was the compassion in his eyes, more than his words, that convinced her. She barely heard him as he said, "I can stop it. I can help your *body* stop it."

Six tried to see past the surface of his eyes, to something deeper, more full of truth. She imagined she caught a glimmer of something honest, but she did not know if she could trust it. "What *are* you?"

Joseph grimaced. She pressed her palm harder on his chest, warning him, but he surprised her. He took his hand off the wheel and covered her fingers, her wrist. He had a large hand. It felt strong. He did not try to pry away her fingers, and she did not move. Too much was at stake.

You could make him stop touching you.

But she did not. Other men had touched her hand, in a far more intimate manner, but this was different. This felt like he was offering comfort, and that was new.

"What I am is complicated," Joseph said quietly. "But the most accurate name is . . . necromancer."

Six stared. "You raise the dead?"

Joseph's hand tightened. "It's not so much a resurrection of the physical, but of the spiritual, the imprint of the soul. Which is *not* the soul, but just the memory of it. It's almost as good as the real thing, though. Especially if you want information."

"And you are being hunted because of this?"

"I'm being hunted because I *refused* to do this. For money. For terrorists. How the vampires got involved is another matter entirely. *That* makes no sense to me."

It made no sense to Six, either. None of it did. She pulled her hand away from his chest. Joseph's expression turned puzzled. "You don't think I'll try to paralyze you again?"

Six wondered the same thing. "I can still disable your voice before you begin to chant. I know what to look for now."

"You're overestimating yourself."

She pointed to a side street. "Park the car."

"Is the military waiting?" There was some humor in his voice. Six merely looked at him, trying to remain unaffected. Joseph held her gaze a moment longer than she was comfortable with, and then pulled down the street she had indicated, away from the lights and press of cars and people. Fireworks spat; peach blossoms made of paper fluttered from lines over the road. Six saw red, everywhere. Made her heart hurt, for a moment. She had few friends, but those she knew had still managed to take time off to return home for the New Year. One rare week spent with family.

Six had never done that. She had never celebrated. New Year, Spring Festival—it was always on her own, or around men and women who had somewhere to be, but could not go. Never much happiness, there.

"Where is your family?" Six asked.

"Are you going to hurt them?"

"No. I was just . . . curious."

He parked the car at the side of the road. The street attendant, an old man in a blue uniform, wandered close. Joseph pulled out his wallet. "They live all over. Mongolia, Beijing, London. Right now, my parents are in Xian. I was going to fly there to visit. My mother is cooking her dumplings for the holidays. Maybe some red bean cakes."

"Can she also summon the dead?"

"No," Joseph said. "That's my father's skill. And his family."

They got out of the car. The old man had his pad of receipts ready. Before Joseph could pay, Six dragged out her identification card, hidden in a narrow pouch inside her pants. The old man took one look at it, nodded his head like there were swinging weights attached, and backed off fast.

"Ah, power," Joseph said, sardonically. "It's heady, isn't it?"

"You would know better than I," Six replied. She felt her two stolen guns press against her lower back, hidden beneath her blouse. Their weight was a comfort.

The corner of his mouth curled. "What are we doing here, really? It's not safe, you know. There are people hunting me. Hunting you, maybe. And I can't imagine your superiors would appreciate you running off like this, without checking in, and with a suspicious character such as myself."

"You are testing me," Six said, concerned by those very issues, but unable to step back, to lay down her desire to know more, to hold on to the old lost feeling of hunger. "We are here because I said so."

Joseph shrugged, and turned around. He started walking. Six matched his pace, watching his throat, his mouth, any sign that he might turn on her. She also watched the people around them, remembering Chenglei—so human, so warm, shriveling into a monster before her eyes. If it could happen to him, no one was safe. Not even her. Not now.

That is what you will become, a voice whispered inside her head. *Monster.*

Joseph's pace faltered. Six took a deep breath. "Assuming, for a moment, that I believe you—which is debatable— what possible use could terrorists have for the spirits of those who are already dead? How in any way does that support their cause?"

Joseph shoved his hands in his pockets. "Here's one example. You want some information from a top-level official, but you don't have the time or opportunity to get it? Order an assassination. Murder the man or woman you want, then question the dead. You don't have to be close to the corpse. And souls, even the memories of souls, don't lie. Not ever."

Six thought of the Foreign Minister's wife. "You said that was just one example."

Joseph glanced at her, his eyes dark, serious. "A necromancer, despite the title, can also control the living. I think you've seen some convincing demonstrations of that."

Six looked away, toward the road, staring at the cars and people. Ten years ago, Shanghai had been an ordinary city, not terribly large or advanced. Still some farms, still some quiet. Now, though, it was all light and flash and thunder—and not just because of the New Year celebrations. Money had been poured into this city. Vast amounts of money and pride and hard work. It had been a beautiful effort, and still was.

Six tried to imagine all of it gone. Blown away. Laid to waste and rubble. It was a possibility. Part of the message recently received. Intelligence reports confirmed that certain extremist cells had begun to focus, not just on the West, but on any example of capitalist success. And China, despite all words to the contrary, was very much a capitalist nation. The iron rice bowl had become a fleeting memory, hardly worth contemplating. Certainly, there were enough people out shopping to indicate that times were, indeed, better. And those better times had to be protected.

"You could make someone carry a bomb," she said quietly.

"I could," he said, just as quiet.

"And you did not have to paralyze me earlier. You could have just forced me to follow you."

"True." Joseph stepped close, forcing her to crane her neck. "But feeling captured is one thing. Violated, another. I took a guess at what you would prefer."

"Neither." Six placed her hand on his chest to push him away. "I prefer my freedom."

He caught her hand, holding it to him. The warmth of his skin traveled through her. She tried to remember the cold he had created, but it was a distant, fleeting memory. She did not pull away.

"I'm going to help you," he said gently. "We're going to help each other, Six."

"No," she replied, unable to look away from his eyes. "You were right. I should not be here with you."

"I don't see you kicking my ass."

"No kicking. Men like you should not be allowed to live."

"Really." Joseph's mouth curved into a slow smile. Six remembered the hot taste of ginger, the spice of his lips. "I can think of better uses for me than killing."

She pulled her hand away from his chest. "Do you have any idea who your rival might be? Who would want you dead?"

"No," Joseph said. "Don't know where to find him, either. Unlike some people I know, we don't run around with tracking devices taped to our chests."

Six narrowed her eyes. "And are you certain you know nothing else about the organization that tried to hire you? You seemed knowledgeable enough about Chenglei's circumstances. You could have told the police."

"Who would have believed me? Besides, I had no names, no proof, no locations. No desire to get involved. I didn't think, ever, that they would find someone to take my place. I can't even imagine how they managed it the first time. Discovering what I could do was supposedly an accident."

"I don't believe in accidents," Six said. "Especially those that happen twice in a row. They knew how to find you."

"I agree," Joseph said. "I can only think that the vampires told them."

"And how would they know?"

"They know. I get around. That must be why they infected Chenglei. Because they knew I would answer his request for a meeting. Easy target."

"So you hunt these creatures."

"The ones who aren't careful. You would be amazed at how many of them work in hospitals, around the dying. It's easy for them to siphon off energy there. Patients are already weak. Problem is, with a vampire around, there's no chance of getting stronger."

"And no one notices? No one sees them for what they are?"

"Why would they? They usually look exactly like you and me. Shifting as they have, in front of us and in public, is extremely rare."

"They did it for a reason, then. To make a point."

"That they're not afraid of being caught?"

"No," she said softly, clarity becoming instinct, fear. "Because they are not afraid of people knowing they exist."

Joseph sucked in a quick breath. "They have a reason not to care anymore."

Six imagined the temperature dropped. It was a good reflection of the way she felt—cold, so cold—and she found herself speaking secrets, things she should not say, because in her gut she knew Joseph was the man who would understand.

She leaned close. "We were warned something was going to happen. The government intercepted a message, a death, but it made no sense. Only we knew it was related to terror-

ist activity in the region, a new cell that we have been unable
to track except through remote contacts, like Chenglei."

"It's the holiday," Joseph said urgently, voice dropping
into a hush. "There's no better time."

"But what do those creatures receive from the bargain?
Freedom? People to feed upon? And where do you come in?
Why pass on your name, *if* that is what happened? Why ally
themselves with a group that would hire someone who hunts
and murders their own kind?"

"I don't know," Joseph said grimly. "But we don't have
much time to find out. A day at the most."

"Why a day?"

Joseph hesitated. "Because after that, you'll start changing."

Six forgot how to breathe. "You said you could help me."

"Yes, but—" Joseph's voice was cut off by the loud wail
of a siren. They turned, but Six already knew what she
would see. She recognized the sound. And for the first time
in a long while, she was not happy to hear it.

A black Audi with military plates pulled to a quick stop
beside them. There were two women in the front seat. Familiar faces.

Joseph murmured, "How?"

Six looked at him. "I did not."

The women got out of the car. Slow and easy, as graceful
as wolves. Taller than Six, though just as lean. Hard eyes,
thin mouths, street clothes that were plain and cheap.

"Ying," Six said to the woman on the left, who had a thin
scar tracing the edge of her lip. She glanced right, to her
companion, the prettier of the two. "Xiu."

"Six," they said in unison, and she could not help but feel
a thread of unease pass through her heart. It startled her,
that emotion; she could not understand it, not when she had
known these women almost her entire life.

Six found herself edging in front of Joseph. "How did you
find me?"

Xiu stopped. "Luck."

"Accident," Ying added.

"Of course, now that we've found you—" Xiu said.

"—we have some questions," Ying finished.

No, Six protested silently. *Not yet. Time is running out.*

But she said nothing, and listened to Joseph sigh.

Chapter 4

Joseph had never thought much about what it would mean to spend time in a Chinese prison, but now that he was actually in one, he really did not know what all the fuss was about. The cell might not be all that clean, but there was a toilet and a bed—albeit, without a mattress—and while the naked springs were rather tough on his spine, at least he was there alone and not in any danger of becoming a poor man's version of some Brokeback bitch. Although a drink would be nice.

He also wanted to see Six. He worried about her. It surprised him, just how much he worried. Out on the street, at the moment of their separation, he had felt inside her a terrible uncertainty. A lack of faith—not in him, but in the people she worked with. She was afraid of losing something, something no one else would understand, and that uneasiness had filled him, as well—though for a different reason entirely. He had, after all, been the one associating with a known terrorist flunky. That, and they had confiscated a very long dagger that no doubt carried the trace DNA of quite a few individuals. Which, frankly, meant that he might as well assume the firing squad position and start thinking about all the people his vital organs were going to save.

The lights had been turned off in his cell. There were no bars, just walls and a door inlaid with a narrow strip of wire-encased glass. Joseph did not mind the darkness. He lay on his springs with his hands behind his head, eyes closed, and searched the surrounding area with his mind. He found very little of interest. Mostly a keen desire to be home, with family; the occasional bout of despair; lust; in the other prisoners, ungodly fear and resignation.

He looked for Six. He thought about her eyes as he searched, the darkness of them, the hard warmth that had finally, at the end, begun to soften when she looked at him. He thought a smile might be next. Just one smile. He wanted to see that very badly.

This is not the time to be thinking about a woman you can never have. Six is not for you. Even if you want her to be.

But Joseph found her. He caught a hint of her spirit and pulled himself along the line of her heart. He tried to see through her eyes, but could not. Her mind was strong. He settled for listening to the edge of her thoughts, and sensed a defensive posture, anger and worry.

He could not help himself; he whispered her name. He did not expect her to notice his presence, but once again, her ability to perceive his mental voice surprised him. He felt her stillness, and then, quietly: *I hear you.*

Relief filled him. *Are you okay?*

I will be fine. You?

Still alive. No one has come to question me.

Soon, she said. *I am being . . . reprimanded . . . for not bringing you in more quickly. They think it is suspicious.*

What have you told them?

Only what I think they will believe. Which is very little. I have tried not to implicate you in anything. Nor do they know who you are. Your lack of identification, or finger-prints in any file, has disconcerted them.

You know my name.

I pretended not to know.

That surprised him. *Thank you. Can I ask why?*

Six did not answer, but he picked up the tendril of a thought; one word: *Believe.*

Joseph heard footsteps clicking down the hall, and he split his focus, trying to identify who was coming and why. He discovered Xiu on the end of his thoughts, though it was hard to get a read on her mind. Like Six, her thoughts were slippery, hard to listen to for anything more than the most basic emotional impressions. In this case, determination, satisfaction, a hint of eagerness.

Great. He was about to get his ass handed to him.

Xiu is coming, he told Six. *Any advice?*

Xiu? She sounded genuinely surprised. *She never handles prisoner questioning. She does not have the temper for it.*

What do you mean, she doesn't have the temper for it? Six—

His cell door opened. Xiu stepped inside. She appeared unarmed, but Joseph was not fooled. He stood, holding his ground, watching her face, studying her mind. He found nothing helpful. All he knew for certain was that she was not a vampire, but that was little comfort.

Xiu was pretty. Her face, however, lacked Six's blunt honesty—and her eyes held a sly light that he disliked immediately. Not straight or true; he felt her cruel streak the moment he looked at her.

Joseph? Six's tentative voice filled his head, surprising him. *What is happening?*

Hold on, he said, wary. *I don't know yet.*

I am coming, she said immediately.

Xiu stepped deeper into the cell. It was small; her movements brought her quite close. Again, Joseph refused to back away. Small defiance. He knew it was not worth much.

"Hello, stranger," murmured the woman. "That is your name, yes?"

"If you like," he said, pouring power into his voice, hoping to hook her. He did not. His power slid over her mind, washing off so easily that for a moment he wondered if he had any kind of gift at all.

"Stranger, stranger," said the woman again. "How interesting that you are here."

"Very interesting," he replied carefully, even more wary now. "I don't quite understand the reason why."

"Treason," she said easily. "Aiding and abetting men who wish to destroy this country and take precious lives."

"I've done nothing of the sort."

"You are calling me a liar, then?" Xiu smiled. "No need to waste your energy on denials. I know what you are. I know who you are."

Joseph said nothing. This was not a fight he could win. Not like this. He pushed harder with his mind, skin puckering with the sudden chill, a side effect. He drew more energy from the room—energy that was heat—and continued searching for a way into Xiu's thoughts.

A process interrupted when she coldcocked him in the face. Her fist moved fast—but he was able to twitch backward. The movement saved his teeth, but his nose flashed pain. He tasted blood, felt the hot dripping rush from his nostrils.

Xiu hit him again. He tried to fight back, but the odds were so uneven he might as well have been trying to take a swing with his arms and legs cut off. He could not even entertain the idea of biting her ankles. She was simply too fast, too strong; like Six, training so long and hard that fighting was the same as breathing.

So he took the risk. He had to. He opened his mouth and began to chant. Low soft tones, a rumbling roar as soft as distant thunder. The language of his grandparents, of the steppes and endless skies. Vocalizing was unnecessary when using his powers—language was not the same as will—but it made a difference to his strength, his focus.

Except nothing happened. Joseph could not reach inside her heart. A barrier stood around her spirit, with not even a tendril free to control. She might as well have been made of stone.

Xiu stood back from him, smiling. "Now *this* is quite interesting. A puzzle."

Joseph stopped chanting. His throat hurt. "Who are you?"

"Just a girl," Xiu said, but there was something in her forced giggle that was so *not* girlish, so much a parody, that Joseph took another hard look at the edges of her mind, and found something so startling—and so obvious—he wanted to slip his head underneath her boot for an added stamp of stupidity.

"You are not Xiu," Joseph said, slowly standing, swaying.

"Not Xiu," said the woman, pursing her lips. "But Xiu enough, I think. Enough to get close to you, *Joseph Besud*. And to certain information I need."

Joseph shut his eyes. He could feel the possession, now that he knew what to look for. Another mind, layered over the woman's. A natural barrier, made by virtue of there being one too many people inside a single body.

"So you're the new hire," Joseph said. "All of this, to help terrorists murder people."

"All of this," said the possessed woman, "to help myself. You aren't much of a necromancer, are you?"

"Enough of one that you want me dead."

"That was part of the bargain struck with the vampires. Nothing more."

Liar, Joseph thought. Xiu smiled. "Professional secrets, Mr. Besud. You cannot blame me for wanting to be the only man of my kind. To be honest, I never thought about what that would mean until I was introduced to this latest opportunity."

Joseph shook his head. "Who the hell *are* you?"

"No one," Xiu said, her voice taking on an odd multitonal quality inside his mind. "No one you need to be concerned about any longer." She leaned forward, her smile turning sly. "Nor do you need to be worried about Six and her imminent transformation. I have plans for that one."

Joseph threw himself at Xiu. He was no match for her strength, but he did not expect to fight—just to touch, to get his hand on her bare skin. That was all he needed. Physical contact always made him stronger.

She let him get close, though the smile on her face turned into a scream as Joseph's fingers grazed her cheek and he shoved a mental spike against the other necromancer's barrier, stabbing it again and again with his mind. He felt a crack, caught the edge of another heart, and tried to latch on, to track, to hunt.

Xiu slammed her fist into his groin. Joseph staggered, throbbing waves of pain spinning lights in his eyes. He tried to straighten, to fight, but another blow caught him in the chest and the impact was so fierce he went down like a rag doll, limp. He crawled, struggling to stand. His body made fun of him.

Xiu knelt, just out of reach. Her eyes were dark, furious. "A poor trick, Mr. Besud."

"Go to hell," Joseph muttered. All he could taste was blood.

"Perhaps," Xiu whispered, leaning close. "Or perhaps I will bring hell here, to you."

Joseph heard running. He felt a familiar heart. The cell door slammed open.

Six entered. Joseph met her gaze. He could not read her expression—smooth, cold—but he felt the edge of her mind and her emotions were neither.

Xiu rose slowly. "Six. Good of you to join me."

Six said nothing. She stared only at Joseph, her gaze traveling from his face and body to the blood on the floor. Her jaw flexed. Her eyelid twitched.

No, Joseph thought, grim. *Not good at all.*

At thirteen years of age, faith had become something of a cornerstone in Six's life, though she rarely thought of it as such. Simply, her existence ran on routine, the steady ticking of a clock that parsed out chores and exercises and studies like some endless heartbeat running concurrent to the one inside her chest, and which could not be stopped or slowed, not at risk of ending her existence.

And then, one day, her faith changed. The clock began ticking to a different beat.

It began early. She rose for breakfast with the other girls, and Aunt was there, waiting. She picked three. Six, Xiu, and Shu. Led them beyond the school walls to a white windowless van. They got in. Aunt sat up front beside the driver, another of their instructors. The van drove for thirty minutes, and when it stopped Six emerged, blinking in the sun, staring at a tall brick structure the size of a warehouse. No windows. Only one door. Aunt made them go in. She said, "I will return later to let you out," and then the darkness closed around the three girls and they heard the lock turn.

They realized, soon after, that they were not alone. They realized, too, that they had been brought there to die.

Six remembered. She remembered men three times her size, moving in the darkness, hunting her. She remembered fighting them. She remembered killing them. She remembered the taste of that first death, how happy she was for it, how proud, because she was still alive, unharmed. Fierce;

the need to survive was stronger than anything she could name.

She remembered, too, the screams. Shu. Broken leg. Cornered. Six had found her, saved her. She found Xiu, too, but later. Very close. Xiu could have gotten there first. Saved Shu some pain. But she had not. She had left the girl, used her as a distraction so she could run and hide.

There were nine men, total. Nine bodies at the end of the day, when Aunt came to unlock the door. She looked at each one, examining the way they died, the killing blows. She said not a single word. No praise, no apology.

She took the girls home. Shu healed, returning to the old routine. Xiu and Six did not. Aunt moved them on.

And here we are, Six thought, staring across the small cell at the other woman, who watched her with a stranger's eyes—eyes that Six knew almost as well as her own—eyes that had betrayed her down in the debriefing room, when Xiu had implied to the station commander that Six might be capable of inappropriate behavior. That she might give up her duty for a man.

Words to kill a career. Words enough to ostracize, blacken, send away—or worse, to put her in prison. A woman with her skills, after all, could not be allowed to run free if there was not the utmost faith in her honor and integrity. A woman like her, after all, would make a dangerous enemy.

Walk away, walk away, said a tiny voice inside her mind. *It is not too late. Walk away and save yourself. Do this and your life will be over. You will lose everything.*

Six gazed down at Joseph's body, covered in blood, beaten. His eyes were still strong, though, cold and dark and hard, and he looked at her as if he could see straight into her heart, as though he could see and did not mind to see, and it struck her how much that meant, how vitally important it was that someone, *someone,* know her. Know her for more than some badge. Know her for more than a weapon.

I know who you are, Joseph said inside her mind, his eyes shifting darker, softer. *I know you, Six.*

I do not know you, she replied.

You'll learn, he said. *We both will.*

Six tore away her gaze and looked at Xiu. "You had no authority to question this man."

"I have all the authority in the world," Xiu said smoothly. "As do you, though I am surprised to see you here. Ying said—"

"—the truth," Six interrupted. "That the wire went dead and I disappeared, that she did not know what happened. You, on the other hand, embellished."

"Also the truth," Xiu replied. "Or do you deny it?"

That you might give up your duty for a man? For Joseph?

Six said nothing. The other woman smiled. Joseph tried to stand. Six did not look at him. Part of her wondered how he had let Xiu hurt him so badly. His throat appeared unharmed. The air was cold.

Inside her mind she heard his voice again, quick and urgent.

Careful, Six. Xiu is not the woman you know. Her mind has been taken over by another. My rival. He is here to gather information for his employers. And kill me.

Sick heat flushed through Six's body. *Is there a way to drive it out of her?*

I'm sorry, Joseph said. *All you can do is make Xiu's body uncomfortable for him.*

Six steeled herself. Uncomfortable. She could do that. No use wasting time, either.

She lunged, fists striking fast, hard. Xiu dodged and whirled, kicking off the wall, coming back at Six with enough speed to break bone. Six cut sharp to the right and jammed two fingers into Xiu's kidneys. The woman grunted, but did not go down. She spun again, her knee catching Six in the gut, her elbow connecting with her jaw. Six dropped, kicking out. Xiu blocked her heel, but Six twisted fast, feinted, and managed to catch her other knee. Bone cracked. Her leg bent backward. Xiu screamed.

Six knocked her down with a hard fist. Pounced, landing on her chest, pressing her elbow against Xiu's throat. She tasted blood, and spat it out on the possessed woman's face.

"Let her go," she muttered. "Now."

"Go where?" rasped Xiu, and her eyes were indeed strange, unfamiliar. "Into you? There will room enough before long. Your soul is going to run away from your body, girl. In a day, you'll be nothing but a shell."

"No," Joseph said, staggering close. "No, I won't let you have her."

Six gritted her teeth. "And you cannot have Xiu, either. Not alive, anyway." And she pressed even harder on the woman's throat, cutting off her air. Xiu's eyes bulged, her face turning purple as she grappled and writhed. Six refused to let go. She was careful not to crush her windpipe, but her strength was inexorable, and Xiu finally went limp.

Six, very cautiously, eased off. Her heart pounded. There was a ringing in her ears. "Did it work? Is Xiu alone in there?"

"Yes," he whispered, staring at her. "Are you okay?"

"No," she said, looking at him. "No, I am not."

Six leaned close to check on Xiu. She was still breathing, though the next time she looked in the mirror it would be an ugly sight. There was also a very good chance that Six had just ended her colleague's career in Squad Twelve. A broken knee was not an injury someone like Xiu could fully recover from. It would be easier for the military to replace her with a younger, newer woman.

Two women, she thought. *You just ruined yourself, as well*.

Fear crushed down on her heart; she could hardly breathe

with it. Six had just ended her own life. Twenty years of knowing nothing else, and now—now—

Joseph touched her. He wrapped his arms around her shoulders and tugged her close until her back pressed against his chest and the rise and fall of his breathing mirrored her own. He felt strong, solid. And it was a comfort, no matter how unfamiliar, or small. His mouth pressed against her hair. "Everything will be fine," he murmured.

Six turned to face him, searching his eyes. "How can you say that? How can you believe?"

A grim smile touched his mouth. "Because I just do."

Because I just do. Another kind of faith. A new clock. Six touched his lips with her fingertips. His blood was still wet. She stood on her toes and kissed him, tasting the hot metallic burn, the spice of ginger. His mouth was hard, as were his arms as he crushed her close and tight.

Six broke away, breathing hard. She glanced down at Xiu, then bent close, rummaging through her pockets. She found keys and took them.

"Come," she said to Joseph. "We have to leave. Now."

She went to the cell door and peered out. There were no guards in the hall. No one had heard Xiu scream—or if they had, no one wanted to investigate. The members of Squad Twelve were not known for needing help. It was a reputation they encouraged.

Six stepped into the hall, and took Joseph's arm. "Head down, look weak, beaten."

"Oh, yeah. Difficult," he muttered.

They walked down the long tiled corridor past gray metal doors marked with numbers. Six heard groans coming from inside some of the cells. She thought about Joseph being beaten and clenched her jaw. Kept her gaze straight and narrow. One turn in the corridor, and the cellblock gate appeared. Two guards in full military uniform stood on either side of the heavy metal door. Another man sat at a desk that held only one phone and a sheaf of papers. All of them stared at Joseph.

"I am moving the prisoner," Six said. "Agent Xiu will be along when she is finished . . . cleaning up. Do *not* disturb her until then."

"Shall I call ahead for a transport vehicle?" asked the man at the desk, who very carefully maintained no eye contact.

"That will not be necessary," Six said. A request for transportation would go through the main switchboard, and be automatically routed to the other members of her squad. "In fact, I would ask that you not call anyone about this prisoner. It is a very sensitive matter."

"Of course," he said, and reached behind him to dial in the combination of the electric lock. He hit a red button and the door clicked open. One of the guards held it for her. Six stopped and took his sidearm. She did not ask. He did not protest. Simply stared into the air above her head. He was very young. Eager to please. Six hoped none of them would be punished too severely for letting her escape with Joseph.

They passed through the cellblock door and entered another corridor that split into three directions. Security cameras hung from every corner, but Six knew they were manned by low-level guards who would know only her face and nothing else. Her face would be enough to grant free passage until Xiu was discovered. Or until Six and Joseph ran into any other members of the team.

They took the stairs. Joseph gave her a questioning look when they started walking up.

"This building is only three stories tall," Six explained quietly. "But there are six sublevels beneath it. We are on number three."

His mouth twitched. "I don't rate a *six?* How disappointing."

"Not really." She let herself smile. "That level is the morgue."

They reached the main floor without incident. Six heard a great deal of activity beyond the corridor, but where they stood was the hall used only by the janitorial staff. Six and Joseph were able to exit through the back door without incident.

Sloppy security, Six thought. She had never paid much attention to just how sloppy, until now, and it embarrassed her. She had taken too much for granted. Twenty years, training to be the best, riding on the laurels of elitism—and now, all of it gone, with the realization that she was still vulnerable, in other ways. It was a taste of humility that she did not need.

The night air was cool and damp. The military offices sat in the center of a walled compound. Most of it was parking lot, filled with military vehicles and the occasional bus. On the other side was a small training ground. Six heard men laughing, followed by the hiss of a burning fuse. Three seconds later, a ball of sparkling flame shot into the air, rushing high above the trees lining the wall. Six heard a whine, followed by a sharp explosion. She could have shot her gun and no one would have noticed.

Six hit the electric lock on the key chain. An Audi beeped back. She and Joseph ran for the car. She put him in the backseat.

They drove out without being stopped. The guards at the gate took one look at her face and waved her on. Six pulled into traffic, hit the accelerator, and there—gone.

"We have only an hour," she said to Joseph, and was stunned to hear her voice shake. She gripped the wheel harder. "Maybe less. Xiu will wake up eventually. I do not know if anyone will hear her shouts, but I would prefer to assume the worst."

"I know someplace we can go," Joseph said. "It's in Suzhou. No one will be able to find a connection to me there."

"You forget, no one knows who you are."

"You think."

"Fine," she said, and then, "We need a plan."

"We," Joseph said. "I like the sound of that."

"You should not," she snapped. "All it means is trouble. I have just ruined my life for you."

Joseph was silent for a long time. The car engine hummed; fireworks crackled against the road. Six had to swerve to avoid hitting some children playing with sparklers.

"I'm sorry," he finally said, softly. "I am, truly. And I am grateful. But Six . . ." He stopped, and sighed. "Was it a life you really wanted?"

"It was the life I had," she replied flatly. "What more is there?"

A strong hand reached from the shadows to touch her shoulder. "You know the answer to that. I can feel it in your heart."

Her eyes burned. "People forget how to choose."

"Not you," he murmured. "Not you."

Maybe not, she thought. But choosing right was another matter entirely.

Chapter 5

At four o'clock in the morning the road to Suzhou was mostly empty, and Six gunned the Audi's A6 engine into a high-speed chase of nothing but ghosts. Just outside the city, though, she took an exit to a rest area and parked the car. Cabs idled on the other end of the lot. She could see the drivers playing mahjong on a makeshift table.

"There are some bottles of water back there," she said to Joseph. "You should wash off the worst of the blood. Maybe take off that shirt you're wearing, too."

"Why do I get the feeling that we're dumping this fine piece of machinery?"

"Because we are," she replied, and got out of the car. Inside the trunk she found some spare clothes, money, and a tool kit. All standard issue. She dug around for a screwdriver, and, after making certain no one was watching, removed the car's plates. She tucked them inside a plastic sack that had very recently contained maps, and then went around to take Joseph's bloody shirt. She tossed him a new one and stuffed the old inside the sack with the plates. There was a garbage can nearby. Six dumped everything inside. It would not stay there long. Someone would dig through eventually for scrap and find the contents of the bag, but hopefully the discoverer would keep his or her mouth shut—and if not—then she and Joseph would be long gone. Or as gone as finding that terrorist cell would take her.

She and Joseph. Six shuddered. She really was thinking of them as a team. And him, still a stranger. She knew nothing about Joseph. Nothing but what her instincts were telling her. It should not have been enough. And yet, here she was, breaking the law.

Not just for him, she reminded herself. *There is a lot at stake here. Too much. Sometimes you must do the wrong thing in order to make right.*

Six thought of her debriefing. The commander had not listened to her warnings about the terrorist cell. Not truly. Intelligence officers had already said that an attack might be imminent. And Six was saying nothing new. Nothing they could use. Nothing she thought she could share. Not without sounding crazy—or ruining Joseph's life.

So she had ruined her own instead.

Joseph approached. His hair was scruffy, his eyes hooded, but the blood was gone and the shirt strained quite nicely over his shoulders. The rough voices of the cab drivers and the rumble of engines drifted close.

"I was thinking," he said slowly. "Xiu only could have been possessed during a moment of close contact. Touching, even. Not only that, but her possessor wouldn't have been able to stay in her body for more than a day. Any longer would be dangerous. Lingering increases the possibilities of becoming . . . stuck."

"Xiu has been in Shanghai all this time. Her . . . possessor might be there, as well." Six's cheek hurt. She touched it, lightly, and felt dizzy. Joseph took hold of her arm.

"We need to take care of that," he said.

"The rest first," she replied.

"It can't wait," Joseph told her.

Six pulled away. "Xiu would not have logged her movements, though I can tell you that she was supposed to question some bankers who work with Chenglei. Their office is near the Bund."

"It's a start," he said. "But it can wait until morning. Right now, all that matters is taking care of you. Unless you *want* to end up like those creatures."

"No," she said, trying to ignore the pure fear that accompanied that thought. Talking helped. "I still do not understand what they are or what they do. It resembles magic, but I know it must be science."

Joseph looked at her as though he knew exactly what she was feeling. But all he said was, "Magic and science are not mutually exclusive. One looks much like the other, if you don't know the difference. In this case, vampirism is similar to a disease. It affects the appearance, although that can be maintained by choice. It gives strength, speed . . . but it also makes the victims . . . hungry."

Six looked away. "Are they evil? Would I . . . become evil?"

Joseph hesitated. "All your emotions, your empathy and compassion, your capacity to love, would be . . . suppressed. If there is a place in the human brain where those things live, it gets shut off. All that remains is something hollow."

"But you can stop it?" She hated the sound of her voice, the thread of fear that crept into it, but Joseph did not seem to mind, nor did he look at her with pity. All he did was squeeze her shoulder and drag her close to press his lips upon her forehead. She let him. Other men had kissed her, but it felt different with Joseph. More alive.

They left the Audi and walked to the cab drivers. The

men did not want to break up their game, but Six offered a one-hundred-dollar note, apart from the fare, to the first person up and ready.

Joseph gave directions, and after a while their cab left the freeway for the industrial zone, a modern area of wide tree-lined roads, modern sculptures, and vast corporate headquarters—some of which seemed to have been designed in some architect's odd dream. Closer to the city core, the scenery changed; water became the influence, canals and bridges splitting roads. The buildings, too, retained a classic charm. Unlike Shanghai, the Suzhou city planners had attempted to maintain the feel of old China in its appearance.

The New Year's celebration was in full swing here, as well. Even in the wee hours of morning, men were still setting off fireworks—albeit half-heartedly. Red lanterns swung gently over the roads, and all the shop doors were plastered with red banners covered in wishes for good luck in the coming year.

Joseph had the cab driver drop them off in the middle of a tiny shopping district. No one else was out. Except for the occasional pop and bang, the air was quiet. Joseph led Six down a side street. They had to cross a bridge over one of the canals—water lapping gently against the stones—and then he guided them left into a well-worn neighborhood where the walls felt high and the streets narrow, and the air grew more still and hushed the deeper they traveled. A good place for a trap, Six thought, but she could do nothing but keep her senses open, ready, alert. It was second nature, but she paid special attention, not wanting to take anything for granted. It was odd, though; the more she concentrated, the more that came into focus. Where there had been silence, now there was noise—so much noise—building into a crescendo of men talking, pans banging, children crying, farts and coughs and pissing in a can. She heard sex. She heard heartbeats. She heard Joseph breathe.

"Something's wrong," she murmured, and her voice sounded like a roar inside her ears. She stopped walking, and held her head. Joseph moved close. He covered her hands with his, and the warm pressure of his fingers moving across her skin, threading into her hair, felt good enough to ease the discomfort bearing down on her eardrums. When he pulled her against him, she did not resist. She pressed her forehead against his chest and closed her eyes. His heartbeat was a roar of thunder.

"It is starting," she whispered. "Whatever it is, I can feel it."

"Your cheek has healed," Joseph said.

Her hand flew up, fingers running over skin. The scratch was gone. No pain, no flush.

"I am afraid," she said, and it was like hearing herself speak another language. She had never said those words, not out loud, but the crush of her fear was so full and thick, she had to express it. She had to tell someone or scream.

I'm here, Joseph told her, speaking into her mind. *Six, I'm here. You're not alone.*

I am always alone, she told him, unable to stop the words that sprang so easily into her mind. *I have always been alone.*

"Not anymore," he promised, tugging up her chin. He kissed her, gently, lips brushing against her mouth with such sweetness, she held on to the feeling with all her strength, fighting for it, suddenly terrified it might be the last time she ever felt that way about another human being. She remembered Chenglei, those other creatures she had faced on the street. Hollow and shriveled, brittle with their hunger for another person's life. Not the men and women they had been born to be.

"Do not let me forget how to feel," she said to Joseph, pulling back just enough to look into his eyes. "I have never asked for anything from anyone, but please, make me feel."

A tremor ran through his body. "Six—"

"Promise me."

Joseph kissed her. He dragged Six off her feet and pressed his mouth hard against her mouth, dragging from her a groan of pleasure as he kissed the fear out of her body, replacing it with a liquid heat that made her writhe and twist against him. Her leg curled around his hip, her arms snaking around his shoulders, binding him tight, and when he backed off for just a moment, she traveled with him, kissing him again, dragging his bottom lip between her teeth. Joseph shuddered. One hand trailed up her waist, sliding beneath her blouse. Her breath caught as he touched her ribs, and then the swell of her breast. A fingernail grazed her nipple. She gasped.

Joseph set her down. She felt his hard heat press through his pants against her belly, which only made it more difficult to let go when he stepped back, breathing hard. "We should move," he said roughly. "It's not safe here."

Which should have been her line. Six swallowed a deep breath. She was losing her head. She had to be careful, or she just might lose more. She had been a survivor too long to toss it all away now.

She followed Joseph a short distance to a small gate covered in red banners. On either side were two pots full of water and tall bamboo. A peach blossom lantern hung from the iron knob. Joseph pulled a small key from his pocket and fit it into the gate. It swung open with a tiny rasp that was met with an answering creak from inside the house. They hardly had time to walk through the gate when the door beyond the small courtyard opened. An old woman poked out her head. She peered at them both, but it was Joseph she smiled at.

"Finally!" she said. "You're home. But what a surprise. I thought you would be going north for Spring Festival."

"Change of plans," Joseph said, pulling Six behind him. "Wenxia, this is Six. Six, my very good friend, Wenxia. She looks after this place for me when I'm away."

"Which is all the time," said the old woman. She moved back into the house with a pronounced hobble. Six looked down and had to take a moment to reconcile her vision. Wenxia's feet were terribly small, hardly the size of a fist.

"Your feet," she said without thinking. "They were bound?"

Wenxia paused, and glanced over her shoulder. "I came from a traditional family. They thought it would help me find a rich husband. And it did. But not much else."

"I'm sorry if we woke you," Joseph said.

Wenxia waved him away. "I was cooking. And a good thing, too! We will eat well today, my boy. Dumplings and candy!"

Joseph kissed the top of the old woman's head. "Six and I have been traveling all night. We need to rest."

"You know where your room is." Wenxia hesitated, her gaze flickering to Six. Joseph raised his brow, and a smile touched the old woman's mouth. She turned around, humming, and left the room.

Six watched her go, then looked at Joseph. "She is your family."

"There are many different kinds of family," he said, leading her up the rickety stairs. "But yes, she's mine and I'm hers, and it's all good. I met her a long time ago through my father. She really was rich, but everything was taken from her during the Cultural Revolution. A mob killed her husband right in front of her, strung him up from a tree. Then she and her son were sent north for re-education on one of the state farms."

"Where is her child now?"

"Dead. He cut his hand on something rusty. It happened early on. She's been alone for a long time."

Joseph pushed open a door at the end of the hall. He stood in the entrance, unmoving, looking at his hands. "You know, if you're not comfortable, there's another room."

Six hid her smile and pushed him gently aside. The room was small and dark, filled with richly carved antiques that gleamed and smelled of lemon oil. A large window looked down over the canal they had passed over. She could see more of it now. The sun was rising.

Joseph did not turn on any lights. He moved behind her, sliding his arms around her waist and tugging her close. He kissed the back of her neck.

"First, we make you well," he murmured. "Then, we see about everything else. Sound good?"

"Yes," she said, and allowed herself to be drawn to the bed. They sat together on the mattress. Joseph made her lie down, and then leaned over her body, his eyes dark, his mouth set in a hard line. Six did nothing but study his face. It had been a long time since she had allowed herself to be in a position so vulnerable. To even be alone with a man for such an extended period of time, let alone rely on one, in any capacity outside her work.

It was not as uncomfortable as she thought it might be. Or maybe she had been around the wrong men. Either way, Joseph made her feel safe. And that was rare, indeed.

"This could be easy, or it could be difficult," he told her softly. "You've been infected, Six. A body can reject that poison, but sometimes it doesn't want to."

She struggled with her fear. "I cannot imagine that."

"It happens." Joseph trailed his finger down her cheek. "But not this time."

"You are very confident."

Joseph gathered up her hand and pressed it to his lips. "Are you ready?"

"What do I do?"

"Just be yourself," he said quietly. "Be yourself, Six, and do not let go of that."

Six closed her eyes. She felt Joseph enter her mind, like a

hand dipping beneath still water. It was an odd sensation; she knew he must have done it before, but this was the first time she was aware, and it was profoundly intimate. A part of her feared the contact, wanted to censor herself, but she remembered his voice—*be yourself*—and she took that to heart and let herself, simply, be. And for a moment she felt the world open up inside her mind, her life spreading before her in all its infinite moments. No sadness. Just wonderment.

But then the pain began, and Six forgot serenity.

Joseph's mother had always impressed upon her son the importance of telling the truth, but of course, his mother had never been able to keep any friends past the shelf life of an honest answer, and so Joseph had learned through example that the occasional white lie was sometimes appropriate—and indeed, necessary—to keeping the people he cared about happy.

In Six's case, it involved a particular omission on the subject of pain. As in, vast unending quantities of pain, most definitely (as he had been told) on the level of giving birth to a baby the size of a large watermelon. And then discovering that you were having twins.

Joseph saw no need to add to Six's burdens.

Unfortunately, he forgot to take into account the fact that she was an incredibly strong woman prone to committing violent acts, and that as the person she would blame for causing her pain, he might just be in for a little of it himself.

"What are you doing to me?" she gasped.

"This is part of the process," he said. "Now, try to relax."

Six glared at him and grabbed his hand. She was not a screamer. She was a squeezer. And she refused to let go.

It was difficult for Joseph to focus past the pain. He was quite certain she was crushing bones. He managed, however, by sinking deep enough into Six's mind that the discomfort became a distant thing, less nagging than a mosquito bite.

And there, held in the darkness, he began to heal her.

The process was different for everyone, or so he had been told. In his experience, he had brought back only two from the brink—another omission he did not think Six needed to know about—and on both those occasions the trigger had been unique. For one woman, it was the remembrance of her child's birth that made her fight the hardest—and for the man, it was nothing more than a random sunset recalled from memory. Visceral reactions—reactions beyond mere fear or desire—infusing bodies with the mental strength necessary to fight off the infection caused by vampire contact.

The mind was more important than the body. It was always more important. Especially when dealing with vampires, whose only weakness was the mind, a lack of spirit. Bolster that, strengthen the roots of the soul, and nothing could take hold.

But Joseph immediately ran into a problem; specifically, with himself. He could not hide from her. His thoughts were open. His memories, fair game. And though she did not search his mind, as he sank deeper he felt her presence on the periphery of his most private mental spaces, and it was an unexpected intimacy that he could not shut off.

You are afraid, Six whispered. *You are afraid of me.*

No, he told her. *I'm afraid of myself. What you see, I see. And there are things I have done that I don't want to relive.*

Like the bones, she murmured, and Joseph remembered that hot flash of her touch in the massage parlor, the memory it had called—a fluke, he thought—but now it happened again, a strike of deep connection, and he felt her gaze once more upon the worst of his memories, years past, twenty-five and on the go, this time to Africa. The Red

Cross, because he wanted to help and they needed people. Sierra Leone, because that was where the need was the greatest.

But all I found was death and rape and atrocity, he told Six. *There was no end to it. And one day, when we were taken to a mass grave to bear witness, I started talking to the dead. I asked them, who. I asked them, where. And when I knew these things I found the men responsible, and I made them—*

Joseph stopped. He tried to suppress the memory, but Six would not let him. He felt her warmth surround his thoughts, unrelenting, and after a moment he yielded to her. He let her see. Allowed her to watch how he had possessed the bodies of murderers and torturers and brought them to the graves of their victims, forcing the men to rest amongst the decay and filth of the dead. And when they were truly buried, he showed Six how he had summoned the memories of the dead, spirits who still wanted vengeance—and shown them what lay in their midst, and that it was their chance to take a pound of flesh.

And they did, Joseph told her. *Not literally, but enough. Those men died. Died of fright, maybe. Or suffocation from the bodies I made them rest under. Either way, I was the one who killed them.*

Are you sorry? Six's question was a gesture of politeness; he knew she was already aware of how he felt. But he said it anyway, because she asked, and it was something he had wanted to speak of for a long time.

No, he said, grim. *I am not sorry at all.*

He sensed her satisfaction with his response. Six was a practical woman. *Why would you try to suppress that memory, then? It bothers you. I see that much.*

Joseph felt a hard cold knot inside his heart, the place where the bones and the death resided. But it was also a place of bitter satisfaction, and there was power in that feeling. Too much power.

Ah, Six said.

It's easy to become a monster, Joseph replied. *Easier for some than others. You can get a taste for it. Righteousness makes it simple. But it's a thin line.*

Much like the one I am walking.

Yes, he said. *Let's take care of that. How's the pain?*

Better, now that I have gone deeper. I apologize for your hand.

Do I still have one?

I hope you like surprises.

Joseph laughed, and it took him off guard. He had never felt so comfortable with another woman; he had never felt so at ease revealing himself, as though her eyes were the same as his, without fear or judgment. He tried to imagine losing that. He could not. It did not bear thinking of.

You lied, Six said, suddenly. *You have only helped two?*

You will be three, he said, and dove into her heart, searching for a memory to save her life. He felt Six try to follow, and he held out a mental hand, tugging her alongside him as he sped through her life, tasting her spirit. No two souls were ever alike—a handful of snowflakes might have more in comparison—but Six was utterly unlike anyone he had ever encountered. Her memories of life were stark and cold, with moments of fierceness interwoven like charms.

But he did not find anything to save her life. Nothing that created a visceral reaction. Not enough to burn out the poison hunting her spirit. He could taste the first tendrils of it, snaking from the darkness beyond her thoughts. Moving faster than he had imagined. If he waited much longer, there would be hooks involved, tearing her apart. Stealing her heart. Making her empty.

No, Six said. *No, Joseph. There must be something.*

You have to fight, he told her desperately. *You're a fighter, Six. You can do this. Find something inside of yourself that's worth living for. Hold on to it.*

He felt, inside her mind, the memory of a window. A window with a view of a wall, and beyond that, rooftops and trees and sky. *Freedom*, he heard inside his mind. And then, beside that window, he felt another memory, this time, of him. Six's first memory, their first meeting, seeing him walk into the room at the massage parlor. He tasted her appraisal of his eyes, his face, and though it was a thrill to know she had noticed him even then, what made his heart ache was that in her deepest unconscious, she equated him with her symbol of freedom.

Is that what you are? Six asked him. *My freedom?*

You tell me.

No, she said. *No person is freedom. But maybe you are a path.*

Then use that path. He wrapped himself around her spirit, holding her. *Fight.*

But instead of fighting, he felt Six grow more solid in his mental arms, and he matched her transformation until he could pretend he was searching her mind in the flesh. Like walking in a dream and feeling the ground beneath his feet; only, he suddenly found himself in that office with the window, standing beside Six as she stared through the glass. They were both naked.

Six, he said, and she turned just enough to kiss him. A hard kiss, hungry, melting right through his soul, scorching his heart. He pressed her against the window, cradling her head in his hands, and he could feel her skin ride against his own, smooth and hot. He grabbed the backs of her thighs and lifted her up, swinging them both around to the desk until he could lay her flat, pushing apart her thighs, moving between them. Six did not hesitate. She reached down and slid him into her body, raising her legs so that her knees practically touched her chin and her calves rested on his shoulders. Joseph gripped her hips and began thrusting hard.

And then, quite suddenly, they were no longer in each

other's minds but on the bed in his room, and instead of being naked they were both in clothes, wrapped around each other, thrusting and grinding. Joseph did not stop. He began tearing off his clothes, as did Six, buttons popping, pants shoved off and caught around ankles. Joseph pulled down the front of Six's bra at the same time he entered her, and the sight of her breasts and the sensation of that first slick stroke almost sent him over the edge. She strained against him, crying out, and all he could do was marvel at the fine, strong lines of her body, the feel of her moving beneath him as he obeyed her urgings and thrust faster, harder, pounding into her as she wrapped her legs around his back, fingernails clawing into his skin.

Joseph had no warning before she turned them, but suddenly he was on his back and she was on top, and that was fine because she lost the bra, and the sight of her bouncing breasts made him so hot that when he touched them he almost lost it for a second time.

Six leaned forward on her palms, thrusting hard. Then she stopped, abruptly, and slid all the way off him. Held herself there as they both panted, Joseph grappling with her hips, and then came down so hard—like that first thrust all over again—that he shouted and sat up, wild, grabbing her around the waist and hips, lifting and squeezing as she moved against him, faster and faster.

He felt her come—rode the wave as her muscles clenched around him—and then took her over the edge a second time with only a few more quick strokes. He came with that second orgasm, emptying himself into her body, and the feeling of being in her arms, spent, was so lush that he wanted nothing more than to plant some roots around them both and never move again.

But as he lay in her arms, he remembered—and slowly, carefully, slipped back into her mind, searching her spirit for the virus that had infected her.

It was still there. Its progression had stopped, the tendrils hard and frozen, but the threat remained. Nor did it appear that it would be disappearing anytime soon.

Permanent and dangerous. Part vampire. Waiting to become whole.

And no way to know what would set it off.

Chapter 6

After the age of thirteen, it became quite easy for Six to reconcile herself with the idea of death. She had, after all, taken lives to save her own, and that was utterly justifiable. As was taking the lives of those who were going to hurt others, however remotely. Indeed, she felt very little remorse about her actions. There was no point. Dead was dead. And she would have to kill again, sooner or later. That was the way of it. That was what she had been trained to do. Her life, no choice.

But now, resting in the darkness of an unfamiliar room, she wondered if this new turn in her life was some kind of karma. A killer without remorse, transforming into the physical manifestation of another kind of killer, also without remorse. Justice, or perhaps a divine joke. Maybe even destiny.

Like meeting Joseph? Six glanced at him. He was finally asleep, though lines of distress still cut into his forehead. He was a beautiful man. Six enjoyed nothing more than staring at his face, analyzing lines and angles and curves. Wanting to touch him again, to feel him inside her. She thought about waking him up, but turned aside that thought. He needed to rest. As did she, though that was unlikely to happen.

Six dressed quietly and went downstairs. She found Wenxia in the kitchen, seated at a fine table with flour scattered, small coins of dough rolled into flat circles. A large bowl of ground pork filled with chopped cabbage, ginger, and shrimp sat by her elbow. It smelled good.

"I'll make you tea," Wenxia said, scooting back her chair.

"I will do it," Six offered, and with some direction, found the leaves. A hot water dispenser leaned against the wall; she let the water flow into a little ceramic pot, and breathed in the steam. She let it steep for a moment, then poured Wenxia a cup. The old woman nodded her thanks.

Six sat opposite the old woman, and sipped her own cup of tea. It tasted good, and she felt herself relax as she watched Wenxia work. Her hands were gnarled and brown, but she made the dumplings efficiently, without sign of pain.

"Can I help?" Six asked.

"Oh, no," Wenxia replied, but she said it with a smile, and Six reached over for a dough skin. It had been a long time since she had tried her hand at making dumplings—there was an art to it—but she wanted to feel the sensation of cooking, of preparing, of putting herself into something other than fighting. She thought of Joseph, and smiled.

"Ah," murmured Wenxia. "You do care about him."

"Are you a mind reader?" she asked, startled.

"No need. I saw your smile. Only a man makes a woman smile like that. You care."

Six saw no use denying the truth. Still, she hesitated. "Yes, I do."

The old woman's mouth quirked. "You have to think about it?"

"No," Six replied. "But speaking of such things is . . . difficult for me."

"You are a product of the state," Wenxia said. "I can see it in your face."

"Does that bother you?"

"No." A dumpling thumped onto a plate. "But it makes you react differently to things some people take for granted. Like making dumplings, for example. You have never spent a holiday with family, have you?"

"No," Six said. "Never."

"Life is isolating enough, but when forced to live under the cold standard of a government machine . . ." Wenxia stopped. "Well, times are changing. One day, you and your kind will be as antiquated as my own generation. Relics. And no one will remember what was suffered."

"No one ever does," Six said, struggling to press the dough around the meat in the center. "And no one will ever care as much as you do about your own life."

Wenxia put down her spoon. "Joseph would care that much. About you. And if you had any heart in you, you would care that much about him."

Six set aside her dumpling. "He doesn't know me."

The old woman's eyes narrowed. "If anyone knows you, it's him. It's what he does. Something I think you're well aware of."

Six said nothing. Wenxia sighed. "Do you know what he does for work? Many things, you know. He makes big money being a therapist to rich men. Giving them advice. Guiding them in their lives. He does that several times a year. Makes enough, and then he leaves. Runs away to places where the people are hurting, dying. And there—*there*—he uses his real power. He makes people whole. He gives them hope. Helps them move on."

"Did he help you?" Six asked, and instantly regretted it.

Wenxia looked down, shoulders hunching. "His father did. He . . . dulled my pain. Made it bearable."

Six did not know how to answer. Wenxia saved her from trying. She leaned on the table, her bright eyes glittering.

"You know the story of the Spring Festival, yes? How a monster would descend from a mountain to terrorize a village year after year, eating people, stealing children. Until finally, someone said enough. And they attacked that monster with nothing but a firework. Boom! And the monster fled! Back to its mountain."

The old woman started making dumplings again. "The New Year holiday is a time of faith, child. Symbols, colors, flashes of light and sound—all of it, *faith*. Faith in a new beginning, in the power of hope. Faith in the ability of people to be more than what they dream. And it is a good dream, yes?"

"Yes," Six said softly. "Precious, even."

Wenxia smiled. "People become so discouraged. There are monsters everywhere, beating them down, stealing their dreams. Except the monsters are such cowards! A loud noise, a sharp light, that is all it takes to drive them away. Face them and be strong, and they will not be able to stand against you."

"And what if the people themselves become monsters? What if *I* am the monster?"

Wenxia gave her a knowing smile, and patted her hand. "Shine a light inside you, child. Make a loud noise."

Six, Joseph, and Wenxia shared a lovely dinner of dumplings, the finest Six had ever had—and the first that she remembered sitting down to, with people other than orphans or military. She asked Joseph if it would be possible for him to learn of her life before she had been taken in by the government, if those memories were still there, buried. He thought it likely. But Six did not ask him to try. Not then. She was not ready to remember.

She and Joseph did not stay long after the dinner. There was too much on the line, and the sense of urgency that pressed upon them was sharp enough to taste. A ruining effect, on an otherwise wonderful meal, though Six felt worse about leaving Wenxia.

They took a cab back to Shanghai. It was difficult to find one, on New Year's day. They directed their driver to take them to the Bund.

"Nothing will be open," Joseph said, holding her hand, cradling it in his lap. He looked handsome, rested, his eyes moving over her face, out the window, searching.

"Maybe not," Six said. "But at least we will make good targets. Perhaps attract the attention of someone who will lead us back to his master." Anger curled through her. "I have been thinking about the terrorists, Joseph. Trying to imagine what they would want with someone like you."

He grunted. "I have been thinking about the same thing, ever since Chenglei first contacted me. Trying to understand what Jihadists would want with someone who most definitely falls outside their religion. Not that I need to understand too much. Hate is hate. Hypocrisy rules. And there is precedent."

"What do you mean?"

"How much do you know about World War Two and the Nazis?"

"I have studied the history," Six said. "But I admit to focusing more on the problems this country faced. I have spoken to many elderly, and they have told me the stories."

"Yes. There are a lot of stories," Joseph said grimly. "But one thing I learned long ago, from the European side of the war, is that the Nazis—and more specifically, Hitler—were so consumed by their desire to win, that they began seeking . . . alternative methods. Inexplicable methods, of an . . . unnatural origin."

"You mean," she said slowly. "Something like you."

"Something like that," he admitted. "Thankfully, they never tapped into anything real, though they came close enough to make some individuals nervous. And not just those with powers like mine, but competing governments who in turn began developing their own programs to explore alternative weaponry within the paranormal. The Russians were the most serious, second only to the Germans. My grandfather was part of that program. He managed to leave it after the war. Illegally, of course. He escaped into Mongolia and never left. He took the daughter of a shaman as his wife, and they had a son."

"A family legacy, then."

"But it doesn't answer any questions."

Shanghai traffic was lighter than usual, but the Bund surprised them by being quite crowded. It seemed to Six that every family had taken the afternoon to travel down to the heart of the city and see the sights. Days off were rare for most; the New Year festivals guaranteed at least one.

"We must stay away from the waterfront," Six told Joseph, after being dropped off by the cab. "There will be undercover military there for sure, and they will know my face. Xiu must have been discovered by now."

As she spoke, her eyes seemed to blur, vision worsening almost to blindness until suddenly, without warning, everything snapped back into focus. Six gasped. She could see . . . everything. The individual pores on a woman's face—who was standing more than fifty feet away. The brand name on the buttons of a man's jacket, far across the street. Her vision swooped and burned like she was an eagle flying, and it was dizzying, frightening.

"Check," she said. "Is the poison—"

"No," Joseph said grimly. "It hasn't progressed. But you're still suffering the side effects."

"Just as long as I do not suffer anything else. I am still me, correct? I still . . . *feel*."

"You have your heart," he said quietly. "I won't let you lose it, Six."

"You will not have a choice, if the poison spreads."

Joseph said nothing. The street they were on was the main artery running parallel to the Bund. The architecture was European in origin, neoclassical designs from the twenties up to the forties. Immense monoliths that had stood the test of time far better than most modern Chinese buildings constructed in only the last few years.

Six and Joseph did not take a walking tour of those massive buildings. Instead, they walked into the Peace Hotel and found a bench in a little nook off the main foyer, crowded with tourists, most of them from America and Europe.

They sat, holding hands. Joseph began a search with his mind. After a moment, he invited Six to join him, and she found herself swept into his thoughts, carried alongside him as he traveled another world, seeking danger.

He found it, almost immediately. Right on top of them. A sickening lurch of knowledge that made them both reel.

There is a bomb in this hotel, said Joseph, horror leaking from his thoughts. *My God. It's a person. A person—*

Six was already running, the location in her mind, the face of the man. She barreled through the crowd, ruthless, battling her own feelings of shock. She had expected this in theory—the Peace Hotel had always been on a list of possible targets to be wary of—but thinking and knowing were two separate things, and there was a part of Six that could not believe it was happening here, now. Not now.

The crowd thickened; she did not think. She jumped. Her body flew over the tops of heads. She heard gasps. She gasped. But there, ahead of her, she saw a stocky man in a heavy coat, and she forced herself to move faster than she ever had before. Faster than was humanly possible.

The suicide bomber never had a chance; he barely saw her coming before he hit the ground. Six did not kill him. She broke his wrists instead, cracked his knees by stomping hard—and then, as he lay on the ground screaming, she flipped open his coat and looked at the bomb. It was not terribly sophisticated; she had trained on harder targets. Six pulled the necessary wires.

Joseph appeared behind her. He knelt, placed his hands on the man's temples, and began to chant. This time, Six stayed out of his head. She stood and pulled out her badge. Showed it to the hotel manager who came running, pale and frightened. Showed it to the crowd, and in her best English, told them to please exit the area in a careful manner. They did, without hesitation. She gave the hotel manager a number to call, just in case they had not already.

"Joseph," she said.

"Got it," he murmured. "There are seven other locations. We can't reach all of them in time."

Six grabbed a nearby man and stole the cell phone out of his hands. He began to protest—she showed him her badge. Dialed fast with one hand. Ying picked up on the second ring.

"The terrorists are planting a series of bombs around the city," she said quickly, and then had Joseph take the phone and rattle off the list of names and locations. Six took back the phone, listening as Ying shouted to someone in the background. She heard the call go up, loud and fierce. For a moment, a feeling of nostalgia, a sliver of regret that could have been grief struck her, but then she looked at Joseph standing beside her, and felt such freedom it stole her breath away. She was making her own path now. Walking her own road.

"Six," said Ying. "What happened between you and Xiu? She doesn't remember anything. You are in such trouble."

"I cannot explain," Six said. "But I am still on your side. Please, no matter what happens, remember that.

"What happened?" Ying asked. "This is not you, Six."

"Goodbye," she said. "Tell the others for me."

Six ended the call and tossed the phone back to its owner. She could hear sirens, and flagged down the hotel manager one more time.

"Guard this man," she said, pointing to the terrorist still writhing on the ground. "Step on his wrists or knees if he gives you any trouble. Do it anyway, for fun. The police will be here in a moment."

"Y-yes," stammered the man. Six and Joseph ran. A police cruiser careened around the corner just as they walked through the revolving doors. Six tugged on Joseph's hand and made him slow to a walk, which they did—very quickly—in the opposite direction. The flow of the crowd made it easy to get lost. A lot of people were leaving the hotel.

"You found something else," she said to him, jostled on all sides by strangers. Her sense of hearing threatened to overwhelm. She tried to subdue the sounds crashing in her eardrums, and much to her surprise, they subsided to something resembling normal. She wished her heart rate would do the same.

"Him," Joseph said shortly. "I found *him*."

He stopped walking. Six bumped against his side. His hand tightened and she followed his gaze to a man and woman standing in the middle of the sidewalk, staring at them. Eye contact was startling; Six felt those two sharp gazes reverberate down to her gut, and she knew without being told that they were vampires. Human shells, hollow cores. Just like her, if she was not careful. If the poison began to move again.

"I wish I had my dagger," Joseph muttered. "I should have kept a spare at the house."

"We will get you a new one after this," Six replied, and that brought a brief smile to his face.

"You and I," he said softly. "What a team."

"Yes," she said. "I like it."

The vampires moved close. Six and Joseph waited. The crowd parted around them all like water.

"Hello, sister," said the woman. "Hello, hello."

"We have a message," said the man. "You should come with us to hear it."

"Really, we're guides," added the woman.

"I think you know who sent us." The man pointed. "It's a short walk."

Joseph and Six did not look at each other. They were already inside each other's heads. And they both knew what they had to do.

They followed the vampires down the long, gently curving street, walking away from the Bund. Sirens filled the city, a wail occasionally interrupted by the shot and blast of firecrackers. The sound made her jumpy, though she tried to hide it. Joseph knew, though. He felt the same.

They were led to an office building that was still fairly new. All glass and steel. There was a security desk, but no one manning it. The woman keyed in a code, the elevator dinged, and the four of them crowded into the small space—vampires on one side, Joseph and Six on the other. She still had the gun she had taken from the guard. Its weight was comfortable beneath her shirt.

"We were sorry to hear that Chenglei passed on," said the man to Joseph. "He was a very good person."

"He had dirty feet," Six said. The vampires frowned. Joseph coughed, holding his hand over his mouth.

The woman gave Six a piercing look. "You are almost one of us now. I think you will like it, if you give it a chance."

Six said nothing. Engaging in that debate would be a waste of time.

The elevators doors opened. The vampires stepped out first, Joseph and Six following behind. His voice rumbled into a low chant. The creatures froze—and then, movements jerky, stepped back into the elevator. The woman snarled, but she pushed a button. The door slid closed.

"That will not keep them away very long," said Six.

"Long enough," Joseph replied.

"A parlor trick, and quite useless," said another voice. Six and Joseph looked up. A blond man walked out of a nearby office. His Chinese had an English accent, and he was tall and clean-cut, clad in a navy suit with a lilac tie. He was followed by three individuals who were, quite clearly, vampires. One of them, however, also wore a suit. His skin was swarthy, his features more of the south, perhaps from Indonesia. He gave her a straight, hard look, and Six felt, from Joseph's mind, the realization that this individual was one of the terror cell's ringleaders. A planner.

"Ah," said the other man. "So you finally see your vampire connection."

"That still doesn't explain why they would want men like us," Joseph replied.

"Control and information," said the vampire. "There was a woman we needed to speak to, but she was too well guarded. She had very private information about how to access certain facilities where she was planning New Year parties. Simple, really. And I knew of your skills. If it makes you feel better, we were going to kill you afterwards."

"Thanks," Joseph said dryly, and looked at the blond man. "And you, Mr.? . . ."

"Doe," he said, with a slight smile. "John Doe, to you. And no, the little bastards won't kill me. I've never touched a single one of them. And if they do try, I've made it crystal clear what will happen in retaliation." He leaned forward, eyes glinting. "Fear, Mr. Besud. You should really try utilizing it in a different manner than you have. You are far too much of a goody two-shoes."

Six recalled Joseph's memories: the bones, the dead, the cold way he had dispatched the vampires during the previous night. Not so goody-goody, she thought. Not at all. The two of them were the same, that way.

"What do you get out of this?" she asked Doe. "Not just

money. You would not want Joseph dead, if it was simply that."

Doe smiled, cracking his knuckles. "Do you know what happens when people die, Miss Six? It is quite remarkable, really. Their souls leave. Everything that ever made a person who they are simply . . . floats away. To Heaven or Hell, or perhaps just to live on a cloud. I do not know, nor do I care. What I find fascinating is not what happens after death, but what occurs *during*."

Joseph paled. "You're feeding off the deaths."

"Do you know how old I am?" Doe tapped his smooth cheek, running his finger down his strong jaw. "Ninety, young Mr. Besud. *Ninety years old*, and my body is still as young now as it was all those years ago. Back home in *Russia*." His smile changed, becoming darker, more feral. "I knew your grandfather, boy. I *trained* him."

Joseph's breath caught. "He spoke of a teacher. Never his name, though. He said that man was great."

"A compliment," Doe said. "I am still fond of him, you know. He was a stunning pupil. I was . . . disappointed . . . when he chose to run away. It took me years to find him again. I thought for sure that he would have used the trick I taught him to stay young, but instead I found an old brittle man with an old crone of a wife, their children aging by the minute. And you. You, with even more talent than my student."

"So you would kill me for that?" Joseph swayed forward. "Why?"

"Because there are no others like us," Doe whispered. "Not anywhere. We are alone, boy."

"And you do not want the competition," Six said, quiet.

Doe tipped his head. "When I was young, nothing excited me more than the idea of my brothers-in-arms, all of us living to use our gifts for pride and country. But it is a different world now, and I like my power being *only* my power."

"You like killing people for that strength," Joseph said flatly. "Only a violent death would give what you crave."

"A little bit of chaos never hurt," Doe said. "China will rebuild. It has people to spare. I'm sure the vampires agree."

Six gritted her teeth. "I would like to kill him now. May I?"

"By all means," Joseph said.

Doe sneered. He lifted his hands, chanting. Six felt a brief tug on her body, but it slid off her like water, and she smiled. Took one step forward, reaching behind for her gun. Doe faltered. The vampires all looked at each other.

"There is a curious thing called possession," Joseph said. "You might have heard of it. Thing is, you don't have to fully inhabit a person in order to keep someone else out. I'm surprised you didn't know that, *Doe*."

Doe paled. He said one word and the vampires lurched in front of him. Six knew what Joseph wanted before he asked; she tossed him the gun and then barreled into the vampires, clearing a path for him so that he could chase after Doe. He did, disappearing around a corner in the long office corridor.

Behind her, the elevator dinged. The two vampires who had escorted them up ran off, snarling. Their human faces had drained away; they stared at her with hollow eyes and black mouths, sharp tongues writhing deep within the maw. The air felt cold.

"Sister," hissed the woman. "I think, perhaps, we no longer want you to join us."

Six laughed. It was too funny. Five vampires against one. She liked those odds.

Doe ran fast, but Joseph did, too. He caught up with the older man. Before he could fire the gun, he heard a low voice fill the air: binding words, pushing against him. Joseph held up one hand and let his own voice fill the air. Double tones, loud and strong. His voice drowned out Doe, and he lifted the gun and took aim. His grandfather had always been good with a gun. So had his father. The steppe made men hardy, that way. Joseph fired.

The bullet caught Doe in the knee. He went down screaming and Joseph stood over him. Doe tried again to use his gift, but the power, while strong, slid away.

"What did you think it would do for you?" Joseph asked quietly, kneeling. "Really, what? Eternal youth? Perfect control over the people around you? And you thought you could beat me with that? You're no better than a vampire. Worse, even. You had a choice. Same choice as my grandfather. As me."

Doe's face contorted. "I should have killed you all when I found you the first time. Made it easy."

"Yes," Joseph said. "You should have."

He put the gun against Doe's forehead and pulled the trigger.

Joseph left Doe's body. He did not watch the man's soul leave. He ran back to help Six. There were four piles of ash on the ground. No doubt all of them had died with their heads ripped off. Vampire strength was obviously doing her some good.

The last vampire alive was the terror cell planner. Six had him pinned facedown on the ground. She had somehow found time to locate a mini-recorder, which she held up to Joseph.

"How do you do that?" he asked admiringly, taking the device. Six smiled.

Joseph turned on the recorder and held it by the vampire's face. He watched as Six questioned him on tape, methodically breaking his fingers every time he refused to answer. And when he still refused, she commenced ripping those fingers off his hand, one by one. The dismembered digits turned to ash.

By the time she reached his pinky, the man had begun

blabbering like an idiot. Helped along, of course, by Joseph's own coercion. He did not feel like wasting any more of their time. When Six was satisfied, he turned off the recorder and slipped it into his pocket. He did not want to preserve, for posterity, the sound of Six tearing off a man's head with her bare hands.

Which she did, quite easily. The vampire turned to ash.

"So," Joseph said. "That was . . . interesting."

"Very." Six wiped her hands together.

"I hope this doesn't mean we're breaking up," he said. "Now that the danger is over."

"There is always danger," Six said. "And no, I am not going anywhere. Not without you."

"Good," Joseph said, the adrenaline finally seeping away, making him shaky. He wrapped his arm around Six's shoulders and pulled her near.

"Happy New Year," he muttered, and kissed her hard.

Epilogue

Three weeks later, Six found herself in Mongolia. It was a nice country. She could admit to herself that she loved it.

It was a beautiful day, cold and crisp. Furs lined her throat. Her leather jacket was heavy and warm. A gun pressed against her ribs, slung tight in a new shoulder holster.

Joseph sat beside her on a motorcycle. It was a Russian model, lightweight, but sturdy enough for two. Good for cross-country riding, unless they decided to buy horses. Unlikely. The animals did not seem to like Six. She blamed the poison still in her blood.

"Life is good," Joseph said.

"Yes," Six said. "Do you believe Ying has been able to use the information that was on the recording?"

"I would think so." He hesitated. "Regrets about leaving your old life?"

"Not really," she said. "I am making a new one."

"In a spectacular way, I might add."

"For a vampire."

Joseph shrugged, but she could feel concern on the edge of his thoughts. "You're only part of those creatures."

"Enough, I think."

"Perfect, just the way you are." Joseph held out his hand. "I've said it before, and I'll say it again. What a team we make, Six."

"Yes." Six trailed her fingers down his chest. "And what will we do next, as a team? I am a wanted woman. You are a wanted man. We cannot ever go back."

"China is a big country, but it's not as big as the world. We'll manage." He patted the back of his motorcycle. "Ready?"

Six hesitated for a moment, gazing down at the valley below her. The land could swallow the sky with its vastness: green and brown and full of lush curves that idled like the clouds.

No walls, anywhere in sight.

Six turned around. Joseph was watching her, a question in his eyes. She kissed him, long and slow, and slid behind him on the motorcycle.

"I want one of these," she said. "I want to fly on this land."

"We'll fly together," he said.

And they did.

MARJORIE M . LIU is an attorney who has lived and worked throughout Asia. She hails from both coasts, but currently resides in the Midwest, where she writes full-time. Her books include the *New York Times* bestselling Dirk & Steele series of paranormal romances for Leisure, and her forthcoming Hunter Kiss urban fantasies from Ace Books.

For more information, please visit her website at *www.marjoriemliu.com*.

The Harvest

Vicki Pettersson

Chapter 1

Zoe Archer had hated hospitals even before she became mortal, and absolutely loathed them now that she was subject to the same capricious whims of the universe as those she used to protect. The sharp smell of disinfectant, and the even sharper underlying emotions, was a bitter reminder that she, too, was suddenly vulnerable to gun-toting criminals and shifty-eyed rapists.

Vulnerable to the rampant evil of *Shadows*.

For God's sake, she thought irritably as she strode from the fourth-floor stairwell, *these* days she was bothered by a mere paper cut. She'd had to find new ways to move through this old world; stepping aside, moving around, and shrinking back instead of barreling through, clamoring over, and standing up. She'd had bruises for weeks after her transformation—bruises!—until she'd finally learned the limits of mortal flesh and blood. She was just thankful this learning curve wasn't being recorded in the manuals. How embarrassing would it be if the agents of Light knew she actually bruised?

How dangerous if the Shadow agents discovered she bled?

Zoe shivered and picked up her pace, her steps echoing through the wide sterile hallway as she settled her briefcase strap more firmly on her shoulder. It was still worth it. She no longer deserved the powers that had once made her extraordinary, and if she'd ever been a heroine worthy of the title, she would've passed on her *chi* before her daughter was almost murdered. But so intent had she been on her mission, her own deceitful life, that she hadn't even considered that possibility. So when it was too late, when all she could do was watch her Jo-baby fight for life—wires and tubes and casts canvassing her young body like she was caught in a web—Zoe knew there was only one title that mattered, and it wasn't *Superhero*.

It was Mother.

And she was determined to prove herself worthy of that. Tonight she'd tie up this final loose end and in doing so ensure the safety of all the loved ones she'd left behind—both mortal and supernatural. Then she'd spend the rest of her life in this fragile human skin as penance, hiding from both ally and enemy alike.

The nurses' station on the labor and delivery floor was eerily empty when she arrived. She heard a woman's cry from down the hall, a sound that had her belly tightening as she remembered the pangs of her own two births, but she needed to stay focused and quickly shook the memory off. Throwing a cursory glance over the rim of her owlish glasses, and spotting no one, she leaned over the admission's desk to thumb through the charts. Yep, there she was. Joanna Archer. Room 425.

Swallowing hard, Zoe headed that way.

She was three doors from her daughter's room when she heard the crying. She slowed, but told herself she wasn't stalling. Just being respectful. Compassionate. *Human*. At least, that was her excuse.

Peering around a doorway, she spotted a young couple dressed in unassuming street clothes, clinging to one another as the world spun heedlessly around them. She couldn't scent their sorrow as she'd have been able to only months earlier, but she didn't need to. Bleakness was printed on their faces—carved in the bend of the man's back as he held his wife, jackhammering her trembling shoulders as she wept.

"Can I help you?"

The voice, sharp and businesslike, came from directly behind her, and Zoe jolted before regaining her composure and turning. The nurse was older than she was, mid-forties probably, and wore her chopped hair in the same red Zoe had favored before being forced to dye it black for this new identity. Her eyes skirted to the nurse's name tag. Nancy was big-boned, her powder-blue scrubs putting Zoe in mind of a giant canvas of sky, and she wore comfortable soft-soled shoes, which was why Zoe hadn't heard her sneak up. Something else, she thought wryly, that wouldn't have happened six months ago.

"I'm Traci Malone," Zoe said, holding out a hand, palm down so the woman wouldn't catch sight of the glass-smooth pads where her fingerprints should be. "Case worker for the Archer adoption."

The nurse's face cleared, understanding replacing her businesslike wariness. She held up her hands, a warding-off motion, before withdrawing them again. "You'll excuse me for not shaking. I just came from delivery, and haven't had a chance to wash up yet."

Zoe's eyes wandered to the couple, still oblivious to all but their personal sorrow. Nurse Nancy saw the look and reached around Zoe to pull the door shut before shooting her a small, bittersweet smile. "Dennis and Andie were another of our patients' adoptees. Their baby didn't survive the birth."

"How terrible."

Nurse Nancy nodded solemnly, then shook it off with a philosophical sigh, just another day on the job. "Well, you certainly got here fast. I just got back from calling your adoptive parents. They're coming right away."

"The family called me first," Zoe lied in a murmur. "They'd like the paperwork and documentation completed as quickly and discreetly as possible."

"Bet they do," scoffed the nurse, causing Zoe to stiffen. "A pregnant teen, some fancy family name to protect. Guess money can't buy you everything, can it?"

Zoe managed a nod. Relatively speaking? Money could buy very little.

"The infant's very early," Nancy went on, motioning for Zoe to follow her. "Just caught the twenty-four-week mark, but she's intubated, and stable enough now that we've got her on the oscillator. Awfully small, though."

"Well, babies tend to come in their own time," Zoe said, following Nancy back to the front desk.

"Sure," Nancy said, but scoffed as she glanced at Zoe. "But an early delivery's more common when the mother has endured such trauma. Raped, you know," she said in an exaggerated whisper, before continuing in a normal voice. "So the child's obviously unwanted, another mitigating factor. Add in a flawed support system—the girl's mother ran off after the pregnancy was disclosed, the father wouldn't even come down for the birth—and you have a recipe for fetal trauma."

Nancy tsk-tsked as she rounded the counter, shaking her head in a way that made Zoe want to rip it off. Instead she pulled out her notepad, and with shaking hands pretended to scribble some thoughts. "What time was the child born?"

"Midnight sharp, actually." Nancy shook her head, flipping through paperwork. "What a novelty, huh?"

Not really, Zoe wanted to say. The Zodiac's lineage was matriarchal. Everyone who was superhuman was born on their mother's birthday, exactly midnight, just as their mother before them. That's how Zoe knew her daughter would be here tonight, even if it was four months too early.

"And the girl . . . the mother? How is she?"

Nancy glanced up, brows furrowed. "You don't need to see her, do you?"

"Why? Is she all right?" *Please, God, please . . .*

"Sedated. The labor was complicated and a shock to a still-healing system, but she's resting easily enough now."

A sigh spiraled out of Zoe before she could stop it, causing Nancy to glance at her sharply. Zoe immediately checked herself—case workers didn't get involved with their clients— and shot the nurse a distracted smile. "No, of course I don't need to see her. She's already signed the release papers, and she should rest."

Nancy was still looking at her speculatively when a crisp bell chimed behind Zoe. The nurse's eyes slid over Zoe's shoulder and her face cleared.

"There are the McCormicks now." She waved them over, and Zoe turned warily, inspecting for the first time the people who would take possession of—no, take *care* of— her granddaughter.

The woman was diminutive; a fussy, fluttery thing who kept clutching at her own hands and holding so close to her husband she very nearly tripped him up. He seemed not to notice, though, chest puffed out peacock proud, a wide smile blanketing his ruddy face as he steered his wife with one large hand, and mauled a stuffed bunny with the other.

"Mr. and Mrs. McCormick, this is Traci . . ."

"Malone," Zoe provided, when Nancy faltered. "I'm with social services. I have your paperwork right here."

"Cutting right to the chase, are we?" Mr. McCormick's

voice boomed unnaturally throughout the still hallways. "But I imagine this is old hat for you, huh? You're probably anxious to get home and to bed."

Mrs. McCormick clutched his arm. "Oh, yes, it's late . . . and so close to Thanksgiving. Everyone's so busy and . . ." She faltered, her eyes going wide at a fresh thought. "Oh, honey! Our first holiday with our baby girl! I just can't believe it! We've been waiting, dreaming for so long . . ."

Mr. McCormick shot Zoe a helpless smile as his wife collapsed into his arms.

"Technically, you won't be with her for Thanksgiving." Zoe's voice came out louder, sharper than she would've liked. She checked it, along with her emotions, and plastered a bland expression on her face. "She must remain in the hospital until she's strong enough to be self-supporting. Another sixteen weeks or so."

"But maybe by Christmas," Nancy reassured, smiling as she pushed away from the counter. "I'll just go make sure the baby's ready."

"Ready?" Zoe turned back to the couple, who were trying—unsuccessfully—to temper their giddiness.

"Oh, yes. Didn't you know?" More fluttering by Mrs. McCormick as her wide eyes searched Zoe's face. "We're having the child moved to the Sheep Mountain Medical Facility. They have the best neonatal unit in town and . . . well, we don't want to risk the birth mother seeing her and, you know . . ."

"Changing her mind," her husband said flatly. "We know she's young. Probably fickle . . . or confused. Obviously not of the best moral character."

"Dave!" his wife slapped ineffectively at his shoulder. "The girl is giving us our darling baby!"

"I'm sorry, sweetie. You're right."

Almost nauseated, Zoe fumbled in her briefcase and reminded herself that she'd picked these people out of hundreds of candidates. She'd researched their backgrounds, those of their extended families, and even did a drive-by on their neat, suburban home. She needed them. And the child needed to be in hiding because of who and *what* she was. She'd be safe with the McCormicks. Safe from the judgment of those who'd fault her for the circumstances under which she was conceived. And, most importantly, safe from the Shadows.

"If you could just sign here," she said, her voice sounding hollow, even to her own ears, as she dropped the paperwork on the counter and moved away. Suddenly all she really wanted to do was get away.

The McCormicks moved in close, chattering excitedly as they each signed the small stack of papers completing the adoption. When they were done, Zoe ripped off the copies and handed them to Mrs. McCormick. She then dropped the rest back in her briefcase, settled her glasses more firmly on her nose, and said, "Congratulations."

Dave blinked and drew back. "That's it?"

"Wow, that was fast."

"The birth mother isn't contesting anything." She shot them a smile. It felt brittle on her face. "Enjoy your new family."

But she'd only taken a few steps before half-turning again. She couldn't help it . . . and asking now would save her the trouble and risk of searching later. "What will you name her?"

"Jenna."

"Samantha."

They answered at the same time, then looked at one another sheepishly, bursting into giggles again. Dave recovered himself first. "We're still working that out."

Zoe nodded shortly and forced an aspect of bored professionalism in her voice before turning. "Good luck."

And she strode away, closing the last chapter on her old life forever.

Zoe's plan was to turn in the paperwork finalizing the McCormick adoption to social services in the morning, quit her job right after that, and lay low until she figured out a new identity to replace Traci Malone. She'd have liked to take a little vacation, get out of town while everyone else was celebrating the holidays, but her finances wouldn't allow it. Every dime she had, and every safety net, she'd had to leave behind. She was starting over for the third time in her life, and doing it with fewer resources than ever before.

But she had seen her family safe, she thought on a sigh, and had secured her lineage for the next two generations. Joanna possessed everything she needed to heal and eventually she'd be better and stronger for it. And now her granddaughter was hidden deep, if in plain sight, and the Shadows would never know of her existence. Yes, thought Zoe as she exited the hospital into a cool November night, it was all worth it.

Caught up in her thoughts, Zoe hardly noticed the black town car glide up to the curb, or the driver hop out to open the passenger door.

"I'll pull around to the side and wait for you there, Miss Olivia," the driver said, holding out a hand.

"Thank you, Brian," his charge said, and Zoe turned to see a beautiful young girl alighting from the car. She was on the cusp of womanhood, with peaches and cream skin and billowing blond hair that stood out like a beacon against her black sweater set. Zoe stared, unable to take her eyes from the girl. It'd been six long months since she'd seen her youngest daughter.

Olivia Archer beelined for the entrance as the car whisked off, her arms so full of bags and boxes she had to peer around the side to navigate her way. Zoe didn't question the need to help, to *see* her daughter. She just moved before she knew she'd acted, rushing to hold open one of the giant glass doors.

Olivia caught the movement from the corner of her eye. Yelping, she shied and ducked, and only belatedly did Zoe realize what she must look like; someone waiting until the girl was alone, charging from the side, attacking in the night. Olivia's packages flew from her arms and Zoe heard glass shattering and bags ripping, while her daughter dodged behind a concrete pillar. Even with her mortal hearing she could make out the ragged breath and whimpers.

"No, no, no, no . . ."

Oh, her poor, traumatized baby.

"Miss Archer?" Zoe cast her voice high, keeping it steady, though it wanted to shake. "I'm so sorry to startle you. I was just going to get the door."

Olivia peered cautiously around the pillar, her blue eyes wide, fear etched on her brow.

Her poor, poor baby.

"H-how do you know my name?" Olivia asked, still wary.

Zoe tried on a smile, but it felt tight on her face, and she let it drop, trying for casualness instead. "I'm the case worker for your sister's adoption. We met before."

Olivia edged out from behind the pillar, recognition dawning in her eyes. "I-I'm not supposed to talk to you. I mean, my father said I'm not supposed to talk about it. With anyone. The baby, I mean."

I'll just bet he did, thought Zoe, cursing Xavier Archer, his greedy heart, his blackened soul. She smiled reassuringly. "I understand. Let me just help you with these."

They bent together and picked up what remained of the dinner Olivia had brought her sister. Turkey and stuffing, cranberries—half of which were splattered across the sidewalk—sweet potatoes and apple pie. Joanna's favorite.

"Quite a spread." Zoe murmured, keeping her head bowed to hide her tears.

"I made it all myself. I wanted her to have a proper meal—the food in here is just awful—and since she won't be home in time for the holiday, and Daddy won't let me come down on Thanksgiving Day . . ." she trailed off, obviously worried she'd said too much. Olivia had never been able to directly disobey Xavier's orders, though she had recently begun to dodge them. As evidenced tonight.

"Well, you did a wonderful job," Zoe said, handing her a final container of gravy. She hesitated, then pressed, "Will Mr. Archer be joining you?"

Olivia flushed to her roots, then swallowed hard and lifted her heart-shaped chin. "Daddy doesn't know I'm here. I snuck away after he left for some party. If he finds out he'll have Brian fired for driving me, but I just had to see Joanna. It's her birthday. I couldn't let her be alone tonight. Thanksgiving maybe. But not her birthday. And not after she so recently . . ."

Was attacked, raped, beaten, left for dead . . .

"Had a baby?" Zoe said softly as she stood and handed a bag to Olivia. "Don't worry. I won't tell a soul."

Relief had the girl sagging a bit. "Thank you, Ms. . . . I'm sorry, I didn't catch your name."

Zoe held open the door. "You can call me Traci."

"Thanks, Traci." Olivia walked through the door, but hesitated just on the other side, not looking back. "She won't talk about it with me."

"She can't. But she's a very brave girl." Zoe waited until Olivia did look back, and held her gaze there. "You're brave, too."

"Me?" Olivia immediately scoffed. "No, I'm not. I . . . ran. I left her. I-I'm nothing."

"That's not true," Zoe said, so vehemently it had Olivia

blinking in surprise. Zoe fought to work a blank expression on her face. "It's not. You're here, aren't you? Taking a chance that you'll get caught. Disobeying because you're *right*. You don't give yourself enough credit. From what I understand you saved Joanna because you *did* run, and fast. There was nothing more you could have done that night. You reacted perfectly to a perfectly horrible circumstance."

Olivia's beautiful face crumpled on itself and tears emptied out over her cheeks. She bit her lip to keep it from quivering, still trying to be brave. "When Jo gets out of here we're going to take a trip to Europe. It'll be a fresh start for her."

"For the both of you."

Olivia smiled through her tears. "For us all. For the baby, too. Dennis and Andie seem like wonderful people."

Zoe thought of the couple upstairs, clutching one another, a stuffed bunny, and long-held dreams of having a daughter. She nodded, but corrected Olivia. "You mean Dave and Andie."

Olivia looked at her oddly before shaking her head. "No, I mean Dennis and Andie. The McCormicks? Don't tell anyone but I looked them up on the computer." She shot Zoe a sheepish grin, though pride lurked beneath the look. "Actually, I hacked into the hospital's registry. I just had to see where my . . . the baby was going. I'm sure she'll be happy with them. Did you know they already have a name for her? Ashlyn. Isn't that lovely? I think it's a family name, but . . ."

But Zoe had stopped listening. She closed her eyes, and let the images come, fast and furious, as Olivia's airy voice faded to the background.

Nurse Nancy shutting the door on a grieving couple who'd just "lost" their adopted daughter. *Dennis and Andie.*

The same nurse warding off a handshake, just as Zoe would've done.

A couple anticipating the long-awaited arrival of their daughter, though, strangely, they hadn't yet agreed on a name.

Zoe dove for her briefcase, fumbling for the papers inside. Typed neatly at the top of the page: McCormick, Dennis and Andria.

Signed below: McCormick, Dave and Andie. Zoe was slow—stupidly inattentive—but she was suddenly catching up fast.

We're having the child moved . . .

"Oh, my God."

She lurched forward and grabbed at the door, Olivia's questioning alarm spiraling out behind her in the wide, deserted lobby. Midnight, Zoe thought, doing a mental head slap. A perfect time to snatch a child. She took the stairs two at a time, her briefcase banging awkwardly against her hip, her breath echoing in the stairwell.

"Nurse Nancy," Zoe said, slapping her palm on the counter in front of a tired-eyed nurse she'd never seen before. "Where is she?"

The nurse blinked up at her. "Who?"

Zoe cursed, and reached across the Formica counter. It wouldn't take much to create a distraction in a hospital. Just a false code 99 raising the alarm that some other patient had crashed. She wondered briefly what ploy the Shadows had used.

"Excuse me! What do you think you're—"

No chart. Ignoring the nurse, she raced for the nursery.

"Ma'am! You need to sign in!"

Zoe skidded around the corner. God, but they'd had their roles down pat.

The baby was gone. Zoe squeezed her eyes shut, and lowered her head to the glass window. There was no Nurse Nancy. No couple named Dave and Andie. If she'd been thinking straight, if she hadn't been so damned close to the situation, she might have noted the small things: the name slip, the way the nurse's nostrils had flared at Zoe's slip of emotion, the couple's forced surface emotions. She'd have seen all of it then as clearly as she saw it now.

"Ma'am, are you all right?"

No, Zoe thought, pushing the other woman aside to charge back down the hall. And neither was her granddaughter.

Chapter 2

In the car on the way to the address scrawled across the discharge papers, Zoe tried to figure out how the Shadows had found out about the baby. She was certain they couldn't scent out the power, the Light, on Joanna. If Zoe had withheld even a smidgen of her own personal *chi*, then maybe, but she hadn't. She'd given it all up, and the very fact that she hadn't scented any of them assured her of that. But they'd taken the baby, and that couldn't be coincidence. So how had they known?

The only thing Zoe could be absolutely certain of was that the Shadows hadn't known who she really was. Otherwise she'd be on her knees in front of their leader right now, begging for her life. Paying for her past.

Zoe shuddered at the thought of the Tulpa, then resolutely pushed his image away. She needed to concentrate on the task at hand, follow the Shadows' trail one step at a time, and go from there. But when she pulled her car to a stop she didn't even need to look at the FOR SALE sign on the lawn to know the house was empty. She yanked her cell phone from her jacket pocket, a slim new model she'd bought on the street, and called the number listed at the top of her papers. Out of service. She then had the operator give her the number to the Sheep Mountain facility, where they told her no baby by the name of McCormick had been admitted that evening. Zoe was disappointed but not surprised. Both sides of the Zodiac force—Shadow and Light—had private facilities with their own medical staff. It kept mortal physicians and officials from being suspicious or curious when the body count rose. It also acted as a place of respite for injured agents until the next splitting of dawn or dusk, when the veil between their two parallel worlds lifted, and they could pass easily into a different, safe, and alternate reality.

So Zoe had no way of finding out where the enemy agents had taken the baby, and even if she had she'd be hard-pressed to take on even one of them in her . . . condition. Mortals were deplorably weak.

But, she thought, biting her lip, there was *one* place she could go . . . one person she could turn to for help. She'd sworn never to see or call upon him again, but if she could catch him before sunup, she might be able to convince him to help her. Because if he ever really knew her—if he had ever truly *loved* her—he'd recognize her even beneath her mortal disguise and without the power that had made her his equal.

And if he refused? asked an unwelcomed voice inside of her, a bitter reminder of what she'd done. Then her lineage, and the legacy of the Archer ended with her, and she'd sacrificed it all for nothing. Including her children. Including, she thought, pulling from the curb, his love.

When Warren Clarke wasn't fighting crime and leading the agents of Light in a century-long battle against supernatural crime, he spent his downtime kneeling in a pew at the Guardian Angel Cathedral. It wasn't that he was particularly religious; like all the star signs in the Zodiac he believed in astrology, preordained fate, and that every life and death was written in the sky. So his regular attendance at the cathedral had nothing to do with penance, forgiveness, or an overabundance of piety. In truth, whenever he lit a candle or knelt before the altar, all he was really praying for was a fight.

Zoe wasn't going to be the one to give it to him. So she lit a cigarette and propped a foot up against the towering white obelisk in front of the cathedral, directly beneath the neon cross flaring at its apex. Staring south down the length of flash and glitter of Las Vegas Boulevard through faux horn-runned glasses, she thought, as she always had, that it was an odd place for a cathedral. But it'd been here since '63, outliving most of the casinos, the mobsters, the Howard Hugheses and Wynns . . . remaining a solid and memorable fixture even though it was unremarkable compared to that long stretch of neon just outside its doors.

A statue of the holy family blessing the cathedral's visitors was cradled in the center of the hollowed-out obelisk, and Zoe glanced at it now. The promise of welcome was a strong lure for both the humans buffeted by the surrounding chaos, and especially for the recent influx of immigrant agents from south of the border. After NAFTA's implementation and the subsequent devaluation of the peso, not only had Mexico experienced martial strife, but the paranormal war between good and evil in that country had taken a decidedly ominous turn. One had only to watch the soaring crime rate, the corruption of government officials, and staggering poverty to realize the balance between the two opposing sides had been toppled, and that any agents of Light still alive in the larger cities would have to flee.

So watch was exactly what Warren did. Because something about Vegas drew the transient and displaced.

Mass would be an unnecessary ritual to those fleeing

agents, but it'd also be familiar, comforting. And if one of them were looking for an ally—someone to perhaps rebuild a troop in this gambler's paradise—then the most visible cathedral in the city was an obvious place to meet.

But troop 175 was already staked out in this glittering valley, and Warren was their leader, so in his eyes, once these displaced agents left their city of origin they became independents . . . or rogues, as he called them. How they got that way, and the fact that they'd once been agents of Light, was of no interest to him. He'd eradicate the valley of the rogues, and the threat they posed to his troop, even if he had to do it one by one.

Zoe glanced at the steel and concrete sign to the right of the holy family. The Guardian Angel had mass scheduled for midnight, which meant it had just ended. There were a few stragglers around the pyramid-shaped building, mostly couples, but they were all exiting. Of the two men she saw entering, one was clergy and the other was with a woman who obviously had the place confused with the all-night wedding chapel. Zoe waited.

Finally her gaze locked on a lone man, hands shoved deep in the pockets of his baggy jeans, the open shirttails of his embroidered Guayabera flapping in the wind. He was young, with smooth olive skin, his heritage decidedly Latin. Zoe straightened and called out to him, smiling brightly, waving him closer. He hesitated, but redirected after a moment.

"Hey, buddy. Got a light?"

He tilted his head, and if he was an agent he'd have scented her out by now—a human, a lone female, no threat. "No in-glés," he said, turning his pockets inside out. "No money."

Zoe sighed and rolled her eyes. Damned newcomers. They all thought hooking was legal in Vegas. "*Dame fuego,*" she said to him, and mimed bringing a cigarette to her lips.

His expression cleared, and he colored even under the kiss of his golden complexion, but his shoulders relaxed a fraction and he dug into his shirt pocket and withdrew a lighter. It was one of the millions sold on the Boulevard, the infamous WELCOME TO LAS VEGAS sign stamped on one side. She flicked him a mildly flirtatious glance from beneath her glasses and bent forward as he flicked the lighter's wheel. It flared on the second try and Zoe caught the smooth gleam of his fingertips, unmarred in the wavering light. Like hers. Like all agents.

Her voice was a throaty purr as she blew smoke up and out. "Gracias, señor . . . ?"

"Solamente Carlos," he said almost shyly, and Zoe felt a momentary pang of regret, knowing what awaited him on the other side of those doors.

"Gracias, Carlos," she said, and let him go anyway, watching him disappear beneath the giant blue mosaic depicting a guardian angel, and God's eye. She had her own problems. And after two full minutes she stubbed her cigarette out beneath her heel and followed Carlos inside to face one of them.

The Mexican agent was nowhere in sight when Zoe entered the Cathedral. She glanced at the spot Warren generally favored, closest to the bishop's chair at the front of the sanctuary, but the pews were empty so he either wasn't in the building, or he was already trailing the rogue agent. Tiptoeing across the white marble floor, she ducked into the chapel of the Blessed Sacrament. While there, she lit a prayer candle. It couldn't hurt.

Thirty seconds later she grinned grimly as a yell ricocheted through the cavernous building, followed by a startled yelp. She stopped grinning at the report of running footfalls down the sanctuary's center aisle . . . four pair, she determined, not two. A Spanish curse spiraled to the building's apex, and if this had been a Baptist church the agent would probably already be burning in hell. But that wasn't what bothered Zoe. Getting to Warren had just gotten twice as tough.

Mortals often witnessed paranormal conflict, though the victorious agents made sure none ever remembered it. Sometimes the humans would wake the next morning swearing it'd all been a dream, or that their dinner the night before hadn't quite agreed with them. Problem was, the memory of the entire twenty-four-hour period prior to the conflict was often erased along with the incident, and Zoe *needed* to remember. Her family's lineage depended on it.

Yet as she stood holding her breath next to the outstretched arms of the blessed mother, all she remembered was what it was like to be *super*. How she could sneak up behind any man or woman and have them unconscious before they took their next breath. How she'd laugh about it afterwards. Now that she'd been stripped of the ability, and was on the receiving end of the body blows, she didn't find it quite as amusing.

Taking a deep breath, she edged around the white marble wall.

The fight was centered in the middle of the Cathedral, though to say that Zoe was watching it would be deceiving. She ripped the faux glasses from her face and shoved them in her pocket. No prescription would allow her to follow these events . . . what she needed to do was *cease* seeing. Let her vision blur as if she was trying to look at one of those puzzles where images were hidden within a picture.

Even still, she only caught brief flashes of action; a limb flying outward before disappearing again, a fist clenching before plowing from sight. The man who wrote the manuals of Shadow and Light had once tried to explain to Zoe how the agents' actions came to him. His inspiration, he said, came in blurred images and it was up to his imagination to supply the rest. Only now did Zoe understand what he meant. It was like flipping through one of those children's books where the cartoon figure became animated the faster the pages turned, only in the life-sized version a few of the panels were missing.

Forcing her gaze to sharpen again, she turned away from the action. Every instinct she had was screaming at her to remain hidden, but she had to trust what she knew of Warren and hope it still held true. He'd be at the center of the melee, and his two companions would be too focused on him to spy Zoe creeping in from the perimeter. Once again, she stilled her breath and began inching forward along the triangular walls. Unlike those involved in the paranormal fight, she moved achingly slow. When in fight mode, agents locked in on quick-moving objects, like eagles soaring over a desert canyon. Of course, Zoe had no delusions about not being caught. Her goal was only to be as close to Warren as possible when that happened.

She probably would have made it if not for the fluted candelabra and its tottery stand. What was it with these Catholics and their gold-plated tchotchkes? The room went still as they all whirled her way. The rogue agent's wild eyes widened in recognition while Warren's narrowed. Zoe didn't bother looking at the other two, she just burst into a full sprint, hoping the unexpected movement would give her time to reach Warren's side.

It worked. Closest, Warren had no choice but to give chase, leaving the rogue to his allies. Unfortunately, Zoe blinked—damned mortal eyes!—and the spot he'd been standing in a second earlier was empty.

Shit. She dropped to the floor, felt arms cushion her fall.

"My hero." It was their favorite endearment for one another, and she said it to no one. If she waited until she saw him it'd be too late.

As it happened, it already was. Warren's form solidified

as he froze, eyes widening in recognition, and then a blur—
the blow slowing—but it was too late to stop entirely. Warren's shocked image shattered as darkness enfolded her in
inky arms, numbness shooting through her body. Strangely,
though, the disappearance into herself was more peace than
she'd known since the last time she'd seen his face.

Chapter 3

The lights in the roadside cafe would've been bright no matter what the circumstances. But with a knot the size of a walnut on her skull, and said knot throbbing like a teen's heart on prom night, they were absolutely blinding.

Zoe pushed away from the ripped vinyl of the red bench, wiped the drool from the corner of her mouth, and faced her three captors. "I can't believe you guys are still coming to this dive. The cook spits in the soup, you know."

"Jesus, it really is her!" The man on Warren's left gaped, dropping his cheap coffee cup back in its saucer with a clatter.

Zoe lifted a glass of water and pressed it to her aching forehead. "Hello, Gregor. Walk beneath any ladders lately?"

He shook his head, his smile almost as wide as his bulky body. Gregor wasn't very tall, but he had the neck of three men put together, and the shoulder span of an angel's wings. He was bald, with one small hoop earring that made him look like a modern-day pirate, and had a superstitious nature to match. "Haven't stepped on any cracks in the side-walk, either. Damn, Zoe, but it's good to see you."

"And worth losing that rogue agent back at the Cathedral," agreed the woman to Warren's right. Zoe smiled at Phaedre. She was the same age as Nurse Nancy, though the similarities stopped there. Actually, thought Zoe, they'd probably ceased in their twenties because that's how old Phaedre looked. Like a twenty-something party girl with lowlights in her mahogany mane and a smile deadly all on its own. The weapon tucked between her ample cleavage helped, though. "Welcome back."

"She's not back."

An uncomfortable silence bloomed and Zoe's heart plummeted. She shifted her gaze to Warren's, meeting head-on the anger she saw living there. His baggy clothing made him look slim, almost slight, but beneath it he was sinewy and tough, though Zoe knew the skin that covered all that compact muscle was as soft as her own. He'd have looked boyish with his short hair springing from his head in straight brown tufts, except that his eyes were hard and knowing, calculating as they rested on Zoe. It was his choice whether to accept her back in the troop or not but that wasn't what he was talking about. Of anyone, Warren knew Zoe never changed her mind . . . or went back.

The waitress's arrival saved her from answer, and the woman let her disinterested gaze travel over Zoe's face, lingering where the throbbing was the worst. "Your girlfriend finally come to?" she asked needlessly, snapping gum the same pepto-pink as her uniform. "Get you some coffee, sweetie?"

Zoe pursed her lips. Why not? Her funds were low, and despite Warren's current appearance—he seemed to be dressed as some sort of street bum this time—he could afford it. Besides, he owed her for the knock on the head. She nodded. "That'd be good. And a short stack . . . side of bacon."

The waitress pulled her pen from behind her ear, and wrote down the order as she walked away. Zoe assumed everyone else had already eaten.

She returned her eyes to Warren, still waiting for her to explain herself. So she did. "I need your help."

Phaedre looked concerned, Gregor interested. Warren continued to stare warily. If she was hurting him by not apologizing—if she'd hurt him by leaving without saying goodbye—he was hiding it well. But it was a superficial sort of hidden; like an alligator stirring up sediment beneath a brackish surface, and Zoe couldn't help wondering when it'd strike.

She made them wait until her food had arrived and she'd gotten a good bellyful before telling them. If she had to chase them out of the cafe begging for help, she wanted to do it on a full stomach. Surprisingly, when she finished the telling—a mortal child had been stolen by the Shadows, and she needed to get her back—they were still there. Cool. She signaled the waitress for a refill.

"So, there must be something special about this child," Warren finally said, cupping his elbow in his hands as he leaned forward. "I mean, to bring you out of retirement."

Zoe ignored his emphasis of the last word, and sipped at her coffee as she shook her head. "I was in the wrong place at the right time. I saw the Shadows take her."

"Didn't you try to stop them?"

"There were probably too many, right?"

Zoe didn't meet Phaedre's eye, or answer Gregor's question. They didn't know about her mortality—they probably thought she was wearing masking pheromones, and that's why they couldn't scent her. She didn't want to relieve them of that notion. Not just yet.

"There were three of them. I was alone."

But Warren could tell she was holding back.

Always holding back, Zoe! Always with the secrets and the lies!

Still Zoe didn't consider for one second telling him about Joanna or the attack her daughter had endured just because the Shadows had scented Zoe on her . . . *in* her. The Seer had been very clear: No one could know about these girls . . . these future Archers. The knowledge could one day be used against them all. Thus, beating against Warren's unspoken accusation was a prophecy that ruled Zoe's days:

You must do it alone.

So she silently willed him to understand that she was still the woman he'd once loved, still Light, but his returned silence was critical, like he sensed her desperation, and he probably did. The unease sitting on both Phaedre's and Gregor's faces told her they did as well. Zoe's lukewarm coffee soured in her belly and straightening, she pushed her cup away.

"Are you going to help me or not?" she said shortly.

"Of course—" Phaedre started.

"Why should I?" Warren interrupted. Not *we*. Phaedre's mouth snapped shut.

"Isn't it obvious?" Zoe said, his imperious tone making her own voice tight. "You're the one with the power."

And don't forget who the hell helped put you in that position, she thought, blood beginning to boil.

"What's obvious," he said flatly, "is that you're doing another one of your disappearing acts, and you want us to clean up after you."

"That's not it at all."

"Oh, really?"

"Warren—"

"Shut up, Gregor." Warren shook off the other man's hand without looking at him and threw Zoe's purse at her. "All your ID is different. You've altered your appearance, hid your scent beneath a masking compound—"

"I'm not hiding it!" Zoe finally exploded, gripping the edge of the Formica table so hard her fingers ached. "I'm human!"

They all fell still, and Zoe felt herself redden.

"I have no power," she said, more normally. "Think about it, smell and watch, and you'll know it's true. I couldn't cross into another reality right now if it unfurled in front of me like the yellow brick road."

Gregor's mouth fell open. "No . . . my God . . ."

The disbelief in his voice had her dropping her head. Only another agent could understand exactly what she'd lost.

Phaedre was just as shocked. "Zoe, what happened? Did the Shadows find you? Steal your *chi?* Make you relinquish it in return for your life?"

Because all those things had happened before to other agents, though not in this troop. Not to anyone under Warren's watch. Zoe nodded. "How else could you sneak up on me without me even batting an eyelash?"

"I was wondering that myself," Gregor murmured, falling back in the booth.

Zoe was so busy reading the pity in his eyes that when her head whipped back, the open-palmed slap coming at her from nowhere, the sting of it had her gasping. The blood that sprayed from her nose had Gregor and Phaedre doing the same.

Pressing her napkin to her face, head tilted back, she regarded Warren over the top of it. "I'd make you pay for that," she said, voice muffled, "but you'd see it coming a mile away."

Warren blanched, which cheered her a bit. "What have you done?" he asked, his whisper ragged at the edges.

"I gave my power away," she said, with more composure than she felt.

"Why? To whom?"

"To someone who needed it more than I did." To someone, she didn't say, we'd all need before long.

"Brave," said Gregor, fingering the inverted gold horseshoe shining from a thick chain around his neck.

"Heroic," Phaedre agreed, on an awed whisper.

"Stupid," Warren said. He shook his head, his expression again shuttered. "Why do you always have to be so stupid?"

Zoe's jaw ached from the effort to hold her tongue and temper. She wouldn't get into a pissing contest with Warren just because he was still nursing hurt feelings. He could deal with those himself. She'd had to. "Look," she said, pushing her cup aside to lean forward on her elbows. "The baby's mortal. We're still in the business of protecting mortals, right? Or are we only interested in slaughtering rogue agents who are doing nothing more than looking for sanctuary?"

Warren colored at that. Good. She was useless physically, but at least her words still had some sting. "*We* protect mortals. You are a mortal."

"Warren," Phaedre chided.

Zoe shrugged like it didn't matter. "That may be . . . but I'm still Light."

Warren just quirked a brow, and when it was apparent he'd do no more than that, Phaedre reached out and patted Zoe's arm. "Of course you are."

Gregor put his giant palm on her other arm, glaring at Warren. They all stared at him, linked and acting as one— even though he was their leader—daring him to tell the Archer of the Zodiac no.

For a moment she thought he'd hit her again. She didn't have to scent his emotions to know how angry he was. "Fine," he finally said, voice frighteningly low. "But let's get one thing straight. You're just baggage, Zoe. You're no good to us—" She flinched; to *me,* he was saying, "—to anyone. We'll get back this precious mortal for you, but after that you disappear for good. And you formally relinquish your star sign."

Zoe sucked in a breath. Formally renouncing her star sign meant another agent born under the Sagittarius moon would fill her place on the Zodiac, in the troop. It would void her lineage forever, and nullify everything she'd sacrificed.

And that just wouldn't do.

But Warren didn't need to know that. So she held her in-drawn breath, and inclined her head. And Warren was just arrogant enough—and angry and righteous, too—not to insist she do it right then and there. He shot the three of them a grim, closed-mouth smile, then threw down his napkin and rose. "Fine. Let's work it out."

Gregor shot Zoe a relieved smile before following, and Phaedre took her hand, helping her up. Zoe wanted to thank her but didn't know if her voice would hold. Besides, just because they said they were going to help didn't mean they could do it.

The Shadow and the Light had been battling in the valley ever since Vegas was just an X on some prospector's map. Each side was comprised of twelve agents—one for each sign on the western Zodiac—and when both sides were full there was balance in the mortal realm. People were then free to make personal and societal decisions uninfluenced by paranormal nudges meant to bring out the shadow or light lurking in their own souls.

As tempting as it sometimes was to interfere in the world's human dramas, agents of Light worldwide had fought to preserve the gift of choice for too many centuries to blithely disregard it. The Shadows, conversely, specialized in that, which gave them a distinct advantage over the mortal realm; it was far easier to cause heartache and mayhem than clean up the resulting mess.

Zoe's life work, before she threw it away, had been to neutralize this advantage. She'd grown up idolizing the elder agents, devouring the manuals that depicted the fight between good and evil. From the moment she'd undergone metamorphosis at the age of twenty-five, coming into her full powers, she'd dedicated her life to infiltrating the Shadow organization. She was patient, wickedly sharp, and determined to use whatever resources she had to fell her enemies: her strength, her craftiness, and eventually her body. She'd spent more years than she cared to remember using that last tool . . . but an effective weapon it'd turned out to be.

So Warren had no right to complain about the means by which she garnered her information or stalked her prey. Hadn't she always reminded him that no matter whose bed she woke in, her heart remained solely with him? "It's what I was born to do," she told him, years ago when they were both still young and arrogant enough to think philosophically about the whole thing. "It's what I'm good at."

And Warren knew it. Maybe, Zoe thought now, that was the problem.

"The child is how premature?" asked the troop's physician, Micah, over the car phone's speakers. They'd called him on the way to the real McCormicks' residence, hoping he'd be able to better deduce where the Shadows would have taken the child. "Well, the nurse—though an imposter—was right. Children can be saved at twenty-four weeks, though it'd help if she were an initiate. One born to the Zodiac is naturally more resilient than a mortal infant."

Zoe knew that, which was why she wasn't as concerned about the child's health as much as her *continued* health.

"So they're hiding her, incubating her, keeping her safe from discovery—"

"Not exactly news to us," Warren snapped, hands tight on the steering wheel. The dueling sides of the Zodiac were constantly shifting their appearances, their occupations, and haunts. Settle in one place too long and you were just begging for a paranormal ambush. As Zoe had discovered.

"Geez," came Micah's voice from over the speakers. "Someone woke up on the wrong side of reality today."

Gregor and Phaedre snickered in the backseat, but Zoe kept staring out the window, careful to keep her expression neutral.

Micah continued before Warren could reply. "We have a couple of locations scouted out. Nothing confirmed yet," he added quickly, and there was a shuffling of paperwork as he searched for the addresses, then read them aloud. Two were located on Charleston, a street where the single-family homes of the seventies had given way to medical and legal offices along both sides of the streets. The third was downtown.

They thanked Micah and hung up as they pulled to a stop in front of a modest two-story in an enclave of middle-class homes. Zoe stepped out onto the walkway, stretching in the morning light, thinking the neighborhood was a good fit for the couple she'd seen grieving the night before. Comfortable, yet without ostentation; orderly, but still welcoming.

Zoe grabbed the briefcase she'd retrieved from her car on the way over, and started up the walk. She halted halfway, causing Warren to plow into and then steady her, though he released her as soon as he'd done so. That fueled her indignation, adding a sting to her words. "Where do you think you're going?"

"You're not going in there without me," he replied, just as coolly, his light brown eyes hardening on hers as Phaedre and Gregor joined them on the walk. Zoe made a point of looking him up and down, taking in his ratty trench coat, tattered hems, and mussed hair. All that was missing was the cardboard sign around his neck.

"Why? You want to scare the poor people to death?" She smiled when he scowled, adding, "Besides, you smell."

His mouth worked wordlessly at that, and a furious blush stained his chapped cheeks. Zoe would've laughed . . . if she weren't so pissed. She'd brought this case to them, and now he was acting like she couldn't be trusted to convincingly play her part.

Gregor, sensing an argument brewing, quickly threw in his two cents. "She's right, Hog. You're as ripe as a maggoty brisket."

Fuming, Warren looked from Zoe to Gregor, then over at Phaedre.

"You stink," she confirmed, and the three of them headed up the sidewalk without him. Even with her mortal hearing Zoe could hear Warren cursing as he returned to the car. Gregor shot her a smile as she rang the doorbell, and she grinned back. It felt good, knowing they were behind her, flanking her, trusting her. It wasn't until that moment that she realized how lonely she'd been.

It was the husband who answered the door. Zoe'd expected that, but what made her heart catch in her throat was the red rimming his eyes, making him look older than his thirty-six years. Making him look ill as well.

"Mr. McCormick, I'm Traci Malone. The caseworker for United Hospital. We spoke on the phone."

Recognition flashed through his eyes at her name, but it didn't brighten them. The guy looked like he'd been extinguished inside.

"Can we come in?" she asked, inching forward. The physical suggestion wasn't as powerful now that she was mortal, but he did take a small step back. "It's about your daughter."

And now the pain followed. He shook himself as if from a dream, and began to shut the door. "You haven't heard, then. We don't have a daughter."

"Ashlyn's alive, Mr. McCormick," Phaedre said, from behind Zoe.

The child's name was what stopped him. Zoe saw that. The rest took a moment to sink in.

"Honey? Who is it?" Andria McCormick must've been

crying all night. She appeared, pale skin blotchy, hair falling out of its loose ponytail, and wearing the same rumpled clothes she'd been in the night before.

"These . . . these people . . ." But Dennis couldn't finish. Fresh worry sprung into his wife's face as she studied his reaction. Then it iced over with protectiveness. Zoe knew then that she'd chosen right. This couple—their love and home—would've been perfect for her granddaughter. *Would be* perfect, she corrected, and straightened her shoulders.

"Mrs. McCormick, we have reason to believe your daughter was abducted from the hospital last night by a couple posing as you and—" Andie gasped as Dennis's head reared up, "—your husband. They were assisted by a nurse named Nancy Allen. May we please come in?"

By the time the McCormicks had led them through the living and dining rooms, Dennis had regained his wits enough to ask to see their credentials. Zoe handed him one of her social services cards, her eyes catching on a *Welcome Home, Ashlyn* banner draped over the glossy dining room table, while Gregor and Phaedre flashed detective badges. Andie then settled them in the cozy kitchen nook while she put on a fresh pot of coffee, and Dennis opened the shades, the morning light invading the darkened house in unrelenting streams. Zoe let her eyes pass over all the baby gear and followed Andie's movements as she pushed aside the preparations for the following day's Thanksgiving celebration, making way for a tray and five cups and saucers. Her attention, however, never strayed from her visitors.

Damn, but Zoe wanted this woman as Ashlyn's mother.

"What we need from you," she said, ten minutes later after telling them all she could about the previous night's events, "is to tell us everything you remember about the nurse who called you last night. Even the smallest detail might help us find her."

The McCormicks looked at one another desperately.

"Nothing stands out," Dennis finally admitted, running his hands over his chin. He looked more composed now, Zoe thought. He'd recovered fast, and concern had replaced his grief, anger superseding his worry. "We wouldn't have noticed another couple, and the birth mother didn't want to meet us, so we never met any of her nurses before either."

Gregor glanced up from where he was pretending to take notes. "Did she try to convince you to have the child moved to another facility? A clinic . . . a private practice?"

Dennis shook his head, glancing at his wife again. She did the same. "Nobody expected the baby to be born so early, though there was clearly a chance of that. Because of the birth mother's . . . trauma."

"Poor thing," Andie murmured, pouring more coffee all around. Zoe lifted her cup to hide her expression, knowing Phaedre and Gregor would've scented the bump in her nerves. This woman's life had just been ripped at the seams and she still had sympathy to spare for her Jo-baby. Sometimes, she thought sighing, she really wondered who was superhuman.

Dennis ignored his coffee, rising instead to pace. "We got the call around eleven last night telling us the baby was coming. We rushed right down, but by the time we arrived it was . . . she said it was too late. I—I don't remember anything after that."

Zoe nearly wept.

"I do."

Four pairs of eyes fastened firmly on Andie's pretty, determined face, and she rewarded them with a tight smile. "The nurse, Nancy, gave me a card. Said I could call her next week to find out the exact cause of death . . . or if I just needed to talk." The smile turned bitter. "I hugged her and thanked her for her kindness."

"Mrs. McCormick," Gregor said, while everyone else held their breath. "Do you still have that card?"

She pushed her chair back and stood with a small, victorious toss of her head. "You bet I do."

The address matched one of those Micah had given them. Phaedre and Gregor disappeared with a hasty goodbye to the McCormicks, leaving Zoe to wind things up . . . and leaving her alone with Warren afterwards. He was waiting at the corner—the others had taken the car—and they fell in stride without speaking, she walking normally, he with the limp from a blow that'd almost killed him years before. As if knowing her thoughts, Warren accelerated his pace. He'd hardly feel it, but knowing she was mortal, he'd also know she would. She gritted her teeth and bore it. The next persona she donned would just have to be extremely fit.

"So what happened to your car salesman identity?" Zoe finally asked, when she couldn't stand the silence any longer.

"What always happens," he answered shortly.

The Shadows had discovered it. "Which one?"

"Taurus."

It figured. That was Warren's sign, too, and if an agent's identity was going to be found out it was usually their opposing Zodiac sign who did it. Just like the old saying, opposites attract. "Breca?"

He nodded, before a clearly satisfied smile overtook his face. "The new one is named Graham."

But when Zoe smiled back, Warren caught himself and turned away. She bit her lip and increased her pace.

"It's your birthday," he said, staring back at a man in a pickup who'd slowed to stare at him. He grinned grimly when the pickup sped away. Both the look and the statement were typical Warren—no preamble or apology or emotion— and it was totally different than wishing her a happy birthday. Zoe was surprised he'd acknowledged it at all.

She shrugged, not wanting him to know the day was any

more significant for her than any other mortal. Most didn't share the day with their firstborn daughter and granddaughter. Besides, she knew he was just warming up, and if she waited he'd finally come around to the heart of the matter.

"Why would you give up your *chi,* Zoe?" he asked, stopping in his tracks.

Because I love my daughter even more than I loved being a heroine. She turned to face him and leaned against a streetlamp. "For the troop, Warren," she answered truthfully. "And its future."

"Bullshit. You've never done anything unless there was something personal at stake as well." He pressed when he saw Zoe's jaw tighten. "Then again, getting out from under my command would qualify, wouldn't it?"

"It's not always about you, Warren," she said, and let the fatigue she felt bloom around her. She knew what it would smell like to him; apples just past their ripeness, and a soft-petaled flower wilting in the sun.

As expected, he pounced. "What happened? Get tired of bouncing from bed to bed?"

She blanched even in the harsh morning light. "You're lucky I'm mortal," she whispered.

"Don't hide behind that."

And don't let him bait you, she told herself as he limped past her so that she, again, had to follow. Because as long as she was doing the right thing, it didn't matter what he thought. He'd know the truth in time. She just wished she could see his face when he discovered how wrong he'd been.

So she swallowed her retort and tried again. "Speaking of hiding, how'd you go from being a salesman to a vagrant? Was becoming a walking cesspool your only choice?"

Stubbornly, he kept limping along. "I chose it because it's the exact opposite of everything you'd want me to be."

"Warren, please," She stopped walking and sighed. "You don't mean that."

He whirled so fast all she saw was the blurred hem of his trench coat. "I do," he said, almost violently. His face was contorted, all the pain he'd been hiding and the anger he'd stored twisting it into a jumble of emotion. His brown eyes were murky and cold. "You're toxic, Zoe. You even believe your own lies. You say 'love' and you mean 'hate.' You don't even know what it means to work as a team or troop. All you know is deceit."

She wouldn't let him get to her or bait her, she swore. And she wasn't going to fucking apologize. Warren had known what he was getting into the first time he'd climbed into her bed. She'd kicked his ass in enough training sessions for him to have no illusions about that. And after? They'd spoken clearly of what they'd give and how far they'd go to conquer the Shadows. They'd give it their all. It wasn't her fault he'd changed his mind about her, or the men she'd already targeted.

Because there had been other men. Two, to be exact. She'd stayed with the last, Xavier Archer, for sixteen years, a mortal who was the human lackey to the Shadows' leader, a man who traded information—and lives—for power and money. That was Olivia's father.

But the first man—if you could call him that—had been the Shadow leader himself. And Zoe knew it was this relationship that bothered Warren the most. Fooling a mortal was one thing—even humans could lie adeptly to one another—but deceiving the Shadow leader took uncommon nerve. Someone with Zoe's particular skills.

She never had found out what Warren found most irritating. That she'd faithfully return to his bed after months of lying in another man's embrace, or that he, just as faithfully, would let her?

All she knew was that every time she returned to the sanctuary they'd end up yelling at one another until their throats were raw. So she never told him when the Tulpa got her pregnant. Or, after she'd changed her identity to go back undercover, when Xavier did the same two years later. Her daughters were hers alone. Not pawns to be bargained with, manipulated, or—God forbid—destroyed because of Warren's jealousy, spite, or sense of duty.

But all of that was in the past, back when she still thought she could make a difference. When she thought she was invincible. Back, she thought as Warren stalked on ahead of her, when she believed she and this smelly, stubborn, and impossibly *good* man still had a future together.

They trudged on in silence.

Chapter 4

Nurse Nancy's real name was Melania. She was the Shadow Zodiac's Libra, firstborn daughter of Treya, granddaughter of Patrice the Cruel, and by the time Zoe learned all this, Nancy was also dead. Not only had she been working at the decoy clinic whe ı Phaedre and Gregor got there, but she'd been alone.

The only problem with this? She was alone. No child, and no faux adoptive parents. But before Phaedre killed her with a fire-tipped wand that burrowed through flesh to incinerate her core, she "convinced" Melania to tell her where they'd taken the babe.

"The Tulpa's house," Gregor reported back, when they'd all gathered at the Smoking Gun Inn, a battered roadside motel dumped conveniently in the middle of town. "And most of the Shadow Zodiac is gathered there as well."

Zoe's head shot up. "That's odd. The Tulpa never allows the Shadows into his home. Or he didn't when I was with him."

And if he'd changed that practice in the years since, Zoe

would've ferreted the information out of Xavier, either with alcohol or sex or both. So it was a recent development. But like the others, she could now only guess at the reasons why.

Yet even odder than that . . . "Why would the Shadow leader take a mortal child into his home?" Warren wondered.

Because she's the granddaughter of his most hated enemy.

"I don't know," Zoe lied, keeping her eyes downcast, weaving the wide straw she'd made Warren stop for at the crafts store on the long walk back to the Inn that afternoon. He'd raised a brow but hadn't asked her why, pretending not to care.

Who knew? Maybe he really didn't by now.

She shrugged off the weight of his gaze and let them debate the pros and cons of risking their lives for one mortal child, keeping her hands moving in an even to-and-fro, like she had nothing vested in the outcome. She'd already made up her mind, so the particulars of their actions interested, but wouldn't affect her.

"Whatever you're doing," Warren said suddenly, "it's not going to work."

Her lips curved—leave it to him to know she wasn't merely weaving—but she didn't stop. Instead she said, "Did you know another name for the cornucopia is 'the horn of plenty'? In the past people would fill it up with fruit, nuts, and seasonal vegetables, and offer it as a blessing when visiting a neighbor's home."

"Zoe—" He sang her name, turning it into a long warning.

She went on, not looking up. "But before that tradition, it was a part of the ancient harvest festivals. See, bringing in the harvest meant stripping the land bare, which left the spirit that lived amongst the crop homeless. A corn dolly—or idol as it was more popularly known—would act as the spirit's receptacle for the winter, until the idol could be furrowed under again at the start of the new season."

Yet in Greek mythology it was a goat's horn, and had the power to give its possessor whatever she wished for. How convenient that it was now associated with Thanksgiving, a holiday—or holy day—that the Tulpa considered one of the best. An extremely superstitious being, he believed celebrations, like ceremonies, gave shape to the days and years of mortals, making their actions nice and predictable as they clung to their rituals. He used to say it kept them in their place, and he loved it when events conformed to his expectations. He banked on it.

Of course, Zoe had already blown that expectation once—blown it like an A-bomb—so she wasn't expecting a joyous reunion. And showing up on his doorstep on Thanksgiving Day was the least expected thing she could do.

But the more she thought about it, the more she was sure it would work. Because though the design of the universe was intricate and mysterious, nothing was left to accident. Here she thought she was powerless to influence anything of import due to her mortality, but by weaving this basket herself, by imbuing her work with her *intent* and passionate belief, she was doing the one thing all humans had the power to do. She was turning her deepest desires into reality.

After all, wasn't that what the man who created the Tulpa had done?

So all she had to do was believe in this task just as strongly as he had. Strongly enough to bend the universe to her will. And that's what *she* had specialized in when she was a troop member, she thought, gritting her teeth. Bending others to her will.

"Thanksgiving is an opportunity," she murmured, more to herself than the others now. "The holiday gives me an opening. The Tulpa will be fixed on gaining power from all the emotions associated with the holiday—hope, joy, *thankfulness*— things humans believe unerringly in. He'll never sense my true intent above all the emotional static. It's perfect."

And she fell back into the rhythm of the weaving, visualizing it now, everything else secondary to what she wanted.

"It's not perfect," Warren broke in. "It's suicide."

She didn't look up; her fingers continued their smooth slide-and-weave, and the basket began taking shape. "Chin up, Warren. At least this time you'll know for sure what happened to me."

He dropped a strong palm over her hands, stilling them. "You're not going. Hear me?"

She remained still, head bowed, voice soft. "I've always heard you, Warren."

He removed his hand quickly. "Then you'll have no problem obeying when I order you to give up your star sign. Tonight."

"I said I heard you." She did look up now, her voice cold as his. "I didn't say I listened."

And he knew that, too.

Warren's chin shot up, and the eyes that'd once followed her every move with an earthy softness were now petrified in an equally unyielding face. "See that she doesn't leave this room . . . even if you have to tie her down."

Zoe returned to her weaving as the door slammed behind him.

"Oh, Zoe," Phaedre said, running her hands through her rich hair on a sigh. "Your plan was to show up on the Shadow leader's doorstep on Thanksgiving Day, clothed in mortality, and bearing a gift cursed with ill intent?"

Zoe shrugged, ignoring Phaedre's use of the past tense. So it didn't sound like such a great plan when stated like that. But she would still go through with it. "I'll charm him into opening his door for me."

Because if she could get inside, get him alone for even a moment, it would work. Getting in without getting killed might be more of a problem.

Phaedre had turned her back, ostensibly fixing her hair in

the dresser mirror, but Zoe knew she was studying her. "Except this time he'll be on his guard. He'll sense an attack coming a mile away. He'll be expecting it from you."

"He'll drop that guard once he sees my humanity. My vulnerability." She said the words to convince herself as much as Phaedre, flipping the straw horn on her lap, starting a new row. "Everyone is always on their guard around him—"

"Because he's the psycho kingpin of the paranormal underworld."

"—and he hates it." She looked up to meet Phaedre's disbelieving stare through the mirrored pane. "He does. It's one of the reasons he loved me."

Phaedre turned. "You weren't on guard because you'd already gained his confidence."

"And so when I say I changed my mind and ran away from the agents of Light, he'll believe I've been hiding from you all these years, not him. He'll believe what he's always wanted to when he looks at me."

Phaedre leaned against the dresser, crossing her arms. "And what is that?"

"That I love him," she said, setting the corn idol aside. "That we're destined for one another."

"Zoe—"

"Trust me, Phaedre." She stood, brushed off her pants, and headed to the door Warren had exited through.

The movement was quicker than the human eye, so Zoe found herself sprawled facedown across the bed without knowing how she'd gotten there. Phaedre was straddling her, so close Zoe could scent the mint on her breath and the powder of her perfume; pleasant, were it not for the wand tip pointed at Zoe's throat.

"Warren said you stay," Phaedre murmured in her ear, meaning the bodily assault wasn't anything personal.

Zoe craned her neck to peer into Phaedre's face, despite the risk of a fiery death. "And what the troop leader says goes, right?"

Annoyance flickered behind Phaedre's jewel-green eyes. "I understand it might grate, Zoe, especially considering your former status, but maybe it's time you listened to someone other than yourself."

Zoe dropped her head and lay limp, knowing she'd get up only when—if—Phaedre allowed it. "You want to put your conduit away? It's a bit of overkill."

Phaedre shifted atop her, but that was for her comfort, not Zoe's. She inched the wand closer to Zoe's left eye, her favored point of insertion. "Bother you, does it? Make you nervous? Because the Tulpa doesn't have a conduit, you know. He *is* a conduit. A whole being through whom energy is conducted, amassed, multiplied. That's why he can affect the weather, move things with his mind, manipulate environments and—most importantly—read your intentions."

"I know all this," Zoe said, testily. She twisted again and this time Phaedre got up, letting her turn. "I'm the one who told the rest of you, remember?"

"So then you also know that he's been working on the time/space continuum, using special relativity to attempt to return to the past?"

Zoe pushed herself to her knees. It was evident from her silence that she hadn't known. So how had Phaedre? "The manuals?" Zoe guessed.

Phaedre inclined her head. "He's conducting experiments, gathering energy around him to return to the moment of his gravest betrayal. When you, Zoe, exposed *his* vulnerability."

"That's not possible," Zoe whispered, kneeling in the ratty bedspread, mind whirling. *Was it?*

Phaedre pursed her lips wryly as she rose and tucked her conduit back in her pocket. Zoe gave an inward sigh of relief.

"He thinks there's only a finite amount of energy available on this earth, in this valley in particular, and since he's bound to Las Vegas and can't derive energy from outside this city, he's working on creating more of it here, storing it. Hoarding it, if you will, for himself."

"And that's what he'd use it on?" Zoe asked, noting she looked as bewildered in the opposing dresser mirror as she felt. "Saving Wyatt?"

Phaedre laughed humorlessly and shook her head. "He's not going back to save his creator, Zoe. He's going back to kill you."

And even as Zoe's mind whirled with disbelief, she knew it could be done. Anything was possible, if the mind believed strongly enough . . . and the Tulpa possessed an iron mind. "He'd need a tremendous amount of energy," she murmured. So how was he getting it? What law of physics or powerful magic—or *both*—would enable him to contract time and alter the terrestrial setting?

Phaedre shrugged. "We haven't figured it out yet. All I know is if you show up on his doorstep, plain as day and clothed in mortal skin, you'll save him the trouble of having to find you in the recesses of time. And you'll die for nothing."

Not nothing, Zoe thought, standing. Because now she was more determined than ever to get her granddaughter back. Whatever the Tulpa was doing and however he was deriving power, she was sure it involved Ashlyn.

"I need to speak to Warren." Zoe started, then smiled grimly when Phaedre took a warning step forward. "He can hold me down himself if he's so inclined."

It was Phaedre's turn to smirk. "He just might," she said, but motioned to the door.

The manuals Zoe had referred to recorded the battle between good and evil in the Nevada desert as it'd gone on for the past millennium. In the mortal world the manuals were called comic books, and were devoured by the young minds that lived the stories out in their imaginations, and in turn, gave energy to the agents and troops through their detailed daydreams and belief. The connection between reader and agent was very much a partnership, and without one the other would fail to thrive.

So everything Zoe had done—both accomplishments and defeats—was recorded in either the Shadow manuals or the Light, depending on the sensitivity of the information there. Any knowledge that could give one side dominance over the other, thus unbalancing the Zodiac, was omitted. That's why Zoe's pregnancies hadn't been recorded on either side, and why neither the Tulpa nor Warren knew where she'd gone when she disappeared.

Thus, every agent had secrets they knew lay solely in their own minds, and even the most senior troop members couldn't help but wonder about their allies' lives as well as their enemies. What wasn't being revealed?

So what exactly were the manuals omitting about Zoe and her relationship with the angry, stubborn man on the other side of that door?

Well, it wasn't the part about the bond they'd forged growing up as teens in the paranormal safe house known as the sanctuary. The bloom of their subsequent love affair, around the time she was nineteen and he twenty-four, was also well-documented—much to their embarrassment at the time—as was the bloody coup that'd led to Warren's meteoric rise in rank to become the youngest troop leader ever. Zoe had been pictured firmly by his side.

No, the omissions began after all that, when Zoe herself had taken up her star sign and began to hunt the Tulpa, a task that would make her famous for her bravery, single-mindedness, and willingness to give up personal happiness in return for their enemy's blood. Maybe what angered

Warren most wasn't that she turned her back on him in order to fulfill these duties, but that the original assignment had been his idea. He'd ordered her into the Tulpa's lair and life—and bed—with his blessing. And in time it became his curse.

Because the manuals *did* record how good she was at her job. They showed in exacting detail how clearly the Tulpa, and later Xavier, fell for her ruse. Soon, every small, helpful, important detail she brought back about the Shadows' plans and machinations was met by her troop leader's knowing and bitter sneer. Eventually Zoe stopped coming back at all.

So the wedge between the two former lovers grew with time, expanding with secrets until the girth that lay between them was too wide for either of them to attempt crossing. And when Zoe disappeared this final time—after the daughter Warren knew nothing about had been brutalized by the Shadow Aquarian—she hadn't even considered telling him why she was leaving, where she was going, or what she intended to do. She didn't want to argue, and besides, she barely knew the answers herself.

All that mattered now was that Joanna and Olivia were safe. She'd given up her *chi* and her place in the troop to ensure it. And now she would hunker in close by, watchful, as she'd failed to be the first time, and wait for the moment when Joanna would rise up and stake her claim in the Zodiac. Because Zoe's greatest secret wasn't merely omitted from the manuals, it was the one the Seer had told her never to utter, not to Warren, not even aloud to herself.

Her eldest daughter was both Shadow and Light, and when she was ready and had overcome the tragedy that would shape her future, she would be mightier than all of them put together.

So Warren and Zoe didn't have a love story that began with "Once upon a time." And, inevitably, it wouldn't end with "happily ever after" either. But Zoe had a job to do, and she was still enough of a heroine to see it through to the end.

"Are you ready to listen?" Zoe began, moving across Warren's dim motel room. He'd stiffened as he sensed her presence, but hadn't looked up from the paper he was pretending to read.

"I'm ready to *hear* you."

Touché, thought Zoe, with a wry smile. She crossed the dingy room to stand in front of his chair. Hearing was a start.

"You need to let me do this."

"Why?"

"Because I can. Because I'm the *only* one who can. The holiday doesn't just give me an excuse, it's a powerful time. The holy days join the old world beliefs with the new. The possibilities that opens up are endless."

He lifted one shoulder, unwilling to admit she was right. "Christmas is coming up. The troop can figure something out by then."

But Zoe had to get Ashlyn out of there now. "Let me do this. I'm already on the outside. Why risk the life of an active star sign when you have me ready to go in willingly?"

"Why do you care so much about this one mortal child?"

"Because *I'm* mortal!" She pounded her chest, then clenched her fist at her side. "It's all I have, don't you see? This life, this skin, the breath in my lungs, it's all that separates me from death."

"And yet you're so willing to give it up," Warren said, watching her now. "Because that's what you're asking to do. One foot on the Tulpa's doorstep, and he'll slay you where you stand."

"Because I betrayed his love?" she asked.

"Yes."

"You haven't killed me," she pointed out.

Because her betrayal of him—their betrayal of each

other—had been greater and deeper than any ruse concocted to topple their enemies.

Warren swallowed hard. "I've wished you dead."

"And I, you," she said matter-of-factly, stepping closer. Warren opened his mouth, but she put a finger to his lips and held it there. "It's not the same thing, and I'm willing to bet my life that the Tulpa feels the same."

His face crumpled in on itself and he shook off her touch. "You would compare me to *him?*"

"I didn't mean that—"

"You said it. Which means you were thinking it. And we both know it's the thought that counts, don't we?"

That's what they'd told one another when she had returned to his arms, his bed. It was the thought that counted most. It was the most powerful thing in the universe.

"Warren . . ." she began to protest, but stopped.

"What?" he said shortly.

"You're right," Zoe said, and the surprise that flashed across his face must have mirrored her own. She laughed mirthlessly. "Maybe I am toxic. But I had to stop feeling anything for anyone in the time I was with the Tulpa. I couldn't just turn it back on when I returned to the sanctuary. I had to close down because I needed to save a small place inside of me that was mine alone." She'd been a possession, she remembered with a shudder, she'd belonged entirely to the Tulpa. "Sometimes I even forgot why I was there—that I was even, or ever had been, super."

She backed up and sank to the edge of the bed, realizing for the first time that it was true. She'd disappeared into her role as the Tulpa's woman and instead of remembering that she had chosen to be there—that she could choose to leave—she'd begun to feel small and weak, like a shell with only the pretty memory of something vital living inside. As for her idea of love, well, the Tulpa had twisted that as well. She'd had to stop feeling real love at all just to survive it.

Zoe looked up when she felt Warren's weight drop down beside her. "Whatever he took from you, Zoe, you gave willingly. You had to have seen and felt it happening."

"So did you," she said sharply, wiping at her eyes.

"And what was I supposed to do?" he shifted, putting distance between them without really moving. "I couldn't contact you, and even if I did I couldn't order your withdrawal, nullifying all the years you'd put in up to that point. Do you realize you've spent more accumulated years outside of the sanctuary than in it? You grew up there, but it's not your home. Your home is your will and desire, and what you want. It's all that matters. It's all that ever mattered."

She turned toward him, and after a long moment, lifted her tear-streaked face to his. "You mattered."

It wasn't what he'd expected, and he jerked back before he could stop himself. She stayed him with a hand on his arm, and when he didn't shake it off—just swallowed hard as he saw her intent—she shifted closer. Ran her hand up his shoulder to curl around his neck. Used the same smooth, liquid motion she had before she was reduced to mortality to pinion around, above, and upon him; the weak cradling the strong as a tear raced down his moonlit cheek.

"You mattered," she whispered again, and wrapped her limbs around him so she wouldn't have to see it, put her head on his chest and shut her eyes, resting there until his arms finally came up to encircle her.

This, she thought, was home.

She sucked in a deep breath, and scented only what her mortal nose would allow: the menthol rub he used on his bad leg, the fainter scent of his soap, and beneath it all, the warm, earthy wisp of the man she loved. She tilted her head, pressing her lips against the first available patch of bare flesh that offered itself to her, his biceps.

"I missed this so," she murmured, voice muffled.

"My arm?" His voice was softly teasing, as it used to be.

She'd missed that, too, she realized with a smile. Pulling away to peer into his face, dry now, doe-brown eyes deep pools of softness in the moonlit room, she knew that no place—sanctuary, safe house, mansion or motel—was more linked in her mind with home than his arms. She straightened her spine and pressed into him so that he sucked in a needy breath. They were fused at hips, her small breasts pressed against his wider chest, and he tilted his jaw up to find her lips. The need in that first kiss illuminated all the hard words between them, showing them for what they really were . . . smoke. Camouflage to protect the emotion they couldn't put into words; the "I love yous" and "I miss yous" and mostly "I can't . . . not without you."

So they abandoned words for the tangible, and Zoe found she'd been missing a lot more than just his arms.

Warren lifted her and Zoe didn't rail at him for manhandling her like she would have with anyone else. She didn't fight to assert her own control over this lovemaking just to prove she could. She just let herself be swept up and away, because the weakening of her knees, her limbs, the numbing of her mind and thoughts, had nothing to do with his otherworldly strength versus her much-hated humanity. It was just Warren loving Zoe as he always had. Loving *her,* she thought numbly as his mouth found hers, and not what she could do . . . what she had done, and would do yet. No, this night was all about being cradled and cherished by the only man she'd ever taken into her with no ulterior motive outside of giving as good as she got.

Which is what she did now.

Humanity hadn't stolen her agility, and when he swung her to her back, her legs whipped up and around his waist. His response, to grind against her, was automatic, as was the moan coaxed from his throat and into hers. Problem was, she was still clothed—they both were—so many of the soft growls and needy whimpers that escaped them both in the next few seconds were driven in part by frustration. The rest were spawned by sudden sensations—a palm cupped just there when her simple cotton shirt was finally lost, a hunger emphasized by the bite above the breast, a surprised laugh at the responding pinch. And a slow melt into the heat of each other's flesh as the rest of their clothes fell away.

Zoe had dreamed of this moment and these sensations for too long to rush. She arched against him whenever she got the chance, but kept it light and unhurried, just a caress of thighs, a skimming of skin, a slow glide from her belly to her thighs to show him she was already wet and ready for him. That she'd been ready for years now, waiting even as duty had kept her away.

One didn't need supersenses to quantify need, and Zoe felt Warren, too, straining to stay himself. He slowed his hands to a languid caress even as the need to race along her sides made him shudder. He tasted her with breathy and heated lips—not just sampling, but drinking her in like her skin was a sweet liquid and vital to his very existence.

This was what she missed most, Zoe thought as she eased over him, blanketing him with her core, lacing his limbs with hers. It wasn't her lost strength or the vitality leached from her world with the stripping of her extrasensory abilities. It was the union of mind, body, and spirit with the man who'd known her so long, understood her so well, and frustrated her so completely.

Zoe eased up, Warren shifted, skimming hips, and smiled as he slid home. Zoe swallowed hard. She could swim in this liquid motion, just let herself drift away as a body both outside and inside herself determined the beat of her steadfast heart. She rocked, feeling like she was mere driftwood on a vast open sea, and the only thing keeping her from floating away entirely was the knowledge that their time together was finite—that the sun would rise and their bodies would part, leaving behind slick thighs and a hollowness where he once resided.

Zoe wiped at her eyes with the back of her hand on her way to caressing Warren's cheek, pulling him closer and deeper as she pushed the thoughts away. She didn't want to swim in these feelings, anyway. She wanted to drown in them. And that wasn't allowed.

"Zoe—"

She pressed a finger to his lips, knowing he sensed her pain. She recalled the ability, and the way emotions burned on the air. He wanted to console her, but words weren't going to fix it, and besides, he felt the same way. She saw it in his eyes, felt it in his tensing fingers and the way he pulsed inside of her.

And that was comfort enough.

She smiled, being as brave as the moment would allow, and his image blurred beneath her. The first tear fell as she refitted her body against his, opening to him further, and inviting the hard and the soft, the warm and the wet. And when they came together, the tendons in his neck straining as he cried out below her, Zoe knew she wasn't just sating him, she was completing him. Because duty aside, Zoe Archer and Warren Clarke were simply made for one another. And when she collapsed atop him, the long smooth length of him still filling her, warming her, she knew that Warren had come home as well.

Later, when he was as bone-weary with the need for sleep as she, Warren wrapped his arms around her from behind, spooning her body with his own.

"You're wrong," he finally whispered, and she knew he would let her go.

Zoe smiled bittersweetly as his hands warmed her breasts, nuzzling back, cocooning herself further. Safe for now. "If I am you won't need to ask me to relinquish my star sign again. It'll be someone else's for the taking."

A sigh hollowed out his body.

She turned in his arms because it felt like there were suddenly acres and canyons and miles between them, and quickly drew close again. "But I'm not wrong. I have prophesies and legacies and adventures left to fulfill."

She had a daughter, a destiny . . . and at the end of it all? Maybe she still had this man to come home to.

So she wouldn't fail. She promised him that, then pressed her lips to his, trying to kiss away the worry that had returned to furrow his brow.

"And if you do?"

It was too practical a question for her liking. She rose, straddled him, and he immediately fell silent, while she shrugged the question away. It didn't matter either way. Death was preferable to a life without meaning, and for the first time since leaving the troop she had a purpose again. That alone was worth giving thanks for.

So she held back the words he wanted to hear—*I won't go*—once again putting away any chance at personal happiness, and merely smiled as dawn rose on a beautiful Thanksgiving morning.

"We'll see," she told him, flipping her hair back, dropping her palms to his chest. "We'll see who's giving thanks by the day's end."

Chapter 5

White was the symbol of holiness and purity in Tibetan Buddhism. It represented prosperity, too, so it was no accident that the Tulpa's home was achromatic from rooftop to doorstep, a blank slate against the sea of pastels and dusty stuccoes that otherwise dotted the valley floor.

It wasn't, however, an ivory tower. The Tulpa was reluctant to remove himself from the source of all his energy and strength. Human emotion, particularly negative, fueled him, though most mortals steered clear of the soaring pale home without even knowing they were doing so. Even Shadow agents didn't darken the doorway without invitation. Zoe had been the only agent of Light to even get close enough to peer in a window, and since her infiltration sixteen years earlier, paranormal sensors and precautions had been added to further secure the place.

But, as Warren drove her to the drop point a block away, she didn't worry about those. She was mortal, and the only monitor that would pick her up was attached to the security camera tucked high above the entrance's alcove.

On the surface of it, Warren was right. She hadn't seen the Tulpa in sixteen years, plenty of time for bitterness to crust over any soft feelings he'd once held for her, and she had no doubt his hatred had further cemented the emotion. But no sense in worrying about that now. Instead, her lips moved in an almost rhythmic chant as her fingers nimbly played over the cornucopia she'd woven.

An observer might have thought she was praying, but Zoe Archer knew too much of other worlds to put stock in any one deity, and let her whispers spiral out into the universe as affirmation instead. She had, at one time, been a fervent student of Tibetan culture and lore, studying the transitional realities called *bardos*, learning the self-control and discipline needed to succeed with tantric work, including hours of meditative practices, prostration, and mantra recitation. Because that's what a man named Wyatt Neelson had done, devoting fifteen years of his life to visualization in order to create a being so vivid, real, and evil that the thought form eventually morphed into reality and became the Tulpa.

It was this being's arrival on the paranormal scene that upset the valley's metaphysical balance. The Tulpa sought influence over the mortal realm—to control their thoughts and actions and dreams—and absolute dominance over the paranormal one. The agents of Light fought, of course, but they'd never faced a *created* adversary before, and suddenly balance became a secondary concern. Survival was all-consuming.

The Tulpa didn't age. He couldn't be killed—not even by the conduits that were so deadly to the agents on both sides of the Zodiac—and he assumed the physical form of whatever the person looking at him expected to see. It was this that most worried Zoe. God forbid he look in a mirror while standing next to her and see the demonic monstrosity that still came for her in her dreams. Then he'd know she was misleading him again and he'd skin and flay and bury her with her bones outside her body, heart still beating atop a living pile of flesh. He knew how. She'd seen him do it before.

So while weaving her cornucopia, Zoe had focused her thoughts on the way he'd once allowed himself to be vulnerable with her, turning those tender moments into a new story for herself and a new past for them both. She wove and thought, and invented and wove, until she had the minutest detail engraved upon her gray matter. She memorized this new past and then began to believe it. She believed the Tulpa was as before, that he loved her and would readily welcome her back. She believed, as before, that she loved him as well, and that she wanted nothing so much as to be in his arms once more. She created this story as she created her gift—with focus and a studied and purposeful intent—and by the time she'd finished she knew she could walk into the Tulpa's house with complete confidence.

Because there'd been one chink in the Tulpa's impenetrable paranormal armor. And Zoe Archer was it.

She was stepping from the car even before Warren had come to a full stop, and the crisp November air greeted her brightly as the morning sun hit her face. It was easy to turn nostalgic on a day like this, a holiday when one should be with family and friends, feasting and giving heartfelt thanks for this life's blessings. She hugged her homemade cornucopia tight to her chest, and its weight and scent and purpose grounded her, giving her strength to push those wistful thoughts away. Leave them for the mortals who had use for such things.

She slammed the car door and had already begun walking away when she stopped. They never said goodbye. It was considered bad form, indicating a deficit of confidence, and was usually unnecessary. But she didn't want to just walk away from Warren, not again, not without at least some solid sense of closure. So she backed up and waited until he'd lowered the driver's side window, then stared down into that face she'd loved almost as long as she'd breathed.

"There's something you should know, but I can't tell you—" She couldn't really tell him anything. Certainly not the truth. "It's about the legend. The rise of the *Kairos*." The woman who was both Shadow and Light, and whose powers would forever tip the paranormal scale in favor of good or evil, whichever she chose.

Whichever her daughter, Joanna, chose.

Zoe squinted against the light as Warren sat back, studying her carefully as she measured her words. "The Kairos lives. She's going to rise up under your command. Watch and listen for her. She doesn't know it yet, but she's hurtling toward her destiny even now."

Warren had fallen stock-still. He was listening, and hearing, her now. "Where, Zoe? Tell me how to find her."

She shook her head and quickly held up a hand, staving off his protest. "She's in hiding, Warren. Even from herself. You won't find her until her metamorphosis."

"Which is when?"

That head shake again. "I'm sorry, but that's all I can tell you."

She thought he'd be mad, start railing about lies and secrets, trust and duty. But he simply leaned back against the leather seat and squinted up at her in the sharp morning light. He could see it out here, she thought. The veil between worlds was wide enough on this hopeful, thankful day that her intentions were clear in the light. And clearly Light.

"I didn't say it before," he finally said, admiration and, yes, love sharpening his words. "Happy Birthday, Zoe."

She gave him a wide smile, then turned to face the long walk leading to the stark white house, up the steps that were almost silvery in the brilliant sun, where she casually rang the doorbell. When it opened, she said what she'd been thinking; her wish for Warren, a vow for the day's work, a final goodbye. "Happy Thanksgiving."

The woman who answered the door was named Lindy Maguire. She was frumpy, matronly, favoring lace collars and long skirts, and she was also the Shadow's Leonine sign on the Zodiac. Like all Leos Lindy was ruled by the sun, and like most, also ruled by the heart. She had long ago set aside personal aspirations in order to remain as close as possible to the Tulpa, so it was natural that Lindy was acting as vanguard for his home. Natural, too, that she hated Zoe.

Lindy's delicate nostrils flared as she examined Zoe, scenting out humanity as she ran her eyes skeptically over the cream slacks and overcoat, though she didn't place her until Zoe opened her mouth.

"Damn, Lindy," Zoe said, studying the woman's beehive. "Still stuck in the sixties, I see."

Recognition had barely flashed in Lindy's eyes before Zoe found herself crushed against the wall, blood welling in her mouth as she thought, *I used to be that fast . . . but I hit harder.*

"Uh-uh-uh," Zoe said, shaking her head as much as she dared. Lindy's conduit was out—Zoe hadn't seen her draw that, either—and the honed nail file was pressed against Zoe's larynx, so that breathing was no longer the best way to stay alive. Zoe shifted her eyes to the camera trained on them from above. "Don't want to ruin all his fun, do we?"

Lindy cursed under her breath, then let up, but not before flicking the file just enough to draw blood. Zoe hissed at the flash of pain—it still surprised her—and Lindy's frown turned upside down.

"I must be dreaming, because every sense I own tells me the mighty Zoe Archer is a mortal." She wrinkled her nose as she said the word, like it befouled the air around her. And while she was gloating, reveling in being the first to know, and at holding her longtime foe at a distinct disadvantage, Zoe discreetly shifted her weight . . . and plowed her fist into Lindy's already flat nose.

She probably felt no more pain than a pinch, and the blood was only a trickle, but Lindy's eyes watered as her nose mended itself, shifting back into place with an audible crack. Zoe smirked and picked up her toppled cornucopia.

"Mortal doesn't mean pushover."

"No. It means walked-over."

"Just tell him I'm here," Zoe said curtly.

The house quaked like the hills of San Francisco.

Lindy grinned as she swayed. "He knows."

As, it seemed, did everyone else. As Zoe was escorted beyond the foyer and into the core of the house, doors began to swing open. She didn't make eye contact as speculative whispers turned to hissing, and curiosity turned hostile. Instead she let her eyes stray over the shoulders of her enemies—Raven was here, she saw, and Polly and Damian; they leered at her as she passed—but she ignored them all and searched out the rooms she remembered and recognized by layout, pretending to look for the Tulpa. There was neither anything resembling a nursery, nor any sign of a child. He'd called these his drawing rooms when she was living here, and she was surprised to find nothing had changed. Not even the furnishings. Even after Zoe's infiltration that first time, even though he knew she'd returned to the Light and reported every secret detail of his lair—and she knew them all—he'd stayed put.

Arrogant bastard, she thought, as Lindy smiled back at her from over one slim shoulder. That arrogance would be his downfall.

She wiped away the thought like cleaning a slate in her mind. Imagination was what was needed to keep her alive through the day. So instead of thinking that the Tulpa was stupid as well as manipulative and cruel, she thought of him as trusting and hopeful, just waiting for the day Zoe would return to him.

"I'll take that." Lindy said, holding out her hands for the cornucopia once they'd reached the end of the hallway. It was an unnecessary precaution. Nothing on the physical plane could injure the Tulpa. But Lindy wasn't about to release Zoe without letting her know she wasn't trusted. Zoe almost thanked her. It was a good reminder after the relative ease of the entry.

"It's a gift," Zoe said lightly. "and it's not for you."

Lindy could've easily wrested the cornucopia from Zoe's grasp. Instead she reached out and deliberately plucked the finishing piece, a sugared plum, from atop the carefully arranged mound, leaving a hole where the fruit had been. She bit into it without breaking eye contact, and juice ran down her chin as her mouth curved upward.

"Attractive," Zoe commented dryly. "And the manuals still speculate why you've no heir to your star sign . . . or prospect of spawning one."

Lindy's expression snapped, anger pulling it tight at the center, but she didn't use the fist clenched at her side, and she didn't tear the cornucopia from Zoe's hands. Security tapes had shown Zoe entering with the piece. If she didn't walk in with it now the Tulpa would wonder why.

And if there was a weapon hidden in the cheerful basket, he'd want to shove it down her throat himself.

There was a pedestal perched next to the door, one that had once held a fern, but now sported a blood-red scripture box with twin dragons on each wooden side, a lone bright spot in the long bare hallway. That was *one* difference, Zoe thought. She hadn't seen any living thing—plants, animals, humans—in the house. Because Shadows didn't count, she thought as Lindy slid open the box's ornate lid, and pulled out a pair of gold-rimmed aviator glasses. "Put these on."

Zoe screwed up her face. "I'm not going to meet the Tulpa in glasses that make me look like I'm stuck in the eighties."

"Put them on," Lindy repeated, her voice brittle.

Zoe sighed, shifted her gift to one arm and accepted the glasses, her confused gaze winking up at her from the mirrored lenses. "Why?"

"Because I said so." Lindy rapped the door twice with her knuckles and it immediately swung open to reveal a dim and deep interior. It wouldn't have been intimidating . . . if there'd actually been someone manning the door. Lindy saw Zoe hesitate and the cruel smile was back on her face. "Have . . . fun."

Zoe wondered at the deliberate word choice, but slid the glasses over her eyes like she hadn't noticed, and smirked. "We always do."

Zoe would've given her life just then to be able to smell the bilious jealousy she knew was seeping from the woman's pores, but the cursing and chattering behind them told her the other Shadows *did* scent it. Knowing an impending riot when she saw one, she stepped smoothly into the room and watched as the door swung shut on the demonic faces glaring at her from the hallway.

Then the vacuum of silence was absolute.

The glasses accentuated the room's dimness and Zoe thought that was their purpose. So she emptied her mind and tried not to let it unnerve her; tried, too, not to think of all the empty space around her, or how she could be cut down where she stood without even knowing the blow was coming. She knew fear stank like something pickled and old, and the Tulpa fed on that fear.

Zoe was determined to make him starve.

Still, she jumped when a movement flickered across from her, freezing as she did. Swallowing hard, she cradled the curved horn like it was a talisman that would ward off injury, and took a step forward. Three beings across from her mirrored the movement. None of them spoke.

"Babe?" she said, using the same endearment she had all those years before. No answer. She stepped forward again. The Shadows across from her drew closer as well, still silent. She tilted her head, and saw two of them imitate the movement. Cutting her eyes to the third, she realized that figure, also clad in owlish lenses, had as well. She lifted her hand as if in greeting, and they did the same.

Mirrors. A relieved sigh scuttled from her throat, but caught when a wispy shadow rose up behind her, kept rising in a tower of smoke that burned even in her mortal nose, and was tripled before her eyes. She froze as it suddenly retracted, leaving vaporous tendrils to dissipate in the air as it solidified over her right shoulder like ash caught in a mold.

Even as she strained through the dark glasses to make out his features, she knew she was the one creating them, expectation and memory joining forces to construct the man she remembered, like an architect building a house from the bones up. He wasn't much taller than she, and slighter than one would expect of a man of great power. His hair was a sandy color—not quite brown, but not blond, either—and he had deep hazel eyes, like the moss of a clouded swamp. With a wide face and full lips, he couldn't be called unattractive and that was no accident. Zoe remembered thinking that if she had to bed down with unadulterated evil, he could at least be good-looking.

Once he'd fully materialized, he slipped his arm over her shoulder, around her neck, his fingers coming to rest on her opposite arm. He squeezed lightly, pulling in tight to whisper in her ear.

"Darling," he said, his endearment for her returned. His voice was raspy, pure male, and honed.

But his embrace wasn't as cold as she remembered, his breath not as septic sour, and though Zoe knew it was only because her senses were blunted with mortality, it made it easier to ignore the rot she knew lay ready to engulf her if not for the fragile membrane of his skin. Before she'd been able to scent out festering venom and bacteria, and at the end she'd even begun to expect infection, like she too was contaminated, even though she was super. But now she could anticipate nothing about him, including this unexpected welcome.

Realigning her thoughts—and Zoe was a pro at that—she let go of the knowledge that he could kill her with a swift snap of those gentle fingers, or crack her like a walnut between the lever of his strong arm and body, and turned into him instead. The sigh that flew from her body was one of relief, not fear. Her arms clung to him with gratitude, not entreaty, and she lifted her lips to his icy ones as she'd done countless times all those years past to utter her heartfelt lie.

"I knew you'd allow me to return."

He pulled away to study her face, taking in the changes since he'd last seen her—few, as she'd aged well—though he studied her eyes in particular.

No, not her eyes, she realized. His reflection in her glasses. Her thoughts as they materialized on *his* face. So she let memories wash over her, easy now that she was seeing and scenting and touching him again, and his features sharpened further. His brow grew in smooth, the whorls of his earlobes became delicate and defined. She thought she saw his eyes flash dark, but his expression brightened as the room did, degree by degree, until they were standing face-to-face in a room of reflected angles and light.

Have fun, Lindy had said, and now Zoe knew why. This was the one room in the house that had undergone a complete renovation, and it was why he hadn't needed to move. Here—in the place that'd once been the Tulpa's bedroom, where Zoe had lied time after time, and betrayed him the night she'd gone to kill his creator—he'd built a funhouse, full-sized mirrors to reflect a true picture of the inhabitant's intent. Reflect it upon, and for, him.

It explained why no one had accompanied her inside. It was harder for the Tulpa to solidify when multiple people projected their expectations upon him, and it was uncomfortable for him to exist under the weight of too many people's gazes at once—he'd actually feel himself mutating and changing under their conflicting emotions. So only the person he was most interested in reading could initially face him directly. Now that he had fully solidified the others could come in, pick up on it without risking influencing the image, or causing any embarrassing mutation. But she hoped they wouldn't. She had a better chance of convincing him to spare her life if they remained alone.

So they stood as a couple, reflected back on themselves in dozens of shapes, sizes, and angles so that not an inch was omitted or hidden from his sight.

"You are the most clever man," she said, letting her realization play out on her face as she caught his eye through one of the mirrors and smiled seductively. "In addition to being the most handsome, of course." She whirled back toward him, intending to draw him closer again. "God, how I've missed you."

He caught her arms, stopping her short—again, gently—and held her in place. It was something Zoe had forgotten. He didn't move from one position to another. He glided. And that wasn't something she had to imagine. He had the ability all on his own. "Oh, I've missed you as well, Zoe," he said, smiling back.

She shut her eyes and held her breath as panic threatened to thread through her veins. She let him sense her uncertainty. It was only natural for her to question whether it'd been a good idea to come here, so she let him feel that hesitancy as well. When she opened her eyes again, he was staring over her shoulder at his mirrored self, waiting to see what emerged. But there was only the Tulpa as she'd always seen him, and she suddenly felt like she'd never been gone, or escaped him, at all. "Please, baby. You have to let me explain."

"Explain why you betrayed me?" he murmured, only now that she'd spoken of it.

"Explain how I managed not to," she replied, and willed him to believe her with eyes, voice. Her mind. He must have felt it because after a moment he appeared to soften.

"And is this a peace offering?" he asked, eyes flicking down to the cornucopia she still held.

A small smile lifted one corner of her mouth. "Merely a centerpiece for your holiday celebration. I remember how you enjoyed Thanksgiving."

He had. It was his favorite holy day.

"Then you plan on staying for dinner?"

She lifted her free hand and removed her glasses, raising her head to gaze directly into the cold black depths of eyes she'd never thought to see again. "I was hoping," she said softly.

He nodded after a moment. "Good. Then over dinner you can offer your explanation to us all."

And he glided to the door to usher in his sycophants, movements impossibly smooth . . . and entirely too quiet for Zoe's liking.

Chapter 6

Dinner was held in the same mirrored room, the hollowed out center suddenly taken up with an elongated black marble table, the cornucopia Zoe had made centered like a bull's-eye. A gleaming table setting of mirrored plates, china, and crystal winked in the studded light of two shining candelabras. The Tulpa could now see himself above, below, and in the mirrored glasses of his half dozen guests. He'd become even more of a control freak since Zoe's hard betrayal, which she understood. Ignoring the fact that he was the epitome of everything she despised—that he was the coldest, hardest heartache in this world—she instead pitied that he felt the need for it, and grieved for the suspicion thinning his lips. She sorrowed, mostly, that she'd been the one to put it there. Her eyes teared as she thought of the pain she'd caused, and she discreetly wiped the tears away behind the mirrored frame of her borrowed glasses, donned again like everyone else at the table.

Across from her, Lindy glared at her from behind her own, much cooler, lenses.

Zoe ignored her, as well as the disbelieving snort from the Shadow seated to her right as he scented her emotion. There was another man she didn't know leering at her from her left, and two other favored agents flanking Lindy, but Zoe didn't try to engage any of them in conversation. They took their clues from the Tulpa, and even though homicide lived in their mirrored faces, they'd stay their hands as long as he did.

"Fruit?" Damian offered, plucking an apple from the cornucopia.

Zoe swallowed hard, hands shaking slightly as she cut through white meat. "It's decorative," Zoe informed him. "I didn't mean for it to be . . ."

He took a bite of the crisp skin, his thin lips littered with sugar.

". . . eaten," she finished on a sigh. She looked to the Tulpa for support, but he was busy watching himself in his mirrored wineglass. He wouldn't let them injure her, yet, but he'd let them have their fun. "Choose one, then. It doesn't matter to me."

"Really? Then it doesn't matter to me, either." He lifted the entire basket and deposited it in front of her so that a few nuts rolled loose. "You choose."

Zoe considered before gingerly choosing a ripe pear, scooping up the loosened nuts and depositing those on her plate as well. Then she set to righting the cornucopia, making it look as ornate—if less stacked—as before. Damian snickered and immediately yanked free a grape bunch before passing it around the table so the others could do the same. Zoe pursed her lips, but said nothing. The Tulpa had steepled his fingers, observing them all over the top like an amused parent watching his children at play.

Zoe decided to begin. "You care nothing about this—or me—I see."

"On the contrary, darling. Time hasn't lessened my feelings for you. It's strengthened them."

Lindy popped a handful of berries in her mouth, snickering.

"And mine for you," Zoe said softly, looking down, pushing a walnut across her plate with her index finger.

"Then why hide from him?"

She glanced up to find the man directly across from her leaning in, feigning interest. Licking his lips. Wasp thin, he reminded Zoe of a snake, that tongue seemingly testing the air, tasting it, honing in on her. His grandmother had been one of Zoe's first victims after she ascended to her star sign. His name was Ajax; he was the new Shadow Virgo.

Zoe leaned back and blotted her lips with her napkin. "I wasn't hiding from him . . . or any of you. I was hiding from *them*."

Everyone looked toward the Tulpa. Zoe waited. Sixteen years was a long time to have hidden from both sides of the Zodiac, but she willed him to believe it. Willed them all. The Tulpa stared, blank-faced, before motioning for her to continue. So she told them the story she'd rehearsed, the past she'd invented, the history she now believed, passing it along so they would believe it as well. It was true that Zoe had killed the Tulpa's creator, Wyatt Neelson. But her intent, she said, wasn't to destroy the Tulpa, but to strengthen him.

"Do you remember the way we spoke of him?" she asked, stopping to address the Tulpa as the others listened carefully. "About the way he clung to you even after you broke free of him to assert your independence. You said he was dead weight, like a stone attached to the string of a kite that would otherwise sail free."

"So you decided to sever that weight yourself."

"No," Zoe shook her head. "I went to convince him to give you a name."

The Tulpa froze and silence settled heavily over the table. Because even though Wyatt had visualized the Tulpa to construct a fully developed consciousness, he'd refused to give the Tulpa a name. There was power in a name. It was why Adam named all the earth's creatures in the bible, giving himself power over all of them. Why in Jewish tradition a child's intended name wasn't revealed until after they were born. It was why cultures all over the world were superstitious about sharing names, and why all parents chose their offspring's names so very carefully.

And it was why the Tulpa desired one so very badly.

Zoe reminded him of that now. "You'd refused to see him for months, and that had taken its toll on his psyche. He was unkempt, mumbling like a crazy man about abandonment, and having nothing to show for his life's work. When I told him what I wanted, that we even had a name picked out—" Here the others looked back and forth between them, curiosity stark on their faces, but Zoe continued on blithely. "Well, he only laughed, then spat at my feet. It angered me."

She bit her lip and the tears welled. "I snapped. I told him *I* was the most important person in your life now, not him. That he may have created you but I was also supernatural, and that we were creating something new between us. That's when he lunged." She swallowed hard, drawing a shaky hand across her brow before letting it drop. Her voice fell to a whisper. "I don't know . . . I guess I'd begun to think of him as one of us, as having powers, being able to detect intent. Plus I was furious with him for his crazed rebuff. I swear it was only meant to be a slap . . . but it was enough to kill him . . . and to reveal that I'd once been Light. I knew once you found my psychic imprint on the kill spot you'd be so enraged you'd never hear me through. So I fled."

Zoe stared at her hands like she couldn't believe she'd done it, and the others studied her—and the Tulpa—from behind their safe, shining lenses. The Tulpa continued watching his own reflection, and waited for Zoe to finally look up.

"So it was all an accident?"

She nodded, eyes trained on his too-calm face, like he

wasn't listening, though Zoe knew he heard every word. All syllables. Every breath drawn in between. "And all these years I've been wracking my brain, trying to think of a way to return to you and prove it'd been unintentional. I needed an excuse that the agents of Light would fall for, or a mission that would bring me back into your arms. Then I realized you'd never believe me. Not if I showed up here as before, with power, ability. Light."

"We don't believe you now," said one of the others.

Zoe's frustration showed even from behind the dark glasses. "Why would I lie? Why would I walk right up and ring the doorbell if I didn't want this more than anything in the world?"

"It is a conundrum," the Tulpa finally said, voice still too gentle.

Which meant he was indulging her out of curiosity. She took a bite of turkey and felt it catch in her throat. But curiosity was a good start, she told herself, swallowing. Curiosity could be turned into concern. Concern into desire.

Zoe shrugged one shoulder, and hugged herself. "I finally decided the only way to convince you of my sincerity was to come to you on this, your favorite holy day, when mortal observance and emotions could be tapped and channeled for your benefit and strength. If you use that power you'll see I'm telling the truth. I've returned to you out of love. I miss you. I just . . . want to come home."

She held up her hand when two of the Shadows opened their mouths to speak. "But I also knew that wasn't enough. I had to prove myself, lose something irreplaceable, as I caused you to lose the creator. It took me a year to get up the nerve to actually do it. But I've shed it all for you—my past, my *chi*, my near immortality. I come to you with a basket of fruit to commemorate this holy day of bounty, thanks, and forgiveness. And I come to you only as a woman."

It was all she had, and it was the truth. The Tulpa leaned

back, lifting his cup, and finally smiled. Lindy's head swiveled back and forth between them, her confusion and growing anger magnified on every mirrored surface. "Bullshit!"

Zoe's eyes never left the Tulpa's face, longing and hope naked on her own. "Just a little clue, Lindy . . . if you've had fifteen years to seduce this man and still haven't made it into his bed, chances are it's not going to happen."

Lindy was fast, but the Tulpa was faster. A flick of the wrist and another mirror sprang up in front of Zoe, halting Lindy's lunge with a resounding crack. She grunted and fell back into her seat, and the mirror—all the warning she'd get—disappeared.

"Returned with a woman's weapons too, I see." the Tulpa murmured.

Zoe looked at Lindy, who was straightening her glasses. *Her* hands were shaking now. "They're all I have. I'll be damned if I die without them."

"You may be damned yet."

"Shut up, Ajax." The Tulpa finally took a bite from his own plate, continuing while he chewed. "You weren't here before so you don't know, but Zoe and I have always had a strong bond."

"Opposites attract," she agreed, before sadness again overtook her face. "Though it seems that too has changed. Like you."

Again he checked his reflection in the mirror, studying what Zoe had created there. "I look exactly like before."

"I mean on the inside. I don't need extrasensory power to see you're holding back."

"And do you blame me?"

"I understand it," she said, shaking her head. "But I regret it all the same."

"Oh, for fuck's sake . . ." Lindy half-rose from her chair, but the Tulpa held up a hand. Her mouth snapped shut, the words scuttling off into a growl. Zoe held back the smile that wanted to visit her face. Still, she knew they all could sense her satisfaction. It didn't bother her, and it didn't seem to bother the Tulpa, either. He pushed back his chair and stood.

"Walk with me," he said, holding out his hand. The others stood. "Only Zoe."

They floundered, looking around at one another. "Sir, please . . ."

"Shut up, Lindy."

Triumph thrilled through Zoe, warming her so thoroughly she didn't even feel the chill of the Tulpa's palm in her own. She smiled up at him, let him gaze into her glasses to see himself as she saw him—handsome, healthy, *hers*—and they exited the mirror room alone.

Zoe took it as a very good sign.

It was three in the afternoon when the Tulpa escorted Zoe from his mirrored room, and a part of her was aware, and surprised, that she'd lived that long. Trapped in a house with supernatural enemies who could snap her neck as easily as she had Wyatt Neelson's, she'd expected the high drama of her return—in whatever way it played out—to have climaxed by now. Instead she'd gotten to explain herself, have dinner, and was now taking a promenade around the grounds. She was *so* in. She linked her arm in the Tulpa's, squeezing lightly, thinking this might just be her best Thanksgiving yet.

Then she saw the boy.

He couldn't have been more than seven, and he rounded the corner struggling with all his might against the hold of two women in long dark robes, their eyes as large as silver dollars and completely overtaken by blackened pupils. Their appearance, however, wasn't what made Zoe's heart stutter. They were ward mothers of the Shadow children, charged with raising and schooling the Shadow initiates until they metamorphosed into full-fledged agents, and Zoe'd seen them

before. But this was no initiate. It was a mortal child with fat
tears rolling down his cheeks, and fear etched on his face. He
caught sight of Zoe, probably the only normal person he'd
seen in this gloomy mausoleum, and lunged for her. "Help
me, please! I want to go home! I want my mommy!"

Zoe had to force herself not to run to him as one of the
ward mothers knelt in front of him, her blackened eyes drawing a scream from deep within his tiny chest. "Now, now.
Let's behave. You don't want to scare the other children, do
you?"

"Others?" Zoe said, before she could stop herself. The
Tulpa only put one finger to his mouth, shushing her.

"Put this on, and you won't be afraid anymore," the ward
mother said, pulling a wooden mask from behind her back,
and slipping it over his eyes. Zoe had seen masks like this
before. Countless Himalayan artifacts such as these adorned
the Tulpa's living areas, creations of that region's animist
tribes. It made sense that the Tulpa cherished objects created by people who believed souls inhabited ordinary objects as well as animate beings. But why put a middle hills
tribal mask on a living, mortal child?

Well, the boy immediately calmed, Zoe saw, and why
not? He could no longer see the woman looming over him
with no eyelids, no tear ducts, no reason or inclination to
blink. If he had, he'd see her looking up as she knelt before
him, nodding once. Her partner nodded back, then in one
swift motion slammed her palms on the sides of the child's
head, like a school marm boxing the ears of a naughty pupil.
Zoe jolted, but the boy didn't cry out. Instead he immediately stiffened and fell unnaturally silent. Then the mask
appeared to begin melting, thinning out like the finest leather
until it molded itself to the child's face, encasing it fully
from forehead to chin. The ward mother rose and, for the
first time, acknowledged the Tulpa.

"A new recruit," she said serenely as they steered the

now-docile child to the left, and disappeared behind a pair of great oak doors, which shut with a sharp click.

"You're distressed," the Tulpa said, patting Zoe's arm and drawing her closer.

She nodded stiffly and fought for control. "I'm just . . . confused. That boy was mortal, wasn't he?" At the Tulpa's nod, Zoe tried for a lighter tone. "You've never allowed mortals in your home before. And what was the mask for?"

"Would you like to see?" the Tulpa replied, motioning to the door.

She didn't. She knew that much. She wanted to run from whatever was being done to that child behind those doors, but she thought of her granddaughter and nodded instead.

"It's fitting that you should see this today, on Thanksgiving," he told her before throwing open the great doors and spreading his arms wide. "Because this is my first harvest. And it's a bumper crop if I do say so myself."

They were lined on the floor in rows of five, wearing dark brown robes in the fashion of the ward mothers, each masked like the first boy, uniform but for their heights. They were all children, and from size alone Zoe guessed their ages fell between three and ten. Except for those along the wall, where another unblinking ward mother stood guard. There, cribs were lined up for the smallest of them. Zoe, aware of the weight of the Tulpa's stare on her face, tore her eyes away. "I don't understand."

But she was beginning to. The horror of it was slowly sinking in as she watched a ward mother read to the silent, unmoving children from the Shadow manuals, introducing the mythos and lore of the paranormal world into impressionable young minds encased in living wood. Zoe pocketed her shades, bent, and passed her hand in front of the child nearest her. The girl didn't move. That's when Zoe saw the tiny pins anchoring the mask in place. There was a slot next to the temple where a perfume vial was cradled, half-full.

Zoe swallowed hard. Not just a mask to keep out the light, then. Or one that merely limited expression. It was shackled to their skulls, and the drug did the same to their minds. Because children, she thought, as she straightened, should never be this unnaturally still and silent.

"It's simple, really," the Tulpa was already explaining. "It's children's belief in us and our mythology that grants us the energy to battle the Light. Problem is, children grow up. They become adults and stop believing in comic books, star signs. *Me*. So I came up with the idea of harnessing their minds, and of harvesting all that potential energy and intelligence and natural curiosity. They think solely of the Shadows. They study our history. They worship me."

Zoe couldn't help herself. Despite her mortal senses she suddenly recalled the smell and taste and touch of this creature's festering spirit. Her Thanksgiving dinner spoiled in her stomach. "So they're your slaves."

"They're my family," he corrected smoothly.

"And the babies?" she asked, her eyes instinctively searching out Ashlyn in one of the cradles. At least they had no idea she was a child of the Light. They'd merely stolen her because the opportunity presented itself . . . as they'd stolen all these children from their families. "Surely they're too young to contribute?"

"Oh, no. They've the most concentrated *chi* of all." The Tulpa smiled. "I'd take them from the womb if I could."

Zoe was glad they were no longer in the mirrored room, because for one moment his image flickered and the skeleton that flashed from beneath his skin wasn't human. It was scorched bone: tooth, fang, and the invisible power that reared up from the bowels of midnight. Zoe quickly realigned her thoughts, glancing around to make sure none of the ward mothers had noticed.

The Tulpa, oblivious, went on. "Think how devoted the mind would be if we could form specific neural pathways and manipulate a person's thoughts from birth on. My children," he said, arms again wide, "will make Wyatt's mind look like a shrunken head."

And that was how he planned on manipulating time. Using the *chi* of dozens of young, trained minds, he would bend natural law, and make reality conform to his wishes. Why not? Stranger things had happened.

"But how do you keep them so docile?" Zoe asked, playing dumb as the Tulpa motioned her to the front of the classroom.

"We limit their choices and experiences." He grinned as he whirled to face her. "And we provide examples of what happens to those who attempt treachery."

The Tulpa's grin dropped, along with the floor beneath Zoe. She yelped, free-falling, and above her the previously mute children let out a collective cheer. Somehow, the evidence of health and life didn't warm her.

Chapter 7

The drop was short, and she hit solid concrete, unsettling enough dust to have her coughing in the complete dark. Her first hint that she wasn't alone was the threatening growl that came from her left. As if she didn't already feel threatened enough. She swung around as an insistent whine and heavy panting emerged, closer to her right.

Wardens.

Fear reared instinctively. The animals sensed it, and the whining strengthened. But fear can still be attributed to my humanity, Zoe thought, whirling blindly again. Who wouldn't be afraid, trapped in a dark underground pound?

"Uh . . . babe?" she tried, revealing her fear and all-too-human nerves in the shake of her voice.

"Still alive, then?" the Tulpa asked casually from directly above. Zoe looked up and saw his slim outline blocking the dim light from the children's classroom.

The question was telling. It meant he hadn't expected her to be. She felt a sniffling along her arm, a wet nose, then the tentative lick of a very large tongue. The Shadow wardens were dogs, paranormal pets that could scent out enemy agents and rip them apart in seconds. They were the only things, other than conduits, that could actually kill an agent. Well, thought Zoe, looking up again, conduits, wardens . . . and the Tulpa.

"Clearly. But, and this is just a wild guess, I take it you have some other questions for me?"

"I have one." Then his voice was in her ear. "Who the fuck do you think you are?"

And one after another, four giant spotlights boomed to life, flooding the cave with light so bright Zoe had to cover her face. The wardens whimpered, their claws scratching as they scampered blindly away. Zoe fished for the shades she'd dropped in her pocket and slipped them back on. Her eyes still teared as the light assaulted her from beyond the lenses, but she could finally make out the perimeter of the room . . . and it chilled her to the bone.

It was a stupa, a building in the Tibetan tradition meant to honor Buddha. The Tulpa had always meant to build one . . . but his, he'd said, would be dedicated solely to himself. Zoe had researched the subject when she'd lived with him, so she knew there were three types of stupas: ones to commemorate events or occasions in Buddha's—or, in this case, the Tulpa's—life. Ones erected to gain favor . . . but those were generally small and this was anything but. Finally, there were those used for the burial of relics from a funeral pyre. Zoe felt the grit caked beneath her fingernails from her abrupt landing and swallowed hard.

Yep, she thought, looking up. The room was cone-shaped, indicating solar worship. There was also an altar to her right. And while most burial stupas held vessels containing the bones and ashes from a crematorial fire, Zoe didn't look for them. The entire room was the vessel. All that was missing was fire.

"I mean, you must think I'm stupid," he went on, voice

circling her like a vulture from above. He was circumambu-
lating, walking in a clockwise direction, reflecting the movement of the sun and rotating planets. Zoe fought back the
whimper that wanted to come. "I have to admit you caught
me by surprise, just waltzing up and knocking on the door
that way. That was a stroke of brilliance, as was the way
you've obviously clothed yourself in humanity. But it only
means you're that much easier to break . . . I'll have to be
careful if I want our time together to last."

She wrapped her arms around her middle. "So you don't
believe me."

The understatement of the year.

"Believe that you went to my creator intending to free
me? To *name* me?" Outrage made his voice shake, but his
outline above had gone unnaturally still. "No, Zoe. I know
you went there believing that his life, and death, was linked
to my own."

She jerked her head. "But you'd broken free of him! You
already had enough consciousness and ability to rule the
mortal and supernatural plane. I knew that. So why risk killing the creator only to leave behind my signature scent?"

"You didn't know. You expected me to weaken and die."
He paused and his exhale rolled over Zoe, pushing her hair
back from her shoulders. "And you never loved me."

Sweat broke on Zoe's forehead, though only part of it had
to do with nerves. "Then what am I doing here now?"

Three of the spotlights powered down, and his voice was
again in her ear. "That's what I intend to find out."

Zoe whirled, but he wasn't next to her. He was across the
ash-strewn chamber, outline obscured, but eyes glowing red.

"Why can't you just believe me?" she asked him, shaking
her head.

"Because look at me!" he bellowed. "I look exactly as I
did before! You have created me in the same image, even the
same fucking clothing! Which means your intentions are the

same as well. But you will die for your betrayal this time, and your death will benefit me."

And as the temperature suddenly soared in the spherical chamber, she knew there was no way to sway him. He'd sought a way to get to her for too long now, and she'd just walked in and given it to him.

Zoe lowered her head, bit her lip, then slowly lifted the glasses from her face. She looked at them for a long moment, then threw them to the ground in front of her. When she looked up, her face was resolute. Slowly she began to walk toward him, the mirrored lenses splintering beneath her heel.

"I gave it all up; my *chi*, my place, my legend and legacy among the star signs of the Zodiac." She swiped a damp tendril of hair from her forehead as she came to a stop in front of him. She ignored his blatant anger as he ignored the bitterness coating her words, and reached out to take his icy hands in hers. They felt wonderfully cool in her sweaty palms, and she lifted them gently and dropped them around her neck like an executioner's noose. She shrugged in the confused silence. "What is my life in comparison? Take it, as I took Wyatt's. Because I no longer want anything to do with this world if I don't also have your love."

For a moment his face remained impassive, a blank slate. She thought he was making her wait, prolonging the moment, making her suffer. But then that petrified stare twisted, first with fury, then anguish, and finally a wild and open need. Those icy fingers splayed wide, bracing her from her hairline to the base of her sweaty neck, slipped lower to her collarbone, beneath her shirt, rising to grasp her damp shoulders. He pulled her to him so quickly she lost her breath, and continued to fight for air as his icy lips found her heated ones, cold tongue probing in her warm mouth. She managed one great inhale of that icy breath, and it shot through her like quicksilver, freezing her lungs, and then she was kissing him back, pouring heat into him, both of them fighting for balance, and equilibrium. They clung to one another the same way they both clung to life, with a greedy and self-centered zeal, a perfect match in that respect.

When Zoe finally opened her eyes again, she gasped aloud. There was the man she loved.

It was Warren's face she caressed, the homeless mien she'd seen most recently. *His* cheeks were the ones she lovingly ran her smooth-tipped fingers over, catching on the stubble, curving at the jaw. They were his lips that her eyes caught upon and his Adam's apple bobbing under the weight of her gaze. It was Warren alone that she saw, even as soulless black eyes flared beneath the bones.

"You do love me," she told him, her whisper choked with tears and truth. "And I love you. And living without that love is a far worse fate than any momentary pain. I welcome death over the half-life I've been living. I'll burn, and I'll do it with your name on my lips."

The Warren-face winced.

"And my bed?" he rasped, the Tulpa's icy breath blowing her hair back again from her shoulders. It felt like a welcoming spring breeze. "Do you return there willingly as well?"

"Not just willingly," she whispered back, her eyes drinking him in as her hands moved lower. "Desperately."

She didn't add that she'd have to be desperate to return to him at all. He had immediately turned and she was too busy following and reimagining him, erasing Warren's image before anyone else caught sight of him. And too busy wiping away her tears. If only she'd said those words to Warren while she'd still had the chance.

It was only after she'd already gone through with the unthinkable, allowing him on top of her and inside of her as she had all those years ago—that he wanted to talk. Zoe was huddled beneath the covers, shivering with cold from her core on out, though she told the Tulpa it had to do with relief . . . and because she'd barely touched her food earlier. So he brought the cornucopia she'd made to their bed, the gesture showing Zoe how much he wanted to trust her again. The sentiment made her smile wobbly, and moistened her eyes. He was like one of the children he stole off the streets, curious and hopeful . . . and so very gullible.

"The timing is curious, though," he was saying, as he popped a ripened fig into his mouth. He was propped up beside her on his elbow as she lay with her dark hair splayed on his pillow, her image reflected back at herself from above.

It turned out it wasn't only *his* reflection he liked to watch in the mirror.

"What's curious about wanting to be with the one you love on the holidays?" Zoe said, running a hand along the fine hairs of his arm. He fed her a bloodred berry, approval in his eyes as he watched her eat, and she nibbled lightly on his fingertips. "It's a time to be with family. I wanted to come home."

"I don't mean that." He smiled down at her, looking infinitely younger. "I mean that after years of no word or sighting of you, you pop up after reports of your capture and death."

She had no idea what had been reported back to him, so kept her response deliberately vague. "I told you. I've been trying to find a way back to you for a long time now. If I've been sighted lately it's because I've been working toward that. Toward this."

He almost grinned as she continued to stroke him, but shook his head. "Not a sighting of you, not like this. Reports had you posing as a young girl who was caught and killed in the desert."

They thought she'd been posing as Joanna, Zoe realized and almost shuddered at the easy way he spoke of her death. "And did you believe them?"

"Oh, no. I knew you were still alive. I felt it in my mind and core, no matter what Joaquin said."

Joaquin, she repeated, committing the name to memory.

The Tulpa mistook her silence for confusion. "He's always been one for hyperbole."

"Then you've . . . reprimanded him?" she asked, hopefully.

"Oh, yes. He knows how I love children."

And the reminder was all she needed to shore up her nerve. "Fruit," she asked sweetly, holding out an apple. He smiled down at her and took it willingly.

Zoe watched him bite into it, imagined it as the juiciest and sweetest fruit he'd ever tasted, the crisp skin smooth against his tongue, the juice trickling down his throat. She put all her energy into envisioning this as she watched his eyes flutter half-shut as he swallowed and she rose up to her elbows, placing the cornucopia—the horn of plenty—on his belly as he reclined, trance-like, the scent of ripe fruit rising to permeate the air.

He came back to himself slowly, so that by the time he realized what was happening it was too late. The cornucopia, once a tool of the Greeks, the pagan farmers, was now a tool of Zoe's will, melding with the traditions of the past. The wicker unraveled as those ancient powers merged and the straw was once again a living thing, slipping around the Tulpa's body, burrowing through the bed and deep into the earth. The growth was slow at first, but it sped up as Zoe's excitement soared . . . and the Tulpa's spirit was enslaved in the narrow tip of the horn.

His eyes flew open, black searing to red, only to be snuffed by Zoe's power. She smiled, closed-mouthed, then rose—fruit and nuts, pomegranates and gourds, peppers and artichokes all spilling over the bed and floor. Each grew stems and spines and burrowed into the earth, both rising and falling, vines weaving among themselves to bind the Tulpa where he lay. Zoe knew the fruit he'd already eaten was doing the same to his insides and smiled again, feeling his eyes follow her as she dressed. When she was done, she turned.

The Tulpa's throat worked, visibly paining him, but he managed a deep breath, even as an emerging leaf shot from his mouth. "But . . . you're . . . mortal."

Zoe brushed the remains of someone else's ash from the crease in her slacks. "You forget what mortals are capable of, Tulpa dear. We can use belief to create, imagine, wish, and will things into being. And those of us with extremely powerful minds believe anything is possible."

She leaned in close to whisper in his ear. "You asked me before 'Who do you think you are?' But I never got to answer, did I?" She licked her lips and despite himself, the Tulpa's gaze flickered down before he drew it back to her eyes. She smiled knowingly. "Well, I'm Zoe Archer, dear. The woman who can break you at will. And the real question—you name-less, formless fuck—is who the hell do you think you are?"

His enraged howls were muffled as a miniature gourd spilled over his tongue.

"I'm leaving now. I'm going to bring in your so-called har-vest and return those children to where they belong, but keep one thing very clear in your mind." She flipped her hair back from her shoulders, knowing she was planting another seed, this one in his mind. "I can and will get to you again. Mortal or not, on this plane or another, anytime and anywhere."

Dozens of images of her smirking saluted her as she turned to leave the room, but before she did she glanced over her shoulder one last time. "Oh, and next time, *babe?* You'd bet-ter have a castle and a moat. Because I'll have learned how to kill you by then. And *I* won't be stopped by a mere kiss."

And with that she strode out the door to find Lindy slumped, anchored against the wall by the woody growth of a cranberry vine, the hard bitter fruit spilling like bright marbles from her mouth. Immobile, her eyes alone followed Zoe as she stooped to meet those hate-filled orbs. "You're lucky, Lindy. The cornucopia's powers won't hold you all long enough for me to both kill you and still get away." She paused as relief played across Lindy's face, then shrugged. "So I'll just let the agents of Light take care of that for me. Have *fun*."

Lindy's protests were berry-choked as Zoe strode down the long silent hallway, back to the classroom where the children were now sleeping, curled up in the same even rows they'd occupied before. The ward mothers awoke when she entered, stood in tandem, but did nothing to stop her. They weren't warriors, and that wasn't their job. Zoe wove through the children, searched out the one she wanted, and lifted her sleeping granddaughter from her crib.

"He'll find you, you know," one of the mothers spat. "He won't stop this time. Not until your blood runs like a river."

"Yeah," Zoe said, drawing out the word as if considering it. "That's what you said the last time."

Then she left the room, and threw open the front door of the Tulpa's house. Chaos erupted behind her as the alarm sounded, the house coming to life too late, and a piercing whistle rang through the night as Light descended on the mansion. Her former allies, felt rather than seen, rushed past her, war cries pealing like bells in the cool air, but Zoe had already fought her battle. She turned her back on it all, and gratefully, thankfully, *finally* took her granddaughter home.

Chapter 8

She laid low for an entire week. Her cornucopia's magic had held long enough for her to get away, and since that was all she wanted—and all she believed was possible—the agents of Light and Shadow had fought yet another epic battle. She'd pick up a manual at one of the comic book shops later so she could get the Cliff Notes version of what went down, but she already knew the Tulpa had escaped with his life. Like him, she could sense his existence in her marrow, and knew she always would. She didn't waste time regretting it, though. She was already plotting how to double back and give him the "next time" she'd promised. She might be mortal, but the word that still summed up Zoe Archer best was *single-minded*.

The McCormicks paid daily visits to the facility the agents of Light had set up just on the outskirts of town until Ashlyn was strong enough to return home with them. They had no problem forging the new identity papers Micah had prepared for them, and immediately put their home on the market as Phaedre instructed. They were still under the assumption that Phaedre, Gregor, and Zoe worked for the government, that Ashlyn was at risk and needed to be placed in a witness protection program, so they told no one where they were going, and left no forwarding address. But Zoe knew it, and she planned on keeping a close eye on them, as she had the night the moving van came and they loaded up all their belongings. She couldn't be there for her daughters any longer, but she could at least watch over Ashlyn.

But what she really needed to do was finally, fully, embrace her humanity. There could be no more dipping into the paranormal world she'd left behind, no lamenting all she'd lost. In order for her to be a whole woman, and a person who could act and move through the world with purpose, she had to accept her limitations, just like anyone else. She had to release once and for all her knowledge of what went on beneath the veil separating this reality from the next.

But this time she would say goodbye.

So the following Thursday found her pacing the walkway of an apartment building just one block from the Guardian Angel Cathedral, hands shoved deep in the pockets of her black slacks, the collar of her winter coat turned up to shield her face from the whip of an angry wind. The weather had turned suddenly, and the streets were empty because of it. Zoe inhaled a deep breath of the biting wind, and as she blew it back out she thought of the Tulpa, naked but for the vines and leaves canvassing his body like living entrails. It was so satisfying, even now, that her laughter stilled her in her tracks.

"You went blonde."

And even though she'd been prepared for him, Zoe jumped. Warren grinned when she turned.

"And you took a shower," she said, noting his smooth cheeks and shorn hair. He was dressed like her, in black, his peacoat flapping open in the wind. He motioned to a stairwell next to the apartment manager's office, and Zoe ducked beneath it.

"I'm trying on a new persona," he said, following her. Her eyes traveled down his long body. "Respectable business-man. What do you think?"

"I like you better as a bum. I could track you down even with this poor mortal nose. Plus it keeps the girls away."

His smile was fleeting. He knew she was saying goodbye. "And do you think you'll need to? Track me again, I mean?"

"I'll want to."

"But you won't."

They didn't look at each other for a time, and Zoe knew he was considering every obstacle facing them, and like her, was unable to see any way around them.

"The children?" she finally asked, turning to him.

He nodded. "All freed. Returned to their homes and families. They'll have nightmares, of course, but they'll outgrow them in time, and there'll be no permanent damage. We also stole the masks the Tulpa was using to control them. He won't be able to do it again."

Zoe thought of the young boy she saw wailing in the Tulpa's hallway. "Good."

"His home was burned to the ground," Warren said, and she nodded to let him know she'd heard. He finally sighed. "So that's it, Zoe? You can just walk away and leave it all behind?" *Leave me behind,* he was really saying.

Zoe ran a hand through her shortened hair. "I'm not walking away, Warren. Every day that I'm out here on my own I'm ensuring our troop's legacy. I'm carrying out a prophecy that will benefit us all."

Warren's eyes fell shut. "Why do I have to love a woman who always puts duty first?"

She placed her palms on his cheeks and waited for him to look at her. "Because if I didn't you wouldn't have loved me at all."

When he finally nodded, she worked a wide ring off her finger. "You know what to do with this, right?"

He looked it over, studying the grooves that gave way to hinges around the stone. "I'll put it away for you . . . or for the next Archer. Are you sure you don't want to keep it, though? It's all you have left to remind you of our world."

"No." Zoe smiled bittersweetly, thought of her daughters, and granddaughter, now safe, and shook her head. "I have myself."

And before his eyes could glaze with pain, before he could get out the words, *And that's all you've ever needed,* Zoe exhaled the wistfulness she held in her soul—the sharp hunger she'd been staving off since they'd made love, and the despair she'd felt in the Tulpa's stupa when she thought she'd never lay eyes on this face again. Warren's mouth still opened, but it stuttered and eventually closed as he inhaled deeply, tasting of the air and of her. And then he sighed. She wished she could smell his feelings on the air, too. She wished she could bottle them and carry the bottle, apply it like perfume or a balm that would melt against her skin and seep into her pores so a part of him would always be with her. Warren scented this, too, and finally it was enough.

"Goodbye, my Phantom," he whispered, and though his face remained tight—brows drawn, jaw clenched—his eyes were suddenly wet and luminous and soft in the icy air. Zoe choked out a laugh at the shared pet name, stolen from a superhero that didn't exist, given to ones that did. To anyone else it had always appeared to be just that, a nickname, but it was much more . . . and it was an endearment she'd never expected to hear again.

My Phantom Limb, the ache that is you existing outside of me, the pain of every moment spent apart, the empty throbbing that remains behind.

And Warren did leave after that, in a movement too fast to catch with mortal eyes, leaving Zoe slumped against the stairwell wall, scenting and seeing nothing in the cold December night.

Then she stopped feeling sorry for herself.

She straightened and turned her thoughts to the Tulpa.

Narrowed her eyes and considered what she'd learned about the power of imagination.

If she was right, what she was planning would take months, seasons, years. It'd take stubborn belief and the doggedness required of Tibetan monks, and all those mortals who most valued long-term goals. But Zoe had a purpose again, and a plan. And she was still alive. She could suck in the cold air and blow it out again, no worse for wear. And as long as she could do that?

There was hope.

After ten years with the Tropicana's Folies Bergere, Vegas native **VICKI PETTERSSON** traded in her sequins for a laptop, but she still knows all about what really happens behind the scenes in Sin City. Her first two novels, *The Scent of Shadows* and *The Taste of Night*, were published in March and April 2007.

For more information, go to *www.vickipettersson. com*.